GOODBYE FREDDIE MERCURY

NADIA AKBAR

GOODBYE FREDDIE MERCURY

PENGUIN

An imprint of Penguin Random House

HAMISH HAMILTON

USA | Canada | UK | Ireland | Australia
New Zealand | India | South Africa | China

Hamish Hamilton is part of the Penguin Random House group of companies
whose addresses can be found at global.penguinrandomhouse.com

Published by Penguin Random House India Pvt. Ltd
7th Floor, Infinity Tower C, DLF Cyber City,
Gurgaon 122 002, Haryana, India

First published in Hamish Hamilton by Penguin Random House India 2018

ISBN 9780670090365

For sale in the Indian Subcontinent only

Typeset in Adobe Garamond Pro by Manipal Digital Systems, Manipal
Printed at Thomson Press India Ltd, New Delhi

www.penguin.co.in

Farrokh Bulsara.

Freddie Farrokh Bulsara, my faithful friends and countrymen.
Does anyone know who the hell I'm talking about?
Born in 1946 to dal-eating, finger-flicking desi parents just like yours and mine.

Farrokh flippin' Bulsara, ladies and gentlemen! That's right, I said it, Farrokh!
No need to delete. No need to shut this thing down.

The name is sacred, my friends—like a saint, like a sinner, like a flaming celestial superstar.

Before he was the great Freddie Mercury, ladies and gentlemen, he was simply Farrokh.
Once a young desi bachcha playing with his aloo ka paratha,
Now the paragon of all that is good and holy in this dusted Desi World.

Classless, raceless, beyond culture or creed, beyond reproach or repeal,
And they all think he's white, for Farrokh's sake!

He is the realization of all our deepest human dreams, yaar.
To connect, to belong, to be of value in this world.

Brown and buck-toothed and beautiful.
And he's ours, yaar, he's ours . . .

—RJ Bugsy, *The Rocket Launch*, Radio FM84

NIDA

I try to imagine her before the killing, scanning the comments on her latest Facebook selfie, fake-blonde honeycomb waves of hair, the crablike tapping of lacquered fingernails against keys, stiff lines of black eyeliner gleaming on screen. My brother used to say I have a morbid imagination, which is true. So I picture tubes, brushes, a grimy eyeshadow palette, flesh-soaked sponges lying scattered and open like surgical tools. This is how I imagine her last day, her last moments. Perhaps she was lying asleep in her bed, or reading a book, or stepping out of a warm shower, but I imagine her sitting in front of her computer, looking at her picture, waiting for people to comment on her virtual life.

The photo, making the rounds on the Internet, which my *fundo* sister Fatima has no good words for, is your typical beauty shot—head tilted, fingers tangled in hair, lips pouting, eyes angled ever so slightly away from the camera lens. She's feigning indifference, her face plastered with whitening cream in the hope that fairness might authenticate her beauty—the highlights, the grey-blue contact lenses for all the Pakistani boys who fantasize about pretty white girls. She wears a black halter-top she's made herself, cutting the sleeves off a cheap T-shirt, fabricating cleavage with a well-disguised laundry pin. A tiny golden nose-ring, wrist encased in a peacock of glass bangles, pursed red lips buttered with a coat of cherry gloss.

If she's anything like me, she's probably scrutinizing the photo, cringing at every imperfection. I imagine she hates her large nose, the wide, dark, cavernous nostrils. And she's already rethinking the cleavage. She's hoping her mother doesn't find this picture. It's one of many she's posted, behind the wheel of a neighbour's car, posing in front of a steamy bathroom mirror, hugging a tree, her chubby brown fingers clutching her neck as the cotton kameez clings to her rain-soaked body.

She hopes that if enough people comment, click the 'like' button, she'll be discovered and her smile will be miraculously everywhere—on mobile phones, the television, gracing billboards where she arches her wide back on a stay-firm MoltyFoam mattress, drinks Coca-Cola, waves the last phonecard that you'll ever need.

There are 354 'likes' already. Someone calls her 'Hotness'. 'You like blue movies?' Bilal69 asks. His phony profile picture: Tom Cruise from *Top Gun*. Another boy begs desperately for her phone number. She smiles, scrolls down.

Perhaps Atif Aslam warbles 'Tere Bin' through cheap computer-speakers and she sways her shoulders, mouths the words, daydreams romance. It has grown dark in the room, but she hasn't noticed. Above the computer screen looms a massive Lollywood film poster, maybe a joke from a friend—*Beghairat Hoon* in red and skin and lime caricature, the woman bent in tears of shame, the man's chest naked and rippling, machine-gun bullets lashed across his torso like a Miss World sash. Faded paper hearts and night-glow stars are glued to the ceiling, an old line-up of Barbie dolls shoved low in a cubby, taped-up local-magazine cut-outs of Kareena Kapoor, Angelina Jolie and Katrina Kaif. She hums and tap-tap-taps the arrow key, scrolling down the swelling comments. Behind her in the darkness her deranged brother stands and seethes. He is holding a knife.

Last week it was front-page news: 'Brother Kills Famed Sister for Honour'. Now it's been relegated to the *Lahore Daily*'s Metro section. I flip the long, unwieldy pages, searching, and find an anaemic column in the upper-left corner. My fingers are already filthy with newsprint. The brother is missing, his friends helped him escape the local thana. They all agree that murder for honour is a worthwhile crime. He won't be found because no one will be looking for him.

I hear the peculiar sound of my sigh echo off the hard plastic walls of the bathroom stall. My jaw hurts from grinding my teeth, the pain radiates into my ears. The college bathroom is quiet this time of night. I toss the newspaper on to the wet floor beneath my feet, the corners grow dark and soften, the floor reads a transparent film of news—the Syrian war, China's Nicaraguan Canal and our upcoming national election. Salim Chaudhry, our current prime minister and election candidate, looks up at me bald-headed, with a crooked, mashed eye. The pages lie wet and mottled against the stall corner, fusing with the coarse pink Rose Petal toilet paper. The ash from my hashish joint hisses, the little gold water-tap next to me—in case a butt-washing is required—gently drips on to the floor.

I am hiding out, trying to get high while the annual Lahore College concert drones on below, two quads down, in the Allama

Iqbal Auditorium. Cigarettes acceptable, but hashish requires a quick trip to a secluded bathroom. I inhale and hold the pleasure in, the smoke caressing my lungs, and release a milky cloud above my head. I feel the sweet release of tension, the heat building. I lean back against the toilet tank and rest my head. I still have a few quality puffs left and I'm going to enjoy it, to hell with the May heat and the armpit stains. I stare at the peeling acid-green ceiling and let my facial muscles go slack.

Shahnaz Bajwa, that was her name. Her Facebook profile was Sheena. She was two years older than me. Her pictures were quite popular online, constantly reposted by friends, mostly poking fun at her gaudy neon make-up, her awful *paindu* leopard-print skirts and velvet bustiers. But now she's not so funny. No one is making fun of her.

'Brother Cuts Off Penis, Restores Family Honour'—that's how I would like to see it play out. That's the kind of headline that would really make my day. And probably do a better job of restoring honour to the family.

I take another long drag of hash and feel my facial muscles twitch, the right corner of my lip rises. Sheena's brother stabbed her six times because he couldn't take the neighbourhood's taunting. I wonder if my brother would have felt the same. Would he have considered killing me for getting stoned? Or if he found out I wasn't a virgin? Would he love me so little? I can't ask him now, he's already dead. But what a terrifying thought. Who can you trust if not your own brother?

The bathroom door slams open, hitting the concrete wall with a loud crash. It makes me jump. I almost drop the joint. I hear someone loudly shush another and then a quiet rustling. I hold my breath and hope no one looks under the stall, or wonders where all this smoke is coming from. I hear a boy's and a girl's voices, the sound of kissing, the sound of a zipper sliding, the swish of clothes coming undone, a belt hook, a dupatta whispering to the floor. She and I had the same revolutionary idea, but she brought a friend.

In my pocket my mobile phone vibrates. I pull it out so quickly it almost falls to the dirty, wet floor. As I slide my twitchy finger across the screen I accidentally trigger Google Maps and the world flashes up at me, moving slowly closer, all bruised and blurry. I'm the blue dot, arrow facing east, fast zooming into Lahore, Pakistan, Lahore College, Third Floor, Engineering Building, Last Wretched Ladies' Bathroom Stall. I press the back button until the map disappears and I can see my friend Saadia's message.

> *Nida, where the hell are you? Did you fall in or something?*
> *I'm coming. Five minutes.* I quickly type back.
> *This show is shit. Hassan is picking me up. I'll msg you later. Byeee.*

Now that Saadia's dumped me for her fiancé, there's no point staying any more. I message my cousin Ali to pick me up. Outside the stall the heavy breathing continues. I wait and sweat. I don't know what they're doing out there, whether it's sex or just some heavy petting, but the boy finally groans loudly. The sink tap turns on and through the narrow seam in the stall door I can see them moving. They talk in whispers, kiss, he laughs a tired, sated laugh, and then I hear them leave, the faint electric-guitar echo of the concert below wafting into the bathroom. I'm alone again. I breathe out and straighten up in the stall, legs shaking. Sweat trickles down my back, my jeans cling heavy. I tug my T-shirt collar, blow some warm air down my shirt, and go back outside.

Ali sits slumped in his battered white Santro, tight as a mini fridge on wheels, his hair wild and dishevelled and wet, curling madly behind his ears and neck. God, I'm happy to see his silly face. He's unshaven and looks half asleep, which is his regular state of awareness—perpetually stoned. His eyes are glassy and red, his eyelids heavy with lethargy. I smack him against the face lightly and tell him to wake the hell up.

'What, man? Why'd you do that?' he exclaims, rubbing his cheek dramatically.

'Wake up! I've just spent the last thirty minutes locked in a bathroom stall listening to two first-years dry-shagging. So light something up, yaar. Blow me away.'

He grins widely, his gums darkened by years of tobacco, his teeth a rotting disaster. No decent girl is ever going to kiss him with that mouth. No, I'm wrong. I think somewhere in the rat corners of this city Ali finds desperate druggie chicks to shag. Free drugs seem to swing open all kinds of doors. Ali services all the best parties, where the rich kids put him to work rolling their joints and crushing their cocaine on CD covers. He tells me all the stories, how he steals their imported vodka, flirts with the girls and charges more than the drugs are ever worth. According to Ali it's his personal drug-making services, along with his product, that make him one of the more popular low-end dealers in the city. People know him by name and his number by heart. People don't even know their own mobile numbers, but everyone knows Ali's. Despite all this, Ali is always broke.

I look back, out the rear window. Lahore College is out of sight.

'Maybe I'll come chill with you next week,' he says. 'Sit in some bathrooms and try to get lucky.' Sometimes he likes to pretend he's in college. He sits in on lectures with me, hits on the girls, offering them free 'studying' drugs, and sells garbage hash to the boys at ridiculously elevated prices.

Ali presses the horn, letting it sound for a few seconds. A group of ditch diggers on bicycles, tools in tow, grudgingly creep out of his way. We've finally made it out of Mall Road traffic, with the help of some dubious shortcuts and traffic violations.

'God, I can't believe how boring it was,' I say.

'Then why did you go?'

'I thought about not going, until I realized all I'd be doing instead is sitting at home. Alone. I mean, it was still better than listening to Fatima proselytizing or enduring Abu's *kabza* over the television.' I sigh dramatically and rest my head against the seat. 'God, why is living in Lahore such torture? When will it get better? I can't take it any more.'

'Not all of Lahore is shit. There are parts of it you won't believe.'

'I seriously doubt that. After twenty-one years of living in this city, I think I'd know if there was a cooler, alternative Lahore hiding behind some smelly chinar trees.'

'Don't be so sure, Nids. I think you'd be surprised. It's really just about who you know.'

I shrug nonchalantly. I know he's talking about all the rich houses he visits to sell his stuff, and I'm sure they're quite magnificent, but all those people still live and breathe in the same city as I do. I highly doubt their air smells any sweeter.

Ali just smiles and hands me a limp new joint. For someone who makes his money rolling Js, he sure makes lousy ones for himself—droopy ones that sag in the middle, the roach sliding out halfway through. He rolls the windows shut.

'Sorry, no AC.' He grins sheepishly.

'Really? You mean this wonderful toasty air isn't air conditioning?'

He takes an air swipe at me and we settle into our smoking-up silence. The car fills with the sweet smell of hash and tobacco.

Smoking, we sweat through the traffic lights and brush off the bent beggars tapping irritatingly at the windows. We pass the joint back and forth, savouring the slow smoke. Sweat builds on my upper lip and drips between my breasts. We inhale and exhale until there's no oxygen left, then we crack open a window. The high runs down my thighs and pools at my feet, where slowly the sensation builds, climbing up towards my chest, my neck, my face, my lips, my nose, my eyes.

Ali turns on the music. It's always one ancient heavy-metal cassette after another in his car. He's apparently never heard of iPods, Bluetooth, digital streaming, MP3s or even CDs, for heaven's sake. His glove compartment is a scrapyard of old mixed tapes. He wears his musical preference—proudly and on full display—black heavy-metal T-shirts shirt with jagged silver writing and a leathery open-jawed skull. He says that the good music, the old stuff that America and the UK used to produce, is the kind of music that burrows a hole in the back of your brain. Like a parasite, it sits there for the rest of your life, feeding. Ugh, I think it's something desi boys never grow out of.

I listen to Metallica smash on for a few minutes, silently working myself through my paranoia until the high takes full effect and I feel better. Then I turn the noise off and flip through radio channels.

Ali gives a shout.

'Sorry, but your wobbly cassette was starting to drive me crazy,' I say.

'Whattt? What's wrong with you? That was Metallica, yaar.'

'Yeah, yeah, I know. My apologies to the band, but if I hear "Exit, light/enter, night" one more time, I'm going to cut you.'

He laughs loudly. 'How rude, yaar.' He ejects the battered cassette and tosses it in the back seat along with the rest of his junk.

I scroll through the four decent channels to FM84 and leave it there. A song ends and a charged male voice comes on.

And The Rocket Launch *continues, with me RJ Bugsy on Radio FM84, 'Where You Get More!'—more music, more requests and, of course, more me. I'm still on a mission to try and find your most loved rock songs of all time—the ones that haunt you as you sleep, the ones you just can't live without. So keep your phone calls coming, we've still got an hour on the clock and our playlist is looking fit . . . We've got some Aerosmith, some Junoon and, eventually, some Queen, of course . . . But to start off this hour, how about my favourite Canadian super-trio . . . This is Rush with 'Bastille Day' . . .*

He's speaking English with a polished American accent, like some late-night TV host. His voice is light and filled with energy. He sounds sexy.

'I love this show,' Ali says excitedly. 'He always plays the most *alla* music.' He turns up his car stereo as loud as the crap speakers will go. The bass distorts the song and I can feel my seat vibrating.

'This shit is amazing, yaar!' Ali shouts as the high-strung feminine voice of the singer begins wailing. Ali headbangs, looking like an idiot, his unruly nest of hair flopping in slow motion. I can't help but laugh. He begins to twist the car around the narrow roads and purposely hits every speed bump in sight. With every bounce he yells and wriggles in his seat, miming the unknown lyrics. I laugh and start to really enjoy the high, tossing my own head around. And then his car conks out with a hiss.

'Fuck! *Bhenchod* shitty *bakwas* car.' He slaps the dashboard and pulls over, then turns the car off. But instead of stepping out to open the bonnet he pulls out a pack of cigarettes and pushes in the car lighter. He looks at me and shrugs sheepishly.

'Just chill, it'll cool off by itself,' he says.

'Yes, I know. I've been in this shit wagon before. Light me one too.'

He smiles ruefully and pulls out another K2. He lights one with the other, tip to tip, and holds both of them between his long, bony fingers. I can see bits of hashish and tobacco stuck beneath his fingernails. He puts the pack carefully back in his shirt pocket, takes a long slow drag of one of the cigs, then hands it to me.

'Cigarette tax,' he says cheekily when I glare at him. 'Smoke slowly,' he tells me, 'this damn pack has to last all week.'

I look over at Ali, his crooked teeth and goony long neck, spindly limbs and thin trembling fingers clutching the steering wheel. I feel bad for him. He's the sweetie of our family, always ready to make you laugh, ready to pick up and drop you off from opposite ends of the city at any time of day. He may look like shit but he's a really good guy. As children Ali was the one we'd dress up in girly clothes and play tea party with; he's soft and gentle and totally incapable of the so-called masculine responsibilities left on him by my brother's death. Honestly, I always thought it would be Ali who would die tragically young, with his drug dealing and party lifestyle. I thought it would eventually catch up with him, sooner or later someone would shoot him or rob him or he would overdose on some *jaali* cocaine.

I look away, suddenly sad, and puff lightly on the filter, sucking the tobacco out slowly. Outside a donkey cart passes us, the animal pitifully braying, his grey coat lit in a purple neon glow by Lahore Broast Chicken across the street. I rarely allow myself to think of Kasim. It's too painful. Two years later and I still can't believe he was killed in something as stupid as a helicopter crash. And I can't believe how quickly a family falls apart—almost instantaneously—within seconds of such news. I look over at Ali, who's checking his messages, his phone constantly ringing or vibrating with possible deals. I reach over and give him a hug. He looks surprised but pleased.

A beggar woman taps at my window; she's young but looks broken and worn like all Lahori beggars. She's covered her thin black hair under a loose ratty shawl, and beneath the wrapped fabric a tiny child clings to her breast. I look away but she knocks insistently, her voice loud enough to be heard over the passing traffic. She makes pitiful faces, begging expressions, and holds out her hand for money.

'Ali, she's eating my head. Give her some change, yaar,' I say finally, unable to resist.

'Are you kidding me?' he says. 'I see her every day, that baby isn't even hers. The other day she had a bankroll larger than mine. Ask her if she can fix my radiator.'

I sympathetically shrug my shoulders at her and gesture that I have no money. She gives me a dirty look. I'm not surprised but am a little offended. What does she think, that the two of us, sitting like squatting *dungar*s in a fuming Santro, have money to spare? She moves on to a Land Cruiser.

Ali punches out a message and turns towards me. 'Nids, sorry, yaar, but duty calls. I have to drop off some stuff right now. Do you want me to drop you home or do you wanna come with?'

'There is no way in hell I'm going home on a Friday night, so wherever you go, I go.'

'Okay, fine, but we might be there a while. The guy's having a get-together and who knows when it'll end.'

I tell him I'm up for it and he drags back on to the road. He's furiously sending and receiving texts. As we drive through the city, leaving behind the roadside restaurants, the broken roads, the cluttered rickshaw and donkey-cart intersections, the houses begin to metamorphosize into well-tended lawns and towering walls, where chunks of jagged glass and razor wire keep the riff-raff out. Trees thicken and crowd the roads. The potholes shrink in size and the beggars have long disappeared. The gates grow more elaborate, wooden and wrought-iron, tall with carved intricate patterns. I strain my neck to peer through the gates, above a low wall, catching a glimpse of a gleaming Mercedes. A servant washes a pristine driveway, a gardener prunes a luxuriant rose-bush. I've been to a few rich houses with Ali in the past, but usually he doesn't like to take me along. I think he feels like he has to babysit me and finds it easier to work solo. I'm surprised he's so casual about taking me with him tonight. I must look really miserable for him to offer.

'So where exactly are we going?' I ask him.

'You'll see when we get there.'

'Why? Is it a secret?'

'Sort of. Maybe.' He winks and breaks a red light, honking furiously at a man on a motorbike with a live goat balanced precariously on the handlebars.

Ali pops his head out the window and shouts, 'Yaar, let the goat drive!' It's so silly it makes me giggle. The hash is in full effect. At this point I feel good enough that most things will make me giggle.

'I don't think I'm dressed for a party,' I say, suddenly aware of what I'm wearing. 'And I've been sweating all day.'

He looks over at me. 'You look fine. I have some cologne in the dash if you want.'

It's some rubbish knock-off for men called Intense Wood. I can't control my laughter. I spray a little on my neck and under my armpits and hope it doesn't have the intended effect. Then I toss it back among his Rizla papers, cheap roadside plastic lighters and scratched tapes. I twist his rear-view mirror towards me and fix my make-up, or whatever's left of it, and find an old black eyeliner pencil in my purse.

'I just need to stop at a gas station first and pick up the stuff, then we'll go, okay?' he says, readjusting the mirror. 'I have to take good shit. This is a client to keep. Just lay low, maybe crouch down when I do the pickup.'

'*Haan, haan*, the same as usual. I know the routine,' I say.

He drives into a bright Shell station and parks near the back, where the carwash hose lays dejected on the floor. He turns off the engine and instantly we're engulfed in a dry baking heat.

'So tell me, what's the secret?' I say. 'You don't usually like to take me along, so why now?'

He gives me a loony grin, nasty teeth and all, acting mysterious all of a sudden. 'Nope, not going to tell you anything, except that it's a famous politician's house. Bas. That's all you get. And that it's some house.' His eyes widen and he nods in emphasis.

I sit up in my seat. 'Really?'

'Get down!' he yelps.

I slump down into the seat until I can't look out the window any more. I rest my shins on his dashboard, knees pressed against my face, butt dangling in the space between the seat and the floor. I can smell his stinky shoes and see that his roof upholstery is torn.

'Which politician?' I whisper. 'Just tell me that. And why is the house amazing?'

'Wait *karo* and you'll see. I think you'll fall in love with it.'

'Seriously? Why? What's so special about it?'

'I'm not going to tell you any more, Nida, so shut up. It'll ruin it. I know you're bored and depressed sitting at home so I thought that next time I go I'll take Nida. That's it. Now stay put, he's here.'

Ali steps out of the car and walks towards the service shop. I can hear him greeting someone. I stay scrunched down in my seat and daydream of palaces.

BUGSY

Omer's massive house looms before us, a hideous beast we've nicknamed the Dodge Mahal. Its sprawling lawns, tacky water fountains and faux baroque furniture makes it look like Louis XIV took a giant gold-plated shit in the middle of Lahore. The nickname pisses Omer off, but what can he say. His father, the infamous Iftikhar Ali, right hand to current PM Salim Chaudhry, is well known and admired for his public looting and rubbing of tax rupees against his balls. It's good to be the king.

To any Pakistani lucky enough to bicycle past the mansion, their only glimpse of the monstrosity is the Disneyesque castle wall topped with copper spikes. This is as close to a Pakistani fairy tale as they will ever get. It's like a giant middle-finger to the impoverished masses of the city and, even worse, an open asshole to the feudal rich—corrupt government money always beats corrupt land money in the Paki version of Miscreant Monopoly.

Faisal honks impatiently at the gate and the guards scurry like mice when they recognize his X5. Faisal and I met years ago in elementary-school art, both of us expecting an easy pass, both of us failing. Faisal couldn't get past his obsession with painting Rubenesque nudes, and I was equally hopeless. Only Faisal appreciated my cartoon-like portraits of famous female political figures—Hillary Clinton, Margaret Thatcher, a young Benazir Bhutto in shorts. A lasting lascivious friendship was forged.

And we've had the mixed fortune of knowing Omer since primary school, when he was a younger version of his current party-horror self. It goes without saying that, of course, the only son of the most influential political mover–shaker in the country would be a *chut*. His school years were largely spent driving up and down Canal Road in a canary-yellow 300ZX, buying off teachers and chasing grammar-school ass. His school lessons revolved around pranking teachers, weekly pissing in some unfortunate nameless boy's locker, texting lewd photos of his dubious conquests and, worse, faking an interest in cricket. He was the only sports captain in the proud history of our prestigious prep school who couldn't tell you the difference between leg side and onside. Despite the slack, like every spoilt rich kid in Pakistan, Omer's half-baked dedication to his father's severely low expectations have paid off. He can be a douche, sure, but in Lahore, with another sweltering summer looming, there's nothing to do but party, and the fact is that Omer throws the most outclassed parties.

Faisal balances a tower of cigarettes, bought last-minute on the way here, and leaves the keys in the ignition.

'Bugsy, yaar, can you take one pack and put it in my back pocket,' Faisal asks, his hands full.

'Fuck off, do it yourself. I ain't sticking my hands anywhere near your ass.'

'Don't be such a dick, yaar. Just do it.'

I shake my head and watch him struggle, cradling the boxes in the crook of his arm, dropping a few as he tries to claim a pack for himself. I ignore him and walk towards the back of the house, towards the pool and Omer's den of debauchery, isolated from the main mansion, with views of the swimming pool and Mughal lawns.

Tonight's GT is looking pretty typical. Omer's grand detached apartment is filled with milling wannabes, seedy partygoers and all the drunken goons and freaks that represent the most influential and dishonoured families of Lahore. Inside Dodge, Omer's huge and throbbing red apartment is filled with smoke, faces barely visible in the dark red room that he has further amplified with red lighting. The windows are open, the air conditioners on full blast, but the smoke refuses to push out. Cigarettes are lit one after another until people fade into a haze of horny boob swipes and drunken sways. Omer's usual sickening brand of hard trance thunders overhead, young female voices chirping in the same endless grinding beat. I nod my head in quick hellos to a few random faces as I make my way to the bar. Faisal goes off to give Omer the stack of cigarettes.

The bar is near the back corner of Omer's enormous room, in the darkest crotch of the red interior, where his usual weird and motley collection of friends assemble—politicians' young sons and obscure relatives, a few strange dealers, a mashed-up collection of recognizable school friends and fashion models . . . all appearing from nowhere, with an equivalent tendency to disappear.

A few of the shady characters stand by the bar and swallow their drinks in large gulps, not wanting to stray too far from the free booze, hoping to quickly get drunk and mumble nonsensical sexual innuendos to some willing chick. Behind the bar in his white uniform is my main man James, handing out drinks with a smile.

'Jamesji, what's up, yaar? Where have you been?' I ask, happy to see him. He's looking fresh, his white hair slicked back with gel, his beard trimmed neatly. I've been seeing James bartending at parties as long as I've been drinking, but lately he's been MIA with a heart attack.

'How are you, Bugsy Saab? I've made a full recovery,' he says with a smile, patting his heart. 'Do you want your usual, Scotch and water?' I nod. He pulls a new bottle of J&B from beneath the bar and cracks the seal.

'A new one, just for you,' he says, and pours it into a short square glass, grabbing ice from a bucket with his bare hand. Faisal, who's back, ripping the plastic off his cigs, the crumpled wrapping carelessly fluttering to the floor, asks for a vodka–Coke.

'So, James, have you been playing anywhere cool lately?' I ask him.

As well as being the best Christian bartender in the city, James plays a mean jazz saxophone. He was quite the musical big-shot on the seventies Pakistani club scene, way back when there were nightclubs and open bars and, apparently, (according to James) women in pink hot-pants grinding to live disco. This was way before Zia and the death of public nightlife in the eighties. Forty years later and the nation's still parched; desi prohibition trickles on, except for a few interlocked rings of partiers circling like thirsty vultures at the watering hole, pecking and devouring themselves in a bootlegged frenzy.

James shakes his head sadly. 'There's nowhere to gig, Bugsy Saab.' He hands me the drink and I take a sip. Perfect, as always. I savour the icy warmth, the sweet ashy taste that leads to conveniently forgotten misbehaviour.

'Well, you can certainly play my birthday party, James. It's coming up soon. I'll give you a call, achcha?'

'Of course, Bugsy Saab, just let me know when.'

A young pimply kid comes up to us at the bar as we're surveying the scene and asks for a Bloody Mary. James silently hands him a screwdriver. The kid stands close to me, untouched drink in hand, and whistles as a group of girls walk in.

'Hot-ties!' the kid says loudly, and then turns to me as if we're old buds. 'Hey, Bugs, great show, yaar.'

I absently nod to him. I've never seen him before, and the fact that he calls me Bugs instantly irritates. A girl with big tits, red lips smiling invitingly, gives me a girly wave. I give her an across-the-room glass-raise. Six months ago I was face-diving into her tits somewhere in the damp grass of Omer's yard.

'I'm recording an album, you know,' the kid says, standing way too close. I edge towards Faisal.

'Achcha?' Faisal says, pulling his eyes off the painted red for a minute, immediately drawn to the subject. 'You don't say. What kind of album are you recording?'

'Well . . . desi rock-pop, I guess. It's fusion, of course.'

'Of course it is,' Faisal says, winking at me. 'So, Bieber, what's your band's name?'

'Itifaq. I'm Itifaq, so that's the name.' With his palm he smears the sweat that's gathered on his forehead back on to his gelled hair.

'That's a good name. Ite-Fuck. On point,' Faisal says, and gives me a look that says *This is too good to be real.*

Every GT someone announces the start or finish of an album, a book, a band, a movie, and yet nothing ever seems to surface. Everyone claims to be a star, but it's mostly bullshit. It's the easier option. Pakistani parties are the perfect platform for personal and historical reinvention. One minute you're a goon, the next a rock star; one minute you're sitting on your bedroom floor eating greasy French fries off a newspaper, the next you're lunching with Johnny Depp at the Ivy. And no one ever calls you out on your bullshit. Pakistan's a nation of short memories.

The boy now stands uncomfortably stiff watching us sipping our drinks. We look past him, through him, over him, at the girls strutting and kissing everyone hello—red lipstick passed around like a hundred-rupee note. I almost feel a touch of sympathy for the boy, he's trying desperately to reinvent himself into someone cool, someone he thinks fits at Omer's party. He doesn't realize we're all goons and freaks.

Someone grabs my arm and I turn around to see Aliya inches away from my face, my part-time-when-she-feels-like-it-rich-and-spoilt-girlfriend. She kisses me hard on the cheek and then wipes the smear of lipstick off roughly.

'Where the hell have you two been?' she says. 'I've been waiting forever, talking total bakwas with random losers. You were supposed to be here like an hour ago.'

'James's gonna blow some tunes at my party,' I say to her.

'I hope that's all he blows,' she says under her breath and then smiles brightly at him. 'White wine, James. That's a great idea, Bugsy, if your mother and four hundred sisters don't mind.' She rolls her eyes. She likes to give me shit for having three sisters. In my house, my birthday is more a family celebration, where everyone except me has a say. I shrug—who cares? They can figure that shit out amongst themselves. The sax plays.

'So Bugsy's in for the rally,' Faisal tells her. 'Now can you please ask Sara to come along too?'

'What! Bugsy, you asshole! Why the hell did you say you would go to that damn thing? Shit. Now I have to go too. Thanks a lot, Bugs. And I thought I could count on you.' She grabs her wine glass and pulls me and Faisal away from the bar, walking us slowly towards Omer's sitting area. Once Aliya is around, she's in control. If you're smart, you follow her and, sometimes, good things happen—like a high-school-style BJ in a parked car.

'He's obsessed,' I tell her. 'He wouldn't shut up. It was torture, I swear.'

'Hey, that's not true,' Faisal says, following. 'I was talking total common sense, and you know it. Stop exaggerating, *Bugsy*.' He loudly emphasizes my name. We've been reduced to children.

'Oh shut up, Faisal,' she says, pushing him. 'Great. Now we're both stuck going to some boring political rally. And I have to ask Saba along too. Faisal, can't you handle your own damn love life? Just call Saba yourself and ask her. I'm sure she'll say yes. I'm sick of being your go-between.'

'Please, Aliya, come on, yaar . . . Just this one time, please.' In two seconds flat Faisal's ditched his self-respect, gone the begging-dog route, all for a mediocre hump. I give him the look: *Pathetic*.

'Okay, whatever, let's go sit down,' Aliya says, dragging us towards Omer's sitting area, smack in the middle of the room. 'There's a new girl Omer's sinking his green hooks into—full throttle. It'll be fun to watch the poor thing. She has no idea what she's getting into.'

We weave through the crush, more hugs and hellos, exchange quick kisses, briefly fired synapses of conversation, promises of phone calls and dinners that will never happen. Always exclusive, Aliya stomps past everyone without bothering to be polite, still pulling me by the arm.

'That's her, next to Omer,' Aliya whispers, elbowing me hard in the ribs. She's pointing towards Omer's seating, his massive square of sofas and armchairs where he likes to hold court, where his new flavour of the month has somehow rattled Aliya. In the thick haze of hashish smoke I can barely make out the old faces, let alone the new. And then I see her, sitting comfortably next to Omer like she has always been there, petite and slender beside his scarecrow legs and fat head. She looks up at me curiously, at

Aliya, and then smiles. I'm surprised. She's not what I expected. I smile back.

Everyone in Lahore knows the type of girls Omer likes. Most girls dress to match his sexual deviance. Omer's preference is the paindu schoolgirl type who dresses slutty; girls with legs like automatic doors. But this girl, with a surprising Joy Division tee and jeans, large clever eyes and a look that's as clean and fresh as daisies—is way different. She's hot, but in an understated kind of way, and I'm curious to know what the hell about her is making Aliya and Omer salivate. And I definitely want to engage her in some rock talk—finding a desi chick who knows Joy Division is rare, wearing it across her chest is as unheard of as soup for lunch.

'Bugsy, you slick bastard!' Omer yells loudly, despite my standing a few feet away. I pull my eyes away from the girl towards his flushed face. 'Where the hell have you been? You've missed all the fun. We've been smoking the most sick shit. We even had a joint-making competition. Which I won—obviously. You've missed it all, you loser.'

I sit down next to Aliya on a large sofa-chair. She's already made herself comfortable next to the new girl.

'Shit, Omer, that sucks. I don't know how I'll manage to survive.'

Omer guffaws and grabs his nuts. '*Oye*, RJ, this is Nida, our new and naughty nymph. Nida, this is the infamous RJ Bugsy!' Omer does the introductions with his usual exaggerated swagger. It's like he's on some cheesy American game show, and tonight, in his maroon-striped silk pyjamas, he's dressed for it.

'Hi Nida,' I say. 'I just want to apologize for Omer beforehand, he knows not what he does.'

She laughs. 'This I've already figured out.'

'Good, no worries, then. Just don't say I didn't warn you.'

'I won't. But I like how you presume I'm not as crazy. How do you know, I might not *know what I do* either?' She flashes me a cheeky, flirtatious smile.

Maybe this time Omer's found someone whose brain cells aren't just jiggling in her tits and ass. She's damn cute. I like the ease with which she sits, not cross-legged or theatrically feminine, but normal, knees slightly apart, and how her hair is straight and dark and natural, unlike Aliya's salon highlights.

Omer's talking, his usual drunk, stoned rubbish, and he points at us with his cigarette, ashing on Nida's jeans. '*Oh ho*, now look what I did. Sorry, sexy,' he says and wipes the white ash off her jeans roughly with his palm. 'A little tobacco is good for the fabric.' He's slurring his ass off. He's probably been drinking non-stop since last night—the celebration of Friday starts on Thursday, sometimes Tuesday. Omer's life is one extended streak of drinking, smoking and snorting.

I lean over to Nida. 'I see you're into *Unknown Pleasures*?'

'What?' she says, wide-eyed.

'Your shirt. Joy Division. You know, *Unknown Pleasures*, the album.'

'Oh, yeah, right.' She looks down at her shirt and laughs. 'I totally forgot. It's actually my brother's old shirt.'

'He's got taste.'

'It's a great name,' Omer says, adding his two cents, never liking to be left out of a conversation. 'But wasted on a band. It would be a much better porno title. Joy Division, *Unknown Pleasures*, Part I. Naked female detectives that solve crimes and take it up the *bund*.'

The sycophants laugh. The rest of us just roll our eyes.

'She's dressed as if she's going sabzi shopping,' Aliya whispers to me, unable to stop herself from tearing the girl down.

'She's wearing bloody chappals, for God's sake. I wonder what's going on in Omer's head.'

I don't want to tell Aliya that a pretty girl is a pretty girl, even in chappals. And that maybe, finally, Omer is bored with boinking the same dumb-ass chicks.

'Hi, I'm Faisal.' Faisal half-waves from across the table. He's seated himself in a large chair across from Nida, sneakers up on the table, body slouched and sprawling as if he's home alone with a joint and *The Sopranos*. 'It seems no one wants to introduce us. Maybe Omer's afraid I'll run away with you. He's insecure like that, you know. I am the handsome one in the group. It's common knowledge. We'll make our escape when he's passed out, which will be in . . .' Faisal pretends to consult his imaginary watch, 'Five, four, three . . .' Omer laughs obnoxiously. Faisal winks at her and she winks back. I'm always amazed at Faisal's ability to flirt with random women. He's perfectly hilarious and relaxed with non-threatening girls— Aliya, my sisters, attractive girls at parties—but when it comes to the girls he really likes, usually rich virginal society types, forget it, total bumbling idiot.

'Nida here makes a near-perfect joint,' Omer boasts. 'Here, check this out.' He passes it to me. Nida watches me while I examine it. It's good. It's made with two Rizlas joined together instead of one and there's no sagging in the middle. The roach is tightly packed at the end. 'Not bad,' I say to her, and then grab Faisal's lighter and fire it up.

'Hey, fucker, that's mine to light,' Omer says to me.

'Too bad. Shouldn't have handed it over then.' I take a long drag, and from the corner of my eye I can see Nida watching like we're some bizarre reality TV show. I can't imagine what she thinks of us. If I were new I'd probably think us obnoxious assholes.

But then again, I hang out with us and find it relatively entertaining. Girls love Omer because he's totally *pagal* and obscenely rich. He says bizarre rude shit and doesn't stop partying. He's a character. According to Aliya, who once had the misfortune of dating Omer, it was apparently like riding a busted rollercoaster. She only realized it was broken when she got off and couldn't get straight again.

I take a few more drags and pass the joint on to Aliya. I sit back and put my feet up on Omer's designer glass table where a mass of bachelor junk has accumulated—broken and scratched DVDs, crumpled Rizlas, lighters and a stack of bent and torn porno mags.

Above us, on the enormous LCD TV mounted on the wall, Omer is playing a muted *2001: A Space Odyssey*. Stoned, it's almost like being launched through our own small desi window into the vast endless substance of the cosmos.

'So you're the famous RJ Bugsy?' Nida asks me, leaning forward on the sofa. Aliya does a pathetic job of pretending not to listen.

'I was just listening to your show, on the way here.' She sounds excited. 'I really liked the songs you played. But you're not how I imagined you.'

'How did you imagine me?'

'I don't know,' she says, giggling. 'I guess I thought you'd look more, I don't know, rock type.'

'You mean like that guy over there,' I say, pointing to a grungy-looking dude with crazy hair and a tattered Metallica *Master of Puppets* T-shirt. He's spitting out joints like they're Model-Ts, sitting with a *Hustler* on his lap, covered in tobacco and hash, a cig resting above his left ear. I've seen him before, he's Omer's dealer. He's a new type of dealer that's going around town—younger guys who don't just sell but assemble your shit too, happily puffing it along with you.

She looks over at the guy and giggles again. 'Yup, like him. Less grungy, though. Better teeth,' she whispers, leaning further towards my face.

'Sorry to disappoint,' I whisper back.

'No, no, I'm not disappointed. I prefer the clean and well-groomed. And I like short hair, but . . . it just doesn't feel rock 'n' roll.'

'Yeah, and if it was the eighties and I had a pocketful of crank, I'd look just like that, with long hair and one good tooth to chew my food.'

She laughs loudly with her mouth open and eyes scrunched like the anime chick from *Samurai Champloo*.

'I like the way you look, RJ Bugsy, and now, having seen your face in person, I will listen to you religiously every night before I sleep.'

She's flirting with me. I feel the blood flowing to my face, and other extremities.

'That would make my job a thousand times better,' I flirt back, 'knowing a beautiful girl is listening. And if you want . . . Well, you could always message me song requests.'

'Wow, *requests*,' Faisal interrupts from across the table. 'That's some offer. He never plays my songs, his best friend in the whole world. Now I'll give my requests to you, Nida, and you can message them to him. Then maybe we'll hear some damn Floyd around here.'

'Fuck you and your Floyd,' I say to him.

Faisal blows me a kiss.

Omer sits in the middle of the ornate red velvet sofa, like the monkey king that he is, and starts to throw his shit. He pulls some drunk girls up off the floor behind him. They squeal and fall backwards over the couch, over Omer's head and Nida's, who quickly moves to the corner of the sofa, near me, to get away from a flying heel and rogue knee.

'I warned you,' I say to her.

'I remember,' she says, and quite expertly lights another joint. She holds the roach between her unpainted fingernails and smokes without missing a beat, not a blink out of focus—slow, long drag, holding, exhaling through her perfect nostrils. She smiles confidently. I'm impressed.

'So, RJ, do you like working at the radio station?' she asks me.

'Yeah, it's good.'

She takes another leisurely drag from the joint, holding her lips in a pout long after the smoke has been exhaled.

'So, what do you do, Nida?' I ask her.

'Right now I'm just a student. Lahore College. Economics. Hideously dull.'

'Economics is not dull,' Omer interjects loudly. 'It's important to know how the market works.'

'Oh, please,' Faisal teases. 'You don't know the bloody difference between Free Market and Liberty Market.'

'Fuck off, I do know the difference.'

'Really, what is it?'

'It's the difference between my massive balls and your *kaalé* chestnuts.'

Faisal throws a cushion at him and Omer laughs loudly, howling like a wolf at the chandelier. I watch Nida laugh, open-mouthed and head tossed back, unoffended by Omer's crudeness. I appreciate that she doesn't pretend to be shocked or scandalized, something most desi girls feel obligated to do when they hear anything related to sex, balls, dick or pussy. As if looking shocked magically repairs their hymens. I look over and observe Nida as she surveys the scene like it's a memory game, taking in everything as if she were going to be tested on it later.

'So, Nida, what would you rather do than study economics?' I ask.

'Anything else. Who cares, cleaning the floors would be better. Economics is soul-crushing.'

'So you'd rather be a maid?' Aliya says, being catty. 'I'm sure that could be arranged.'

'Shut up, Aliya,' I say, giving her a weary look.

'I love films,' Nida says, ignoring Aliya. At least she knows how to do that, and I applaud her for it. 'I would love to somehow be involved in that process, but I have no idea how. It seems hard to do.'

'Film is really great. Would you want to act, write, direct?'

'I don't know. I think direct. Maybe write. I'm not much of an actress.'

'That doesn't stop anyone here on PakTV,' Omer says. 'Those bitches act until their assholes fall out, literally.'

'Omer! You foul shit,' Aliya says in shock, scolding him. 'What a fucked-up thing to say. What's wrong with you? Some of those girls are here tonight.'

'What? I didn't mean it in a bad way. I was just commenting on all the sexual favours they have to perform to get those jobs. It's true. Why are you acting all high and mighty, you said the same shit to me yesterday.'

'I did not.'

'Oh, yes, you did. I may be drunk, but I'm not deaf.'

They argue back and forth like siblings. I depress further back into the spongy sofa. I'm starting to get fucking high.

Every two minutes someone passes me a fresh J, and James is continuously refreshing my drink. I look down and, presto, fresh ice and fresh J&B. I stare into the TV where Frank floats in space repairing the failing radio transmitter. I love this movie. Omer likes to play random movies during his parties, it's his GT screensaver. Sometimes the movies are more interesting than the party, and we end up turning up the surround sound and smoking up to *Apocalypse Now*, *The Doors*, or anything by Wes Anderson.

'Bugsy, do you only play rock music?' Nida asks me.

'What? Yeah . . . mostly.' I'm still a little lost in space with Frank. Suddenly I have this urge to leave. To get up and take Nida with me, go home, start the movie from the beginning, and sit in a cool dark room with her warm perfume pressing against mine.

'I don't know much about rock music,' she says, oblivious to my zoning out.

'That's a real pity,' I tell her. 'It's the only music worth listening to.' I give her a lazy stoned smile and slide down a little further on the sofa. I feel as if I'm talking to her through a clear plastic membrane. I don't know how she has such energy after chugging so many butts. She must have the tolerance of a horse.

'Maybe you can recommend some bands. I'm bored with all the music I have.'

'Sure, no problemo. I can totally do that. Have you heard of Queen?'

'Oh ho, Nida,' says Faisal, eavesdropping on our conversation again, 'you've got him started on Queen. You poor girl. Now he'll never stop.'

'You daft *lumbhu*, buzz off,' I say.

Nida giggles. She has a sweet laugh. It sounds great when I close my eyes. She's nothing like the giggly annoying girls that are endemic to Omer's parties.

'You should come check out the station sometime,' I say.

'Oh God, Bugsy, why the hell would she be interested in seeing that miserable bunker of yours?' Aliya interjects.

'Actually, I would love that,' Nida says to Aliya. 'I've always wondered what a radio station looks like. It seems so exciting. Maybe I can sit in on your radio show.'

'Abso-fucking-lutely. Any time, babe,' I say. 'You'll love it. Hey, maybe you can even be a guest. I'll interview you—Bugsy talks to a fan. Something like that.' Aliya digs her fingernails into my arm. She's not so into my invitation. Her fingernails feel like jagged glass. I yank my arm away and rub the deep red marks. Crazy bitch.

'That would be fun,' Nida says. I give her a thumbs up.

'She's pretty fucking cool, isn't she?' Omer gloats, wrapping his arm around her shoulder. 'Just remember, I found her first.' He says it like Nida's bought and paid for. He gives me the look, the one I've seen a million times before, whether it's a new car or video game, the look that says: *This is mine and no one is to touch it.* And no one does, because Omer can be a vindictive bastard.

Nida glows with the attention. Then she looks over at me and winks. I grin like a schoolboy. What's this chick up to?

'Oye, Bugsy,' Aliya says, smacking me in the back of the head. 'Wake up. It's time to go. Alfie will be pissed if we don't at least show our faces after his fashion show. You know how pissy he can get.'

'You guys go and call me and tell me how it is,' Omer says to us. 'Then I'll see if it's fucking worth it.' He gives Nida this look, total Omer sleaze, like there's no way he's going to leave her tonight. It's too bad. She's seems nice.

I drag myself up off the couch. Nothing to stay here for any more. 'Okay, fine, let's go.'

I shrug at Nida, who just smiles and shakes my hand goodbye. Her fingers are cold.

'Hey, my birthday is in a few weeks . . .'

'Don't worry, she'll be there . . . with me,' Omer interrupts, grinning cheekily at me, his million-dollar dimples in full force.

Not exactly what I had in mind. Bastard.

'Okay, okay, *chalo na*. Come on, Faisal, you lazy bugger, get up,' Aliya says impatiently.

Outside I take a deep breath of warm air. It's thick and heavy and smells like chlorine but at least it's less toxic than Omer's room. Aliya stands by the fountain and yells loudly for her driver. Eventually, he jogs towards us from the front gate and she tells him to follow us in her Merc to Alfie's.

Inside Faisal's X5, Aliya slides up from behind so she's sitting with her face between us, her manicured fingers on the back of our seats.

'I wonder if this girl will be Omer's new toy for the summer,' she says.

'Probably. He seems plenty interested,' Faisal replies. I don't say anything.

I fiddle with Faisal's radio. It's late, house music is playing on a loop at the station. The throb of the backbeat gives me a headache, but I don't turn it off. Any music is better than no music. Faisal and Aliya discuss Nida's fate, both enjoying the new opportunity to gossip. I open the window and turn the air-conditioner vents towards me. Warm and cold air washes over me, one after the other, like satin ribbons stroking my face.

NIDA

In Pakistan we shop to survive.

To survive miserable marriages, inconsiderate in-laws and ungrateful offspring; to survive a husband's sexual indiscretions, monetary hardship and death; to survive the regret, the shame, the blasphemy. The Ultimate Survival Guide for the Desi Woman begins with *kapra*. We salivate over salwar-kameez like famished at a feast. Last year it was the skintight salwar and ultra-short kameez, this summer it looks like long salwars are back, paired with a ridiculous billowy parachute. The long dupatta–short dupatta controversy rages seasonally like a virus.

Aunties visiting from the west—Birmingham, Bedford, Jersey City—stand out like wilted lettuce in yesteryear trends, gawping at the modernity with their sleeveless and high ankle-slits, horror-stricken that the nation they left behind hasn't remained the conservative closet they imagined.

At the start of this summer, sanctimonious punches were exchanged by seemingly respectable society women over a shortage in designer printed lawn. Fashion is passion. Fashion is why we have holidays, weddings, dinners, get-togethers. Fashion is the queen's currency in a kingdom where a woman's scorn comes cloaked in submission and pink chiffon paisleys.

And this is how it works: Pakistani women buy fabric—available in multitudinous abundance from air-conditioned floor-to-floor multiplexes to the intoxicating tight open-air shops of the Old City with dreamy Mughal names like Ichhra and Anarkali—and tailor it themselves. If you're wealthy, a tailor sits waiting in your basement, available at your beck and call, making dinner napkins during seasonal downtime. If you're truly fortunate, you buy off-the-rack designer trends with fancy beading and exotic thread-work, wear them once and discard them. For everyone else there is the long, hot walk through the gullies of Main Market and Liberty, bargaining and haggling with sweaty impertinent tailors.

In Pakistan we shop to forget.

To forget the lost luminescence of youth, the schoolgirl days, the comfort of a father's home; to forget last night's unsatisfying love, a lost girlfriend, a loved one, a dead brother. We hoard leather sandals with zebra-patterned heels and diamanté-clustered toes to forget our crumbling economy, warm imitation pashminas during winter sales to forget our corrupt government filled with cowards and snakes. We buy swathes of floral-printed foot-fungus-scented linen, stretching from Peshawar to Peking, to forget that in the winter there is no gas for heat, in the summer no power for air conditioning. We shop and forget that the monsoon rains now come with shifty little mosquitoes that host dengue. In Pakistan, everyone is shopping for their own personal amnesia, stockpiling their closets with junk still encased in its plastic, treating them as if they were bottles of bootlegged Smirnoff smuggled from the back of the Ambassador Hotel.

My family is no different. In my family we shop to forget my brother Kasim. There's no drinking, no drugs, no windswept midnight motorbike rides. At least not for my parents and my sister Fatima. The destruction is still molten within their chests. I watch my mother inhale cheap Chinese fabric like McDonald's fries. It's her fix, a monthly needle in the arm to forget that somewhere scattered along a mountainside in the Swat Valley, not far from where we vacationed as children, his army helicopter is a burned-out shell, his body returning slowly back to the earth beneath a rubbish bit of shrapnel.

In my family, we shop to forget the dead.

The barefooted Khan—the name my mother calls all fair-skinned salesmen from Peshawar—unfolds a ream of blood-red silk and spreads it out before us. He bows his head melodramatically as he awaits her reaction. She sniffs and wrinkles her nose in distaste, tells the Khan she's looking for a cloth that's both cheap and high-quality.

'What, I look like a common beggar to you?' she says in irritation, tossing the red fabric back towards him. As Ami ages she loses all her social graces. The Khan suppresses a smile. I'm surprised he's not shocked, but then again, he deals daily with women exactly like my mother. I'm sure they all speak bakwas. I'm sure they're a royal pain in the bund to attend to.

She leans back in her chair and mutters under her breath, loud enough for the Khan to hear, 'To think we've been coming here for so many years, and this man still takes me for a fool. Find another shop, Nida. Look on your phone and find some place that will value us as customers. Why waste our time and money here. Chalo, look.'

I pull out my phone and pretend to be looking for another shop. I don't even know if Lahori fabric shops have an online presence. Instead, I scroll through Facebook.

'I thought maybe your daughters would like it,' the Khan says defensively, taking an edge of the red fabric and laying it across his shoulder. He models, covering his chest with the silk, letting the light bounce off the shimmering folds. He's standing on a short wooden platform, behind him is a multicoloured wall of fabric shelves stuffed with elaborate materials and patterns. The colours are almost blinding. My mother rubs the crimson fabric between her fingers, as if having second thoughts. Then she holds it against her arm, seeing if it makes her skin look fair and young. It doesn't. She huffs again like an agitated buffalo and purses her lips at him. She's sweating through her flimsy cotton kameez, the stains expanding out towards her belly rolls from beneath her vast armpits.

'Are you going to show me what I want, or waste my time with this rubbish? And look, it's stained.'

Only the stain knows it's there, because the fabric is stunning in its two-tone hint of gold embedded between the threading. I gingerly touch it, rub it between my fingers and feel its cool, smooth tautness. Between the buttery silk there are patches of rough, and as I examine it closely I notice that in a slightly darker crimson, almost imperceptible from afar, there are dragons in the folds. This fabric is much too expensive for my mother—it is an incantation from abroad, and I know she will insult it until it darkens into the dull tawdry fabric she wishes it were.

She grabs a light-blue piece from the mound of cloth before us and yanks it upwards, the colour cascading around her, fabric spilling like water, pooling in a dejected heap at our feet. She raises the cloth, embossed with pink flowers repeated in a haphazard circular pattern, towards the Khan.

'This is no good either. What do you think? That I was born yesterday? You're leaving me no choice but to visit your competition.' She pouts childishly, employing her best theatrical chops. She could win a bloody Oscar. If she were prettier, younger, less worn out and mangled, she could get one of the younger Khans to help her, the ones who don't look as if they'd rather be a suicide bomber than a fabric salesman. But she's not. She's still wearing her plastic house slippers and her toenails are long and uneven, yellowing with neglect. Her fingernails are bitten to the bone, a tiny eclipse of maroon nail-polish clings to each nail, like a drop of dried blood. Everything she buys today will sit in her closet, still in the store shopping bag, dejected and gathering dust in the back with all the other bags, waiting for the moment someone feels joyful enough to claim them, find a tailor, care enough to wear them outside.

I sip my free Fanta, an offering from the shop owners to stretch our spending, and wonder: What's the fucking point. I look at my mother, my sister sitting robotically at her side, nodding in bovine agreement as my mother continues to insult the fabric, the Khan, the shop, China.

The Khan, irritated by my mother's patent aggression, sighs deeply and goes off to find something cheaper, something that will fade away in two washes. He's an old man, someone who has spent a banal lifetime handling women such as my mother. He's tall and skinny, oily-smooth, with squinty kohl-rimmed eyes and a pencil-thin moustache hanging from saggy facial skin. He's been in the sun too long, probably outside on the Liberty Market roundabout, loafing with the other useless shop-wallahs, complaining about customers like my mother.

We've been coming to Bliss Fabrics for as long as I can remember. From a small one-storey shop, it is now country-famous, with five storeys bursting with the scent of shawls, summer lawns, Chantilly laces, Chinese silks, organza, chiffon, cotton and goddess knows what else. The first time I remember coming here I was five and my brother Kasim nine, when my father was at the height of his career at PakTV. My mother beamed as she walked through the large doors, her hands proudly caressing the wooden banister, her back straight and tall as she made her way up towards the expensive Mulberry silks, wearing her best, and only, pashmina.

'To buy expensive, you have to wear expensive,' I remember her saying. 'Otherwise the shop-wallahs waste your time with junk. And we're not here to buy junk, are we, Nida?'

I'll never forget it. She gently tousled my hair as we walked up the stairs, caressing it, telling me how she was going to find the perfect Eid outfit for me. Her gold bangles clinked against my ear as I balanced myself on every step to match her, making sure no sudden movement on my part caused her hand to leave my head. Kasim ran up and down the steps like an excited puppy, drank four 7UPs and set a world record in burping. I understood then what it was to be a Pakistani woman, to be a part of the club, so to speak. To speak the language of desi fashion. Although I still can't tell if nylon is for the summer or winter, if organza is a local fabric or foreign, if khaddar scratches against the skin when worn.

I look around the massive shop extending away from me until I can't see the colours at the end, the fabrics lining the walls like books in a library. Next to us, serving a younger mother–daughter combo, the salesman is kind of cute. He's young and fair with a dark mop of hair that falls over his light-hazel eyes. He's cute in a Pathan sort of way, probably dumb as wood. He smiles patiently and continues pulling fabric off the shelves, searching for something bright but not too bright, flowered but without too many flowers, something that may eventually please the lady. He smiles and attempts a low-key flirt, knowing the mother will leave buying enough to grant him a decent commission. She whispers something to him and he walks towards us, separates the crimson fabric out from beneath a hideous mustard-coloured monstrosity my mother is admiring. For a minute I want to stop him and I grab a corner of the cloth. He looks up at me surprised. His eyes explore my chest. He's squirrelling a quick boob-shot away for a private moment later. I look down at the toppling mountain of fabric. He has secured the fluid red silk, my dragons, with his feet. His toes are hairy and unkempt, the nails dark and jammed with grime. I caress the fabric for the last time and let go. He trods all over it as he drags it back to its rightful place.

The woman drapes it across her shoulder and oohs in pleasure.

'Look at that,' my mother says, elbowing me lightly to get my attention. 'Wasting her husband's hard-earned money on such bakwas. So easily fooled by something so gaudy. It's perfect for her. Good, let her buy it and get it out of my way.' I hear the bitterness in my mother's voice.

'*Jee*, Ami,' I say miserably.

Since my father's retirement, he doesn't come out shopping with us any more. He's embarrassed he has no more money. Not enough for dragons on Chinese silk anyway. Not enough for fabrics that are never going to be worn. And there is no son to supplement his pension, no son to make a father proud, to buy a mother expensive gifts. It's just two girls, two burdens. And there are just two cheap bundles of fabric for us to settle for.

The Pathan sneaks another quick look at me, his hazel eyes intense, focused solely on my chest. I try to imagine him naked, not all that impressed with what my imagination conjures up, when suddenly an image of Omer from last night flashes across my mind—Omer dancing around drunk in his underwear to The Vapors' 'Turning Japanese'. I laughed until I choked, clapping along to his hilarious faux-femme Thai fingernail dance. He then snorted a mound of cocaine, stood on the table and imitated every single one of his ex-girlfriends. He keeps calling me every day, and every night I see him. Usually it's with his friends—his need for social approval is ridiculous—but last night he kicked everyone out early and it was just us. We never got to finish the movie we started.

'Nida, stop daydreaming and tell me what you think of this,' Fatima says, tossing a brown-patterned fabric towards me.

I look up at her as if through deep layers of sleep and she gives me her best you're-such-an-annoying-sister look.

'Yes, I don't know where your head is half the time, Nida,' my mother says, irritated. 'Always dreaming of who knows what. Half listening to us, half somewhere else. Where are you? Is it better than being with us? Because if you're not interested in shopping with us, don't come. But stop wasting our time.'

Fatima looks over at me smugly. For a brief second she's on the same team as my mother; the two of them against me and my defiant daydreaming. Thank God they can't read minds. I scratch my nose with my middle finger and Fatima instantly loses the smirk.

Ignoring Ami, I yank at a swathe of cloth. I pretend I'm examining the intricate embroidery and inhale the odours, searching for the scent of Chinese cotton fields, the exotic musk of Laotian textile mills, but instead I find the same sad foot-odour of Nathia Gali, the must of Lahori dust. What a buzzkill. The joint I smoked earlier in my bathroom has completely worn off, leaving me with an empty crackly feeling. I sip more Fanta.

Finally the Khan returns with something dull and grey, the flowers minuscule pink stains, and my mother's face lights up. He unrolls the fabric theatrically, like he's showing us Queen Elizabeth's inaugural robe. Ami nods happily. It's just what she wanted—cheap and ugly. Something no one will remember, something she can silently fade away in, float away like an invisible kite. She proudly displays it to my sister for approval, holding it up against her chest.

'Well, what do you think of this one?' she asks, although she already knows its fate—sitting in her closet, dejected, with all the other greys. Although Ami does wear some of the more industrial-strength prints, so this one might stand a chance of seeing daylight.

My sister shrugs and gingerly runs her fingers over the fabric. She wrinkles her nose in distaste, and with the most lethargic movements pulls out something cheerful the Khan had shown earlier.

'I prefer this for your lovely skin, Ami,' she tells my mother, making sure to toss in a little bootlicking while she can. My mother pays no attention. She asks the Khan to cut for her and Fatima enough for two kameezes. I gloat openly at Fatima's horrified expression. She glares at me and makes a nasty face. Before we came to the shop, and all through the car ride, Fatima had attempted to condition Ami so she would buy her something colourful, a fabric that didn't scream tight-arse nun. Clearly it didn't work. I smirk some more, thoroughly enjoying Fatima's irritation.

'And this too, it's just lovely,' my mother says, massaging some diarrhoea-coloured fabric between her finger and thumb.

'Nida, what do you think?' She yanks the fabric towards me, spreads it out so the hideous violet leaves are visible against the chartreuse background. I gingerly caress the cotton. It's paper-thin, so flimsy and coarse that it scrapes roughly against the burn on my index finger. Omer made me roll an endless number of joints last night. He even made me roll him some before I left—'To remember you by,' he had said, with kisses.

'We'll take this too,' Ami says about the nauseating multicoloured fabric.

It looks like soiled pyjamas, but I'm not going to cry about fabric patterns that match the curtains in a blind villager's house. I remind myself I don't have to wear it. It can join last year's shopping tragedies in my morgue drawer.

I look down at my phone and message Omer.

Attention! Maharani in danger of becoming wrinkled fabric-suffocated Auntie—send expensive sports car and courtesy cannabis post-haste for emergency medical evacuation.

He hasn't replied to my previous texts. Knowing him he's probably stoned with friends, engrossed in some random pirated movie he'll forget about an hour later. He was quite amused when I told him that today was reserved for family-kapra shopping and told me a long story about how he had taken some girls there who had gone mental and practically bought the store. For the shortest second ever I contemplated asking him to join us. But then I saw my mother, who hasn't washed her hair this week, and Fatima, who would be happy to spill all my secrets, and realized what a daft idea that was.

If I had to choose between being stranded on a deserted island—starving, salt-crusting my butt—or going fabric shopping with my mother, I'd bend over for that wave any day. I don't really want to be here. After my brother's death, Fatima and I bit our tongues and tried to make Ami's life easier. We did what was expected of us without complaint. So every month Fatima and I go shopping with Ami, we indulge her, wait patiently, accept what she chooses for us, because we feel bad for her—there's nothing worse in Pakistan than a mother having lost a son. Except maybe a mother with two unmarried daughters. But right now I'd give my big toe to be at Omer's house. Sitting in his cold air-conditioned room, stoned, watching a movie, killing zombies on his Xbox or making out. His friends randomly appearing, without a call or question, and we all laugh and smoke some more, flirt and show each other the funniest videos we've collected on our phones.

I message Omer, willing him with all my energy to look at his phone.

'Khan, why does this cloth smell like kung fu chicken,' Ami says. 'You said this wasn't Chinese, but it smells like dirty noodles. Are you lying to me?'

Fatima leans forward and looks at me over my mother's lap. We roll our eyes at each other. It would be funny if she wasn't our mother and we hadn't heard her say stupid shit our entire lives.

I aimlessly flip through my phone, slide through the smiling lives of others and their loudly voiced political opinions on my Facebook. My phone vibrates. It's Fatima.

Want some kung fu later?

I look over and she's looking at her phone screen, laughing.

I reply. *LOL. Maybe some dirty noodles. This is torture.*
Fatima says: *You want torture. Wait till you wear that hideous print. Now that's torture.*

I look over and grimace. She gives me a wide grin. Ami is nearing the end of her kapra spree. There isn't a single scrap of fabric left she hasn't insulted. The poor Khan has lost the equivalent of his weight in sweat. We've now reached the point where my mother claws through all that she's already discarded in case some treasure has been left behind.

Fatima messages me.

Maybe you can find a husband who appreciates the finer aspects of floral-printed diarrhoea.

I lean behind Ami and smack Fatima on the head. She fills her straw with Fanta and blows it all over my face and hair, getting some in my ear. Ami gives us both a grave look—that we're embarrassing her with our jungli behaviour and that if we don't stop she'll come at us with her plastic chappal.

I dab Fanta off my face with a pretty pastel chiffon dupatta. Might as well get some use out of something pretty. As we get older, we can't help but judge our mother in a harsh light. Her washed-out face, the puffy bags beneath her eyes, the unwaxed fuzzy upper-lip, the dead-eyed stingray look she gets when she sees us. I visualize generations of women exactly like her, clones standing in a line behind me, bending around the cowpat corner in genetic variations of my DNA, my paindu ancestors—village women transported lost and confused to the city, their only source of power their marriage and motherhood.

My phone vibrates again and I pray it's Omer. It is.

How goes the shopping fun, meow-mix?

I send him four poop emojis. That should explain it all.

Hahahahaaha. What you doin' after? wanna hang? i mis ur face.

I sigh in relief.

God, yes. Rescue me!

I can pick you from Lbty corner bookshop? whn u dun?

20 mins. Faster if i can help it. I'll wait for you outside.

Sweet. Keep a look out for a handsome devil. lol. Cya.

My heart begins to beat in anticipation.

I quickly message Saadia:

Call me. Quick. Waiting.

By now we're experts at lying. She understands I need an excuse. Bloody hell, after all the lying I've done for her this past year, making up stories about how she's in the bathroom with the runs instead of with her fiancé, she owes me big time.

The phone rings and Saadia is on the phone, loudly asking me to help her with some wedding outfitting and saying she'll pick me up. I hold the phone slightly away from my ear so my mother can hear Saadia's high-pitched fast-talking. Then she spends five minutes actually eating my head about her wedding outfit, which is too tight in the boobs.

'Ami, it's Saadia,' I whisper, as Saadia chatters on. 'She wants me to help her with the dress and some other shaadi-related things. She's going to pick me up, okay?'

My mother just nods. She's too busy making sure the Khan doesn't cut the fabric too short and cheat her out of a few extra inches. She likes Saadia, and thinks maybe Saadia's obsession with marriage will infect me like a virus. She's worried about my wedding prospects, how I'm starting to edge past my bride expiry. Right now, if all was well in Ami's world, I might have had a line of balding mediocre suitors of my own to choose from. Instead, I'm helping Saadia manoeuvre the puzzle pieces of her life without any heed for my own. Personally, I have no problem with this, having not thought twice about my own marriage. However, for my mother, who lives in a world of Lollywood dramas and anxiety-ridden social expectations, she thinks that encouraging me to bask in the glow of another's impending nuptials will help my own plight. Where else can one meet eligible marriage-ready bachelors?

I kiss Ami goodbye. Fatima knows there's no Saadia picking me up, she's too *tez* for that, and she gives me a hostile glare for abandoning her during Ami duty. I shrug and mouth sorry, hoping to make it up to her later.

Outside Bliss Fabrics the heat is sweltering, melting the mascara off my eyelashes as I blink. Sitting inside the air-conditioned shop, I forgot the outside world of Lahore in June. Otherwise, I would have told Omer to pick me up from the store. I carefully wipe away the dark mascara smudges with my fingers and hope I don't have raccoon eyes. I take a left, walking in the shade of the shops that curve in a crescent towards one end of Liberty Market. Now it's starting to get busy, more and more shoppers emerging out of their cool generator-humming houses. I pass ready-made clothing shops, leather shoe shops, vendors with pretty plastic chappals and glittering hair accessories. Women are starting to crowd the entryways. A shoe salesman stands on a tall ladder and drops boxes of shoes down from the storeroom— 'Seven, red heel with flower; eleven, golden sandal!' he shouts. I stop at a small side shop and examine a hairband studded with glittering stones, a delicate emerald jewelled butterfly perched on one side.

'Only one hundred and fifty rupees,' the man says smiling, and shows me another hairband with a tiny ruby ladybug. 'From London.'

'These are not from London,' I say.

'How do you know? They could be, if you want them to be,' he tilts his head to the left and examines my face. 'On your face it would look beautiful.'

'No, thank you,' I say and put down the hairband. 'London is a little too expensive for me.'

'Then let's go to China and call it one hundred.'

I shake my head and walk away, hearing him lower the price to seventy and then fifty.

I pass the narrow Dupatta Gully where we used to buy our Eid bangles, available in every colour imaginable, to match our outfits. I think the bangle-wallahs tried to defy nature with their colours. Ami, our cousins from Rawalpindi, Fatima and I would all spend hours mixing and matching bangles, making our very own patterns, getting creative with the glitters and the neons. And then when you finally had the colour mix you wanted, you picked two large silver or gold ornate bangles to place on either side of the stack, sometimes thinner silver or gold to separate the colours and make a pattern. They were beautiful. And

then invariably on Eid we'd trip on our dupattas and shatter
the delicate glass hoops, crying as the blood dripped down our
wrists.

Once-great memories, now just depressing episodes from our
past. Last Eid we did nothing. Ami and Abu slept through the
afternoon. Fatima and I lay around the house in our night-suits
and watched the same dozen episodes of *Friends*. No one came
to visit us. We went nowhere. Instead we rotted, listened to our
neighbours' cries of joy and Eid Mubarak.

I walk around the horseshoe of Liberty Market and
stop at the end where Omer will pick me up. Behind me a
relatively new three-storey concrete plaza squats like an ugly
square pig. Already some of the glass windows on the top
floor are broken and taped together, the building's silver metal
exterior is darkened by dust and a dark ubiquitous grime
that seems to cover everything along the street. Even inside,
the shopping plaza is littered with cigarette butts and candy
wrappers, strands of fallen hair, long and black, lie clogged
in the corners. Lahore has a way of wearing everything out.
We are born and then proceed to wither under the unforgiving
Punjabi sun, the circling dust of the salinized farmlands
driving its way through every ass, crack and crevasse in the city,
settling between the lines of ageing faces. Beyond the plaza
doors children squeal in excitement as they climb up and down
the broken escalator. It's not working, but somehow it's still a
novelty.

A few feet ahead and there's the traffic of Noor Jehan Road,
where cars, buses, donkey wagons, rickshaws and bicycles pass
in a mad, disorganized rush, everyone honking from their
vehicles and yelling from windows like loons. Across the road
is the famous Karachi Paan Shop Omer likes to frequent late

at night, and to my left the stationery store and the strange ice-cream place which gave me the runs. Grown men holding hands stare as they walk past me, amused at the sight of a strange girl in jeans. As if *I'm* the odd one. They laugh and blow me kisses, their kameezes fractal-patterned with salty sweat stains. I ignore them and keep a lookout for Omer. I hope he hurries. I don't want to get into his car with a stinky, sweaty T-shirt.

I sweat and wait, feeling faint. I could really use a smoke. A skinny teenage boy stands on the steps behind me and smokes openly. He's wearing a faded *Terminator 2* T-shirt that has holes in the shoulders, Arnold Schwarzenegger's partial cyborg face peeling. The boy's severe hair gel still stands strong in the heat, he's tucked the shirt into his cheapo pin-striped pants and stands proudly in a pair of greying rubber flip-flops. He's thirteen and forgettable, but despite all this, the little prat can light a cig whenever he wants and go nuts. He can puff until his lungs turn black. If I pull a smoke, the stares would burn right through me, and some Good Samaritan uncle would materialize, telling me that girls shouldn't smoke. God, I wish I had a smoke. But before I can seriously contemplate asking the boy for a *sutta* I hear the whine of Omer's Porsche and then his obnoxious honking. He stops right in the middle of heavy traffic, not bothering to move to the side, and yells from the half-open window for me to hurry up. I quickly weave between traffic, avoiding all eye contact and the dirty looks from the waiting, honking drivers, and jump in. The car is so cold it shocks me, sucking the sweat off my chest like a vacuum and hardening my nipples. Lazily Omer leans towards me and smiles. The traffic flows around him. He's the elephant in the stampede.

'What's up, cutie kitty?' he says.

'For God's sake, Omer, drive,' I say.

'Don't worry, my eggy muffin, they'll never hit me. Expensive cars are scary.' He honks and presses down on the gas impatiently, then brakes hard. There's no space for him to speed through. He hates waiting, but has no problem making others wait.

'I missed you, Powerpuff,' he says. 'Give me a kiss.'

'What, here, in the middle of Liberty?'

'Tinted windows, babe. We can judge them, they can't judge us.'

I kiss him on the mouth, his lips freezing against mine, and feel his tongue lick my teeth. Despite the dark windows, I feel uncomfortable kissing him surrounded by the masses. Omer doesn't stop, however, not until he's felt every single one of my fillings.

'God, what a day,' I say after he's pulled away. I wipe his saliva off my chin and sit back, slipping off my sandals. 'Bliss Fabrics—never again.'

'That bad, eh?'

'Well, it's over now. What have you been up to?'

'Not much. A little of this, a little of that. You know, the usual. But I have something for you,' he says. He rummages in the back seat and hands me a plastic toy—a cheap Hello Kitty doll. *Made in Taiwan* is stamped on the back of her head. I squeeze it lightly and it squeaks. It's a McDonald's Happy Meal toy.

'It's cute, like you,' he says, pleased, as if he's given me the Koh-i-noor diamond. Hello Kitty in her little red bow and blue overalls. I thank him but he doesn't hear me; instead he is jamming his foot on the accelerator and overtaking a Suzuki.

People stare and jump out of the way, yanking their motorbike handlebars away from Omer's Porsche. The last thing they want is to scrape any of the black off his expensive paint-job. I clip Kitty to my brother's flight-bag zipper, where she hangs expectantly, without a squeak or sound.

BUGSY

All week I've tried to weasel out of this political rally. The faithful, fanatical, agitated, patriotic Pakistani politicos have already driven themselves into a froth preparing for this rally on the streets and TV talk shows. This is *the* Mian Tariq rally in Lahore, apparently history in the making. And because of Faisal's non-stop guilt trip and desperate demonstrations of sexual frustration, I'm going to be a part of that wretched history. Now in Faisal's X5 we're being driven ever so slowly through the horn-blaring traffic of Mall Road, snailing through a seething human flow of lingering pedestrians.

Today there was another suicide bombing in the inner city and the rally was relocated; now a hundred thousand perspiring desis in the throes of a May swelter will be squeezing into Race Course Park. Faisal's driver follows in a rickshaw, ready to park the X5 at a nearby friend's house until we need him. It's a rarity when Faisal prepares for anything, and Gulaam Driver following close behind is a true testament to his commitment to God and country.

The bastard refuses to let us listen to music or the radio. He wants to discuss politics en route. As soon as we got into the damn car he started with, 'No music today, Bugsy, yaar, okay? I don't want to taint this event with anything Western.'

Ironic, given Faisal's innate inability to live a West-free life.

'You mean inside this imported hundred-thousand-dollar German fucking SUV?' I say, smirking. Aliya and Saba giggle from the back seat. I give them a wink in the rear-view mirror.

'Yeah, Faisal,' Aliya says, egging him on. 'And is that Western mousse I smell in your hair?' She rubs her hand roughly over his puff of styled hair and smells her palm. 'Strawberry. Smells very L'Oréal-ish to me. What do you think, Saba?'

He instantly pouts and fixes his hair, gingerly recalibrating the stray strands back into the original pomp-fade. We love fucking with a fired-up Faisal. He ignores us and continues talking.

'Mian Tariq is the answer we've been waiting for, you guys, and you're too idiotic to know it. He's our political messiah, no doubt. I have total faith he will pull us out of this mess.'

'Can't we just go to the rally first, *then* discuss?' I say, irritated. 'I'd like to at least see the man speak before I raise him to Jesus status.'

'It's not what he sounds like, Bugsy, you idiot, it's his political platform, yaar.'

'Yeah . . . his platform: No Corruption.' For added effect I wave my hands in the air as if I'm a magician about to reveal a secret. 'Somehow it seems a little thin, don't you think? An entire campaign based on one idea, and that too a concept that no red-blooded Pakistani could possibly make sense of. It's like having a platform based on feng shui-ing the parliamentary offices. What does it even mean, yaar? How can a million corrupt politicians, bureaucrats and businessmen suddenly decide: *Oh no, I've milked enough money from this miserable country, thank you, now I'll finally do the job I'm not trained for and have no idea how to do, and become an honest man.*' I lay on a thick Indian accent for effect, complete with hand gestures and head bobbing.

'He does have a point, Faisal,' Aliya says from behind, moving up between us. 'I mean, corruption is in our blood. It's a way of life. It's how we survive. You know that. It's too tempting, and anyone who believes that this nation can be corruption-free is . . . well . . .'

'An idiot?' I pipe in. She lightly shoves my seat from behind. She doesn't want to get an already-heated Faisal any more riled up.

'No, not an idiot. Naive is what I was going to say,' she says.

'So a hundred thousand supporters—and that's just Lahore—are all naive? They're all idiots. Is that it? Idiots for wanting something more from their country?' Faisal says emotionally. I can see his knuckles whitening as he grips the steering wheel.

'They have hope,' Saba says quietly. She's been staring out the window the entire time, and hearing her soft gentle voice mellows us all out immediately. Aliya moves back and there's a moment of silence.

'There's nothing wrong with that,' Saba continues. 'If we don't have hope, if we don't at least want a better nation, then what's the point of being here at all? We might as well all be Indian or Persian or Saudi Arabian.'

'You mean we're not Saudis?' Aliya says sarcastically. 'Who knew.'

'Yes, yes,' Faisal says impatiently, annoyed at how far we've strayed from the patriotic conversation he was optimistically anticipating. 'This rally represents hope, as Saba has stated so brilliantly . . .' He pauses and gives Saba an adoring smile through the rear-view mirror. She smiles back softly. Aliya pinches my shoulder from behind, making sure I'm not missing any of the romantic drama that's unfolding around us. 'And our support of Mian Tariq is really support for a better, stronger, more economically viable nation,' he adds.

'Keep dreaming,' I say. 'There's no way he's going to win. It's impossible. A hundred thousand isn't even a drop in the desi bucket. Even if he had a million, two million supporters . . . There are billions of little people, like fire ants, crawling in the villages and countryside. Salim Chaudhry is a big-shot feudal, with more money than Bill Gates. There's no defeating him. He has enough money to pay every man, woman and child to vote for him twice. Nobody says no to free money.'

'That's true, of course,' Saba says from the back. 'The masses vote for the tangibles—food, water, shelter—not ideas. But you never know. Crazier things have happened.'

Again Faisal nods his head vehemently, agreeing with her. They both seem to happily be on the same stupid page, Faisal with his staunch masculine support, Saba with her requisite feminine hope. It's like a bad Bollywood romance, all they need now are matching denim jackets and a field of tulips to run through. Again Aliya pinches me, but this time I swat her hand away.

'Oh ho, why can't we discuss something interesting?' Aliya says lazily, her American-school accent dropping a little and her words lilting in Urdu sing-song.

'We were discussing something interesting,' Faisal says, hurt. 'I'm sorry politics is not interesting enough for you Miss Fucking Lifestyles of the Rich and Famous.'

'It's not,' she says in her best spoilt voice. 'But I'm going to this damn rally, aren't I, and in this boil no less. I think that's enough of a commitment.'

Faisal has been bleating on about No Corruption politics for weeks, and we're all worn thin by his enthusiasm. Despite the blasting air-conditioner my arm burns as it lies against the hot window. I think I can smell my arm hair burning, and this is just the late-afternoon sun.

I have no one to blame but myself. I should have expected this form of religious fervour from Faisal. Faisal lives for a cause. WWF pandas at twelve, waste recycling and plastic collection at fifteen, a short stint into socialism in college . . . and, of course, every female he's ever had a crush on since the eighth grade. He's the kind of guy who hones in on something he likes, then blindly obsesses about it until there's nothing left except the shattered pieces of his dignity. It's the rich-boy curse: no cause equals any damn cause. The girls and the environment I can deal with, but it's this new devotion to Mian Tariq that's troublesome. It won't be fun dealing with him if Mian Tariq loses.

I try to shut out his voice, which is starting to grate. Let them talk it out. Outside the rich tree-lined mansions of the distinguished Government Officers' Residences surround us. The houses are hidden behind the throngs of bamboo, peepul and chinar trees, but we can see dark gates, exposed driveways, a car or two in residences that once housed officers of the British Raj. I doubt this neighbourhood is pleased at the relocation of the rally. So much for powerful government influence.

A fat man in a greasy sweat-stained banian attempts to miraculously squeeze between pedestrians and cars on his motorbike, his handlebars scraping the paint off a red Honda. The woman driver yells at him and thumps his helmet through her window. It's a heightened chaos—usually reserved for Chand Raat or a citywide protest. Despite the insulated and elevated soundproofing of the X5 we can still hear people yelling Mian Tariq's name, waving his red-and-green campaign flag, their horns blaring in unison in an attempt to show a uniform solidarity.

'Faisal, this is ridiculous,' Aliya says. 'We've been in the same spot for an hour. I can see the damn park's entrance from here. Come on, let's just get out and walk.' With that, and without a pause of confirmation or agreement from us, Aliya opens her car door and steps out. In a scramble for Faisal's driver, who throws money at the rickshaw quickly and takes Faisal's place, we follow in a wash of traffic noise and oily engine smells.

It's Lahore high on industrial-scented crack: diesel, petrol and CNG, pungent underarm-sweat, cheap perfume, airborne dust, the taste of iron against my tongue. There's the familiar Lahori smell of burning rubber and the stench of smoking garbage, sweet paan and popcorn wafting from the park. My nose and ears burn from the excess. Every horn created by man is firing today—Japanese, German, American, Korean. The long horse-whines of vans, the short squeaks of small cars, motorbike put-puts and rickshaws all driven forward by the large booming aggression of Land Cruisers telling us to move off the fucking road. We're pushed from the comfortable womb of the X5 into a world none of us remembers how to negotiate any more. Aliya takes the lead, interlocking her arm with mine and pulling me on to the dusty curb—if a burnt rail of grass and some uneven bricks can be called that.

It's hard to describe Third World chaos. It just looks like shit. A family of five pushes past us, the children holding hands in a line. The mother digs an elbow into Aliya's ribs as she shoves her aside. Aliya's curses are ignored in the tumult. It's difficult to breathe. Along the median, among discarded cigarettes and gum wrappers, I see a young girl's lost gold sandal. A beggar woman tries to sell Saba a balloon—'A pink balloon to match your pink kameez, pretty girl? If you buy a balloon you'll marry a rich handsome man with a moon face.' Faisal protectively grabs

Saba's arm, afraid Moon Face might appear any minute. Aliya keeps plunging boldly through, still holding my arm, weaving between noisy families. I barely manage to keep up with her as she drags me through the narrowest of spaces between two trees. The long floral dupatta around her neck flaps about the trunk. With the park's gate in sight I speed up, tripping over a small rock. A teenage boy with a fuzzy moustache on a cycle smirks at me and I give him the finger—his smile grows wider, exposing a mouthful of uneven teeth.

At this point, I confess, I'm a little nervous. The crazed traffic, the overzealous political supporters, the throngs of Lahoris who have emerged from God-knows-where like locusts at a plague party—I feel almost claustrophobic. I feel anxious taking the girls to such a large public event. The last large gathering we all went to—an Ali Azmat concert at the Pakistan College of Design— Faisal got smashed in the head by an airborne crook-lock— twenty-five stitches and the end of parental permission to see mass musical events. That was almost a decade ago. I don't know what it is about Pakistani crowds that bring out the jungli in everyone. It seems the larger the gathering, the more dangerous the results. Maybe it's in our blood, a century of British repression, and now the only person we want to punch in the face is ourselves. And I won't even bother thinking about the terrorist-attack possibilities. Once that fear sets in we might as well break our own legs to stay at home. I take a deep breath and slowly follow the massive laughing breathing blinking coughing complaining perspiring talking crowd through the large iron gates of Race Course Park.

I look around at the dust-laden leaves of familiar trees, the worn cobble pathways, the burnt grassy hills and odd rock formations and, suddenly, I feel a bit nostalgic. That's the thing about living in the same city for a lifetime—the memories are varied and vivid, and endless. I remember a school trip, when we were twelve and the park was a massive sprawl of free fuck-around space. Faisal was an idiot even then, but he bowled a hell of a game. We ran wildly and behaved badly, chasing girls behind the canteen and stealing their ball. It was awesome.

'This is so exciting, isn't it?' Aliya says, squeezing my arm. 'I haven't been to Race Course in years. This is going to be fun.'

Faisal turns around and gives us a thumbs up. He's grinning like a mental monkey. He's probably recalling the girls we attempted to hook up with a few years ago behind the park's many trees, his lame attempt to appear cool in a white linen suit, the late-night jaunt through the curling pathways, pitiful, sweaty hand-holding, the beating wings of enthusiastic fruit-bats, some wet kisses and the two *kusra*s we discovered humping behind a bush.

Faisal's Diesel jeans are hanging loosely off his waist, the bottoms dragging in the dirt as he tries to quickly manoeuvre through the crowd. Saba practically has to run to keep up. The fool wants to stand right up front, the worshipper position, so if anything happens he can make sure he won't survive it.

'Let him go,' I tell Aliya, pulling her back. 'We're bound to lose him anyway. We'll find them again. He'll be the tallest, dumbest flag-waver around.' Aliya laughs and we slowly circle the massive fields, trying to find the easiest entry towards the stage. I can't remember the last time I went to a park in Lahore. I feel out of sorts. It seems as if the parks are no longer for us but for the real people of Pakistan, who don't live in chilled glass-houses and smoke hash all day. As children this would be the highlight of our week, my sisters and I, my mother, the vast green sprawl of open fields, the evening's jogging Aunties, the bizarre misplaced water-fountains. We didn't give two shits about class or education.

If you could bat or bowl, you were in for a day of fun. Now we stay indoors, play video games and watch copious amounts of television shows, and pretend we're above it all.

As we get closer to the big field we hear chanting and yelling, voices in unison, louder than at any rock concert I've ever been to. Down the winding path and around a corner and suddenly there's a sea of humanity before us; wave upon wave of red-and-green flags fluttering in the air, voices undulating and crashing together with the name of Mian Tariq and his bullshit party. So many people are gathered that for a moment I'm speechless, a little overwhelmed despite the surprising warmth and smiles around us. Aliya grabs two flags from a young vendor and thrusts one into my hand. She's already part of the swarm, chanting Mian Tariq's name, pulling me roughly into the storm of faces and sweat. I find myself scanning the chaos for Faisal's head. I realize that I was wrong, and that I probably won't be able to spot his gangly ass among this massive living, breathing ocean. People roughly push past us into what seems a pit of endless human steam. Far out in front, past a layer of dusted atmosphere, there's a high, wide stage with podiums and chairs, microphones and wires criss-crossing, dangling in mid-air, above the crowd. Giant colour posters and flags are propped behind the stage—Mian Tariq's face magnified in an almost movie-star glory.

'Oye, yaar, hurry. Let's get closer to the stage,' a man says, passing me. 'I want some tip-top photos.'

High on makeshift metal cranes, men with television cameras perch and wait for the spectacle, their dangling legs suspended in mid-air. I give them a wide berth. I'm not risking anyone falling or dropping their shit on my head. I stop Aliya, holding on to her arm tightly. She turns and looks at me, annoyed. 'What?' she asks. I can tell she's enjoying the gush of energy. It's like a full-blown rock concert, but I'm not sure I want to push through a thousand elbows and fingers, people so close I can smell their breath on my face, their sweat, their chicken handi dinners. I know if I lose sight of her I won't find her again.

'Maybe we should wait back here for a bit,' I say to her. 'Where the crowd's less like a mosh pit.'

'Are you kidding me?' she says. She doesn't wait for me to answer before looking away, merging back into the crowd. She's mesmerized, unable to look away—the stage, the colours, the lights and sounds of a hundred-thousand Lahori auras humming in excitement, gathered in one place for the first time in our recent history.

'Faisal's right, the front is the place to be. I want to see the sweat drip off MT's face,' she says. 'Otherwise we might as well have seen this shit on TV.' Then she looks at me closely, surprised. 'Bugsy, what's wrong with you? You're the concert junkie, Mr RJ. Don't tell me you're claustrophobic.' I shake my head. What am I going to tell her? That at a concert I'm usually high off my ass on the music and a fine cocktail of mood-altering substances, and that if I'm squashed to death at least it's in the name of rock 'n' roll, not some dingbat politician and his campaign rally.

'This is a virtual riot. In Lahore. In June. So, no, I'm not crazy,' I say to her. She rolls her eyes and drops my hand.

'Will you stop being such a wuss? God. You'll live.' And with that she moves purposely forward, roughly parting her way through the dense crowd. I glance down at the flag clutched in my hand—a small rectangular scrap of cloth divided horizontally through the middle, red for Mian Tariq, green for Pakistan, the half-moon and star, our national symbols. It's attached to a cheap wooden stick, like in an ice lolly. A simple symbol—a flag, cheap two-rupee fabric, a splintering piece of wood, and all the weight of a nation's history waving precariously in the wind.

Surrendering, I run to catch up with Aliya, excusing myself and apologizing for all the feet I trample and people I push. In the middle, where the crowd is densest and I can smell musty fabric pressed against wet flesh, I hold my breath, sucking air through my lips. The crowd is swelling, growing, pulsating as I move closer towards the stage. The park has disappeared above the hordes of pressed shoulders, a few treetops the only indication that there ever was a park in the first place.

'When will the band come?' I overhear a boy ask.

'There will be a new song just for Mian Tariq,' another answers. 'That is what they said on FM84.'

What band? I didn't know there would be music at this rally. I guess I haven't been listening to my radio ads lately. I hope to God it isn't some dorky wannabe pop band, out of tune and out of date.

'Why do they always start so late, *hain*? It's going to get dark before he arrives,' someone complains.

I stand in a small pocket of air, a miraculous hole in the surging crowd, and gather my bearings. I allow myself to breathe. The stage is so close it has occluded my view, the massive posters and spotlights my only orientation. Aliya has disappeared amongst the supporters who, tired of waiting, have started to sit in the dirt. A fat woman next to me fans herself with her flag and talks while lazily chewing gum.

'The mosquitoes will eat us alive if they don't hurry,' she complains.

'Mosquitoes? In June? In this heat? Are you pagal?' someone else says.

'No, you're pagal. Of course there are mosquitoes. Where do you think you are? In the Ing-land?'

Next to me, too close for comfort in this heat pit, a girl holds a very unattractive baby on her hip, pointing different things out to him while he squirms to get away. A few people grumble, wipe the perspiration off their lips and noses, but most are smiling, faces beaming with sweat and the anticipation of Mian Tariq's arrival, flushed with the possibility of hope and change.

I continue to search for Aliya or Faisal, craning my neck, closing in on the front, almost beneath the stage. I spot them with a few other friends standing in a semicircle to the right of the stage—Aliya jumping up and down like a madwoman, waving her flag, screaming Mian Tariq's name in mock excitement. They're impossible not to see situated near the podium and the band, where Mian Tariq's face will be at an angle, his left side clearly visible to us. The band will probably be loud enough to pop an eardrum, with crummy desi PA and sound reinforcement. I don't know why the hell Aliya has to stubbornly stand right in front to see everything—her father is friends with Mian Tariq, and she's met him personally on countless occasions. But, no, she stands right in the front, and yells to some teenager, 'Oye, you, move! I can't bloody see. Is there a reason your big fat head is in front of me?'

'So is this thing ever going to start?' I ask, joining them. I'm relieved to have found them. They inform me that the band is on its way, stuck in rally traffic on Jail Road. Nothing in Pakistan starts on time, so why should this? Despite Mian Tariq's nation-transforming platform, it seems efficiency and organization don't quite fit under the No Corruption umbrella.

Aliya furiously messages people on her phone and takes selfies, tweeting and posting her location on Facebook, showing off her appearance at her first political rally. It's a notable event for her socialite fan base.

'Give it a rest,' I say to her, 'before you get carpal tunnel.'

I look around at our position—at the crest of the wave—
and I'm glad Aliya dragged me up here, where, in case of an
emergency I can jump on stage and escape via a back route. At
least now I'll be able to hear what the hell Mian Tariq has to
say, figure out the drug of Faisal's addiction. We wait. Aliya
sits on the ground, gets up, sits again. The girls gossip and do
a rundown of every Pakistani fashion disaster in the last six
months, every extramarital affair, every twisted and broken
relationship. My ears perk up when they discuss Omer's new
girlfriend, Nida. She's what Aliya refers to as Omer's 'Menu Del
Dia'. He's apparently seeing a lot of her, possibly even likes her.
I snort, as if Omer could ever like anyone but himself. Faisal
attempts to interrupt the girls by laying some tragic moves on
Saba—a movie invitation, a party, dinner with the gang post-
rally? She shrugs. He's not as interesting as Aliya's spewing of
one-eyed jagged-toothed gossip—she's our local E! News. I
shake my head at Faisal, he's just not a closer.

We light countless cigarettes, a hip flask is passed
indiscreetly. And then there's a stirring, as if the wind has
picked up. The rustling of leaves, the creaking of a thousand
bones as people get up, turn their faces forward towards the
noise of the stage. The mic screeches, making eyes water and
mouths groan. We hear the crowd's cheer building, growing
louder and louder until I can feel it in my chest, a heat rising.
The band members, skinny kids in jeans and black tees, run
up the steps and start to plug in their instruments, perform
a quick—at this point useless—soundcheck. The singer, who
has a maroon Tele strapped to his back, taps the mic hesitantly.
The speakers squeak obnoxiously loud, right in my fucking
ear. I recognize him from an earlier desi-rock creation, he's

Aamir Khan from the now-defunct BrainStorm, once a Lahori rock staple. This is his new—and apparently improved—band of rock 'n' roll goons.

'Soundcheck 1, 2, 3.' The drummer takes his seat, pounds out a few notes, the keyboard player fingers the ivory. And then it's on. The crowd gets louder, the sweltering heat and their frustrations lost. The band busts out a few off-key songs, their instruments squeaking periodically through the massive speakers, their voices barely a croak over the roaring of the crowd. And then they play Mian Tariq's theme song. It's loud, in key—for once—and decent. Not amazing, but I'm impressed. The song has a strong patriotic ring, anthemy, with some elaborate drumming, and a guitar solo that's a desperate nod to Journey's Neal Schon. I was expecting a song that would lead us all to suicide. Luckily it isn't so shit. I would never play it on *The Rocket Launch*, but it doesn't make me want to stab my ears out with a BBQ skewer either. All in all, disaster averted. New respect for Mian Tariq's band choice Kabzah—not a great name, especially if the last two diarrhoea-spelling letters are left out, but hey, you can't have it all.

There's silence. The band bows and leaves quickly. The excitement for Mian Tariq builds. He makes us wait. His party members slowly walk on to the stage, take their seats behind the podium. They receive rock-star cheers, despite being a motley collection of fat uncles in various stages of balding. They're all corrupt men who jump parties like they jump hookers. Each one waves like he's the bloody Queen of England, proudly sitting upright and gloating. These are the faces that disgrace the No Corruption slogan, faces that we've all seen since the seventies in one disastrous political party or the other.

And then he steps up on stage, Mian Tariq, a sharp contrast to the toads behind him—tall, handsome, clean and fair, with a starched-white salwar-kameez and gelled movie-star hair. An all-encompassing cheer moves through the crowd like wind through wheat, building from behind until it becomes a gale force. People scream, shriek his name, their voices hollering, then coming together to chant: *Mian Tariq, Mian Tariq, Mian Tariq*. I cringe at the roaring of a hundred thousand people, but find myself chanting his name along with everyone, just as loud, the flag circling above me as I wave the damp popsicle stick.

Mian Tariq walks up to the podium, his face displayed on the multiple projector screens, so large his teeth are visible, white and perfect as he smiles. He raises his open palms up in modest appreciation. He waves to the crowd and everyone goes apeshit. A lady next to us, a hijab covering her head, face barely visible, inserts two fingers in her mouth and whistles so loudly Aliya and I jump in our skin. Mian Tariq stands there, his smile probably starting to hurt, outstretched palms hushing the crowd until slowly an easy silence descends. Behind him the main members of his party stand, all in kameezes of grey and black, looking a little too *sharif* and subdued, their eyes sharp, determined, taking everything in, assessing the crowd. It is because of this small handful of powerful and corrupt men, who MT has managed to convert from other prominent political parties, that he is standing here before this massive support.

Mian speaks to the semi-hushed masses, a few still hoot and holler. His voice comes out strong and smooth through the cheap Chinese microphone. There is no electric squeaking this time. His voice is hard, urgent, and it rises above us and circles like a storm. I can feel it physically pressing against me, the thickness of his emotions surrounding us with their message. He sermonizes in Urdu, English and Punjabi—all spoken perfectly, blending so harmoniously, it's as if he's creating his own language. The shifts are almost imperceptible. He starts small—with introductions, gratitude, admiration for the support—and builds to his vision of a new Pakistan, a new future: a place where corruption is defeated. I listen, sceptically at first, judging his every word. I don't believe in No Corruption. The idea is utopian and impossible, like asking a master thief to start stealing hundreds when he's used to millions. Or asking American CEOs to forgo their bonuses in lieu of a workers' retirement fund. It may be for the greater good, but it's so unrealistic it's laughable.

'Corruption is the disease eating our country,' Mian Tariq says with power, his voice laden with emotion. 'It flows through our rivers, seeping into every aspect of our lives—from our crops to our businesses, our government to the military. Corruption has become so much a part of our lives, we are now blind to its evil. We think it is a part of our culture, when, really, it is the *disease* of our culture.'

He continues to talk of this endemic corruption we've all grown accustomed to and explains how it is not our fault, we have been manipulated by our leaders—generations of prime ministers, presidents, generals and intelligence directors. We've been manipulated by the West and their desires to conquer and control us; decades of manipulation by the likes of India, Saudi Arabia and now even China. Apparently our brand of evil is not our own doing. He talks of making Pakistan a working state of liberal economics with the abolition of feudalism, an anti-militant state, with decreased bureaucracy and with the implementation of anti-corruptions laws.

'I am a wealthy man,' he confides in us, a tight fist raised in the air, 'and I have no need for more money. I want to live my life in my country freely. I want my children to grow up Pakistani. To be proud to go anywhere in the world and declare they are Pakistani. I say to you all today: I am an open book. Read me as you will, but I assure you, with me there is nothing to hide—no secrets, no buildings or housing developments in Dubai, Geneva or London. These investments I leave for the others,' he says, smiling wryly, a subtle hint to his competitors.

'What you see before you is what you get, and I will keep my promises!' he yells. 'As a nation we must create a culture of accountability and transparency, and this culture begins with me!'

People go mad. Flags are thrown in the air and caught again, children are hoisted on shoulders, flashes of cameras wildly spark in the now-reddening sky of dusk. It's definitely a rush. I don't know whether it's the deafening cheering of the crowd—the people I am surrounded by daily, my fellow countrymen, finally, now, for the first time united by a cause, for the betterment of our nation—or whether it's Mian Tariq's voice that is causing the pressure to build inside my chest. Aliya is tearing up next to me and she squeezes my hand tightly.

'He's amazing,' she says dreamily, as though she were watching Freddie Mercury live at the Budokan. Faisal grins at me like a love-struck fool, and I have to smile back. There's something to be said about a massive crowd of cheering people that really makes you feel alive. My heart's beating wildly, the impossible possibilities of life feeling somehow closer, and I feel, well . . . patriotic. I'm laughing along with everyone. I'm not crying, fuck no, but I do find myself wondering about the possibilities a leader like Mian Tariq presents. I don't know how much national support Salim Chaudhry currently has, how many dollars he has stashed away in Swiss bank accounts or under his mattress, but the hundred thousand voices in Race Course Park don't seem to give a shit.

BUGSY

The front doorbell rings sharp and loud, signalling the first in my father's tedious line-up of military cronies. It's the evening of my twenty-fifth birthday, and I feel like standing on my bedroom sofa, where I am watching downloaded episodes of *Breaking Bad*, and throwing a lopsided salute. I can hear my father's booming 'command' voice echoing up from the front corridor. My room, along with my elder sister Nosheen's, is upstairs, where we share a large communal living area surrounded by two bedrooms and one guest room, the stairs our demarcation line to divide us from my parents—they rarely, if ever, bother to make the climb. In Pakistan this is as good as it gets for troubled flat-broke youth; it's a virtual penthouse.

Our district of the city is aptly named Defence, all military beneath the manicured suburban surface of tended gardens, red-brick walls and hideous Greek columns with Kalmas inscribed carefully in gold plating on each pediment. As the black market grows, so does the housing construction in our area. To my father's disdain, he and his fellow army elite now find themselves surrounded by the slow invasion of suburban Pakistani civilians: the close-walled houses and their shouting servants, children on bicycles, the squawking of unknown neighbours wrestling with the night, listening to Lata and Rafi on their transistor radios that infiltrate my father's conquest dreams with three-four waltzes and images of shimmying hips and glossy lips in Filmazia Kodachrome. Defence even comes equipped with its very own neighbourhood McDonald's and a three-floored KFC.

On nights like tonight my family's responsible for the night-time cacophony as much as anyone—an odious blend of East meets West. Beneath the celebratory tent in my parents' garden a quartet of tabla, harmonium, violin and saxophone winds its way in a timeless din. Downstairs in the parental soirée, heavy middle-aged military wives occupy all furniture, stuffing themselves on pakoras, samosas and fresh juices, while the men stand at parade rest—avoiding the wives at all costs—tanking up on whisky and vodka and discussing politics and cricket in pure old-fashioned segregation.

Upstairs my friends will soon slowly amass for our own kind of celebration—a party that is decidedly integrated and all about getting ass. It's here that the garden twang of violins will disappear in a wave of drunken howling and Bose surround, and it is here that I will celebrate *my* birthday.

'Happy birthday, Bugsy darling,' Aliya says flirtatiously in my ear, coming up behind me and wrapping her arms around my waist. I'm still in my room, last-minute hair-gelling and deodorizing, ignoring the early-bird auntie–uncle arrivals. Aliya's the first one up here, and hopefully will be for some time. My loser friends are always late and arrive half-cocked, pre-partying until they realize they could be copping my parents' free booze instead of their own.

She kisses my neck from behind, and I turn my face towards her, trying to meet her lips. 'I wanted to come before all the thirsty alkies,' she says, smiling, kissing me lightly on the lips. She kisses carefully, not wanting to smudge her lipstick, and slaps my hand away when I try to touch her hair. She masterfully slithers away, straightening what appears to be a very expensive peach-and-gold sari, and lights a cigarette.

'Why'd you come early if I can't even touch you?' I say to her, annoyed.

'To fuck with you, why else?' she says, teasing. 'Don't worry, you'll get your present later.' She winks. I move towards her, attempting at least some grinding action before people show up.

'You're going to ruin those khaki pants if you keep this up,' she says, giggling.

'Fuck the pants,' I say, digging my face deeper into her soft, perfumy neck and tasting its bitterness.

'Whose pants are fucked?' says Faisal as he kicks the door open, holding two bottles of Absolut Cranberry. 'Where is everybody? All the auntie–uncles are rockin' it downstairs.'

'Highly doubtful,' I say. 'And why the fuck do you insist on coming so damn early?' The bastard just grins and wipes his sneakers clean with the wet towel I have draped on the sofa.

Aliya has already slipped away to fix her face in the mirror. She's like a slippery fish you just can't get a hold of. I think she prefers the tease to the real thing. Our relationship is largely based on the mutual exchange of sexual hints and suggestive petting, a lasting but hollow flirtation at parties. By tonight she'll be too drunk to remember the juicy specifics of her birthday offer and the sex will be, as it always is, drunken and desperate, performed quickly in some awkward dusty location away from the prying eyes and ears of our friends. Happy fucking birthday to me.

'I'm not early. It's already . . .' he checks his oversized ass-rapingly expensive designer watch, 'ten thirty. So are we getting drunk or not, yaar? And why the fuck are you dressed like some old-ass auntie, Aliya? Feeling a bit mature today, now that your Bugsy Wugsy is twenty-five? Are you hoping to impress Auntie Bugsy for a shaadi proposal?'

'Suck it, Faisal.' Aliya gives him the finger. 'I can wear whatever the hell I want, and a sari is incredibly sexy.'

'She's right there,' I say, agreeing, and swipe a quick feel around her bare belly as I grab the chilled vodka bottles from Faisal. They're numbingly cold, the product of a quality car cooler. Faisal's only this organized when it comes to booze. He's useless at everything else.

'All the mixers are outside, go figure it out. I'm coming,' I tell him.

'Where's Saba?' he asks nervously, suddenly realizing Aliya's here alone.

'Relax, my driver's gone to pick her up. Just chill,' she says.

'Yeah, Faisal, chill,' I say, giving him shit. 'Now go outside and organize.'

Aliya laughs and touches up her hair with my hairbrush, her highlighted long brown hair static-clinging to my shirt as I try to cop a feel, attempting to capture one solid sober memory of ass for later. She pushes me back with her butt and grins wickedly at me in the mirror.

'Are you sure you don't want to give me my present right now?' I ask, wrapping my arms around her thin exposed waist, pulling her close to me. It's driving me crazy. A bare female belly is a rarity in Lahore, like petting a blind porpoise.

'What, with Faisal outside?'

I shrug. 'Oh, please, it's just Faisal! He'll cycle through the music and silently pickle himself in cran-vodka.'

She adjusts her blouse, lowering the V-shaped neckline and exposing the tops of her tits, the fair skin and the mole you can only see if the top is low enough. I run my hands roughly over them like some monkey in a zoo and she smiles mischievously at me, wags a finger and slips away. She's done with her preening and teasing. This is all I'm getting for now. I feel young and desperate and incredibly helpless, like it's my fifteenth birthday instead of my twenty-fifth.

'Oye, are you coming?' Faisal yells from outside. 'I'm waiting. And bored.' He has a gift, I swear, a cock-blocking gift. He's a fucking master.

Aliya laughs. 'Silently drunk, eh? Yeah, right. The only girlfriend he has is you. You two are made for each other. Come, let's go.'

'Fine,' I say gloomily.

'Don't worry,' she says, noticing my dejected face. She softly runs her fingers over my cheek. 'I promise it'll be worth it. Plus, it'll give you something to look forward to as you drink and greet your guests.'

I might cry if it's gift-wrapped.

The first part of the night moves quickly in a whisky-laced sprint. Upstairs it's a PhD in polarity—loud-ass music alternating between eighties rock and some crap party songs my sisters keep recycling, the decisions between a whisky drink or a vodka drink and, of course, sex and the desi female disease of saying No but wanting Yes. The girls stay classy throughout the night while the boys start to fall apart after the first few shots. At the end everyone will blend into one bad bruise and then it'll really begin.

Downstairs the music is full desi and sobering, the chatting guest voices high and aflutter, like canaries in a cage. The uncles have stepped out to smoke in the tented area despite the stifling heat. It's my birthday, it's once a bloody year, so I have to make the rounds and meet and greet. First come the aunties, who all fawn and touch my face and leave the imprints of their cheap lipstick on my cheeks. I get envelopes of birthday money—the only plus—and exchange short bursts of polite conversation with an auntie or two. They mean well, and some look pretty fucking fit, with ample bosoms on display. No complaints there.

I spot my sisters Noshie and Bano talking to some random relatives. They're doing their duty masterfully, smiling politely, their faces masks of attention and tolerance, answering question after tedious question, probably about marriage. Most of my sisters' sexually depraved female friends are upstairs getting wasted with my friends, hoping to get felt up before their curfew. My sisters signal for me to join them, but I quickly dodge out, stepping into the heat of the tent to say hello to my father's friends.

Right at the doorway, halfway between the air-conditioned cold of the inside and the blistering heat wave outside, Elahi Chacha stops me and drones on and on about my cousin's savvy investments in America. His very gay investment banker son, just gotten married, is, according to common gossip, flaming all over New York while his wife sits confused at home playing with her Prada. Another uncle stops me on the stoop to reminisce about his own twenty-fifth birthday, persistently insisting I must enjoy life before I blink and I'm fifty and *my* wife spends all *my* money filling her lips with collagen and ass with Botox. Cheery thoughts. Uncles never censor their thoughts when they're drunk. They really should. The poor dude looks like cancer; could probably use some fillers himself. A series of quick conversations, some agreeable nods shared with a few uncles-shunkles, and I make my way to where my father, The Brigadier, is holding court: a small group of officers sweating together in their garden civvy-suits. Here goes nothing.

The men stand in a loose circle, posture erect, eyes sharp, ready to observe and be observed. The fattest is Colonel Pervaiz, The Brig's closest friend—whose son was on the shortlist of marriage possibilities for Noshie but was rejected because of some serious halitosis. Standing next to him is the Air Vice-Marshal, a real kick-in-the-balls hard-ass who wears his expensive Japanese off-colour toupee proudly, like it's a mink stole. There's also Lieutenant General Kaz, who doesn't talk much and seems like a nice guy except that The Brig can't help showing off around him at my expense. He spots me and motions to me curtly with his hand to join them.

The circle expands slightly to include me in a carcinogenic ingestion that includes busting my balls about my life decisions, future lack of decisions and past vices, with the occasional Sweet Uncle protection. I take the brace position: legs slightly apart, hands balled at my sides, shoulders squared. Also known as the military butt-fuck position.

The uncles smile behind well-groomed moustaches and dole out the perfunctory birthday greetings, referring me to their wives for the money-filled birthday envelopes. I know these retired military men well, and alone they are nice-enough dudes who go hunting and fishing with The Brig and bitch about their wives, mistresses and genital herpes—or so I presume. But together they can't seem to escape their military rankings, the hierarchy of stars and stripes patterns their DNA—and the anal prod gets long and hard.

There's a new short little man standing with them, not much older than me, dark, with a little black moustache and hard hair gelled so severely it looks like he's wearing a mortar shell. He doesn't say a word, just observes us closely, squinting like an idiot. Maybe he'll be tested on it later.

'So, Bugsy, you are keeping yourself out of trouble, right? Not partying too much, I hope?' Colonel Pervaiz asks me. His well-meaning but heavy hand is on my shoulder, pressing fingers into the bone, refusing to let go.

I groan inwardly. 'Jee, uncle,' I reply quickly. Questions like that instantly make my teeth hurt.

'Well, that's good to hear.' He smiles and shakes me a little with his fat hand.

'So what is it you want to do with your life now that you're entering twenty-five?' the Air Vice-Marshal asks. This has been more or less his standard question since I was twelve. Back then I would say I wanted to join the air force and he'd beam with pride and slap my back. I've really missed that boat.

'It seems he's written off marriage permanently,' The Brig angrily complains. Trust my father to exaggerate everything. I'm a perpetual disappointment, especially in front of his military friends. I'm his punching bag, the only son, apparently the only one who matters. He rarely talks of the girls or their lives. It's always just me.

'What! Written off shaadi? How can that be? *Nahin*, *beta*, nahin, that's just wrong.' That's the Colonel again. He speaks in fatherly tones, always-dramatic, fluctuating feminine variations.

He has an incredibly high uncomfortable laugh, a bit like a horse whine, which I'm sure the neighbours can hear through the walls.

'Marriage is the only institution that keeps one sane, young man. It's how you mature and become the man you're supposed to be.' That's the Air Vice-Marshal. 'Without marriage you're always a kusra, never a man,' he says, and they all laugh. Cheap gay shot. Nothing new here.

'That's what I keep telling him, but he refuses to listen.' The Brig adds his two cents, fuelling the fire.

'I haven't written off marriage,' I say, bristling slightly. 'I'm just not interested right now.'

'Look at Major Anwar here,' The Brig says, familiarly grabbing the young man by the back of the neck. His whisky sloshes in the glass. The entire time the little man has been studying my face intently, looking me up and down, assessing my every article of clothing, his narrow eyes darting back and forth throughout our conversation. 'Major Anwar has just had his second child and is on his way to becoming Lieutenant-Colonel.'

I congratulate the little man; he gives me a brief acknowledging nod. He's not as young as I previously thought, but the ass-kissing expression is bang on.

'The Brigadier tells me you're on the radio, doing some show?' Major Anwar asks.

'It's apparently all he wants to do,' my father adds, 'play music, day and night. Get drunk and play music.'

'You're on FM84,' Major Anwar says, more of statement than a question. 'I think I heard your show the other day, late evening, during my drive home. That was you? RJ Bugsy?'

I nod.

'It was pretty good. Not my kind of music though.'

I celebrate this small victory in my head.

'I have a small suggestion for you . . .' He leans forward, moving close to me, as if relaying a secret. I can smell his lemony cologne. 'I think you should play more jazz on your show.'

I stare at him, wondering if he's fucking with me, and if he could take one of my right crosses. He seems serious.

'My broadcast is a rock show only,' I tell him in the nicest, softest, most patient way I can, as if I'm talking to a small, dim-witted child. 'That's the point, in those three hours, to only play rock music.'

'I don't think a little jazz would hurt anyone,' he says, smiling at my father and his friends. 'And it'll benefit your show, trust me. No one likes so much rock, one loud song after the other. It gives people a headache.'

I don't know what to say. No question, the midget goes down with even the slightest glancing blow. How the hell did this dodo make it to major? I imagine his little head rattling around in an Al-Khalid tank, shooting at bloodthirsty Taliban. Not a chance. They'd have him for breakfast. Major through some major ass-kissing, that's for sure. I try to hide the disgust and tell him it's a good idea and next time I'll consider playing some jazz music on my exclusively-rock-music show. Everyone seems pleased by my response.

'So, is this all you're doing now? Radio?' the Air Vice-Marshal asks. 'Where is the career?' And there it is—the question. The question with no answers. I consider answering, but there isn't enough time to go through the entire list I practised while in the shower. I just shrug and smile weakly. No answer is good enough anyway. It's a trick question. He fills in the blank spots left by my dignity.

'Did you know my daughter wanted to be a doctor?' he says. Major Asshole looks dramatically interested. 'She told everyone since she was five that she was going to be a surgeon. I paid for her to go to university in America where she took organic chemistry, failed and decided she'd rather get married and sit around the house all day with three children and the maid.' The Air Vice-Marshal's face doesn't move a muscle as he talks, dead serious like he's bombing Bangalore. I've heard this daughter disaster tale before. He doesn't mention that when she failed he made her come back. No doctor, no America. If she were a boy it wouldn't have mattered if she failed or not, she could have jerked off until graduation and everyone would have been proud. But he tells it as if it's a personal affront, his daughter's life choices. He talks as if he's imparting stock tips or insider-trading secrets instead of his harsh and often irrelevant opinions. His daughter got knocked up and his son sells cocaine at parties, case closed.

'You know, Bugsy, you better decide soon what you're going to do with your life—before it's too late,' he says. 'You kids today don't know this, but there is a cut-off time, and then it is too late. You're either too old or too inexperienced for anything worthy. You can't be a DJ all your life.' He chuckles at this last part, as if in his head he's imagining me a balding dancing pot-bellied DJ spinning tunes at some kiddie party.

'Why didn't you join the army, Bugsy, if you don't mind my asking? Your father has had a very distinguished career,' the Midget Major says. 'I'm sure The Brig would have supported your army career. You might have been a captain by now.' I just can't escape that damn question. Every fucking year some douchebag asks, and every year I stutter and spit a pathetic answer, unable to fully articulate my dislike of the military because of my father.

'Um, well . . . I'm not really interested in the military.'

'He's just not the army type,' The Brig pipes in. 'His mother and sisters have spoilt him soft. It's my fault. No discipline.'

Ouch. Major Pain just nods, a smile playing his lips, and I imagine him going down with a single-nudge jab, nose bleeding down his cheap powdery-blue shirt.

Col Pervaiz feels for me. I can see the sympathy oozing out of his plump, round maternal face. 'Well, it takes discipline to be a boxer, and Bugsy was a damn good boxer when he was younger. Doesn't matter, children are children,' he says soothingly. 'My son is getting married in December,' he tells me, changing the subject. 'Did you know?'

'Of course, uncle, congratulations,' I say, relieved by the change of subject, able to finally swallow all the rage that's flooded my mouth.

'You'll have to come to all the functions,' he says. 'I'm sure there will be lots of pretty single girls.' He winks at me.

'That would be a miracle,' The Brig pipes in. 'Plenty of single girls prancing about everywhere, and the boy still can't make up his mind.' He's done his fake-disappointment routine, which means I can escape soon. The birthday scrutiny and ass-raping is almost over.

I stand next to him uncomfortably as they continue talking around me, about Swat and the Taliban, about the army adding another brigade to Special Group, the Air Vice-Marshal complaining about the lack of spare parts and equipment for his F-16s, and how without them The Brigadier and the army would be a lost band of well-dressed, disciplined halfwits. He's right there. And then the little Major brings up Mian Tariq's name and the whole group starts jabbering, and for once I am interested.

'He's not going to be able to stop the drone attacks. Impossible.'

'What, and piss off the Americans? Never.'

'His hands are tied. He will be like all the others in this matter. Talking a good game isn't the same as playing a good game.

And his platform is weak. Where are the real reforms? The ones that this country desperately needs. Anyone can promise No Corruption, but try to execute it and see what happens. It'll be chaos.'

'Maybe we just need someone new,' I say, adding my two cents. 'Maybe just having a change is good enough. A new face. He can't be any worse.'

'He won't win. He just doesn't have enough national support.'

'But if he does he'll leave the heavy lifting to us and start promising intervention and decreased attacks like the rest of them. We'll have to support another lame duck.'

'He doesn't know politics. He's too busy talking of No Corruption to even consider what the country is going through. He's cut off from the military and has no connections. He's living in a dream world.'

The men huff and puff, their discussion heating up about the losses in the army's past operations against the Taliban in Swat. Their drinks dwindle. I take my cue and quickly say goodbye; they hardly notice amidst the mushrooming opinions.

Inside I spot Noshie and Bano sitting with our cousins on a sofa, whispering to each other. The aunties have stampeded off to the dining room to eat, dinner served early for them, before midnight, and then later for the men.

'What are you girls *khusar-phusar*-ing about?' I ask them.

'Auntie Zenaib is hanging from the curtains again,' Bano tells me.

'Isn't she like eighty years old?' I ask them.

'Age eighty, liver 140.'

I look over at poor Auntie Zenaib, who has kicked off her heels and is trying for dear life to remain upright. She's probably only fifty, but her affection for cheap booze has wrecked her.

'She's married to fat Colonel Sheraz. Although he's not too bad.'

'I don't know why she behaves like that,' Noshie says.

'Because he probably drives home in his tank and drops a big fat bomb on her every night,' I say. The girls laugh and make disgusted faces.

'That's our future, ladies. Enjoy it,' Bano says.

'Not mine,' my cousin Shireen says. 'I'm marrying well—rich industrialist with a small painless one.' She wags her little finger and the girls burst out laughing.

'Okay, I think I've heard enough,' I say. 'Aren't you coming up? Your friends are probably all smashed and de-virginized by now.'

'Ewww!' Bano says. They all give me dirty looks. Mission accomplished.

My lounge is filled with smoke, drunkards double-fisting multiple cigarettes at once. Some pretentious idiot has lit a cigar and the apartment is a wash of tobacco, colognes, perfumes and the dank scent of sexual desperation. A few girls I don't know are dancing solo in the middle of the living room, sloshing sexy in drunken sashays, tripping on the rug, slipping on the tiled floor. I spot Faisal, who is attempting a quick make-out in the last few minutes before Saba has to go home. Desi girls, no matter how liberal or conservative, have ridiculous curfews, but the illusion that they are chaste virgins is decidedly false. At parties there is always a bathroom shag or the messy BJ in the linen closet. We've all placed in the Pakistani House-Party Sex Olympics. Past notable events have included the ironing-board bend-over, the spiral staircase suck-off and the garden shrub butt-plug—because, in the end, some desi girls do indeed like to preserve their *wurginity* for their wedding night. Fortunately, Aliya is one of the rare chicks with no curfew, which at first was a big plus in my pursuit. Later I realized she wasn't all that into the actual sex part, the freedom just gave her more time to break family rules and lead me around by the cock.

I spot Aliya in the corner of the room. She gestures for me to join her and Alfie as they walk into my bedroom.

'It's snowing in Bogota!' Alfie sings dramatically, one hand on his hip and the other gesturing us to my bathroom as if he were waving a magic wand of homosexuality. The bathroom is where you do all the fun shit at parties—the drugs, the sex, the real hard-core gossip—where we read both the bleak and powerful future. I'm lucky that my bathroom is bigger than most and has an air conditioner. In here many a lewd and lascivious thing has happened, and I am proud to report that many important social issues have both been instigated and resolved from the comfort of my toilet seat.

Alfie sits on my sink counter, hair styled in an Elvis-esque bouffant, a colourful Louis Vuitton scarf tied around his skinny neck and tucked into his white button-down Polo shirt. Aliya sits on the throne—seat down—with her legs crossed, shoes discarded on the floor, a cigarette dangling between her fingers, looking like Audrey Hepburn next to the Trevi Fountain. She can make herself at home anywhere. Their faces lean together, they're talking softly about something.

'What's going on?' I ask them, knowing full well. I close the door behind me.

'We're waiting for Omer and what's-her-name to join us,' Alfie says. He snaps his fingers, trying to remember her name.

'She's quite charming, totally unexpected. I thought she'd be another one of Omer's pathetic horny experiments, but I kind of like her.'

Aliya nods absent-mindedly, smoking.

'Surprising,' he says, to no one in particular.

The door opens roughly and Omer presses in.

'Yo yo yo, where's the blow, Johnson?' he says merrily, stumbling half drunk into the bathroom. It's his new summer thing, calling everyone Johnson, including his servants, and then laughing hysterically at the confusion. He's holding Nida's hand, a full glass of ice whisky in the other, pulling her eagerly behind him as he closes the door and locks it. He doesn't like to share his drugs.

'Has everyone met my little meow-mix pussycat?' he asks, pulling Nida close and kissing her cheek roughly. Omer looks around the room, his eyes half shut, taking in our faces as if trying to recognize us out of some faded drunken dream. He's completely wasted. Nida has her hair up in a pony and is wearing silver hooped earrings that somehow make her seem effortlessly fresh in a way that Aliya never does. She reminds me of a hot desi Natalie Imbruglia.

Nida smiles and exchanges polite hellos. We lock eyes and she says, 'I really like your house, Bugsy. I met your mother and sisters downstairs. They are really sweet.'

'No one can believe he has three gorgeous sisters,' Alfie says. 'I don't think they taught him a thing. He's such a macho boor. You know, Nida, you'd look great in a red-gold number I just designed,' he says without pause. 'You must come by my boutique and check it out. Maybe I'll take a few pictures of you for my collection.' His voice is like a machine gun warming up.

Nida's eyes widen and she glows. 'Really? I would love that.'

'Absolutely. It's made for your skin tone. Give me a call.'

Nida's introduction into Lahori high society is now officially complete, she's hooked up with a rich slack politico, and now she's met and been invited by Alfie Kareem, fashionista and gatekeeper to all that is chic and debauched in Lahore. From here it's only up, up, up, and down, down, down.

I move over on the bench next to the shower. 'Would you like a seat?' I ask her. 'All I have to offer is this wooden bench, this wet bathtub, or the fine marble counter next to Alfie. Aliya, as you can see, has already occupied our illustrious throne.'

'Sink is good,' she says and jumps up deftly, sitting on the counter across from me. My toothbrush falls clattering into the sink.

'Don't worry about it,' I reassure her.

'Alfie, pull out the yay-yo, yo! And don't be a fucking *cheapster*, yaar,' Omer cracks obnoxiously. Omer is Alfie's cousin and the two can invariably be found at any given event locked together in some party bathroom snorting copious amounts of dodgy glass-and-Disprin-laced coke. At Omer's house you don't have to hide it, you can get drugged and drunk right there out in the open. Everywhere else you pretend to be discreet and lock the shitter door. I'm not really much of a snowblower, but I don't discriminate either; everyone has their own poison.

Alfie rolls his eyes with an exaggerated reluctance and pulls himself off the counter. He rummages through his skintight jean pockets until finds the small baggie of white powder. He's a skinny little guy and there's not much jean pocket to rummage through, yet Alfie always seems to have deep pockets filled with foreign treasures.

'This is my only shit, okay, and it has to last until tomorrow, so don't shove it all up your nose, Omi!' Alfie scolds, pouring a stingy amount of powder on to the counter and starting to mix and crush.

'Damn, Bugsy, what's up with all the *Archie Comics*?' Omer says, sitting on the edge of the tub, nosing through my bathroom magazine rack. 'Where are we, middle school?'

'Oh my God,' Nida gushes, 'I haven't seen one of these in forever.' Omer throws her a *Jughead Double Digest*. 'Wow, these are really old. My brother used to read these exact same ones. They're the original thick ones, from, like, the sixties.'

'Yeah, back when Veronica's bikinis really were scandalous,' Alfie says approvingly.

'I think Bugsy's been collecting these since he learned to read,' Aliya says, joining in on the Bug bashing. 'Which wouldn't be all that long ago. Here's a *Betty and Veronica Double Digest*,' she says, holding it out to Nida. 'Feel free to take as many as you like.'

'Amazing, smell the paper,' Nida holds it out and Omer inhales dramatically. 'It's like a time machine.'

'I'm glad you're not pushing your brain too hard into the realm of the intellectual, Bugsy,' Alfie says. 'We wouldn't be able to recognize you if, God forbid, you read an actual newspaper or magazine.' He says this while making four anorexic parallel lines of coke on my sink counter. He uses his gold credit card, sliding his tongue over the edge greedily when he's done, hard gumming with his fingers.

'All right, all right, are you all done busting my balls? It's not like you fuckers are reading anything more intellectual. *Saturday Weekly* and *Punjabi Fashion* don't count.'

'Touché,' Alfie says after his first go at the cocaine, all quick and through one nostril.

'I always wanted to be Veronica,' Nida says wistfully. 'But I was always boring Betty.'

'Our Aliya here makes Veronica look like a fucking angel,' Omer says, and shoves Alfie aside. He inhales quick, wipes his nose with a flourish, rubs the remaining powder into his gums. Aliya reaches over and gives him a punch and he laughs like the devil and smacks his lips.

'Now your turn, kitty cat,' he tells Nida. She slips up off the counter lightly and takes the rolled-up blue thousand-rupee note from him, looking at him expectantly.

'Don't worry, you'll be just fine,' Omer says to her.

'I'm not worried,' she says.

'Do it just like me, half through each nostril. It's better that way. Think of it as icing on a cake. It's like having a wonderful cake shoved up your ass and actually tasting it. Trust me, it's delicious.'

'What kind of cretinous description is that?' Alfie says, laughing. 'That's fucking disgusting—and I should know!'

Omer wobbles, thinking about it. I can see the thoughts slowly crawling through the molasses that is his brain.

'Omer, you're classic. A classic fucking moron,' Aliya says, shaking her head in disbelief, unable to stop her laughter.

'Well, that's very sweet of you, darling,' Omer says sarcastically. 'Please feel free to suck my cock, which, as you well know, is also made of pure sugar.'

Aliya hits him again and Nida leans down, snorting it half through each nostril like a pro. Omer claps and lifts his glass in mock celebration, spilling his drink. 'Welcome to the dark side, my little meow-mix,' he says.

'If you need to use the bathroom, let us know,' Aliya says to Nida. It's her weird way of being nice. 'Cocaine always makes me want to poop.'

'Brilliant!' Omer says, toasting us. 'Let's all discuss our shitting habits. Why not?' he says with ironic disapproval. He looks at Nida.

She nods, pupils wide and alert, and lets him know she's okay.

'Great, we're off to enjoy the festivities!' he says loudly. He unlocks the bathroom door and pushes Nida gently through. 'See ya, suckers.' She quickly waves goodbye to us and, poof, she's gone.

The night passes in a blur. People refuse to leave a party until the alcohol runs out. Around 3 a.m., with still a sizeable group of partiers left upstairs and downstairs, a small waiter in uniform white comes up to me. He's weaving, looking lost amongst the drunken skunks, and tells me to call my sister's mobile. I step away from the noise and call her from my cell.

'I just thought you should know,' she tells me, 'Moby's here.'

'What?' I ask her, startled. 'Are you serious?'

'Yeah, I just saw him. He's on his way upstairs.'

I don't have time to think or process the information before I see his shadow on the wall, a slow climb, growing larger and larger until he's here. He's looking as he always did, tall and skinny, a wide smile on his face, and in his usual costume, still the same after almost a decade—all-black Trent Reznor, as if the nineties never left; black jeans, slightly wrinkled untucked black shirt. His dark hair's still spiked, but I can see the spotlights reflected in his greasy scalp, and his neatly trimmed goatee has turned salt-and-pepper. Eight years have passed, but he looks the same. He stops at the top of the stairs and laughs as soon as he sees me. It's the same laugh I remember, husky and dry, and a little unpredictable.

'Bugsyyy, happy birthday, yaar,' he says to me in a slow drawl. His voice is deep and gravelly, sandpapered by long years of tobacco use and filtering the smog of Lahore's inner city.

I gingerly walk towards him, hand out for a shake, but he yanks my hand and hugs me tightly. I return the hug uneasily.

'I can't believe how big you've gotten, yaar,' he says. 'The last time I saw you, you were a twig, a little stick of uncontrollable punching youth.' He pushes me back slightly from him and examines me. 'It's good to see you, yaar. How are you?'

'I'm good. Great, actually,' I say. Seeing Moby has thrown me for a loop. I just stand there like an idiot, feeling awkward.

'I know, I hear you on the radio. I love your show, never miss it. It reminds me of old times, yaar.'

'Cool. It's always good to know people are tuning in,' I say. 'So, what the hell are you doing here?'

'I'll tell you. But first, where can we go where I don't have to see these *chutiya* drunk strangers,' he says lightly. Some dude I barely know grins stupidly at us and asks if we have a joint. I blow him off and lead Moby into Noshie's room, the only semi-quiet place in the house.

Moby senses my discomfort and slaps my back in an attempt to thump out the tension.

'Let's have a joke,' he says.

We sit down in Noshie's reading nook, in two floral armchairs, a coffee table stacked with yoga books and Ayurvedic bakwas between us.

'If you only knew all the times I wanted to call you when I heard a crackin' one, yaar, if you only knew.'

I nod at the surrealness of it all.

Moby leans back, foot resting on his knee, and gets comfortable. From his pocket he extracts a pack of Marlboro Reds and lights one. He exhales slowly. He hands me one and I join him. Noshie is going to kill me for smoking in her room.

'So there's this Pathan, and he finally gets married,' Moby begins. 'On the wedding night he goes into his wife's bedroom, and she's sitting on the edge of the bed. He goes and sits next to her. He has no idea what to do. He just sits there on the bed looking at his wife. So the wife takes the initiative and kisses him, and he kisses her back. Then she hugs him, and he hugs her back. Finally she takes her shoes off, and he takes his shoes off. She takes her blouse off, so he takes his kurta off. She takes her salwar off, and he takes his pyjama off. She takes her bra off, and he takes his banian off. Finally she takes her panties off, and he takes his dirty chuddies off. She lays down on the edge of the bed, and he lays down on the edge of the bed. She lifts her legs up in the air, and he lifts his legs up in the air. Finally the wife says, "Listen, Khanji, go down to the corner snooker club and get two young men—one for me, and one for yourself."'

I laugh, and Moby laughs with his typical shaking shoulders and a fist held up to his mouth.

'I knew you would like it,' he says. 'It made me think of you.'

'It is a good one,' I say.

'It's good to see you, yaar,' he says, suddenly serious.

'It's good to see you too,' I say, almost feeling it.

'It's been a long time, Bugs. I need your help, yaar.'

'What's up?' I ask.

Moby pulls out the pack of cigs again, his half-smoked Marlboro still dangling from between his dry lips, and draws out a joint. He must really need my help because the joint is fucking hung. With his head tilted sideways he lights it, the silver Harley-Davidson Zippo—the same he's had for decades—throwing sparks. Some things don't change—the way he lights the joint hasn't changed, or giving a fuck where he's lighting up. Noshie is really gonna whoop my ass tonight. I don't say anything. Instead, I study his face. It's a futile attempt. Moby's intentions were always indecipherable, and it's been so long I can't decode them any more. He looks at me, meeting my eyes, and I see the same sharp, penetrating look, as if he knows everything before it happens, as if he knows what I'm thinking and is one step ahead. He smiles, displays his tobacco-stained teeth, his lips a dark purple-grey.

'I know this is not the time or the place, yaar, but I need a favour. You're the only one I can trust, Bugs.' He hands me the lit joint.

I take a long, slow drag and hold it in. I get the feeling I'm gonna need to be pretty fucking high for this. I can feel a distant paranoia already. Moby is here. Sitting in my sister's fugly pink marshmallow of a room. And he's not pissed or upset with me for cutting off all communication after the accident. Almost a decade, and he's the same, totally chill, like we saw each other yesterday. Then there's the timing of my birthday. The joke. It all seems too rehearsed. I nod, prompting him to continue, wondering what kind of favour, eight years later, he could possibly need from me. Knowing it's definitely not playing Nine Inch Nails in my next playlist.

'I could have called, but I wanted to come and see you myself after all these years. You're my brother, you know, no matter what, and I've missed you . . .' he pauses. He sounds emotional. He talks more, about how we'll always be brothers. He waits for me to respond, and when I don't, we sit silently, passing the joint back and forth. There are things to say, questions to ask, possible excuses for my eight-year absence, but I stay quiet. I'm reluctant to break the seal of silence. The music filters in softly through the semi-closed door and the end of the joint glows bright amber in the dimly lit room. Then, after a while, when I don't speak, he continues. 'It's a small favour, nothing to worry about, but I can't talk about it here. How about my house, Friday night, say, ten thirty?'

I nod without thinking, remembering his haveli in the Old City. I've missed his house and its dusty smell, the sound of his wife yelling down the stairs, the cramped neighbourhood and narrow streets, the view of Lahori lights from the rooftop.

'Good, Bugs. Thanks a lot, yaar. I knew I could count on you. We have a lot to talk about.' He stands up and puts his hand on my shoulder. 'But I didn't just come for a favour, you know. I wanted to wish you a happy birthday in person, and I brought you something.' He reaches inside his pocket and pulls out an old brass AK shell, and I know exactly where it came from. 'For old times. Happy birthday, yaar.'

I walk Moby to the gate, fingering the cool metal casing in my pocket.

'It's good to see you, Bugs. You look good, yaar. I'm proud of you,' he says, hugging me tightly.

Most of the aunties and uncles have left by now. The Brig is probably in bed, fast asleep. I watch Moby start up his Pajero and turn left at the end of the street. I walk back inside feeling strange. I haven't seen him since the car accident, after which I never wanted to see him again. There was a time when we would spend every day together, morning to night, getting stoned and shooting the shit. But that was a long time ago. It almost feels like it happened in another life. I look down at the bullet casing. I grew up with an army father, yet Moby was the one to show me how to shoot a gun. He was the brother I never had. The bullet is a reminder. But what's so important he had to come to my house? What's he going to tell me on Friday? I try to imagine the worst but somehow my imagination can't conjure up what the worst could be. If it's money trouble or he needs my father's military connections, he's barking up the wrong tree. What could I possibly offer, except moral support?

At the foot of the stairs Noshie is waiting for me. 'What's going on, Bugsy? Why was he here?' she asks me, worried. She's wary of Moby, believes he was a bad influence on my young and impressionable mind. Which isn't too far from the truth.

I momentarily think of telling her about the Friday meeting and her smoke-filled bedroom, but decide against it. 'He just wanted to wish me.'

'So after all these years he just shows up, randomly, to wish you a happy twenty-fifth?' she says. 'Bullshit, Bugsy. What's going on?'

'I'm serious, I have no idea. He told me he wanted to wish me a happy birthday.' All this was true.

'And that's it? He just wished you and left?'

'He smoked a cigarette, said I looked good, told me a Pathan joke. That's all. Are you satisfied? Are you done busting my ass?'

'I don't buy it,' she says, narrowing her eyes in suspicion.

'I don't know what to tell you, Nosh,' I say, starting to walk up the stairs. 'Maybe he was nostalgic. Maybe he has cancer and wanted to say a last goodbye.' She follows me up. She yanks at my shirt and gives me a hard look, lips pursed tightly, eyes squinting. The persistence of her suspicion is impressive.

'Fine,' she says, letting go of my shirt. 'But be careful. He's trouble.'

'Just relax, will you?'

I walk up to the noisy party, still in full drunken decline. Someone's turned off all the lights, and I can see a couple making out in the dark. Some dull trance plays in the background. Most are still drinking and dancing. Aliya comes up to me and snuggles against my chest, kissing my neck.

'Where have you been? I missed you,' she purrs. Maybe I can sneak Aliya into Noshie's bedroom for my real birthday present. Inside my pocket I finger the brass casing.

NIDA

Alfie Designs is squeezed into a sleepy square amidst the criss-crossed tree-lined neighbourhood lanes of Gulberg. People who live in Gulberg have always boasted of their elegant townhouses and shaded bungalows. In this elite neighbourhood the sounds of children yelling as they play road-cricket are absent. There is no smell of onions frying or food being cooked. Here the chowkidar sits inside the house instead of picking his toenails right out front. These particular houses are not large—they share a wall, a small lawn and a haughty post-Partition affiliation. In front of his boutique, in contrast to this cultivated sophistication, sits a large banyan tree with a swing where a sleepy maid pushes two young girls.

Omer parks outside, behind a black Mercedes, and tosses his keys to Alfie's driver, who has hurriedly stamped out his cigarette to greet him.

'Are you going to stay with me?' I ask Omer.

Omer shrugs non-committally and puts his arm around me, absently massaging my shoulder. His body continues the relationship—hugging, kissing, touching—while his mind wanders. He seems to be on relationship autopilot most of the time.

I'm not sure what to expect from the boutique. Alfie's fashion is so astronomically expensive I've never even been to his store, and have only seen the ghararas, lehengas, saris and other fancy bridal dresses flaunted on the pages of the best fashion magazines. An attractive young woman with a small boy, trailed by a Filipino maid pushing a pram, walk out the front door, engulfing us with cold air and pulsing lounge music. She greets Omer with a flirty cheek-kiss, which he is only too happy to return. And then we enter Alfie's domain, where, suddenly, everything is blindingly white, from the curtains to the marble floors, the wall paint, even the upholstery, everything is a bright-white splash. Everything looks untouched, immaculate and pristine in its virginal bleach. I'm stunned for a minute, trying to adjust my eyes, my body to the freezing cold. It's like arriving in the polar Arctic. As I look around I realize that the reason everything is so ridiculously white is to allow the clothes hanging in rows against the walls to stand out in all their colourful splendour.

'Wow,' I say to Omer.

'Tell me about it,' he says. 'It's like being in an Albino's asshole.'

'You're horrid,' I say, giggling, and he grins like a pleased little boy.

The studio is largely empty, summer not being peak shaadi season, with only a few women milling about, lifting heavy kameezes to their plump bodies. Omer seems at home, walking swiftly through the studio towards the back, where the offices are located. He doesn't knock.

'Oye, Johnson!' he bellows loudly. 'We're here.'

A dark girl in a plain blue cotton salwar-kameez slips out of a side door.

'Hina, where's the *harami*?'

'Alfie's with a client right now,' she says, smiling, tiptoeing up to kiss Omer hello. She introduces herself to me as Alfie's lead designer and shakes my hand. 'You must be Nida. I've heard a lot about you. If you wait here, Alfie will be down soon.'

'Well, tell him to hurry up,' Omer says impatiently. 'We're on bloody time for once.' And then without pausing or waiting, Omer grabs me by the hand and moves up a flight of white marble stairs. I follow, my face inches from the red Nike swoosh embroidered on the butt of his trackpants. He walks fast and I stumble to keep up. The stairs wind up in a semicircle, wide and slippery.

Upstairs my senses suffer another psychedelic assault—it looks like a scene from some libertine novel, a stark difference from the polar-bear sophistication of downstairs. This room is stuffed with antique furniture—a purple bureau with Oriental trees and flowers, matte-gold-painted chairs, a long teal velvet sofa, heavy black-brocade curtains and Persian carpets. And large square cushions of crimson raw silk are scattered on the floor. The lights from various Victorian-style lampshades glow soft and diffused, amber beams cascading gently on the black marble floor, creating a mosaic of gleaming glass. In the centre of the ceiling a massive chandelier hangs with black-and-plum-coloured droplets. It's ready-made and set for the Marie Antoinette fantasy alive in every auntie and bride-to-be from Lahore to Liverpool.

'Bloody hell, Omer,' I say.

'I know, right,' Omer says. 'It's a right whore's palace. I keep telling Alfie this is the party place. Imagine girls laying on those red cushions, half naked, half drunk. Dionysus himself would blush, but the dipshit refuses to let us party here.' He casually flops on to the teal sofa. I walk around slowly, carefully admiring the artwork—Alfie's designs and sketches in gold frames, his many magazine shoots and covers.

I hear Alfie before I see him.

'Auntie, stop worrying and just trust me, it will be to die for.' He's stepping out of an adjacent room, holding the door open as four women enter.

Seeing the ladies in tow Omer surprisingly straightens up, pockets his phone and stands at attention. Once all the women are in the room I realize that only one of them can be qualified as an auntie —a squat woman with black hair dyed blonde, the thick dry roots clasping to her scalp in a final stand. Her make-up is bad, too much and too young for her face, the shimmer on the eyes highlighting the wrinkles, the fuchsia lipstick tawdry against her dark skin. The other three appear to be younger versions of her.

'Salaam, auntie,' Omer says as he approaches her. He's suddenly put on an oh-so-sharif expression, his posture dipped in a slight bow, matching the saccharine of his voice.

'Nice to see you, ladies,' he says to the other three, who all nod hello, smile as if they know him well and then proceed to give him no lift. But they all seem very interested in me, giving me a long and thorough once-over. They are not pretty girls. I let them gossip, let them have something to make up for their piggy eyes and pudgy faces. Alfie really has his work cut out for him.

'Omer,' the auntie says coolly, giving him an acknowledging nod.

'Are you enjoying the shopping?' Omer asks, then feigns a laugh of politeness. His hands are clasped behind his back.

The auntie grunts. 'If you call this shopping,' she says, and then glances at me disapprovingly. It could be my loose jeans and plain white T-shirt, the unpainted toenails, the hair I didn't bother to style but just brushed out of the shower. I'm getting the full appraisal, complete with disapproving lip-purse. I just look down at the floor, waiting for her to either leave or make her point. She says something to Alfie, and I ignore her, concentrating on Alfie's artwork instead. There's no point in saying hello, she hasn't identified me as anyone important, although I can tell she has scanned her memory, in case I turned out to be someone in the Lahori social scene.

'I'm sure you'll find something you like, auntie,' Omer says disingenuously. 'Alfie's designs are in a class of their own.' She purses her lips as if she disagrees. Omer keeps his cool and attempts a humble smile, but his discomfort is palpable. It's the first time I've seen Omer wear this diffident mask—I imagine it's the one he wears for his mother's friends, his schoolteachers and principals—in which he appears innocent, wrongly maligned by society.

The auntie doesn't look in my direction again; she walks around the room touching the few clothes Alfie has displayed on headless mannequins. She's not an attractive woman, paindu, not a lot of education but a shitload of money, or so it seems from the massive diamond she's wearing on her ring finger, the golden bangles, the mammoth designer handbag slung on her shoulder like a small suitcase. She fits perfectly into Alfie's bizarre decor and I realize she is who Alfie has decorated his studio for—rich paindu women attempting to camouflage their weathered bodies with the fashions of *Vogue* and *Asiana Wedding*.

'Achcha, Omer, it was nice seeing you, beta. Now move out of the way,' the auntie says, stepping towards the stairs. 'Alfie, make sure it all fits in one fitting. I don't have time to keep coming back. And keep it decent, we don't want to look like one of your vulgar models.'

'Bye, auntie, can't wait to see you again,' Omer says cheekily to their backs. The girls give me one last disapproving look as they disappear down the stairs.

Omer throws himself back on the sofa and starts laughing. 'Is it just me, or are the girls getting uglier by the minute?' he says to Alfie.

'Who were they?' I ask.

'You don't know?' Alfie asks, leaning in close, in full-on gossip mode. 'That was Salim Chaudhry's wife,' he explains. 'Mrs Prime Minister.'

'No way,' I say, shocked. 'That lady is Salim Chaudhry's wife? The daughters don't look anything like him.'

'No one looks like him,' Alfie says, laughing. 'Unless you're a hobbit.' He sits down on a chair and stretches his skinny legs out in front of him. He's wearing a pink shirt and skinny jeans with a red scarf tied around his neck, bright cherry-red with a pattern of large grey razorblades.

'Well, Shaista does looks like him a bit,' Omer says. 'Same piggy face and body. Now, Arooj, she used to be hot, once upon a time. You should have seen her five years ago, before the divorce wore her out. Now she's just a bag of saggy titties.'

'Oh God, Omer,' I say.

'You wouldn't roll your eyes if you knew what they're saying about you right now,' he says.

'Saying about me? They don't even know me.'

'So? You think that stops anyone. We are the kings of passing quick and harsh judgement on the less fortunate. Get used to it. Get thicker skin.' He's leaning back on the sofa, his head tossed back, staring at the ceiling like he's some contemplative Sufi poet. He likes to talk loftily, as if there's something of significance going on in his giant coconut other than his next joint or drink or hamburger.

'Is that why you acted like a schoolboy caught with his dick out?' Alfie says laughing. 'Is that your thick skin?'

I laugh with him. 'Yeah, Omer,' I say goading him. 'No one wants to see that skin.'

He rolls his eyes and continues with his nonchalant charade. 'If Arooj would just lose ten pounds she'd be amazing again. She's my favourite out of the ugly stepsisters.'

'All girls are your bloody favourite!' Alfie interjects. 'Ugly or not.'

'That's not true. I would never do the two fat ones. But the auntie, maybe, just to say I fucked Salim Chaudhry's favourite hole.'

Alfie pretends to gag. 'Wouldn't his favourite hole be the one in his mattress, where he hides all his American dollars?' Alfie says.

'Suck it, Alfie.'

'Isn't your father Salim Chaudhry's right-hand man?' I say. 'I mean, your father's entire career is based on backing him.'

'So what does that have to do with anything?' Omer says.

'I mean, don't you all support Salim Chaudhry?' I ask.

'Support? What the fuck for? They don't need anyone's support—ignorant fucks. The way I see it, Paki politics is run by monkeys. Apes, chimps, gorillas, whatever . . . Monkeys who sit around and, I don't know, knit all day. And we, the public, look at their knit work and say, 'Wah, wah, *kya baat hai*. Wonderful! Beautiful!' But in the end, all it is is a wretched, fucked-up thing made by a bunch of shit throwers. It's not my job to kiss their asses. They have plenty of douchebags doing that already.'

'Really? Because I recall you bending your head as she talked to you,' Alfie says. 'I think I even heard tiny sucking noises come out of your mouth.'

'Oh, that's rich! I don't think you, Alfie, of all people, have any right to talk about the demerits of sucking ass,' he says.

'Someone is pissy today,' Alfie says to me, winking. 'Nida, you must understand that our Omer here has some serious daddy issues. He spends all our hard-earned tax money getting high so he can forget that it's the politics that's making him high in the first place.'

'Go fuck yourself,' Omer says to Alfie, still staring up at the ceiling.

'Come on, Nids,' Alfie says, getting up. 'Let's leave him to stew in the vapours of our obvious mental superiority and get to work. He can sit here like a bump on a log and imagine all the fat naked Aunties he wants.'

Omer smirks and gives Alfie the finger.

I follow Alfie into another room, similarly decorated with transparent plastic chairs amongst the ornate sofas, a glass table with scattered magazines, and a floor-to-ceiling oval gilded mirror straight out of Snow White. Alfie leaves the door open and I can see Omer outside. I can hear him call downstairs for a Coke. I can hear the impatience in his voice and feel his restlessness.

'Don't worry, he'll stay,' Alfie says, watching me watch Omer. 'He'll find some lint to chase.' He goes into a smaller room, a walk-in closet, while I wait outside.

I sit on a chair and examine Alfie, his delicate bird-like frame, as he rifles through hanging outfits encased in plastic. He shakes his hips softly to some hip-hop song playing in the background and mouths the words. He's a unique character, like Omer and Aliya. All of Omer's friends are like film stars. They're all funny and irreverent and so comfortable being themselves. I've witnessed Alfie and Aliya exchange an entire dialogue across a dinner table with just their eyes. I'm not a part of the group yet, just a visitor Omer brought in to mix things up. This photo shoot is the closest to the circle I've ever been.

'I have four outfits I want you to try,' he says, carrying long bags of plastic on hangers. He gently places them on the sofa arm. 'Then we'll see what suits you. Try this one first.' He hands me the heavy kameez on a frail metal hanger. 'If you need a zip-up, give me a shout.'

Slowly, a bit self-conscious at being naked in a strange room, I take off my shirt and unwrap his clothes from the plastic. The outfit is beautiful but expensive and heavy, thick golden embroidery down the front. The sharp edges catch in my hair as I pull the kameez over my head. It has a dense smell, earthy, metallic from the burnished thread.

Outside I hear Omer talking loudly and Alfie laughing. There's a strange girl's voice as well. I quickly put my legs through the salwar and adjust the hook at the side of my hip. Then I organize my clothes, place my T-shirt and jeans so they are hanging over the chair, make sure my shoes are lined up evenly. I step out barefoot and stand uncomfortably while Alfie walks around me, talking to himself, complimenting me.

'It looks fabulous. This strawberry baldachino is so you. I knew it would be.' He zips me up, inserts a few pins at the hem and makes me turn. All the while I watch Omer, who, after briefly glancing at me and giving me a thumbs up, is busy entertaining some girl. She's wearing the tightest jeans possible. She can barely sit. In a fitted black T-shirt that is diamanté-emblazoned with *Hard Rock Cafe Dubai*, she is turned towards Omer, one leg crossed beneath her, and as they talk she touches his shoulder. She's laughing at one of his jokes.

'Great, Nida, now go try the purple one,' Alfie says once he's done with the poking and pulling. 'And careful with those pins.'

After I've tried what seems like a dozen outfits, most of the heavy bridal variety, I flop down exhausted into a chair next to them. Two more girls have joined Omer, emerging out of the woodwork like termites. He's now surrounded by three adoring fans. Alfie watches, amused, as if it's television, and winks at me.

'Who are the girls?' I ask Alfie in a whisper.

'Models, groupies,' he says, with a nonchalant wave of his hand.

'Whose? Yours or Omer's?'

'Anybody's. Everybody's,' he says. 'They'd be yours if you flaunt Louis Vuitton and offer to buy them lunch.'

Omer and his increasing gaggle of groupies occupy the sofa, Alfie and myself on two chairs watching them flirt in true Bollywood style, filmi body gestures and hair-tossing. My body itches from trying on so many different outfits and I rub the pin scratches wearily. My make-up has probably rubbed off by now and my hair is a bloody mess. The girls look as if they just stepped out of a salon, their shirts unwrinkled, their make-up seems airbrushed, hair immaculately blow-dried. They glance at me briefly but offer no introductions.

'So, Nids, I think the baldachino is a go for sure,' Alfie says. 'And maybe the midnight-blue lehenga. The tailor's working on it now. We'll try them on once more sometime this week and then I'll set up a time for the photo shoot.'

I just smile, exhausted.

'We'll do it with all the other models on location. It's for my new winter bridal collection, so the shoot won't be until after summer.'

The girls squeal with laughter and there are more hands running all over Omer.

'What are you guys talking about?' I ask them.

'Last week's party,' Omer says. 'That floozy who jumped in the pool. Remember?'

'Someone needs to tell these slutty-butties that desperate girls never get the husband,' Alfie says. 'Poor girl, I feel for her, I really do. She's been drunk everywhere. The first time I saw her she was running half-naked on someone's lawn, floppy boobies bouncing everywhere.'

'After she's all fucked and sucked she'll probably go faux-fundo, hoping someone will forget those flapjacks and marry her,' Omer adds.

All the girls nod and laugh as if this is common wisdom.

'That's so sad,' I say. I hear the dismay in my voice and try to extinguish it with a cool laugh.

'It's okay, love,' Alfie says and pats my knee. 'You'll get used to it, like a bad tattoo.'

'Yeah, like having Billy Bob drilled into your pelvis with red ink,' Omer says.

The girls talk amongst themselves as Omer leans his head back on the sofa and stares into space, finally ignoring them. Alfie next to me scrolls through his phone, swishing through one Instagram post after another. I watch them as if they're onstage. Will I ever understand these people? Or better yet, is there anything to understand? City states with their own flags and anthems residing within my borders.

'Omer, shall we go?' I ask him finally.

'Sure, kitty,' he says, sitting up. 'I'm starving. Who wants pizza?'

'We do!' the girls chorus.

I look over at Alfie. He just grins, unsurprised, and shrugs his shoulders at me.

'What can you do,' he says to me. 'Impossible to change an ass into a thoroughbred.'

'Please say you're coming too.'

'Why not,' he says, getting up. He tugs on his pants and adjusts his belt. 'I'd like to see where this all ends up.'

I follow them down the stairs, imagining the girls tripping, carrying each other to the hospital, palms full of bleeding teeth.

BUGSY

Some shit never changes: Moby's doorbell, the same cheap sing-song electronic warble echoing through his high-ceilinged haveli. How many times have I rung this whack-sounding Chinese bell? A hundred? A thousand? The potted palm next to the door I used as an ashtray, and once as a urinal, is gone, replaced by its squattier, dustier brother. There's one lone cigarette butt in this one, a sad, lonely Marlboro Red. Under the porch lights sits a brand-new Honda Civic, silver in a brilliant shine.

I wait at the door, ears straining for the sounds of footsteps inside, familiar voices. But all I hear are neighbouring televisions and the sobbing in the nightly dramas; the pure tone of an inner-city azan sparking above the honking cars and the buzz of a cut-rate electric light bulb above my head. The door rattles from the inside and the latch is released in a grinding screech.

'Bugsy!' Ayesha, Moby's wife, squeals as she opens the front door. '*Uff* Allah, look at you, so grown up.' Her hug is tight and familiar, with an excited breathlessness. I lean down to return her hug and am overpowered by the pungent odours of desi cooking. She always made wicked spicy chapli kebabs. She pushes me towards the light to examine my face, her fingers pressing into my shoulders tightly as if I'll run away. She shakes her head in disbelief. 'I can't believe it has been so long. You never came to visit. You broke my heart.' She says all this with a wide smile on her face. She doesn't look heartbroken. She's always been a bit filmi from all the Bollywood she watches. Behind her, a little girl with big brown eyes clings to her salwar leg.

Ayesha looks the same—her eyes still big and filled with humour, her round face wrapped in a pink headscarf, the ends tucked neatly beneath her chin.

'Well, come bloody in,' she says, smiling, her Birmingham still thick and direct.

Inside things look the same, smell the same—a combination of food and furniture polish and old-house dust. I'm surprised how little has changed. Next to the front door sits the same old-ass foyer table, with the standard cut-glass bowl filled with keys and matchboxes, a pastel-blue rotary telephone. I don't know what I expected. A different Moby and Ayesha? Less nostalgia, maybe?

'I can't believe it's been eight bloody years,' Ayesha gushes. 'God, how time flies. I'm so old. You're still young. God, it's hellish.' She laughs and then looks down. 'This little monkey here is Nour,' she says, introducing the shy little girl who squeezes her round face further into her mother's leg. 'She's a terror, just like you,' Ayesha says, poking my chest, leading me to the drawing room, talking a mile a minute. 'You'll both get along swimmingly, once the initial shyness wears off. Isn't that right, Nour?' She looks down at the girl and rubs her head. 'Do you want to sit with Uncle Bugsy?'

Fuck me, I've been promoted to uncle. The kid looks terrified of 'Uncle Bugsy'.

The drawing room is nice and cold, the air conditioner running. 'I'm so glad you're here, I've really missed you,' Ayesha says, squeezing my arm. 'It's been quiet without you yelling up and down the stairs for Nimco and masala chips.' Again she laughs, as if it's bubbling uncontrollably out of her. Is she nervous or just excited? I'm happy to see her too but I'm not overflowing with giggles. She wasn't always this enthusiastic. I remember her pissy-faced at night, waiting for us to leave while we sat on the roof stoning our asses off, polishing off the last of the snacks she had brought from the UK.

'Moby really misses you, you know,' she says softly, as if revealing a secret. 'It's been bloody tough for him to not call or see you, but he knew it would be best to let things naturally take their course.'

I look around the drawing room, still decorated like my grandparents' house in the early eighties—velvety brown couches, hideous gold-embroidered cushions, nauseating beige curtains, their thick valances and panels suffocating. All patterns have faded after years of use and sunlight. Ayesha motions for me to sit on the sofa, where I perch uncomfortably and stare at a table in front. Every desi table in Lahore is, without fail, covered with the same bizarre assortment of crap—weird crystalline animals in mid-pounce, ceramic dancing girls, Versace knock-off ashtrays and, always, a massive empty glass plate or bowl sectioned off for nuts and dry fruit. I remember Moby telling me once that the drawing room is where all family gifts and decorations go to die. He wasn't kidding. A grand rectangular depiction of the Kaaba hangs across the room, apparently watching and judging as I do the same.

'Do you want something to eat or drink? Should I bring some tea or a Coke?' Ayesha asks.

'Coke is great, thanks,' I say.

I sit in Moby's dull-ass drawing room reluctantly, the Clash hitting me with a 'Should I stay or should I go?' Why the hell does Moby want to meet me in his drawing room, like we're some old formal motherfuckers? Why aren't we on his roof hitting a J? That's Moby's style—chill—or *was* his style, the last time I hung out with him. The whole drawing room and tea bakwas is throwing me off. I'm starting to feel uncomfortable. What exactly does he want from me, and since when did I become a *guest*? Worse, an *uncle*?

Ayesha returns holding a tray, balancing a glass of Coke, jug of water, plate of biscuits and bowl of Nimco. 'Eat, eat,' she says. 'Moby will be home any minute. He just called.'

I sip the Coke, annoyed that Moby isn't already here. *He* called *me*, so he should be here, the fucker. All the good feelings on my birthday, seeing Moby again and remembering the good times, are slowly replaced with apprehension. Why the hell did I come?

'He's just been really busy with the lands ever since his father died,' Ayesha explains, probably seeing the look on my face.

'Oh, I didn't know his father died,' I say, suddenly guilty. 'I'm sorry to hear. When?'

She shrugs nonchalantly. 'About six months ago. You know what he was like, but everybody dies, and, of course, Moby got all his lands, and now he's going insane trying to figure out what to do with them, how to run them . . . you know. He's been travelling to the village and back almost every day.'

I nod, knowing full well how Moby's family works—two sisters, one son, the lands, a slightly insane feudal father. I've seen Moby's lands, stayed at his small dishevelled farmhouse, ridden his bony one-eyed horse. His lands are more salinized dustbowls than anything else, acres and acres of dead farmland, a few puny orange orchards. But I don't tell Ayesha that.

I hear crying from upstairs, a shriek. Ayesha rolls her eyes and walks out of the room. I lean back against the sofa and stare up at the cracked ceiling. There's that same yellow wavering crack, long and lonely and present in every desi house from Bahawalpur to Bannu. It slithers its way across the ceiling and down behind the curtains. I don't know why I'm here. What could Moby possibly want from me?

It's been almost two years, maybe three, since I've had reason to come into the Old City. The last time I ventured out this far was to buy a video camera for The Brig from Nisbet Road. All the rocking haveli parties of our youth are coming to a standstill, now mustered into exhausted houses behind Cantonment barbed-wire and checkpoints. The rest of this ancient city lies untouched like a silent nude behind glass doors. I don't know what it is, the smell of this place, the cow-dung colours, but I want to get the fuck out of here. I can't help but think of the past, the slow cauterization of my friendship with Moby. The car accident was a giant fuck-up. Moby's dumb-ass drunk friend couldn't stop showing off about his Mercedes-AMG, pissing everyone off with his general douchebaggery. It was late, around 4 a.m., Moby was supposed to drop me home, but for some reason he thought it would be smart to have the drunk friend drive us in his brand-new black dick. Moby sat in the front, me crunched into the back seat. We raced down an empty Main Boulevard; Moby yelled 'Faster!' and he went faster; we howled with our hearts in our mouths; the driver raised his glass, sloshed his drink in his lap and cursed loudly; my fingernails dug into the leather seats as we became airborne. I screamed. I heard Moby's hoarse cry, and like a rocket we crashed into an electrical transformer and landed on to the Liberty Market roundabout. I heard nothing, the world was a blur. But someone managed to wrench me out of the back seat and I crawled on to the grass, tasting blood, pain shooting through my arm and neck. Moby was there next to me. We lay there for an endless time, breathing, unable to believe we were alive. And then Moby got up, limped around the wreck. I heard him crying and cursing. I had never seen Moby cry before. The driver was gone. No seat belt, no life. And a sleeping man, some old homeless dude minding his own business, happy to have found a comfortable dry patch of grass on the roundabout—a temporary safe-haven from the riotous summer days of Lahore's pedestrian and traffic mayhem— was wedged beneath crushed metal. 'Go, Bugsy,' I heard Moby say. 'Get out of here. Run. Go! Go home.' He pushed me away, not letting me get near the car. 'You weren't here,' he said. I could see the man beneath the car.

I stumbled down Main Boulevard and, eventually, somehow, called Faisal. My father, my family, never the wiser. Nothing was broken, I was just a bruised mess. I went to visit Moby a few times after his release from the hospital. He never told the police about me. And he never said anything when slowly I got busy with school, went to the States for college and just didn't see him any more.

I check my watch. It's almost eleven. I hear the putter of rickshaws on the road outside. I contemplate leaving. I've waited twenty minutes. And then I hear Moby's voice outside, loud and sonorous. The front door slams and I hear him asking Ayesha if I'm here. He pushes open the drawing-room door and I get up to greet him. In the bright lights his goatee is whiter, his hair thinner, the dark circles around his eyes deeper, but he's still the same. The same Moby who patted my shoulder like an elder brother when I got high for the first time and threw up on his roof.

'Bugsy, yaar, I'm so glad you came.' His voice is relaxed, sounding genuinely happy to see me. He comes forward and hugs me tightly. Then he sits down and pours himself some water. He's not being formal, asking if I'm comfortable or if I've eaten anything. It makes me chill out, seeing the same old Moby, even if we are sitting in his stuffy-ass drawing room.

'I know you're dying to know what the hell is going on,' he says before I can speak. 'And I know you were reluctant to come here.'

'No, it's not a big deal, yaar,' I say, acting casual.

'No man, it *is* a big deal. You think I don't understand?' he says. 'It means a lot to me that you're here, Bugs. It's not easy, going through what we did. And you were just a kid. I let you have your space because you needed it.' He wipes the edges of his mouth with his fingers thoughtfully. 'But things are changing. Things have changed, Bugsy.'

'I heard about your father. I'm sorry, yaar.'

'Haan, haan, it's okay. Shit happens. He was old, he had to die at some point. I can't believe he lasted this long. At least now he's resting in peace.'

'Yeah, but which piece?' I blurt without thinking. Moby looks up at me, surprised, and then bursts out laughing. He knows his father was a notorious womanizer.

'That's why I missed you, Bugsy, yaar,' he says between laughter, slapping my back. 'You say it like it is. I've been bullshitting so much these last few months I've forgotten who I am. But not you, you can see through all that shit. You're not afraid to tell me the truth. That's why I came to you, yaar. I know I've made the right decision.'

I sit back and take a sip of the sweet flat Coca-Cola. It feels a bit like old times.

'Anyway, he's gone now,' Moby says. 'He left quite a bit of money, and his lands, of course. I've sold some of it and am trying to cultivate some. I've been receiving some great advice and made some major decisions.' He pauses for effect.

I wait.

'I'm going into politics.' He looks expectantly at me, but I don't know what to say. What is with these people and their damn politics? The idle man's job, I suppose. I mean, I'm not totally surprised at Moby saying this, he voiced political aspirations in the past as a kind of joke, but now he seems serious.

'You don't have to look so shocked,' he says to me, sounding slightly hurt.

'I'm not shocked. I guess I'm just surprised. So what are you going to be? Some beggar-pushing *nazim* stealing old ladies' zakat?' As I say this I try to imagine him as the mayor of his shitty little *gao*—the king of dung, dirt and dhotis.

'Maybe. I don't know yet. I've just started considering it. A few people are advising me.'

I don't ask who these so-called advisers are—I don't want to know. Some shit is best left unsaid and unknown. 'I hope you're not joining Salim Chaudhry's shit train?' I joke.

'No, of course not Salim Chaudhry's. His party is near-death, foaming like a mad cow. I'm thinking more along the lines of Mian Tariq.'

'Seriously?' I ask, surprised at the rapidly growing size of MT's bandwagon. 'I was just at his rally. It wasn't bad. He even exceeded my subterranean expectations. Are you sure you're up for it? MT seems serious. It's not dinky politics.'

'That's exactly why I'm thinking of his party. You know how it's always been, Bugsy—the corruption, the dysfunction. Only now, with my father's lands, do I fully understand the extent of it. It's like a fucking epidemic, a bubonic plague of lies and suffering. We need to break this cycle, yaar. And the only way we can do it is if we break that bhenchod Salim Chaudhry, his greedy relatives, his crooked cronies. We need to find someone new, someone with balls. This is the time for action, yaar. If we don't act now, then fuck it, let's just grab our limp dicks and play with ourselves,' he says bitterly.

His melodramatic delivery makes me want to laugh, but I remain silent. Moby likes his long-ass orations filled with drama-*shama*. The more you engage, the longer the monologues, and I want to get to the point of this meeting before tomorrow dawns.

'I'm fed up with no gas and no electricity. Before my father died I could barely afford a generator, let alone the diesel for it. Soon we'll have no clean water. We're moving steadily back into the Stone Age, while the rest of the world charges forward. Bhenchod factories being shut down, people laid off in the thousands,' he says, talking fast, spittle flying about as he practically shouts the words. 'We're the mathematical formula for disaster: Pakistan plus yearly floods equals no food and dengue, which equals inflation and Third World strife. Repeat. And that's just one problem in a million. And now with my father's lands, I can't do shit with them. I have fucking lands, finally, and they're goddamn worthless! Everything is either too damn expensive or made in China. We need Mian Tariq to break this cycle. We need something new.'

I nod at him agreeably. He sucks in air after this long tirade and tries to calm down. He sips some water, looks the other way. He's pissed, and Moby is not one to anger easily. I remain quiet, letting him regroup. I've had enough political passion from Faisal to last me a lifetime, I don't need Moby to add to it. What's come over everyone? It's MT fever.

'So far no one has ever come out and talked about anti-corruption this transparently,' he says. I can hear the passion in his voice about the standard party line. It sounds almost authentic. 'Mian Tariq has laid himself out in the open—his party members, family, businesses, all open to scrutiny. It's not what he says but the fact that he's saying it that's causing all the commotion. And it's about time!'

'Okay, I get it, MT rocks. He's a star. He'll swoop in like Superman, fix shit and we'll pop out of his asshole as Germany. Swell. But what the hell does all this have to do with me?' I ask.

He gives me a dirty look, unappreciative of the awesome sarcastic imagery I've just hit him with. I myself am quite proud. I watch him as he runs his fingers through his hair and fixes his kameez. He does an entire scene of dramatic grooming, not meeting my eye, demonstrating his disapproval, prepping me for what he's going to say next. And then he looks at me, his mouth serious. 'What this has to do with you, Bugsy, is that I need your help. I need someone I can trust. Someone apolitical.' He overemphasizes the A, something I'm clearly being judged for. Then he stops and examines my face, looking for what, I don't know, the apolitical perhaps, or some semblance of trustworthiness. Who the fuck knows.

'Get to the point, Moby, for God's sake. You're killing me here,' I say, fed up with all the tortuous *gol-mol* non-speak, now properly baffled as to where this conversation, and my apoliticalness, might be leading.

'It's nothing serious, so relax, yaar. Don't get all irritated before I've even told you. It's just a small favour that's of great importance to me. I don't have many people I can trust, especially now.'

'Okay . . .' I say, waiting for him to continue.

He leans in, looking quickly behind his shoulder to make sure we're alone. I can see flecks of white in his goatee. 'All I need is for you to deliver an envelope, that's it.' He clasps his hands together as if that ends the favour, so simple a gesture, so simple a favour.

'What kind of envelope, yaar?' I say, breaking out into an instant sweat. My internal alarm is going off, but I'm trying to ignore it.

'Bugsy, you've always been like a brother. I would never let anything or anyone harm you. You know this, right?'

He's laying it on thick. He waits for me to answer. I nod slowly, thinking about the accident. Him pushing me away, telling me to go home. My safety and security was one of the first things he thought about, even in his broken, fucked-up state.

'The car accident . . .' he pauses. 'I was a stupid kid too, you know. It was my fault to lead you into such a situation. If I had known what would happen, I swear . . .' He pauses, actually getting choked up. I look down at my hands and uncomfortably crack my knuckles. 'I've had to live with this for eight years, Bugs. If I could change the past, I swear, I would.'

I nod. It's all said and done now. Years have passed and we're still here. 'So what's in the envelope?' I ask.

His face straightens up.

'I can't tell you,' he says, then grins apologetically.

'Moby. Go fuck yourself.'

He laughs. 'I'm sorry, yaar, but chill, it's not drugs or anything illegal. I'm through with that shit. It's just papers.' He gets up and leaves the room, coming back with a large, thick manila envelope that he drops on the coffee table.

'That's it? Just this envelope?' I ask. He nods. 'Why can't you deliver it yourself? Why the hell do you need me?'

'Okay, I'll lay it out for you. The reason I need you to deliver this is because, one, I trust you completely, and, two, you're a part of the elite crowd that I'm not a part of. The details are not important, but it's a question of the right people at the right time. I need your connections, Bugs. You can deliver this envelope and not draw attention. I'm not in the same class of people, yaar. I'd never get access.'

It's true. He stands out like a festering bloodsucking zombie. Moby's the type of guy you hang out with on dark rooftops in viscous clouds of buzzed vapour.

'It's simple, yaar. From what I hear you've become quite famous.' He gives me his best *gaandu* grin.

'Radio infamous at least,' I say dryly, finding myself already spiralling with doubt and pressure.

'This envelope will help Mian Tariq's campaign. It will help me finally make it, yaar—save my lands, change everything for me, Ayesha and Nour, our new baby. Yeah, that's right. Ayesha is pregnant. I need you, Bugs.' I stare at the wall hanging across from us, the intricate headless white figures, thousands of devoted worshippers crowded around the Kaaba.

'Where did you get that from?' I ask Moby.

'My mother, who else. She came by one day and there it was, making this room impossible to use. Definitely killed the sex, if you know what I mean.'

I wonder if it's supposed to be motivational or inspirational. Or if it's just meant to generate guilt.

'I don't know, yaar,' I say finally. 'Let's say I was completely out of my mind and said yes? Who the hell would I be delivering this package to anyway?'

'Salim Chaudhry,' he says, his face a mask of seriousness.

NIDA

So here we are, seated in the only sushi restaurant in Lahore, hidden like a pastel piece of salmon among sea-foam folds of concrete, wrapped within hotel rooms and double-paned windows, high up on the topmost floor of the prestigious Palace Hotel. My glammed-up reflection is everywhere—shimmering in the floor-to-ceiling windows, radiating from my copper dinner-plates, in the slanted glint of the Japanese mirrors. We're even faintly cast in the blue water of the swimming pool outside. A European is the lone swimmer, his pale skin contrasting sharply against the dark tiles. Donning tight goggles, he's executing a perfect breaststroke. Only a white man would be mental enough to swim beneath a burning Lahori sky. Beyond him, past the elephant umbrellas and pool chairs, I can see the silvery trail of Mall Road traffic—serpentine, the median lush with trees, the procession in split rows waiting for the light to turn green.

I once saw a photo of a naked Japanese woman. It was in one of my brother's magazines, the ones he twisted tight like secrets, hidden beneath his bed frame. Her eyes were closed, arms at her side, nipples cold and dark. She was laying on a table, covered in sushi, snakes of perfectly symmetrical rolls circling her stomach and thighs. I don't know why, but I ripped the picture out and kept it in my bedside drawer.

When I told Omer about it he laughed, told me to imagine some Punjabi woman, big-boned, with gelatinous rolls along her belly, balancing chicken biryani between her breasts. Then he made fun of how I've never eaten sushi before.

'Don't worry, chicken nugget,' Omer says, snatching the heavy leather menu out of my fingers. 'I've got this. You just look like a sushi flower for me and smile.'

I shrug and let him take control. He's going to do what he wants anyway. It's easier—and usually more amusing—that way. But I'm not altogether pleased with my new nickname, which for some odd reason has downgraded from 'kitty cat' to 'meow-mix' and, now, to 'chicken nugget'. Am I becoming cheap processed food? Tomorrow it may morph into something further ridiculous, like 'litter box' or 'cough syrup' or 'squirrel nut'. It's very possible that at some point Omer forgets my name. I'm not sure he remembers his own. He's always so high I'm surprised that he can manage the basic human functions.

He glances through the menu, mouthing the names to himself in an appallingly offensive Japanese accent, then thumps it on to the table and takes my hand, holding it right there, openly, on the beige silk tablecloth without the slightest hesitation. He fidgets with my fingers and blows me a kiss.

Life with Omer isn't like normal life in Lahore. He's made Lahore, as he says, 'his bitch'. According to the Gospel of Omer: 'The possibilities one city offers you are contingent on how much you squeeze the parameters. Lahore is no different than, say, New York. The only difference is that in Lahore you have to create your situation, while in New York the situation has already been created by some dodgy fucker before you.'

We were talking about Omer's party lifestyle, how no normal Pakistani is living such a bizarre outlandish existence. He was in his silken robe, rolling an unlit cigar lethargically between his fingers, refusing to shower until I mentioned my lack of sushi experience, which got him running to dress and 'educate me on the finer things in life'. He either sees me as an innocent kid, or as a project—the desi Eliza Doolittle.

'We have great timing,' Omer says, looking around the restaurant. 'It's pretty empty. Better service for us.'

It's four thirty in the afternoon. Too late for desi lunch at three, too early for desi dinner at nine. I nod agreeably and look over at some Chinese businessmen sitting on a long table grabbing food off a wooden boat. They're eating fast, like hungry fish, the food flying into their mouths and down their throats before they can chew.

Omer orders in his usual bossy, confident way, talking faster than the manager can write. Omer never talks to waiters, unless to point at his empty glass. The minute he enters a restaurant the manager is on him, a foot behind, hovering and guarding like a pilot fish, waiting for instructions, hoping Omer will remember him later during a conversation with his father.

'To begin, bring the tempura, nana wings and the gyoza—but fried, not the ones that look like your steamed ball-sack, Ayaz. And then bring the usual spread of sushi. And keep the ice coming, garçon.' He points to an empty glass and winks.

I lean back and observe the crowd at Umami Restaurant. According to Omer the sushi is flown in fresh every day from Dubai. He rolled his eyes and gave me the finger when I mentioned that our vegetables are donkeyed in fresh every day from Sargodha.

I've been to this fancy hotel before many times for weddings, anniversary dinners, engagements; once, for my brother's service academy graduation, we came to the Chinese restaurant downstairs. Lahore boasts two five-star hotels and everything of significance that happens in the city is hosted here. But this is my first visit to Umami, which is hidden like some forbidden oriental jewel, with its dark mahogany tables and red paper-lanterns.

We have a window table, and on the opposite side, lined against the wall, are teppanyaki stations, where chefs are flipping shrimp into the air as fire explodes from the grills. According to Omer they should be called 'tacky-yaki' stations, because only the plebs sit there. I keep my opinion to myself and watch the chef flip his knife, the sounds of clanking metal making my teeth hurt.

'More wine, Nids? Or do you want to continue with the bug-eyed staring?' Omer teases.

'Sorry,' I say. 'I'm just looking around. There's an odd couple sitting behind you. They haven't exchanged two words since we got here.'

Omer twists in his seat to see them. 'Yeah, that's normal for them. He was one year ahead of me in school.'

'I think they're having a fight.'

'Or an anniversary,' he says wryly.

I observe the couple, trying not to look too obvious. They don't notice me, don't even make eye contact with each other. They reach down with their chopsticks and slowly carry the food to their mouths, chewing as if in slow motion. The girl stares down at a bowl of brown rice and looks as if she might cry. She's quite dressed up, with platform pumps, a thick diamond bracelet on her wrist, hanging diamond earrings and even a fancy glittering watch. She's wearing night-time make-up, grey with lots of black eyeliner, and false lashes. The man's cavernously large nostrils keep flaring as he chews. He passes her the soy sauce and spills some on the tablecloth. It's not a pass as much as a shove.

Her bracelet dazzles in the daylight as her chopsticks move up and down, dropping bits of rice on to her plate like tears.

'His father died recently,' Omer tells me, stuffing lettuce with ginger dressing into his mouth. 'He left the entire family in chaos. They're going bankrupt. He converted his factories ten years ago from electricity to gas, which seemed like a good idea, but now there's no damn gas. Ha, what a joke. She's some paindu ex-model who married him for his money. I'm sure she's not too pleased by the downshift. If she wanted to travel economy she would have married her pimp.'

'Shh, Omer, not so loud. They'll hear you.'

'So? I don't give a fuck.' His voice goes up a little as he says this. From a plastic bag beneath the table he pulls out a bottle of red wine and a small bottle of whisky. He pours himself a glass full of each and some red wine for me. I never realized how many people were drinking in Lahori restaurants until I met Omer. You have to bring your own bottle, but they happily provide the glasses and ice. Omer takes his bottles everywhere, even when we park and have paan. He jokes that it's his insulin.

I gingerly sip the dry wine, which is not very good and unfortunately distracts from the taste of the miso soup, which is wonderful and salty. As I lick the salt off my lips, I have a thought.

'Hey Omer,' I say, unsure of how to pose the tricky question. I don't want to ruin his mood by mentioning his father.

'Yes, nugget?' he says, pointing with his chopsticks. 'That's seaweed and tofu, which tastes like shit on its own, but not so bad in the soup. You likey?'

'Yes, it's delicious,' I say. 'But I was wondering . . . we have electricity issues and load-shedding, and that's difficult. And then there's no gas.'

'That about sums it up.'

'Well, why are the politicians . . . like your father . . . unable to mend the situation?'

He stops sucking his spoon and just looks at me, surprised at the question. It makes my heart skip a beat. Then he gives me a wide, crazy grin.

'Because all that shit costs money. And why spend the money when you can keep it?'

'Are you joking?'

'Nope, no joke. It takes actual organization and planning to fix an infrastructure. The dumb fucks in government can't even spell the word, let alone actually sit down and make a plan. Plus, no one seems to rally, so life goes on. You get what you're willing to settle for, and we all seem to be all right with no *bijli* and no gas.'

'But your father . . .'

'My father's been in Paki politics for, like, forty years. He's all jaded and shit. You ask him why something doesn't work and he looks at you and asks surprised, "It doesn't work?" Those dumb shits at Pak Power go home all confused thinking they have it figured out until their damn house lights don't fucking turn on.' He laughs loudly, but without humour. 'Daddy-o is a pro though. His job isn't to make this country better, it's to make the same fuckheads win again and again and again until they die and their dumb-ass kids take over.'

'That's really depressing.'

'Yup, and that's why we eat our sushi and drink our whisky,' and with that he proceeds to demonstrate by taking a giant gulp from his glass. 'And snort all the shit we can until our nostrils blow out!'

He fails to mention why his house has steady electricity, why there's no load-shedding for him. I've noticed that Omer never uses the word 'corrupt', not when we talk about the government, or the state of our country, and definitely never when discussing his father. Omer knows the truth and isn't stupid enough to see pink when something is red. That is how he survives.

The manager comes by with a large tray of sushi, lined in neat rows. I lean forward and examine them, the emerald and coral filling spirals into pearly rice and dried seaweed. The manager adds more ice to Omer's glass and gives him a conspiratorial grin, letting him know that he's no middle-class fuddy-duddy, but also an elite boozer. Omer ignores the look and inquires about Crazy Maki and tempura. The manager grows flustered and fast-walks back into the kitchen.

'Eat, eat,' Omer says, placing a few pieces on my plate with his chopsticks.

It tastes more like boiled rice than anything else, salty rice soaked in spicy soy sauce. There's a slight hint of soft flesh, some unidentifiable-vegetable taste, and when I try the one with the golden-orange eggs, they burst in my mouth with a cod-liver-oil taste I instantly dislike. Omer laughs at my expression and points to the ones that are less fishy—the simpler-looking ones: starter sushi for ignoramuses. I don't like the taste of the green wrapping that Omer has assured me is edible seaweed. It's like eating a notebook lost at sea, but I shut up and swallow the food, hoping what's left to come from the kitchen is an improvement.

More people walk in, a few business types, maybe staying at the hotel, and a young couple holding hands looking very newly married and proud to be going to Umami together, just the two of them. When the boy spots Omer his eyes grow wide and he walks excitedly towards us.

'Omer, how are you, yaar? Long time no see,' he says, shaking Omer's hand a little too eagerly, slapping his back a little too hard.

Omer doesn't get up, like he would for a close friend, but wipes his mouth with his napkin and leans back in his chair.

'Haan, Aamir, how've you been?' he asks.

'Great, just great, yaar. We just got back from our honeymoon—Bali, Bangkok . . . you know.'

'It was fabulous,' his wife adds. 'Such beautiful places. I'm miserable being back in Lahore.' She laughs and gestures with her left hand, rotating her wedding ring with her thumb so the enormous diamond faces forward.

She ignores me completely, her eyes fixed only on Omer. He doesn't look at her twice. He has enough women fawning over him, she's nothing special. I smile to myself and watch them all interact, like I'm watching monkeys at the zoo. The woman is holding a furry black purse, some sort of dead animal, and keeps rubbing her lips together to spread the maroon lipstick she's wearing. She's not very pretty, but with all the make-up one might be confused into thinking she was attractive. It instantly reminds me of a news article I read last night, about a man who sued his wife for deception after he saw her without make-up. It makes me giggle. She shoots me a dirty look.

'Even though Thai food is fucking amazing, we still missed Umami's Crazy Maki.' The boy laughs. 'How pathetic is that?'

Knowing Omer, he's holding back from blurting out 'fucking pathetic'. The guy stands embarrassed when Omer remains silent.

'We must get together, yaar. I'll have a GT soon,' he says. 'You must come. I smuggled in a bottle of single malt that I think you'll appreciate.'

'Yes, Omer,' the wife says. 'You must come check out our new portion, we have the whole upstairs to ourselves now, with a private stairway of our own.' She doesn't know Omer too well, otherwise she would have shared different information, something

Omer actually cares about. He's already bored. He's picking up his chopsticks, slowly lifting up a papery piece of ginger and placing it on a circle of sushi.

The manager is back with more sushi and fried vegetables, apologizing profusely for the delay.

'Anyway, we'll let you get back to your food,' the guy says, starting to sweat. 'But I'll be calling you soon.'

Omer nods, a large piece of sushi stuffed in his mouth, and gives the guy a distracted thumbs-up. They stagger towards their table, the girl stumbling on the carpet with her high heels. They're whispering something to each other. Omer rolls his eyes at me and places a tempura carrot on my plate, pointing out the appropriate dipping sauce.

I look back at the young couple. The girl must be my age. It's hard to be accurate, what with all the thick foundation and contouring. She's excited to be out of the house, that much I can see, away from the watchful eyes of her in-laws, free from their scrutiny, their pressure. She did it, the most important thing expected of her—she got married. There will be no more societal pressure. If she quickly pops out a baby, she'll have completed her female duties. From then on, she's just an extra exhale in society.

'God, what are you zoning out about?' Omer asks me. 'It's just sushi, not base jumping. You don't have to be so damn serious.'

'Was I being serious? I'm sorry, I didn't realize.' I laugh. 'I guess I was just wondering if I should have gotten more dressed up. I feel a little too normal here.' I lower my voice. 'I'm wearing flats.'

'You're wearing chappals?' he says loudly and looks beneath the table at my feet. 'That's style, baby—thongs at Umami. I love it!'

'Shush, Omer,' I whisper. 'Can you please not announce it to everyone? And they're not thongs, they're fancy.'

'*Haww*, how rude, telling me to shut up. And in the middle of your sushi-vushi training. Anyway, fuck them. I still can't believe you were a sushi virgin,' he continues loudly. 'I'm honoured to be the first to de-sushi you, my little California Roll. That's your new nickname, my California Roll. Or maybe my *nangi* unagi.' He tosses his head back and laughs at his own joke.

'Thanks for the view,' I say, pointing to his open mouth. 'I don't just get to try sushi, I also get to see it after it's been mashed and chewed. What an honour.'

He laughs and mixes more wasabi into my soy sauce, explaining it all like some drunken schoolteacher.

'Fuck the chopsticks, just use your hands.' He watches me like a kid inspecting a limp lizard hobble across the floor. I use my fingers to dip it into the sauce. 'Well, what do you think of it all?'

'Hmm, it's interesting. It doesn't really taste that fishy, except for the fish eggs. I don't really like those so much.'

'Yeah, you and most desis. Those were for my advanced taste buds. If sushi was fishy, no Paki would eat it. Plus I ordered all the tame shit. No eel or uni, or sashimi. We'll wean you slowly, like with the booze.' He gives me an exaggerated wink and stuffs a giant crispy prawn into his mouth.

'You know what I read on Facebook yesterday?' he says, changing the subject.

'You should really try to get your information from a source more reliable than Facebook.'

'Why? I like it. It's filtered information. Only the weird makes it through.'

'That's the problem.'

'I read that Pakistan is the number-one country in terms of Google porn searches.'

'Well, we are a horny, sexually deprived culture.'

'Balls,' he says with a full mouth. 'It's all Western propaganda, to show us as some depraved culture. Although I'd like to say that I've personally contributed to the statistics.' He laughs and I am privy to another mouthful of food. 'Everyone is horny, kitten. What, you think the Germans aren't? Or the Japanese? They probably didn't do an analysis of "golden waterfalls", "salad tossing" or poop searches.'

'Ugh, Omer, please! I'm eating.'

'The stats are retarded, and the idiot compiling them is a moron. If only 40 per cent of your population is literate, and literacy means being able to write your damn name, then who the hell is doing all these Google searches?'

'That makes sense.'

'Of course, it does. It's bullshit. I seriously doubt every schoolboy in America, every college kid, office worker, husband and father is just using the Internet for the latest *New Yorker* fiction podcast.'

Suddenly there is a warbling boom. The windows tremble, like an earthquake, and the water shakes in my glass. I look out, the pool water is swaying from side to side. The swimming gora is gone. We hear a rattling that sounds like fireworks. Omer and I stare at each other, wide-eyed. I can almost feel his ears perk up like a dog's. His chopsticks clatter on to his plate, forgotten.

'Gunfire,' he says. 'Automatic AKs. Two. No three.'

We hear loud single shots that follow the rattle, four or five, each followed by a comet-tail echo. Omer pushes his chair back, still sitting, but alert. And suddenly there's a massive blast, violent enough to wobble the windows inwards, as if they were made of rubber.

Omer yelps and jumps up. I'm already on my feet, stepping away from the table towards the middle of the restaurant, away from the windows. People around us are shouting, some running towards the exit. Others are stunned, curious, trying to look out the window from behind the teppanyaki grill. I grab Omer's arm and stand behind him. Outside, towards our right, thick grey smoke starts to billow.

'The Punjab Assembly building,' Omer says to me, holding me close.

'It's the *Daily Post*!' someone shouts.

I see people running across Mall Road, small figures moving in panic.

Omer steps closer to the window, doing his best to peer out the side to see which building is smoking. I try to pull him back but he shrugs me off.

'Don't stand so close to the window, there might be another one,' the friend from earlier says loudly, his voice trembling. He's standing by the exit with his wife in his arms.

'Omer! Omer!' I shout his name. My body is shaking violently. 'Omer, please, let's get out of here.' The restaurant is near empty now. 'Omer. Listen to me. Omer, let's go.'

'Look at that.' Omer points. It's hard to see through the trees, but there's a chase, someone is running, someone is trying to shoot at him and we hear more single shots fired. And then another blast, right there on the road. It's not as massive as the first one, but the windows rattle again, the swimming pool water leaps out the sides like at sea. I bolt, straight out towards the entrance. I tremble in the doorway, shake uncontrollably. I'm afraid I will throw up or faint. Omer is still visible, standing where I left him, not the slightest bit fazed. I'm glad we weren't out on the road. Omer calls my name, then motions for me to come back.

'Nida!' he yells. 'Come back. You have to see this. It's fucking crazy. There are bodies down there, cars are burning. I think there's even a donkey cart that's been split open. Goddamn fucking fundos. It's okay, you can come back now. It's over. We're safer in here than outside anyway.'

Hesitantly, I step back in, still keeping a large distance between myself and the windows. I can't believe they didn't shatter. Omer seems to have no fear, he stands right up to the windows, his nose pressed against the glass. 'Come here. A suicide bomber exploded,' he says, looking thrilled. He seems to be enjoying this, and I don't appreciate it, especially when all I want to do is get out of this damn hotel and cry.

I shake my head no.

'Relax. Come on, meow-mix. It's over. The glass is shatter-proof. Trust me. Come look, at least.' He comes to me and wraps his arm around my shoulders, gently steering me closer to the window. I stop when we get close enough for me to see out. I stand on tiptoe and try to get a better view. I can't stop shaking. His arms are warm around me.

'Jeez, kitty cat, you're all shaking and shit. Relax. We're so far away and high up. Plus we can't get out of here, anyway, with the road all fucked-up. We'll wait, and when it calms down, we can leave. Okay? We're safe here, don't worry.' He kisses my forehead and absently rubs my back, his eyes still on the scene below. I can hear sirens.

I sit down on a chair and try to control my trembling. Two waiters watch us from the kitchen, their faces visible through the glass porthole.

'Shit, what am I thinking? I should be recording this,' he says. 'I can't believe we didn't film the action. I guess we'll just have to settle for the clean-up.' He does a quick pan of the restaurant and me. Then he stands in front of the window holding his phone, pointing it down, zooming in closer.

From his large phone screen I can see the wreckage, the donkey cart on its side, the man buried beneath. I can't see him clearly, but the donkey . . . it lays in an expanding circle of blood, legs blown apart, a crater exposing everything intimate that once belonged inside. Omer zooms in and out, his phone capturing every horror in explicit and terrifying detail. A small car has gone over the divider and hit a tree, the wheels spin in the air. The camera records all this, and more. I turn my head away. The building next to us continues to burn. The sirens sound closer. I sip someone's water. A sliver of abandoned salmon lays on the plate like a dull slab, all life drained, the vibrant colour leeching out slowly.

BUGSY

I'm speeding down a desolate midnight Raiwind Road, not a truck or lorry in sight, the envelope lying on the seat next to me like a self-made noose. Moby talked, as Moby does, in concentric circles, about politics, the future of our nation, our long, dusty friendship. Not once did he reveal the contents of this envelope. Repeatedly he asked for my help. Repeatedly he told me it was safe, that I was his truest friend, that it was better if I remained ignorant.

In the end, I took the damn envelope.

I'm en route to Salim Chaudhry's farmhouse. One phone call to Omer; it was as easy as that. The truth—I'm asking for trouble. Trouble is too damn interesting. Trouble is an integral part of the desi lifestyle. It's what we do. We see a sticky situation, sniff the danger and plunge headfirst with eyes open and thumbs up. We're all fucking skydivers. I feebly lie to myself—*It's for the greater good, Bugsy; for the nation, for our future; your debt to a friend*—but really there's a big part of me that just wants to see Salim Chaudhry's face, that wants to see what happens when the envelope is delivered. Moby knows this about me. He's always known. I will regret this—that I am solid on—but right now, I just drive and try not to overthink it.

The scent of crushed roses and woody cologne linger at the front door. I hear the *chun-chun* of bangles and a classic Bollywood tune—the same type of sappy song The Brig listens to in his Land Cruiser on his way to the Punjab Club. Inside, music and a cacophony of slurred voices, the din of men cheering and clapping to a shuffling dhol beat. To my surprise, it's a full-blown *mujra* happening at the farmhouse residence of our esteemed prime minister. With the thick envelope in my hand, I walk with feigned nonchalance through the wide entrance towards the commotion, my polite uncle-face on full ass-kiss mode. There will be uncles here who know The Brig. There are always uncles who know The Brig. The first thing I see is the semi-famous Chanda, belly exposed, hair whipping, dancing her skinny ass off in something sheer and shimmery. As she turns she blows me an air-kiss, courtesy of Faisal and a very interesting twenty-fourth birthday. I give her a wink.

The oval-shaped living room is packed with men sitting on *gao takiya*s and other embroidered floor cushions. The carpet is covered in a white sheet, and in the centre a plumper girl dances. She flips her long brown hair like a rope, her thick arms held out wide in an imitation hug, massive *bazonga*s exposed to all, her hips jiggling to the quick beat. The music is loud but the men's howling is louder. They toss cheap banknotes at her, stand and wave them above her head, and at the girl's feet lie piles of red and green, scattered like corrupt confetti. Another

slightly-better-looking girl in turquoise and gold jumps into the
dancing circle, twirling her long tresses in a manic arc, almost like
she's lost in a Sufi trance. As she spins, her long skirt splays out
around her like blue flower petals, her feet feverishly moving. Her
legs are bare beneath the skirt, knees worn and grey, *ghungroo*s of
silver bells chiming around her ankles. Frantically picking up the
money, trying to avoid the spinning whirls, a young boy in an
embroidered Balochi cap hops like a frog around the floor. He
holds his shirt out like a pouch, stuffing it with money. Once it's
full he empties it out for an old woman in the back sitting cross-
legged near the wall, counting their mountain of petty cash.

'You, girl, come here! Come to me!' a fat uncle yells, waving
a wad of red notes. Red is cheap, blue is what she wants. But
she graciously moves forward, leans down, plants a quick kiss on
his old greasy forehead. He has an owlish face, round eyes that
protrude slightly, a moustache of sweat on his bare upper lip.
I recognize him from the newspapers, he's our flipping foreign
secretary. He pulls more money from his kameez pocket and her
eyes glow. A kiss on the cheek, more money, on the nose, more
money, until finally he just flings all the cash up in the air. He's
making it rain, desi-uncle style.

The mujra is as old as civilization itself. A ritual for the lewd
and lascivious, uncles with dull wives and deep dirty pockets. The
songs are old-is-gold favourites and the girls keep it simple. Heart
attacks are to be avoided whenever possible. There are always
sexual relations going on in some random unfortunate's bedroom,
but it's mostly dancing and middle-aged boners.

I walk around, say salaam to an unavoidable friend of The
Brig's, a minister of the National Assembly, wait uncomfortably
next to him as he tosses drunken spittle my way and slurs his
words. He points to the plethora of women beginning to surround

us, pestering me to join their dancing. There are the dancing girls, then there are the other girls, the prostitutes, dressed in tight disco clothes, cheetah and zebra prints, overdone lips and hair coiffed in heavy-metal plumes that would put David Coverdale to shame. A large fat man with a handlebar moustache, who I instantly recognize as the head of the Pakistan Electronic Media Regulatory Authority, giggles like a boy as a woman licks his ear. He bounces on his chair as he flings rupees towards the dancing circle, his light-brown toupee askew on his liver-spotted head. The colour of his toupee doesn't match the black of his bushy eyebrows or thick moustache. It's ironic, especially because he's no doubt spent his entire day censoring songs for the radio and making sure there are no nipples on TV.

I move away to the bar and light a cigarette. While I wait for my whisky–ice I can't help but revel in the ridiculous scene. These are men people take seriously during the day. Men who appear on solemn talk-shows and political debates, men who lead the government and decide the fate of our national economy. These are men who meet UN dignitaries and foreign diplomats, the US President, Angelina Jolie, for goodness' sake. The man with the twisted toupee once shook Obama and Sarkozi's hands at an international summit. The chinless bug-eyed man now prancing about the dance floor like Frodo on crack with the pretty fake-blonde is an esteemed member of Parliament. If only the public got to see this *Planet of the Apes* gang fuck.

I sip the alcohol. It tastes like the real deal, not a bottle pirated and poured in Peshawar. But I could be wrong. I remind myself that having money is not the same as spending money.

The home's large high-ceilinged rooms connect, one den of inequity leading into another. I walk around, searching for Omer, my palms sweating from clutching the envelope. A pretty girl with bright-blue contact lenses duck-faces at me while she dances, pursing her lips seductively. I stop and check her out as she dances for me, coming close and flinging her hair in my face. Apparently hair flinging is at the top of the desi seduction list. I pull some of her hair from my mouth, preferring to have been flashed instead of having my face mopped. She doesn't notice or care, and comes in even closer, wriggling her warm pelvis against my thigh, shaking her tits so I can see down her blouse. I take the only money I have, a folded thousand-rupee note, from my pocket and gently insert it between her sweating breasts. She leans in and presses her moist lips against my neck. I can smell her strong cheap perfume and, layered beneath the pungent sweat, beneath the folds of her clothing and skin, the smell of sex and spit and pussy, which no sweet faux-French fragrance can hide. And then she's gone, on to someone else, touching his face with her long fingernails and undulating like a lost wood nymph.

Suddenly I hear my name. I turn to see Omer waving at me. He's gyrating like an old fart to the offbeat. A girl is bent over, her long dark hair hiding her face. She's pulling at her shoes. Her drink sloshes out of her glass. Omer leans down and tries to grab the glass as it slips out of her unsteady hand. She stands up and flips her hair back, turning to look towards me.

It's Nida.

'Hey, it's Bugsy!' she shouts.

Omer attempts to hug me and I push him away, his breath strong enough to scorch my eyeballs. I snatch a quick look at Nida. She looks hot. She's holding an empty glass and her face is flushed, her eyes bright and glassy, her lips wet and red. Her black shirt is low-cut and tight, curved cleavage on full display. She gives me a huge hug, tripping a little over her heels.

'Bugsy, yaar,' she says, 'I didn't know you'd be here.'

'I'm not,' I say, winking. I put my finger to my lips and Nida nods as if she understands. She giggles and attempts to take a sip from her empty glass.

'Oh ho, it's empty,' she says.

'Yeah, no shit. You fed most of it to the carpet,' Omer says.

She laughs.

'It's cool. What's good for the liver is good for the carpet,' he says. He rubs his shoe into the wet patch and smears dirt into the puddle.

'So what's up?' I ask them.

'Shit-all. Just fucking around,' he says and, in demonstration, pulls Nida towards him roughly and kisses her hard on the lips. She squeals, laughing.

'You took your sweet time getting here,' he says to me. 'Okay, enough of this sober-*shober* bakwas. We need more drinks, yo. Where's that damn waiter? Waleed!' he yells out. 'Where is that bastard?'

When no waiter appears, Omer gives me a dodgy smirk, puts his arm around my shoulders. 'Bugsy, my man. Lookin' good. You wanna go get us some drinks?'

'Fuck off,' I say.

'Fine, be a *chut*. I'll do it myself. But you're in charge of my kitty cat. Here—,' and he lightly pushes her towards me. She teeters on her heels, almost falling, then steadies herself.

'Keep the syphilitic uncles away,' he says, stomping through the crowd.

'You won't believe what happened today,' she says. 'Suicide bombers outside the Palace Hotel.'

'I know, Omer sent me the video.'

'It felt unreal.'

'It's nuts, Nida. I'm glad you guys are safe.'

She nods and takes a sip from my glass while it's still in my hand, like a cat drinking from a bowl. I tilt it towards her mouth and some whisky dribbles down her chin. She giggles and wipes her mouth with the back of her hand. I just give her the glass and she takes a big gulp. I can tell she's still in shock, trying to drink past it. As if dating Omer isn't all the PTSD a girl needs.

'How come you're here?' I ask. 'This isn't exactly the type of place one brings a girlfriend.'

'Omer said Ifti was cool with it,' she says.

'Ifti? Wow, already on a nickname basis with the emperor,' I tease. 'Highly unlikely that he was okay with it though.'

'Probably why Omer's been avoiding him all night.' She sways elegantly and leans against me. 'I've never seen so many drunk uncles before.' Her breath is almost sweet, like orange juice. 'Look at all these women in leopard-print pants, so many wedgies. And look,' she points to a tall, large-boned chick whose massive melons are pushed so high they're practically touching her chin. 'I didn't know women like this existed in Lahore. Where do they buy those clothes? I can't believe their husbands would let them dress so slutty.'

I stare at her, surprised. 'Nida, you do know these women are hookers, right?'

'What?' she says, confused, looking up at me, blinking.

'Hookers. Prostitutes. You know, *gashtis*.'

'Nooo! Serious? They're gashtis? All of them?' Her mouth hangs open for second as she looks at the four women sitting on the sofa behind us fixing their make-up.

'Yup, all of them.'

'I thought maybe a few, but others I thought were just . . . I don't know, mistresses, girlfriends . . .'

'The mistresses are all at home, just like the wives. These, my dear, are ladies of the night.'

'Where do they come from? Where do they live? In Gulberg, Johar Town, like everyone else? Or is there some sort of special area? Maybe there's a special house they all live in, like a farmhouse? A massive farmhouse with chickens and donkeys.'

'Wow, how drunk are you?' I laugh. 'I'm sure they all live in a wonderful home together, like in *Little Women*. And play board games, and knit and sew, do each other's hair. That one over there can be Joe.' I point to a neon woman with a giant ass encased in sheer black tights. Nida laughs, embarrassed. She's an incredibly cute drunk, funny and beautiful with her flushed cheeks and large watery brown eyes.

'Okay . . . so maybe I'm a teeny tiny bit drunk,' she says, her index finger and thumb an inch apart.

'Maybe a little more than that,' I say, separating the fingers a bit more.

She sways close to me, then further apart. I lean out and steady her, touching her cold bare arm.

'But I'm not totally, totally drunk, okay? I think that was my third drink. No, fourth. Fifth? I think the orange juice is giving me heartburn. Omer says it tastes like the orange juice in airplanes. I love it though, it tastes so fake.' She grins and her face looks like those perfect anime faces in Japanese cartoons. I wish she wasn't here, exposed to this shit. It's embarrassing, people thinking she's a possible *prosti*, not understanding that Omer's completely fucking clueless. I would kill someone if one of my sisters was brought here.

'You know, you really shouldn't be here,' I tell her again. 'It's not the kind of place a nice girl like you should be brought to.'

'What do you mean *a nice girl like me*?' she says. I think she's teasing me, but I can't be sure.

'You know what I mean. I don't think I would be here if I didn't need to be.'

'So you've never been to a mujra before?'

'Well, no, of course I have. But I would never bring my girlfriend or my sister.'

'Ohh. So it's cool to go by yourself and see dancing girls, but not with a sharif girl?'

I don't say anything. I know she's fucking with me on purpose, and for some reason it's working. She suddenly doesn't seem quite so drunk.

She raises an eyebrow, then takes a step closer and leans forward, whispering slowly in my ear, enunciating every word. 'Relax, Bugsy, nothing is going to happen that I don't want to happen.' Her perfume is sweet, like cotton candy, her breath warm and ticklish. She smiles seductively, looking straight up into my eyes. I stare at her, simultaneously uncomfortable and mesmerized. The lights illuminate her face, revealing the intricacies of her big brown eyes, the bronze circle of her irises. And then she laughs and leans back and says in a normal voice, 'Who knew a mujra could be so tacky. It's fun.'

I pause, I can feel my heart beating faster. An uncle bumps me while passing by. I give him a dirty look, which he ignores. The uncle pulls one of the hookers towards him. She's wearing vinyl leather pants, chewing gum with her mouth open. She gives Nida a professional head-to-toe once-over as she passes us.

'So what's with the envelope?' Nida asks.

'Shit,' I say, almost having forgotten the envelope. I hold it up. 'I have to deliver this bakwas to Salim Chaudhry.'

'I saw him in the kitchen earlier,' she says. 'Do you think all these girls are enjoying this?'

An excited cry goes up as a classic song from *Pakeezah* comes on.

'I love this song,' Nida says.

It's a standard mujra song, ironically, about mujras.

'Step aside, fuckers, the king is back,' Omer says, holding two glasses filled to the brim. He hands me one.

'That was a long fucking jaunt to the bar,' I say.

'Bar via the shitter. And look, fucking water all over my pants. Looks like I pissed myself. Which wouldn't be so bad if I had actually pissed myself.' Omer laughs his loud coked-out laugh 'Has Bugsy Wugsy been a good boy and kept you entertained?'

Nida nods and Omer sloppily kisses her on the lips.

'I love this chick,' he says drunkenly, draping his arm around her. 'She's a fucking cool pussycat.'

Omer hands her the drink and she gulps it like some desert camel.

'Look at her go! Now that's my kind of chick.' Again some more slobbery kisses.

'Okay, I'm off,' I say. 'Going to drop this package off. I'll see you in a bit.'

I search for a kitchen and discover three—bustling with waiters and chefs, large *daig*s of biryani for dinner, bottles of empty booze and dirty dishes—before I find Salim Chaudhry. The last kitchen is small, new and contemporary with expensive German appliances, probably a private one for the family. Around a marble island four men stand with their whisky drinks condensing on the counter. They stop talking as soon as I enter, all eyes on me. Iftikhar Ali, Omer's father and Salim Chaudhry's right-hand man, is standing to the left of Salim Chaudhry. He's tall and fit, with a full head of jet-black hair and sharp sober eyes.

'Yes, Bugsy? How can we help you?' he asks politely. His voice is soft and slow, each Oxford word perfectly articulated. He's wearing a dark-grey pinstriped Brooks Brothers with a light-blue shirt and an inky-purple tie; in the light he looks a bit like a desi James Bond. We used to joke as kids and call him Jam-Es Bund, one lassi, shaken, no sugar. The men around him are in more casual starched-white salwar-kameezes and look a bit like henchmen. SC is wearing a black vest with large, round silver buttons over his kameez. Ifti leans down to Salim Chaudhry, whispers something, and I hear my father's name—The Brig, so and so, son. Chaudhry nods knowingly. I walk up to the counter and say salaam to everyone, shake Ifti and Salim Chaudhry's hands.

I stand and wait, suddenly unsure of what to say now that I'm here. I didn't really think this part through.

'Well . . . uncle, I have this packet . . .' I raise the large envelope. 'I was asked to deliver it by someone I know. As a favour. For . . .' I pause, suddenly lost, unable to find the right terminology to address Salim Chaudhry. Should I say uncle, or Mr, sir, or prime minister? The options are confusing, especially after years of rude nicknames like melon-head, Mr 10 Per Cent and shit-for-brains. But Ifti takes control and takes the envelope from me, handing it to Salim Chaudhry. I can feel myself sweating under the button-down shirt.

'Don't worry, young man,' Salim Chaudhry says, holding the packet between his short, fat, hairy fingers. 'We've been expecting you.'

He tears open the seal roughly and pulls out a thick stack of papers. His eyes gleam. He's a short man with a large, protruding belly, his face composed mainly of pudgy cheeks, a pakora nose and pockmarks. His eyes are small and piggy, almost disappearing when he smiles, which he's doing right now as he squints over the documents. I wait apprehensively, watching his eyes glide over what I can perceive as grey numbers in rows. No one touches their drinks or speaks. Ifti is the only one looking calm, standing next to Salim Chaudhry, reading the information over his shoulder. He reaches the last page, then slaps the papers loudly down on to the marble counter.

'Excellent! This is excellent,' he says, grinning his famous poster-PM smile, his small teeth reddish from years of chewing paan. Salim Chaudhry comes around the island to where I'm standing and smacks me exuberantly on the back. He's much shorter than me and I feel awkward standing next to him. I've seen him on TV since I was thirteen, growing fatter and balder before my eyes, twice prime minister, now a fat failing political figure. That's the problem with most desi politicians, they're all just uncles in the end, one more or less like the other, behaving just as badly as everyone else.

'Come, beta, let's get you a drink,' he says, his hand on my arm. 'You have no idea what a help you've been.'

I cringe at the surprising thought that somehow I may have helped him, at him calling me *son*. I don't know what the papers say, but I sure as hell hope I'm not helping him. What could I possibly have given him that would produce this reaction?

With his hand on my arm he leads me out of the kitchen. Ifti follows. One of his men takes the documents from the counter and walks me through another door leading back into the mujra. I am stunned.

Across the room I spot Nida. She's standing alone. I motion for her to come join me. Carefully she weaves through the dancing girls. Suddenly an uncle rushes over and grabs her, smiling like an asshole, and seats her in a red high-backed armchair. She looks over at me and shrugs. The uncle circles her like a vulture, waving money over her head, placing a few choice notes on her forehead. He holds the rupee and a dancing girl comes by, starts to belly dance before Nida, drawn to the money. Nida laughs, embarrassed. The uncle points to Nida's cheek and the dancing girl leans down and kisses her, swiping the money from her forehead at the same time. The uncle raises his arms in the air and hoots in pleasure. Nida looks at me helplessly and I shake my head. I don't know what's with these horny uncles, but in seconds another is holding a larger rupee note above Nida's head and she receives more kisses, and then more, until she's being kissed by multiple dancing girls and the uncles are cheering in a frenzy. Even the dancing girls are amused, probably preferring to kiss Nida rather than the old farts. With all the city's prosties packed in one room, the uncles choose to lavish their attention and money on the one 'normal' girl. Finally a slow song plays, and Nida gets up, says goodbye to many of her newfound admirers and walks towards me.

'Whew! I've never received so many stale-lipstick kisses in my life,' Nida says to me, wiping her face with the back of her hand.

'Neither have I.'

'Aww, Bugsy, don't be jealous. I'm sure one day you'll have your chance, when you're old and wrinkly. But promise me one thing? You won't wear a light-brown toupee when you have black eyebrows.'

I smile and she nudges me gently with her shoulder.

'What time does everybody go home?' she asks me.

'I don't know. Late. Whenever they want, I suppose.'

'If my father had stayed out this late my mother would have murdered him. Although now he never leaves the house.'

'My father sleeps at nine every night on the dot and then gets up at five to play tennis. He's obsessed. Army-trained, army-obsessed,' I say.

'Your father was in the army?'

'Yeah, a brigadier. Recently retired. Now he's home all day driving my mother and sisters crazy.'

'My brother was in the army,' she says, leaning down to adjust her shoe straps. 'These shoes are murder. All I can think about is ripping them off. What are you drinking?' she peers into my glass.

'Be careful, it's probably poison. This drink was delivered by the troll prime minister himself. I think it's a whisky–Coke.'

'Can I try it?'

I hand her the glass and she takes a big sip. 'Strong,' she says, making a face.

'I know. It's guaranteed to make you feel like shit.'

She takes another sip. And then another. Omer appears from who-knows-where, looking sullen. He's now too drunk to have fun. Soon he'll drink until he passes out. Nida's also partying her ass off, eyeliner smudged, toes red and marred from the uncomfortable strappy heels she keeps adjusting. From across the room Ifti calls my name and comes towards us. Omer mumble-curses under his breath. I'm overcome with sudden anxiety as I see his serious face.

'Bugsy,' he says calmly. He doesn't look angry. He's sober and still smelling like he's stepped out of an Axe commercial. Unlike Omer, Ifti's a big one for maintaining self-control. Despite all the massive floor-thumping parties he throws, I've never seen him drunk once.

'Yes, uncle,' I say, my polite best. I stand up straight.

'Take Nida home, please,' he says to me. 'Omer will go home with me,' he glares at Omer. Next to me, Omer tries to suppress a drunken burp.

'Yes, of course, I'll take her,' I say, relieved that I'm not the focus of his displeasure.

'Now, please.'

With that he glides off, back straight, through the dance floor, through the dancing girls and uncles who quickly part for him with expressions of fear and awe—not dissimilar to my own. Why he supports dumbo Salim Chaudhry is beyond my understanding. My heartbeat returns to normal.

Omer mumbles some more shit. He's fucking wasted. He can barely stand. He grabs another drink from the bar and stumbles over to a chair, flops into it, his limbs loose and acting on their own accord. I look at Nida, who seems as drunk and silly as Omer.

'You're dropping me home?' Nida asks. She wraps her arm around me and leans against my chest. 'But I don't want to go home.' Her voice is muffled against my shirt.

'Leaving you here with Omer is not happening,' I say. 'You heard the orders. I wouldn't want you to end up bussed home with all these girls. You might get your wish and find out where they live.'

Nida looks up at me, her face inches from my own. She's hanging off my neck. She looks as if she's contemplating the idea. Her eyes are half shut. The drunken sloppiness is strangely lovable.

'Come, let's go,' I say to her, patting her head and supporting her up.

'No, I don't want to go home,' she says stubbornly.

'Fine, we'll figure something else out. Let's at least get the fuck out of here first.'

She smiles like a little girl and links her arm with mine. 'Okay. If you say so, Bugs.'

I grab a large bottle of Nestlé Pure Life from the bar and tell her to chug it down, hoping she'll sober up and not puke in my car.

BUGSY

Nida weaves between the haphazardly parked cars, her arms out and waving like a lost Japanese Zero, laughing and running her fingers across the windshields. The press of nauseating bhangra trails us even out here among the drivers, the mass of them sprawled in the open garden, chatting, smoking, enjoying the cool midnight air.

'Which one is your car?' she asks.

I tell her it's a silver Honda. Not difficult to find, I think, the donkey amongst the thoroughbreds.

'Isn't this one beautiful? Like a panther.' Nida runs her hands lovingly over a black Murciélago, the only one I've seen in Lahore, probably driven in by some industrialist chut from Faisalabad— the balls to drive a Lamborghini through Lahore, or any Pakistani city, roaring the engine between potholes, dodging rickshaws and donkey carts, beggars stumped for the first time, unsure whether they should dare to press their grubby noses against the million-dollar windows.

'Imagine living here,' she says dreamily. 'It's a palace.'

'A palace with that fat toad as your king.'

Amidst this driveway showroom the farmhouse is a blazing bordello against the unlit darkness of sugarcane. The driveway is paved a full kilometre long, flanked to the left by a ridiculous artificial lake with swan-shaped paddle boats. Nida walks up to me and links her arm with mine.

'I could learn to speak toad,' she says. 'It's stunning.'

Somewhere in the darkness I hear a Bengal tiger roar, an anguished bellow from SC's own private zoo.

'These damn shoes are ripping my toes apart,' Nida says, leaning on my arm heavily. 'Where the hell did you park your car? Multan?'

'Sorry, but there wasn't anywhere closer.' I point at the mass of cars parked at angles, blocking each other. It's chaos in heavy metal, the drivers as lazy as their masters, parking without sense or logic.

'Anyone leaving tonight better be very drunk or stupid,' Nida says, 'otherwise the drivers have had it. I don't understand why they can't park in a damn line. How do they leave?'

I shrug in the dark. 'They don't.'

Nida's heels click against the uneven driveway tiles—silvery rectangles of gunmetal grey reflecting the haze of the moon. She's tugging at my arm as she walks, trying to use my body as a crutch. I try to hold her up the best I can, stopping every few minutes to let her rest.

'Why don't you just take those damn torture-devices off?' I finally say, exasperated by her constant stop-start foot rubbing.

'The driveway is filthy.' She stops and wobbles towards the grass and falls down. 'Oh, forget it.' She twists and turns her body, unable to see where the strap meets the buckle.

'Here, let me do it.' I sit down next to her on the damp grass and try to find the small buckle, located next to her ankle bone. She has tiny feet. The shoes are strappy and black, the heels frayed at the ends.

'My sisters wear the same ridiculous shoes,' I say. 'For what reason, I can't understand. It's not like you're short.'

'It's for you loser boys, because apparently heels make our asses look better.'

'Oh, please, as if any ass isn't hot—heels or no heels. If you women really knew men, especially desi men, you'd realize how deprived we are. An exposed ankle under a winter razai would get us going.'

She giggles and tousles my hair as I pull the strap out of the tiny buckle, so small I can't see it, only feel it with my fingers. She lets out a sigh of melodramatic relief as I pull one shoe off, then lifts her other leg and places her foot in my lap. She rubs the bottom of her bare foot, kneading her fingers into the balls of her feet and toes.

'God, I hate feet. They're so ugly. I think most women wear pretty shoes to disguise their fat ugly toes.'

'You don't have ugly feet,' I say. 'You have cute feet and tiny little toes. You should see Bano's feet. Huge fat barnacles. I'm always worried she's going to steal my sneakers and blow them out.'

Nida giggles in relief, both her feet finally free, and rubs them against the short-cut grass, as if to scratch an itch she cannot find. I help her up, pulling her slight but reluctant body off the grass, her sandals swinging in her hand. She's not doing too bad for a drunk girl. In the distance we hear an uncle yell for his driver. An engine revs to life. From the farmhouse a Bollywood diva's high melancholic whine is finally fading in the distance. I can hear Nida's breath next to mine as we walk.

'We're almost there,' I say. 'I can see my car.' Luckily no one has parked behind me, blocking my exit.

'Nice car,' Nida says, pitching the shoes on the floor and sitting cross-legged on the seat. 'It's very clean.'

'Thanks. It's no Lamborghini, but it works.'

I start the car. David Bowie's 'China Girl' comes on loudly, the song already in the middle of the second chorus, the guitars heavy, my car coexisting between two clashing worlds—a time machine between the grating rural roads of Pakistan and the past of Bowie's porcelain rasp doing the full Brixton sexy. I lower the volume enough to be able to hear Nida speak and back carefully out of the long driveway, giving the gate guard a quick head-bob goodbye. He ignores me, his eyes follow Nida instead, head tilting slightly to get a better look, a slight moonlit sliver of breast. The advantage of the kilometre-long walk is paying off as we speed out, not having to honk or wait for some old fart to figure out where he left his cell phone or keys, whether he said goodbye to the host, second-guessing a large hooker tip. Sayonara, fuckers.

'That was strangely fun,' Nida finally says as I race down a relatively empty Raiwind Road.

I just smile at her, trying to differentiate where the line of the road breaks from the line of the fields to my left.

'This song is great,' she says, turning it up. 'Who is it?'

'It's David Bowie, baby,' I say in a terrible Austin Powers accent. I give her a wink, she gives me more giggles.

The roads are pitch-dark but clear, except for a truck or two heading into town from the surrounding villages. Their decorations shine fluorescent—hand-painted pink paisleys, elaborate and exaggerated kohl-rimmed eyes, the floating faces of politicians, landscapes of the Punjab framed with coloured reflectors bright against the splash of my high beam. After they have passed away into the darkness we overtake a pallid donkey-cart laden with hay, a loud untuned motorbike vibrating like a mosquito and a few wobbling midnight bicyclists either returning home or heading towards their work in the city. The fields on both sides of the road are vast and flat, peppered by a few new housing districts that loom in the distance, the city lights and its sleeping millions. We pass beneath tall and dust-weathered trees, their shadows clamouring over the car, shading the moon from view.

'So Bugsy, Bugs, Bug-see, Bugsy Wugsy,' Nida repeats. 'Why *is* your name Bugsy? That's not your real name, is it?' Her question catches me off guard. It makes me laugh. I look over at her—she's leaning against the door, head pressed to the window, legs crossed beneath her. It's the first time I've seen anyone look so comfortable in my passenger seat. She looks so familiar that for a second I wonder if we've met before. Lahore isn't such a big city . . . Maybe at a play, a concert, a birthday party when we were kids? Sitting there looking almost poised in her drunkenness I feel as if I've known Nida all my life, smiling from the passenger seat, smiling from a forgotten memory.

'Obviously, it's not my real name,' I say. 'Otherwise my parents were smoking some serious shit when I was born.'

'So then?'

I smile. 'I watched a lot of gangster movies as a kid, and I watched the movie *Bugsy* all the time. It drove my sisters crazy. So, they started calling me Bugsy as a joke, and it stuck. Warren Beatty is one of my all-time faves. Have you seen *Dick Tracy*? *Bonnie and Clyde*? No? The dude's amazing.'

She laughs out loud. 'That's hilarious. You're *so* not gangster. I thought it was because of Bugs Bunny or something. You know, big teeth.'

'You think I have big teeth?' I ask.

'No, no,' she starts to giggle again. 'You don't now. But I thought maybe you had them fixed.'

'Nope, sorry to disappoint. Not Bugs Bunny. And no braces either, I might add.'

She scratches her ankle absently, a mosquito bite from the grass, probably. 'How come you were at Salim Chaudhry's?'

I pause, contemplating how much to tell her. 'I was delivering something for a friend,' I say, deciding to err on the side of safety.

'Are you a fan? Do you support little bald *bona* politicians?'

'First of all, please don't insult the innocent bonas,' I say. 'They've done nothing wrong except to be born short.'

She rolls her eyes and gives my arm a slight shove.

'I didn't meet him, but he seemed pretty harmless,' she says.

'The guy's a dick, most politicians are,' I say. 'What does a guy have to do before people realize he's useless?'

'I don't know,' she says. 'Maybe display his naked goods.'

I turn to look at her, surprised at her answer, and she bursts out laughing. 'What?'

'Really? His goods?' I tease. 'I don't know if they'd be called "goods". "Uglies" is more like it.'

'Or "littles",' she adds and waves her pinkie finger.

'You're funny,' I say to her. 'I didn't expect you to be funny.'

'Thank you, Bugs. You're sort of funny too. Not hilarious, but funny-ish.'

'Funny-ish? I'll take it,' I say.

She cracks open her window and tilts her face up, inhaling slowly.

'I love the smell of farm fields,' she says.

As we leave Raiwind, the last fresh wisps of air leave the car as it fills up with the smell of city diesel and burning rubber. The truck in front slows to a crawl. Nida raises her window. We're passing the last few housing projects before entering Lahore proper. The arched gateway to our right says Eden Project. It sounds like a bad Cold War–era installation. The houses are set back from the road, in neat rows, like an American suburb, and lit like Christmas to fend off beggars and burglars.

'I just don't understand why people keep voting for Chaudhry if they know he's corrupt,' she says.

'Because people are that desperate and ignorant. And he has the deepest pockets.'

'I guess that makes Ifti corrupt too?'

'Yup, it does.'

'It's funny.' She pauses. 'He doesn't look corrupt. I mean, he seems too smart, too put-together to be a cheap crook. The way he acts and talks, how he carries himself and looks. He looks almost . . . I don't know, moral.'

'Everyone looks moral next to Salim Chaudhry,' I say. 'So I'm guessing you don't do politics?'

'No, I don't do politics—just politician's sons,' she says, and then suddenly realizing what she's said she covers her face with her hands and drops her head down towards her feet and groans in embarrassment.

'Jeez! Thanks for the information,' I say jokingly, lightening the mood. I turn down Bowie a bit, more a whisper in my head than a presence in the car. I don't think we need him as a background distraction any more.

'Sorry,' she says, cringing, 'too much? God, I really need to think before I speak.'

'Please don't. It's rare a girl speaks her mind, so please . . .'

'God, I must really be drunk. I have no filter. I was just wondering what you look like naked, but I told myself to keep my mouth shut—and look, I just told you!' She slaps the back of her head and tries to look serious, pulling her face into an expression of respect, but then it crumbles and she bursts out laughing. 'Can you promise me something, Bugs?'

'Sure.'

'Promise you'll forget everything I've said tomorrow.'

'Done. That was easy.'

'I don't know why I'm talking about Ifti. He's just not really very uncle-y. You know? All the girls wonder if he has a six-pack under those suits.'

'Oh my God! I was wondering the same thing,' I say, trying to mimic her. She shoves me again, this time letting her hand linger on my shoulder longer than necessary.

'I know I'm revealing way too much and I should shut up, but the girls in my class at college have this game, where we imagine boys naked and rate them. Ifti would get a high rating. Higher than Omer,' she says and puts her finger to her lips. 'Shh, our secret.'

'I'm sorry, love, but it's not much of a secret. Everyone in Lahore has seen Omer naked.' But I still cheer in my head at the dirt, at Omer's mid-level rating. He's such a douche, thinking he's the desi Casanova, always boasting of a long line of sexual encounters, half of Lahore he claims—yet, to this day no one seems to want to boast about Omer.

I take the plunge. 'So what's my rating?'

'Don't worry.' Nida grins. 'I think you would get a high mark. I mean, I'm only guessing, but . . .' I can feel her dark eyes examining me, but when I look towards her she suddenly looks away, out the window.

'So basically you'd give me a high mark,' I say, grinning so hard I'm sure my teeth are glowing neon. 'Personally I think I deserve a very high rating. Super high, like *Top Gun* high.'

She rolls her eyes in an exaggerated manner and shakes her head at me. 'Okay, Maverick. You boys and your egos. Uff!'

'What? You brought it up.'

'I was only talking, okay? I was just contemplating possible . . . scenarios.'

'What, you and me? You know there's really only one way to find out . . .' I say, sleazing out a bit. She's silent and I reign it back, quickly reminding myself that she's Omer's girlfriend and not somebody I should be tossing lines to in my car in the middle of the night.

'I'm going to come see you at the radio station,' she says, completely changing the subject. I embrace the semi cock-block, expecting it. She puts her feet up against the dash, her fluorescent-pink toenails bright against the streetlights. We're entering the city and traffic has picked up, even at this late hour.

'Any time,' I say, feeling a bit let down at the topic change. I shift my attention to the road, to the continuous melodic honking of a truck behind me. I slow down, letting him overtake.

'I listen to your show, you know. Your voice is kind of . . . sexy.' She says this slowly, with a tease playing on her lips, her head leaning against the seat, her eyes half shut but still watching me from their half-moons of light. I imagine she's still quite drunk, her mind swirling in her pants. My mind is starting to swirl in my pants too.

'I like to listen to you talk about the music. I can hear how much it excites you. I think the listeners can sense it too, your passion. That's what makes it hot. Plus you sound like you're stoned . . . sort of sleepy, a voice from beneath the sheets. I like that.'

'Wow. That's good to know,' I say to her. Whatever she's doing, saying, it's making my heart beat faster. I can't say that I mind, but I would prefer it to lead to somewhere other than me dropping her home. She's watching me while I drive. I can feel her studying me, watching my hands on the wheel, my legs. I wonder if my hair's all fucked-up and try to smooth the sides back.

'You know, you can tell a lot about a man by the way he drives,' she says.

'Really? Like what?'

I remind myself, amidst beating heart and sweating palms, to be cautious. I conjure up Omer's drunk face behind the wheel of his Porsche and try to concentrate on the traffic. And yet I wait breathlessly for her to go on, to hear her sexy drunk voice drown out Bowie's slick howl in the background.

'About his personality . . . If he's chill, uptight, aggressive. How he holds the steering wheel and shifts the gear can tell you a lot . . . I mean, I'm no expert, but it seems to be pretty accurate so far. But I'm still studying you.' She grins mischievously and suggestively licks her lips. I brake hard, barely missing a donkey cart slowly crossing in front of us, and look over at her. She smiles seductively and bites her lower lip. I can feel the heat rising through my shirt collar. I give her a quick wink.

A Land Cruiser coming up behind honks, the noise impatient, high and squeaky, and then whips around and past us heading hell-bent towards the Canal. Probably the uncle we heard yelling for his driver at the party. Asshole's ruined the moment. My concentration is back on the damn road. But I can feel a sexual heat radiating from the passenger seat, Nida's outline beneath the streetlights glowing a sultry red.

Once we pass the outer-city traffic the road grows calmer. We've passed the small shops, bus stops and truck traffic, and now the few cars that remain going into Lahore pass us confidently. I stay in my lane and drive in peace, glancing at Nida without the wild traffic distractions—feet up, head resting against the seat, face towards the window. Her reflection against the glass reveals her bright eyes staring out at the large gates and house walls. Her mood seems to have shifted from the sexual teasing. She's quiet, contemplative. The alcohol may be wearing off a little.

'Drink the water,' I tell her, pointing to the large bottle next to her. 'It'll make you feel better.' She takes a long swig, dribbling water down her chin and wetting her shirt. She brushes off the water and wipes her mouth with her arm.

'Do you have a cigarette?' she asks me.

'Glove compartment.'

She pulls out a cigarette and holds it between her teeth as she uses the plastic lighter I store in the pack. 'Do you want one?' She holds the cig between her right fingers as she lights me one, this time holding it between her lips. She passes it to me, the filter damp.

I adjust myself in the seat and try to avoid thinking of my face between her legs. She started it, and now I have to find a way to stop it. The car is cold, the AC on full blast. I shiver, flick the CD player back to track one, 'Space Oddity'.

'So this is Bowie,' Nida says. 'I like it. I just remember him from that movie, you know, where he has the potato in his pants.'

'*Labyrinth*. Yeah, that was pretty bizarre. My sisters were obsessed with that stupid movie. Poor Bowie, to be remembered by young girls everywhere for his potato crotch.'

'Maybe when I come to the station you can make me hear some of your favourites.'

'Definitely. I'll blow your mind. Especially if you're high.'

She perks up and faces me, smiling, back to sitting cross-legged on the seat. 'Guess what?' she says. 'I completely forgot. I have something from Omer's room.' She rummages through her purse, which is lying forgotten on the floor, and pulls out a thin joint.

'I lifted it.' She giggles. 'I knew it would come in handy.' She flicks the lighter a few times before it gives. She puffs, burning the twisted Rizla paper at the tip and the car fills with the thick sweet smell. 'Now we're having a proper party. A car party.'

'Nice,' I say. 'I'm impressed. It's turning out to be a pretty sweet night. And to think, I could have been stuck with baldy uncles, smelling of cheap perfume.'

'Yes, it is a pretty *sweet* night,' she says, imitating me cheekily. She hands me the joint and I take a deep drag, the steering wheel level in my right hand. We haven't reached the potholes yet.

'So who are your favourite bands?' she asks.

'Oh God, that might take forever to list. So many different ones for so many different reasons . . .'

'I know you like Queen.'

'How did you know that?'

'I told you, I'm a fan.' She smiles at me, her eyes sparkle.

I can feel the joint's tranquilizing effect surging through my legs, slowly rousing the heat circling my groin. It's good, strong stuff, without the usual shit charas paranoia. I sneak a glance at Nida, sitting loose-limbed next to me, sucking on the roach while absently fingering her long hair. She draws the smoke in slowly, some of it swirling up through her nostrils, and holds it in her lungs. We've reached the main city, where streetlights every few seconds illuminate her and then pour her again into darkness, back and forth until she smokes in slow motion. It's like watching her through a haze-filled dance floor, the strobe light intensifying every back arch and hair toss. Time stops and starts as I watch her. The Canal is quiet. The streak of muddy water to my right is like a sheet of black glass, not a ripple, just a calm reflection of the streetlights. Nida sips the water, darkness, tongue and lips, darkness, the sheen of saliva against the pink. She tilts the bottle of water against her mouth, swallows slowly, the long thin expanse of her neck. In splashes of light I see her live an entire existence before me. I've seen her before. But where? Her name, her face, her eyes, they twist and slip through my memory. We pass a brightly lit traffic light and it seems the sun is shining down on her, her hair flaming in the night, the lights streaking stars across her eyes.

I tear myself away from her, concentrate on the grey of the city as traffic merges on to Jail Road. The car brightens. Gate lights and residential windows bright despite the late weekend hour. Lahore is a city of houses. Where they could build them they did, all dust and noise and breathing. I wouldn't want it any other way.

'Would you like to hear some Queen now?' I ask, Bowie's sci-fi pep starting to grate. The CD changers whirr to load my favourite Queen hits I've ripped from the station. 'Play the Game' is first. It starts with Freddie going all Mozart on the piano, hitting the keys with his elbows, the voices of screaming Brits chanting and clapping. And then his soft voice.

'This is the live version,' I tell her. 'From Milton Keynes Bowl, 1982. Can you believe that? 1980-fucking-2'

Nida listens silently, lost in the melody. I turn it up and she shifts in her seat, sits up a little straighter. The energy is full and unparalleled. She looks over at me and gives me a wide smile.

'The live version is different from the original. He's not able to go high into his falsetto, but I prefer this version. Feels real. You can really hear his voice,' I shout over the music, which doesn't seem to bother her. 'It's from *The Game*. Fucking great album.' She just nods, listening.

'He wrote this song for his boyfriend, after they broke up. This is my favourite part,' I yell, as Freddie really gets into it. You can hear him trying to catch his breath as he sings the verse, Brian May opening up his guitar. I turn up the volume until the sharp chords vibrate in my ribs.

'Your car stereo is really awesome,' she says as the song comes to an end. 'I can feel it inside me.'

'I know. Nothing quite like being drowned in the music. Otherwise, what's the point. This song is part of a trio. It's pretty amazing. It's crazy, Farrokh, leaving behind a desi life, becoming something new, someone so wholly one-off and inimitable, and now heard by people back in Pakistan dreaming the same dream but who can't share the same reality. I guess only a few get to live that life. The rest of us just get to climb into the music and pretend.'

'I know,' she says.

By the time she's listened to the trilogy and 'You Don't Fool Me' is winding out with Freddie's *nah nah nah* and Brian May's high-pitched solo once again, decisions need to be made. I don't want to drop Nida home just yet. I'm having too much fun. And, clearly, she's not all that into the idea either.

'Are you hungry?' I ask.

'Obviously,' she says.

'Okay, I know where to go, as long as you don't mind a drive.'

'Drive on, Bugsy.'

It's late, almost three in the morning, but Defence Market is buzzing with neon and all-nighters. Young waiters scurrying about, running after cars, waving menus. This late, most people eat sitting in their cars. School and college boys hanging out, smoking up, waiting for their breakfast nihari; married couples and families parked at the juice bar; green-lit shopkeepers trying to sell cigarettes and chewing gum. Nida sits contently in the passenger seat and chomps on her shawarma, garlic sauce on her lips. Her kebab is still wrapped in its translucent paper neatly, not dripping down her arm to her elbow like mine. She leans over and wipes the garlic mayo off my hand, then my elbow, then my shirt.

'Sorry, I just can't eat this without wearing it,' I say.

'It's the only way to eat,' she says, pulling a long strand of raw onion from the wrap and gently placing it on her napkin. 'I'm trying very hard to be neat. I don't want you to think I'm a piggy.'

'I have three piggy sisters, remember?'

'Good,' she says, and takes a giant mouthful, her cheeks filling up like a chipmunk's. She holds her hand up, shielding her mouth from view.

'So, is Aliya your girlfriend?' she asks.

'I don't think Aliya is ever anyone's girlfriend,' I say. 'She's too busy with herself to take anyone else seriously.'

Nida nods as if she understands. 'She's really pretty.'

'True, but a pretty face can only take you so far. You know?'

The waiter brings our drinks—Fanta for Nida, 7UP for me. I roll down the window and he hands me two ice-cold glass bottles, old-school, with paper straws bobbing out. It takes a few seconds of reworking to figure out where to put them. Nida lodges hers between her thighs, bending her head to drink from the straw. I manage to balance mine in the cupholder.

'You said your brother's in the army,' I say, after a few minutes of silent chewing. 'What does he do?'

'He *was* in the army,' she says. 'He died.'

'Fuck. I'm sorry to hear that.' I cringe at having asked her and sip my 7UP uncomfortably.

'It's okay. It's not your fault. When he joined the army we all knew it was a possibility. Especially when he was sent up to Swat.'

'He was in Swat? That's hard-core. My father had retired by then but I remember him talking about it, about the Taliban and all the pressure to make sure the militants didn't reach Islamabad.'

'His helicopter was shot down near Mingora.'

'That's horrible. I'm really sorry.' I gently touch her shoulder.

'I prayed every night for him to be safe, you know—but it made no difference.'

'That's the army family's life. You live in fear until the day they retire. When I was a kid every phone call made me sweat. Every time my father went to work I thought it might be the last time I would see him. I think it's one of the reasons why my sisters and I are so close. You grow up sharing such a deep fear, no one else understands it but you. It's tough.'

'Yes, it really is. We didn't get a phone call. I came home from school and heard my mother crying in the living room. I knew then.'

I don't say anything. What's to say?

'Bugsy?'

'Yeah?'

She holds up her shawarma. 'I don't think I can eat this any more.'

Nida is silent as I drive her to her house. I feel bad. I shouldn't have asked about her brother. Her head is against the window, her face turned away from me.

'Are you okay?' I ask her.

'Kya? Yes, just tired.'

'It's the joint. Heavy back-end.'

'Yes, I think so. It's been a long day.'

'No shit. Do you want some music?'

She nods and I DJ, putting on something lighter, a compilation of Journey ballads.

I drive across town to where she lives, the dawn light emerging slowly. We don't speak much except to comment on a familiar song, a lyric. It's not uncomfortable or forced and feels natural in its sleepy ease. I slow down at a checkpoint in her neighbourhood and the police wave us through without even looking into the car. They're tired too.

'I've decided I like your music, Bugsy,' she says. 'My father worked for PTV, so I grew up listening to Indian love songs, and Madonna. I didn't think rock would be my thing. I'm surprised.'

'Amen and hallelujah, finally a convert.'

Nida laughs at this and I smile at her.

She gives me directions to her house and in a few turns we're outside her front gate. She twists towards me, almost full-body.

'Thanks for dropping me, Bugsy. I'm glad your name isn't because of Bugs Bunny. But I think we might have to find you a new nickname.'

'Too late now, babe. I don't think Dick Tracy would suit me.'

She laughs softly and leans over to hug me, kissing my cheek lightly. She smells like cigarettes and grilled chicken, a slight lingering of something sweet—perfume? Sweat? Her face hovers in front of mine for a second and I wonder if I should kiss her. Does she want me to kiss her? Would it be a shit move if I did?

But before I can make any decisions she's moved back and is yanking her shoes out from under the seat. She rummages through her purse for the keys. She grunts as she pushes the door open, but before it slams shut she turns, the shoes slapping against the window as she holds the door open. 'Bugs, you never told me, what's your real name?'

'Maybe another time,' I say cockily. 'If you're good.'

She raises her eyebrows, gives me a look—*All right, hero, if you want to play it that way*—and swings the car door shut. I scroll the CD player to Audioslave's 'Like a Stone', turning the volume up. Perfect for the drive home.

I wait for her, watching her stand on her toes to unlock the gate from the other side, her jeans so tight on her thin body I can see the outline of her underwear. Giving me a thumbs up she walks through the small gate and disappears.

NIDA

We drive *Fast & Furious*, me clutching the side door, his police radio bleeping turbulently as we sprint towards the city in slightly less than three hours. Omer is sneaking me to Islamabad, to a friend's dinner party. Instantly gone are the GT Road days of six-hour drives and pit stops to pee in shocks of wheat, a pashmina shawl lifted for privacy, watching the black water-buffalo sluggishly roll in the mud. Those listless days with my brother, counting cows packed nose to tail in open-backed trucks and seeing the crush of tiny villages dripping past in a wash of RC Cola–painted shop sides, donkey carts and mud-cut walls. Despite Omer's white-knuckle driving, the irreverence towards our eardrums with his house beats and the sheer madness of travelling with two cases of smuggled Corona and bottles of Black Label wrapped in newspaper, it's a drive to remember.

The tensions of home slide away as we speed towards that distant destination; the obligations, the guilt, the oppressive architecture of home and society push behind us; what lays ahead is the future, a future as visible as the road rushing beneath, the Salt Range rising, the Punjab farm fields sweeping away in a crimson curling that folds and unfolds upon itself. It's strange, as

I think about it, sitting in Omer's speeding bullet, how a slight change in global positioning, even a mere three hours, can have such a vast impact on one's point of view.

It's nearing the end of July; how fast time flies—I've been with Omer almost two months. He's a bit of a distant island. The distance between us on a sunny day like this doesn't look too daunting, the water so clear you can almost breathe the salt at the bottom, touch the white sands and the idle stingrays. It's beautiful in the distance. But he's here, crazy hair, all cologne-d out, obnoxious drunk-talk and all. He just can't be sensibly reached.

The Islamabad dinner party is held at the base of the Margalla Hills, on the broad and beautiful Khayaban-e-Iqbal road, where immense low-walled houses flank pine trees and scarlet bougainvillea. During the summer holidays my brother, sister and I would fantasize about living there as we passed by on our way to Murree—imagined living the lives of foreign diplomats, the bossing around of servants in tongues unintelligible, the preparation of strange foods and stranger socializing.

'So, Nids, about this dinner party tonight,' Omer begins to explain as we pass through the gate and park in the open driveway, a large square lawn to my right. 'Just a heads-up, Ahmed's a bit older. He's really my father's friend, but since forever we've been hanging out. You'll love him and his wife, Audrey. She's a gori. Norwegian or Swedish, or Dutch, I don't know, some Nordic blonde-chickie type, with nice hooters.' He says this with a cigarette dangling from his mouth as he gathers his things—cigs,

lighter, phone, wallet—and motions for a servant to grab the
bottles from the back. He leans down and fixes his hair in the side
mirror, fixes that look—long face, slack jaw, cheekbones sucked
in. 'But chillax, it's just a party, baby,' he says, kissing me.

'Should be fun,' I say, with a tinge of nervousness I can't place.

'Good, star-muffin. That's why I love you, you're my cool
kitty-cat cucumber.' I stand near the car watching a skinny
servant haul Corona boxes and Scotch bottles out of the back seat
through Omer's slip of a car door.

'Oye, bhenchod jungli, don't scratch the seat covers. Come,
Nids, let's get out of here before I see him doing something else
fucked-up to my car.' He pats my butt and leads me towards the
house.

The front door has an inset of smoked glass distorting what's
inside, and surely distorting us as well. But the door is open. Omer
doesn't even bother to ring the bell—he walks straight inside the
narrow hallway, a ready, plated dining-table to our right, empty
study to the left. We're still early for dinner and the places are
empty. The hallway is long, decorated with paintings and ivory
tusks, Asian figurines and a fat laughing Buddha in gold. Omer,
confident and so tall in his easy-limbed gait, walks quickly all the
way down and descends into a large, sunken living-room. I follow
leisurely, taking in the decorations, miniature faces and bodies
intricately carved—a little wooden fisherman holding a porcelain
fish, a bare-breasted African statuette, a ballerina poised in white
ivory. At the end of the room, tall windows enclose the living space
and outside, a bright swimming pool surrounded by clusters of
tea-light candles. In the mustard–cornflower living room I watch
Omer walk to the bar and animatedly hug a short man with wild
black hair and a potbelly protruding tightly, like a tabla, out of his
white button-down shirt.

I'm disoriented by the music, thrust among a foreign group of middle-aged aunties and uncles with eyes gleaming like hyenas, as I step down on to the soft carpet of jazz. I disappear—grow younger, uncomfortable and fidgety; my designer shirt and heels disappear, shrinking now into jeans and cheap shoes, now into my white school uniform, now into my childhood Pink Panther pyjamas.

'Nida, stop standing there, silly, and come join us!' the short man shouts from behind the bar.

Ahmed is the pot-bellied man. He clearly dyes his hair—it's so black it might be blue—and his face is round and friendly, big-cheeked, thick eye-browed, aware. He hugs me warmly, as if we're old friends, and goes on about his long-time friendship with Omer—of their adventures in Las Vegas and Crazy Horse, something about Monte Carlo and a Ferrari, an incident with an Italian woman that makes them laugh and high-five each other. I watch them politely play out their masculine celebrations. If I was a man then I too could bond over mishaps and misadventures. I jealously listen to their excited voices and recreated rose-coloured past. I listen to their endless drizzle of stories, with Ahmed as Batman and Omer as his Robin. I can't keep up with them, all I can do is nod, smile, appear excited when it seems appropriate, laugh on cue and daydream about places that I will never visit. Ahmed pours me a generous glass of red wine without bothering to ask what I want to drink and thrusts it enthusiastically into my hand. There are no waiters.

'Nida, have you met my wife, Audrey? Oye, Aud, come over here!' Ahmed yells towards a sofa, where I see a tall white woman stand up smoothly, back erect, like she's in the middle of a yoga pose, and walk towards us. She hugs Omer first, putting her hands around the back of his neck, then turns to me formally. She shakes my hand limply. Audrey is a giraffe, almost as tall as Omer, with thick, wild, curly red hair down past her shoulders, and a long horsey face with sharp features. I can't tell if she's attractive or not, but she's pale. Maybe it's all the sharpness of the goris—the scorching blue eyes, the long thin noses, the severe lips with sharp peaks. Our Punjabi faces tend to be rounder, softer, cuter, while her eyes are small, the blue lost in the thin slits, fine wrinkles and freckles, and when I tell her I like her hair she squints harder at me, making me squirm. Her skin is almost papery beneath the make-up, transparent enough to show the blue veins around her eyes and nose. I stand awkwardly in her gaze and stare down at my wine glass, feeling cheap, unsure of how I'm being perceived in these black heels, the jeans and the loose, long silk top that Alfie generously lent me.

'Come, I'll introduce you to everyone,' Audrey says, her voice deep, husky and unexpected. It's such a change from her appearance that I stop and stare at her. 'It's what you get from a lifetime of cigarette smoke and bullshit.' She laughs a wheezy, throaty laugh.

She takes me to a long sofa of soft-brown suede, on which most of the women are sitting, and one by one rattles off names, none of which I can remember. The women mumble reluctant greetings. Most of them are Pakistani, but some are foreign with short boyish hair and sour faces. Audrey sits back down, leaving me standing, and I watch them go back to their chatter while awkwardly looming above them.

These women feel very different from the women in Lahore, who are either loud and welcoming, or loud and bitchy, or loud and pious. Here, they all look serious and intellectual, playing the role of sophistication somehow imperfectly. Their make-up is underdone, their clothes dark and serious, shoes plain and expensive—there's no glitter or embossed embroidery here—their faces alert and honed to a knife's edge.

I drift away from them, mumbling that I need a smoke, more wine; I go back to the bar, where I can hear Omer spraying his opinionated bakwas everywhere, other blowhards jumping into the fighting pit with him. I look back at Audrey, who has returned to her deeply engaging conversation. What could they be talking about? I realize wine is not going to do the trick this Islamabadi evening, and I whisper to Omer for a whisky.

'Oye, Ahmed, bhenchod, *this* is my girl,' Omer says loudly. 'She just asked for a bloody fucking whisky. Meow, baby!'

I'm a little tipsy and hiding out in Audrey's bathroom, biting my lip, trying to feel my body, my teeth in their gums, numb in my cavernous mouth. I can't feel much. I tap at the teeth. I can hear them clicking. They're nice teeth, white and small, and when I smile the gums are invisible. I peer deep into the mirror, leaning over the wet sink and counter to remove the black mascara collected in the corners of my eyes. Desi boys—Omer and his friends, college boys, schoolboys—are merciless critics, dissecting every female that crosses their path with the ruthless precision of a forensic pathologist.

Audrey's bathroom is pink and pompous. My face looks acceptable. The eyeliner is wearing off, but not so bad overall. The sink counter is cluttered with bottles and jars of all shapes, some with French labels. I wash my hands with her soap, the smell of lemongrass and lavender on my fingers as I screw open a lid of face cream—*La Prairie*, as the silver writing reads. Insert finger, rub goo on neck, gummy and wet. Doesn't feel all that special. I guess the skin tightening takes time. I purse my lips in the mirror and fix my hair using Audrey's flat brush, the static strands rising above me like a halo. I make the duck face that Alfie has taught me, nose pressed inwards, lips pursed. Alfie says a good selfie is the key to eternal self-confidence.

Crystal drinking-glasses hold Audrey's make-up brushes, her eyeliners and pencils, combs with long strands of red curls intertwined; her many perfume bottles are arranged together on a square silver platter. Most of them smell awful, strong and candied, but I generously spray on the Chanel N°5 and think of Marilyn Monroe.

I look like a party girl, that's what I look like. Like in the movies. I see myself in the mirror as I sit on the toilet, the back of the bathroom door a giant floor-to-ceiling reflection, jeans bunched up at my ankles, hair down, eyes smudged black, face pale and hungry. I look and feel like a proper party girl, that's what I look like, and it makes me grin. Who would have thought. I wonder if Omer brought some blow.

I hear footsteps, they pass. Maybe it's the maid. Everyone is finishing up dinner, of which I ate almost nothing. I dab my cheeks with some light-pink rouge and smile at myself again, Alfie model-style. I should go out now, I can't hole up in here among the facial scrubs forever.

Outside the bathroom the air-conditioning is cold and I start to wake up. How long was I in there?—because there seem to be fewer guests. The few that are left are dancing. Audrey and

Omer are dancing, slowly, in their matched tallness, their faces close together. I just stand and stare, Omer's nose hidden in her mass of tangled hair. Ahmed waves and walks towards me, doing a little dance, bobbing his head and spinning in a tight circle, a very sad imitation of a middle-aged Michael Jackson. He can't stop grinning and his eyes have sort of shrunk into small slits— everything he sees now is probably half its original size, sliced at the top and bottom, the world cut perfectly down to size.

'Nida, darling, where *have* you been? We thought we lost you in there. I was just coming with a plunger to plunge you out,' he says, and then he giggles. He's been giggling all night. It's feminine and kind of disturbing. He has a schizo English accent, which fades and appears depending on the words he's using. 'Come on, love, dance with me,' he says like a tubby British talk-show host and pulls me into the middle of the living room, moving close to me and putting an arm around my waist, taking my hand and holding it high with his other. I feel like I'm his life-size doll. I notice the music has changed from the faster swing jazz of the evening to a slow, sultry-piano type. We move awkwardly around the room, his face only an inch or two above my own. He looks at me while we dance, his eyes on my face.

'You are a very pretty young girl, you know that? Very, very pretty,' he emphasizes, more to himself than to me.

'Thank you . . .' I say, almost calling him 'uncle'.

The room has grown darker—there is a faint light radiating from the swimming-pool candles and a few dim lamps. All the furniture is shrouded in shadow, people's faces like the moon, only half visible. Omer and Audrey whisper and giggle to each other, his arm circling her waist a little too tightly, her lips a little too close to his. It's the first time tonight I've seen her laugh. Ahmed swings his hips left and right. He's doing all the old fuddy-duddy-uncle moves he can think of. I step away from him and watch, pretending to be amused. He pulls me close again. Maybe I'm too stiff. Maybe I'm taking this all too seriously. I look around, two other couples are slow-dancing. Maybe this is how the sophisticated dance, this is Islamabad after all, so very unlike Lahore, where no one ever slow-dances.

'You have doe eyes, did you know that? Did anyone ever tell you that you have doe eyes?' Ahmed whispers to me. Audrey has burst into fresh giggles and buried her face into Omer's shoulder. He looks over at me and gives me a wink, an encouraging smile, and dips Audrey with ease, like she's his Stockholm Barbie. He's having fun.

'Um, doe eyes? No, I don't think so,' I mutter, busy watching Audrey squeeze my boyfriend's butt.

'You need to relax, Nida. He's only dancing. And you're not really dancing unless you're cheek to cheek.' And, of course, as if on cue, he pulls me close and rubs his chubby cheek against mine. It's surprisingly warm and soft. 'This is dancing. The most romantic act in the world. Even more romantic than lovemaking, which can be so impersonal, disconnected. But with dancing . . .' He swings me a little in his arms, but is unable to fully control me. I wobble on my heels and cling to him. 'Take your shoes off, Nida. You don't need to be tall to be around me.' He leads me towards the sofa and I kick my shoes off. My body is loosening up, my feet feel relaxed and free.

'Do you know Oscar Wilde?' he asks me as we return back to our dance position, his body a little closer now. His hand has moved further down my waist, almost at my tailbone. A few more inches and he'll hit cheek. Omer dances towards us, Audrey holding on to him tightly. He passes us a thick joint. Audrey looks relaxed and happy, probably already high. She leans down, hands still on Omer, and kisses Ahmed on the lips, two inches away from my face. I flinch back, not wanting to be so close to their fusing spit. I can smell her pungent attar perfume and feel her hair brush against my neck. I hear them smack. I expect Omer to kiss me, but he doesn't—instead, he steers Audrey away once more, leaving us in charge of the profusely smouldering J, now in Ahmed's hands. He takes a few slow, languid drags, still dancing, one hand still precariously close to my butt. He couldn't have used that one to smoke instead? Then I get to smoke and everything calms—the alcohol headache I didn't realize I had is gone, the low-grade anxiety smoothens. I feel Ahmed's warmth against my skin, the smell of his spicy cologne, the feel of his hand against my back, which is so hot I feel its heat sinking into my spine.

'Sin is the only note of vivid colour that persists in the modern world,' Ahmed whispers to me.

'What?' I ask hazily.

'Oscar Wilde.'

'Oh. Okay,' I say, unable to get my tongue to fully formulate the words. The joint is so strong I feel as if I'm having an out-of-body experience. I feel a little dizzy. I stop dancing and feel faint. I wonder if it has been laced with opium.

'Are you okay? Nida darling, it's too much. Come, let's get you some fresh air.'

Ahmed leads me out to the swimming pool, where the Islamabad air is cooling. We sit on a pool chair and he rubs my back as I breathe slowly, my face down towards my knees.

'I'm afraid it's a little stifling in there. I forget you're new. Don't worry, take your time.' He says this understandingly, like a father, and rubs my back like my mother used to when I was throwing up. It helps being outside, the nausea passes. I look at the small kidney-shaped pool, the light-turquoise tiles that waver beneath, the dark humped shapes of mountains beyond the house. The water looks so peaceful, so inviting. A bug lands smoothly on the water, his long legs skimming the surface, and then he realizes his mistake, there's a struggle; he grows still. I feel tired.

'Can we go back inside?' I say to Ahmed. I want to see Omer. I want to ask him if we can leave. Or if I can find a TV somewhere. Watching rubbish television always helps when I'm blasted, it helps me relax. Maybe have some water.

Inside there is only one other couple left dancing. Omer and Audrey are still at it, slow-hugging around the room. A white woman who was earlier showing us pictures of her bikini-clad trip to Costa Brava dances barefoot in a long floral skirt. Her husband is quite handsome, younger than the others, with fair skin and hazel eyes. They are kissing, their tongues visibly darting out from between their lips. I look away and unsteadily walk towards the sofa.

'I think I'll sit for a while,' I tell Ahmed. 'Can you leave the window open?'

He nods and kisses the top of my head and then wanders off towards the bar. Another wave of nausea envelopes me. I rest my head back and try to get through it. I breathe deeply and concentrate on the music, trying to ignore the panic that keeps rising. When I look up I can't see Omer and Audrey any more. I search for them, the room seems empty, and then I notice a shape in a dark corner. There's a small sofa-chair in the corner, beneath the hanging miniatures of Mughal-era Kama Sutra scenes, and through the haze and the dancing bodies of the strange couple, I see Audrey kiss Omer on his mouth. I perk up, confused. How high am I? But there's no mistake. Yes, they're kissing.

I stare, mesmerized. Omer's hands are in her hair, up her skirt, pushing her dress all the way up to her neck. I can see her panties, lacy and black, and her matching bra, one breast visible, one hidden in the shadows of the drapery of her dress, hanging around her neck now like a scarf. Her skinny white body gleams in the darkness. I want to say something, to somehow stop them, but I've lost my voice. All I hear is the mouse-squeak that warbles out of my throat. I've lost all sense of myself, of up and down, left and right. And then Omer looks at me, locks his eyes with mine and motions with his hand for me to join him. I shake my head. Ahmed comes to my side and hands me a cold glass of water, which I sip without thinking. No one seems the slightest bit surprised or bothered. The other couple that was dancing walks outside and I see them removing their clothes slowly, still dancing, throwing their shirts and pants on to the floor. He stands in boxers, she in a red bra. A man's dark sock floats in the pool next to the bug corpse.

I want to laugh at the absurdity of it all. I *think* I do. I've never seen naked adults before in the flesh—another woman's breasts, the strange nipples and styled pubic hair. It's too much. I try to avoid looking at the naked man. I look back at Omer and Audrey, his lips on her nipples now. Her breasts are so pale, the hair red and abundant as he yanks on her panties. I feel numb. I know that somewhere inside I should probably feel angry or jealous, but I feel nothing. Like sedimentary layers of evolutionary time splitting and reforming, if I dig deep I might find the appropriate emotions for this occasion, but looking at naked Audrey, her body so thin and ephemeral, I don't really feel anything. Her head is bent back, mouth open, hips gyrating. Her underwear is gone, now replaced by Omer's face. She raises her hips towards him and I look away. I don't want to see this. I take a gulp of water and put the glass down near my feet, and then I see a set of bare feet next to mine. I hadn't noticed someone sit next to me. I can see his hairy knees. I'm almost afraid to turn my face and look.

But of course I do. Ahmed is sitting next to me, leaning back against the sofa, completely and utterly naked. His potbelly is covered in thick dark hair. He's playing with his erection.

I feel like throwing up. I look back towards Omer, who is sitting comfortably on the sofa now, arms over his head. Audrey is bent down, on her knees, shielding his nakedness from me. Omer looks at me and gives me a sleepy smile, a *look*. It's such an odd look but I understand it immediately. It's a very Omer look—one that says so much with just one expression. It's a challenge, one that says: Can you handle this? Are you cool enough?

We drive home around dawn. I don't think either of us want to see those people in the daylight. Night is a passing wave, washing over awareness and custom, no one wants to see what it strips away once it recedes. I'm tired and dehydrated and have a terrible headache. My tongue feels like sandpaper. The sun is out with its usual summer inferno, and I'm sure I look like shit and then some. Omer certainly does.

'God, Nida, you're one fucking crazy cool chick, you know that?' Omer explodes. I'm expecting him to fall asleep somewhere near the Kallar Kahar mountains and crash-kill us both. A small Fiat passes us, children and a grandmother crowded into the back seat, parents up front. They all turn to stare as we pass them, their eyes soaking up every detail of the worn-out couple passing them in a fast-moving Porsche. I can't imagine what they're thinking, but I know it's nowhere close to the truth.

I look wearily at Omer. 'Yeah?'

'Fuck yeah! Goddamn, Nida, we should fucking get married.' He gives me a quick toothy grin before focusing back on the motorway. I wonder if he's serious. Does a bond grow stronger the stranger it gets? I don't want to think about it.

I lean my face against the window and let it soak up the summer fury and remember an Indian movie I once saw as a kid—black-and-white, one specific scene, a man in love leaving his country, but before he leaves he strikes his lover across the forehead with a brick, so that now every time she looks at herself in the mirror she will think of him, so that now she can never forget him, never forget the man-made scar.

Love is a brick to the head.

BUGSY

All right, Pakistan!

That was PJ Harvey with 'Let England Shake', from her Mercury Prize–winning album of the same title . . . You're listening to The Rocket Launch *on FM84, Where We Play More . . . I'm RJ Bugsy, and on today's Launch we're doing something special . . . Today, I want you to call me with your favourite rock bands of all time. That's right, yaar, we're making a Pakistani top five . . . the ones you simply couldn't live without . . .*

Imagine that we're about to pull the plug . . .

Imagine, if you like, that there's some goon in here with a TT pistol pointed at my head saying, 'Main Bombay ka don hoon!'

So which ones do we save? Is it our yaar Bryan Adams? Dreamy Jon Bon Jovi, or shall we sacrifice him? Aerosmith, Zeppelin, The Who? It's your call, 042-444-8484 . . . I'll tell you mine if you tell me yours . . .

And while I'm taking your calls . . . Here's some Heart with 'Barracuda'.

Flanging guitars take over. I increase the volume, sliding the fader up almost to full. I turn off my mic, the small 'on-air' room filling with the hard strumming of Ann and Nancy Wilson, two of rock 'n' roll's most incongruous names, their real faces replaced for me by their hand-painted bobblehead doppelgängers on my console, a small inheritance from some long-disappeared art school RJ from Rawalpindi. Both dolls are now vibrating and rocking out in pure feminine evil, and I nod my head to the music and eye my own contribution to the on-air booth—a full-size glossy of His Holiness Mr Mercury doing his version of the microphone-warrior pose. The listener phone's red LED is flashing eagerly with calls from different sections of the city—Cantonment, Defence, Cavalry, Model Town—the names reading like a laundry list of dirty colonial chuddies. I let it ring.

From where I sit, atop a crescent of outdated and dusty shops that only a pukka Lahori could identify, Liberty Market is in full Friday-evening rush. Far below my porthole view from the eighth floor are distant gaggles of salwar-kameez-clad aunties and their daughters buying bangles and chappals and dodgy second-hand Chinese trinkets. Endless swathes of kapra from Bliss Fabrics is being laid out before them like crack cocaine for addicts. There's so much potential ass and not one able to differentiate between Beethoven and the Beatles. Up here, I might as well be on the moon.

So why be a Pakistani rock radio jockey? The fame and free ladies? Ha! Not in this country. And it definitely isn't the damn pay either, barely enough for a pack of K2s and a chicken–cheese.

No, the only worthy perk is the night-time satellite ride, this broadcast from the dusty crotch of Liberty and Music for All, my own personal music megalomania, my access to badass battle-axes broadcast for the masses. Basically, I love the fucking music, yaar. There's something about it pulsing out to the nation every night that's almost patriotic, almost spiritual.

I put on the Holy Ones in order to illustrate the point: 'Another One Bites the Dust'. In the downbeat and shaking snare rattle, the full-belted tenor of the world's greatest vocalist, the on-air room becomes my rock 'n' roll shrine. I imagine a hundred and fifty million young Pakistanis listening—the cheap-designer-knock-off-T-shirt-wearing Government College boys stuffed into their night-time Daewoo buses; the horny village teenagers in their gaos sneaking a listen beneath their charpoy chaddars; even the young Pashto Paharis in their green turbans dodging bombs and wiggling uncontrollably on their bicycles with their hand-held transistors, weaving in and out of all the luminescent trucks that will eventually squash them. It's a trip. It's a mission.

I check the on-air clock. In here time slows, minutes become long hours in radio time. Between songs I scan the new pirated database on the desktop folder, all the world's music free and available thanks to the clever fingers of some computer nerd in Hafeez Centre, who can take your computer apart piece by piece and put it back together faster than you can order a caramel macchiato. It's mostly junk these days—girlie pop music, Euro-trash rave shit I don't bother with at all, strange hip-hop and rap that would shame Biggie and Tupac and bring them back screaming from the grave. It's all about mining the few rock gems that fall through the cracks—Arctic Monkeys, Black Keys, Queens of the Stone Age.

As Freddie fades out and Whitesnake's 'Here I Go Again' comes on, I know desi boys all over the country are turning up their car radios, thumping their Suzuki horns to David Coverdale's full throttle, imagining their own hair in full guitar-solo flow. With a smile I pull up my hoodie and place the cheap knock-off Beats on the outside. The air conditioner is on full power, protecting the CPU and the motherboards from the nuclear summer's midnight bake. Through the booth window, down the dim hallway, I see the lounge door open and our station manager, RJ Hercules, bumbling towards me. He smiles and waves, does a little peace-sign head bob to the music. Fuck. I try to force a smile back at him, manage an eyebrow lift as he breaks the sacred seal.

'Yo, Bugsy, great summer show tonight, yaar!' First he gives me the double finger-pistols, then shoulder-dances around the table bhangra-style to peer over the computer and check out my playlist. He's wearing red Adidas Classics with gold racing stripes down the sides—fake, found in some Ichhra back gully—a plaid button-down work shirt. I can't look, it's so bad.

'Don't forget to add the breast-cancer awareness spot at the half hour,' he says. I nod, picturing him with his own pair of saggy fun-bags, and adjust the ads.

Hercules is his brilliant RJ name. His real name: Ihtisham Naveed Abrar-Ul-Zaman. It's the kind of ridiculous name you'd find on some bicycling moulvi from Quetta. His minor claim to fame: a decidedly shit rush-hour pop show. His story: once-mediocre accountant for international pharmaceuticals responsible for dodgy Third World drugs and diarrhoea, now chut radio manager responsible for advertising and occupational harassment. In the last few months he's mutated from a cheap-suited, late-thirties manager-type to a disco fan-boy with spiked highlights and pastel T-shirts.

'Bugsy, yaar, you missed an epic rave last Friday in Dubai!' he gushes. 'You should have been there. Oh my God, we got so *tun*. I didn't get home until six in the morning. DJ Spyder from Bombay was rockin' with his cockin' out yaar. It was amazing!'

This is, as usual, complete and utter bullshit. There are no trips to Dubai—past, present or future—for Hercules, no Grammies and no Puff Daddy. This can be instantly confirmed by his wife and two daughters, sitting listlessly at home on a Friday night while some waiter from a nearby tikka shop goes down on him.

'Just remember,' he non-sequiturs, 'don't put the callers on-air. You didn't get previous permission. I need permission from Karachi head office before you can put anyone on-air. Okay? And please don't mention TT pistols or goons again, yaar, come on.'

Desi management kills the buzz.

I purposely put on Rage Against the Machine's uncensored 'Killing in the Name', while RJ Hercules rubs a marker stain off the motherboard with a wet tissue, and shift AC/DC's 'Big Balls' up, so it's the next song to play. He can't decipher the Aussie lyrics, it's like Zulu chanting to him. He hums tunelessly and flips through an old-ass music magazine, holds up a picture of a half-naked Kate Moss in undies for me to see, smiling like a prepubescent idiot. I try to ignore him. I crank the volume. Small victories.

A year ago the station was the Lahori place to be, a planet with its own centrifugal force resurrected from our once-great musical Mughal city. Before gaandus like Hercules took over, FM84 was the prime hangout for young musicians, college students, music aficionados and, on blessed days, even a handful of horny co-eds from the National Arts Uni. Pizzas and plates of French fries, breasts pressed into tight kameezes, Marlboro Reds and bad desi joints smoked in ubiquity in the elevator, in the office bathroom, even in the station lounge. We sat in a benevolent cloud of smoke, religiously high and playing cards, lost between our passion and intellect, our endless arguments returning again and again to hot female singers, always the careful weighing of evidence, the eventual digression into size of tits. Now all has gone to shit with asinine rules—'RJs can only come in twenty minutes before and stay twenty minutes after their shows,' 'No radio call-ins,' 'No food,' 'No stealing the already-pirated music'—rules created simply because some corporate chut couldn't come up with anything original to do in their sad nepotistic lives.

I take a call. 'Yes, this is absolutely *The Launch*. Sure I can play a small request, but first you have to give me a rock band you couldn't live without.'

Hercules vigorously shakes his head, no requests. I ignore him, pretend not to notice. Relieved it's a rock tune and not some filmi bullshit *gaana*, I write down the band—Live—adding it to the minuscule list of real rock bands, and add the caller's request for *Dolphin's Cry* to the queue. Sometimes a great request comes along, just sometimes.

'Come on, Bugs, man, don't play requests, yaar,' Hercules says in a pathetic pleading sort of way. It's his puss way, cajoling instead of demanding. No one listens to him, but I give him a nod anyway, knowing the stooge is just doing his job.

He's pleased I haven't made life too difficult for him and makes an effort to pretend to like my music, while in his head I'm sure he's translating it into something pink and pretty and smelling like used bubblegum, think Katy Perry's 'Roar'.

'How do you like the new time slot?' he asks me, referring to my new showtime. He told me it's due to the popularity of the show—the station wanted to reach the larger audience driving home from work. But my ego just can't quite get on board, suspicious fucker that it is, it knows desi mentality too well to trust a better time slot based on the audience—as if the radio station has a way of monitoring listenership and interest; it's all guess work and no work.

'It blows,' I say. 'I preferred being alone, at night. It's odd playing heavy rock in the afternoon. It feels wrong. And now you're here, popping in to say hello, bugging me about ads and recording-station IDs. It's fucking up my groove.'

He just laughs uncomfortably. 'I know, I know. I told them you'd hate it. You want to know the truth?' He leans forward, arms laid across the counter in front. 'The owner's nephew wanted your time slot for his *After Dark* jazz show. He thought midnight was too late.'

'I knew it! Bastards. My poor night-time slot shit-canned for jazz.' I'm playing it up, much to Hercules' amusement, but I do feel a sudden tug for the old station life, the midnight hour. 'Depressing shit.'

'Sorry, yaar. I was all for you, but you know no one listens to me.'

I do a quick link, reminding all that they're listening to *The Rocket Launch* in a brand-new time slot. I cue the advertisements, stock ones for biscuits and phone companies and foam mattresses, and add a few station IDs for good measure.

'Anything else, Herc?' I ask, lowering the fader.

'No, yaar, I just wanted to say hello. I know you hate this time slot, but I'm happy you're here. We need more of your style, yaar.'

I roll my eyes and he grins. Then he's out, sauntering like he's the birth of cool, his dumb-ass red pants blazing in the hallway lights.

The phones are ringing, call now to get in your favourite rock bands of all time, the ones you just can't live without, like food,

like air, like water. 042-444-8484. Call soon, or they're going to
break my knuckles, shove bamboo shoots under my nails. FM84,
Where We Play More, and The Rocket Launch *continues with*
ACDC, this one's called 'Big Balls'.

That should freak Hercules out. I laugh to myself and queue some
Chili Peppers. I look up and see a small feminine face staring at
me, big brown eyes visible through the small porthole in the door.
She smiles and waves and I realize it's Nida. That's new . . . I wasn't
expecting her to visit. I wave her in and quickly arrange the extra
swivel chair next to me, clearing the desk of all my musicology
files—the *dirty deeds done dirt cheap* histories of rockers fresh and
long-decaying pushed away for a cute face and the sweet scent
of girl.

'Hey, what's up?' I say. 'Good to see you.'

'Sorry to interrupt. I was in the area and thought why not.'

'Of course, silly,' I say, perking up, happy for times like
this—unexpected and brilliant sparks of light in the dullness of a
monotonous Lahore. 'You're not disturbing me at all. Experience
The Rocket Launch first-hand.'

She plops into the chair, looking tired, her face shining with
a thin layer of sweat. She unwinds her dupatta from her neck and
dabs the sweat from her forehead, eyebrows and nose. She looks
worn out, thinner, with rings under her eyes. She's still hot, but
looks as if dickhead Omer's wearing her out.

'How have you been?' I ask her.

'Fine.' She rubs her nose and sniffs a few times. She's probably
been doing too much coke.

'I've never seen you in salwar-kameez before. You look
different. I mean, nice, but different.' She's wearing something
light pink, with small white flowers.

'Thanks. I'm totally soaked though. It's shocking how hot a city can get. I was shopping with a friend, she's getting married soon. She ditched me for her fiancé. Some quality friendship, nahin?' She laughs. 'So I walked over.'

'Wow, you walked. That's dedication to music.'

'It wasn't far.'

'I know, but I don't think I know any women who walk in the summer. Not even my sisters. Not even for jewellery and discounts.'

'Well, it was either this or going home in a rickshaw, eating the smell of toe-jam and gasoline. So I'm very glad your showtime has changed, Bugsy.'

She smiles weakly, not so flirty this time. She's not as bubbly and carefree as before either. Maybe it's because she's sober, or sweaty. I don't mention it, but instead give her a tour of the four-by-eight on-air room, of my computer, the Winamp player, the massive digital folders of pirated music, and then that's it— I've run out of stuff to show off. So I do the next best thing, queue up a mad off-air playlist, one that's just for us—the best of rock music to inundate her with, the classics, the greats, the good, the bad and the uglies of rock 'n' roll. Hell, I even toss in some Bon Jovi to smooth the transitions. I don't wait until the songs wind down but play one right after the other, without a breath, without a pause, without a second to contemplate life, death or taxes. In the background the on-air playlist spins slowly, consistent, approved rock songs for the masses. Off-air I take her on a wicked melodic ride she won't be forgetting soon, with dodgy lyrics and shrill screams and guitar fills designed to blow the mind.

'Wow, Bugs,' she says eventually, slumping down in her chair, head bent back, eyes closed. 'I feel like I've been reprogrammed.'

She seems to like most of it, responding to the massive dose of rock history I'm hitting her with like a champ.

'Well, that was the intention.'

She gives me a crooked smile. 'Well, it's interesting stuff, that's for sure. I didn't realize how rock-crazy you really were. I thought it was just your *shoda* reputation, you know, Lahori style, built on schoolboy bakwas and dreams.'

'Thanks, I think,' I say, laughing. 'I didn't realize I had a reputation, let alone a shoda one. I'll take that as a compliment.'

'You should.' She pauses and listens to Kings of Leon's 'Sex on Fire'. 'Your phone is ringing, you know that?'

'Oh yeah. I was doing a sort of call-in show, the desi rock favourites.'

'Do a lot of people call?'

'Yeah, sometimes, it depends on the day, the hour. Right now is busy. People keep thinking that when we say "call in" it means we're giving something away, so I've been getting all sorts of calls where someone mentions a song and then asks what they've won.'

'Everyone wants free stuff.'

'Tell me about it.'

'What type of people call?' she asks. 'Sorry I'm being nosy but I've always wondered what kinds of people are in Pakistan. Like, who would call and what would they request, their accents, where they are calling from . . . You know?'

I nod, understanding what she means. 'Mostly it's kids and teenage boys, guys in their twenties, occasionally a wannabe cool uncle reliving the seventies or eighties, requesting Pink Floyd or Deep Purple. But the teens are my staple audience. I always make sure to throw in some metal for them. I don't know what it is, but Paki boys love heavy metal. Metallica, Iron Maiden, Sabbath,

Tool, Megadeth. I rarely talk to real adults. I'm sure they're cursing me all over Pakistan, yanking out their car radios.'

She laughs. 'I know my parents would. Lata and Rafi—or nothing. Or then they go the other way to Nusrat Fateh Ali Khan. They don't want to give new music a chance.'

'You should hear my father. God, he's terrible. He's been making fun of my music since I was a kid. He would throw my rock CDs out just so I couldn't play them. I'd always go out and rebuy them, play them louder outside his bedroom. He hates that I do this.'

'Which is probably why you do it,' she says, giving me a sneaky smile.

'Yeah, I guess so. But I'd like to think it's for the music. Otherwise, I'd probably be working in some soul-sucking bank.'

'Well, I'm glad you don't. This is a nice song,' she says about Mother Love Bone's 'Chloe Dancer/Crown of Thorns'.

'Yeah, it's a great song. From a great movie too. *Singles*. Classic. Maybe we can watch it sometime,' I say, hoping for another hangout session.

'Sure,' she smiles, non-committal, and closes her eyes.

'So where's Omer?' I ask her, digging a little. It's the first time I've seen her without him—clinging to her, calling her some ridiculous nickname, falling all over her—and I'm surprised.

She stays silent, eyes still closed, and shrugs. She looks spent. I should do a link, but I don't want to spoil the mood, so I queue up a few more songs and jam a thirty-second advertisement between Tom Petty and Alice Cooper. I feel a gentle touch, Nida's watching me, her hand on my arm.

'What?' I ask.

'Nothing. I'm glad I came to see you. I missed you. Missed seeing someone normal and sober for a change.'

I realize that she's not here for the music. And maybe not even to see me. Well, maybe a little for me, but more for a friendly face than my charming sexy personality. It's standard operating procedure for Omer's girls, he wears them out. Either they get sick, or their parents get worried and take the girls on vacation or butch up their curfew, or they find a place to hide for a while and recuperate. Now this is Nida's hiding place. What a bummer. Omer really knows how to mess up a good chick.

I ask her if she'd like some water and she says she wants to wash her face. I show her to the bathroom and return to the studio. I find Faisal sitting in my chair fiddling with my playlist.

'What's with the Bon Jovi, yaar?' he says without a pause, without a hello or explaining what the fuck he's doing here. Typical Faisal. 'You're turning into a pussy. What's with your playlist? It's like a chick fuck-list.'

'Kiss my ass. I have an audience, you know, a responsibility. I play for all sorts of rock aficionados. And that's the off-air list, dipshit.'

'Yeaaah, sure, whatever.' He smirks at me and cuts 'Free Falling' off halfway, replacing it with Soundgarden's 'Slaves and Bulldozers'. 'Let 'em think their radio is skipping. So what's up? When you done? I need shoes, wanna go check out some stores?'

'No.'

'Asshole.'

I yank him out of my chair and remove the Pink Floyd he's queued up next. 'I already played Floyd, fuckface. Stop screwing with the list, man, it's sacred.'

'Aren't you done already?' he says in his usual pushy voice, the overpowering stench of his Armani cologne saturating the room and burning my nostrils. 'So? What *are* the top desi rock songs?' he asks, flipping through my notes. 'You stopped talking about it after the first hour. What the fuck? Your audience is disappointed,' he says, pointing to himself.

'Shit, I totally forgot about that.' I quickly queue up a link. Faisal watches as I reintroduce myself, let them know there's thirty more minute of rock music, and remind them to call in for their top rock songs.

'Lemme guess,' he says once I'm done, 'Queen somehow managed to make number one.'

'Not this time,' I say. 'I think people caught on that it was my addition.'

'No shit,' he laughs and pores over the list, making a sour face when he gets to Deep Purple.

'I added what I thought people would like, not what you like. Fucker.' I add the swear for good measure. 'I made the list last night. I thought I'd announce it at the end, adding a song or two that someone actually requested.'

'It's not the best list I've ever seen, but not terrible either,' he says, handing me back the notebook. I just shake my head. Trust Faisal to come up and analyse my show, critiquing everything. He can't help himself, our boundaries are blurred to the point of nonexistence.

'Any chicks call in?' he asks me.

'What do you think?'

The phones are still ringing, less but constant, and will continue until about half an hour after my showtime, when people finally realize the show really is over and I'm probably not sitting here any more. Faisal slides the desk chair back and answers the phone.

'Hello,' he says sleazily, attempting a deeper voice, 'This is *The Rocket Launch*. What can I do for you? Really, I do? Well, thank you,' he fake-laughs. It's a girl, otherwise he would have hung up immediately. He looks over at me and whispers, 'She says I sound better on the phone than on the radio.' He shows me his massive mouth of whitened choppers. 'Yes, of course I can play Madonna's 'Like a Virgin', it's totally my favourite song too.' I roll my eyes at him and kick his chair away from the desk.

'Chutiya,' I mouth and get back to the playlist. He flirts with her on the phone, asking her what school she goes to, her age, if she likes coffee. He gets a phone number and pockets it smugly.

'I don't understand your issues, yaar,' he says to me. 'That was damn easy. What's the point of being on the radio if it doesn't get you ass?'

'It's because I'm a fucking professional who works for a living, unlike some people.'

'Excuses, excuses,' he says, still grinning.

Nida returns, looking fresher; some colour has returned to her face, and Faisal gives me The Look: raised eyebrows, lips twisted in a cheeky horny smile, eyes wide with respect and surprise—*Dude, you have a chick here, you dodgy lucky sonofabitch.*

'Hi Faisal, I didn't know you were here,' Nida says, coming over and giving him a hug.

'I didn't know *you* were here either,' he says, still wearing that cheeky cheapster smile. 'You're having a regular party here, aren't you, *Bugsy*?' he says, emphasizing my name, like I've been a bad boy. 'And you didn't invite me?'

'I don't need to invite you, you show up anyway.' He grins like a show monkey with cymbals.

'So how have you been, Nida?' he asks. 'Has Bugsy been entertaining you here at FM84? I hope you got the grand tour.'

'It's been educational, that's for sure. And I just met some of your fellow RJs outside, Bugsy. Nice guys. Friendly.'

I leave them to talk while I finish off the last of my song list, adding all the advertisements and station promos.

'Let's get out and have a quick smoke,' I say. 'Two and a half hours and I'm dying. My lungs haven't felt this fresh in years.'

Outside, in the battered RJ lounge, I'm surprised to find a group of RJs, despite the head office's crackdown measures. Apparently no one is paying much attention to the ridonculous 'no RJ's twenty minute before or after their show' rule. I imagine some fat aunty in florals, a cousin or *khala* of the owner, sitting in some squalid Karachi office chewing the end of her Piano pen and coming up with random rubbish to ruin the buzz. Razzle-Dazzle, Mania and Flash are sitting around in a cloud of tobacco smoke, shooting the shit. They get up and we hug, exchange handshakes, give each other shit for not making an effort to meet up outside the station.

'Bugsy, yaar, where the hell have you been, man?' Mania asks. 'I only know you're alive from your show and this crap music you're playing. What is this *Pulp Fiction* bakwas?' He's wearing camouflage combat pants, his white unbranded tennis shoes are up on the table.

'It's Dead Kennedys, you tone-deaf monkey. Would you prefer it if we all huffed some nitrate poppers and pranced around to Tiesto?' Mania laughs at this and gives me the finger.

'Bugsy's too cool to hang out with us now,' Flash says in his slow desi drawl. He's the tallest of the bunch, a giant hairy bear, and not someone you would want to fuck with.

'What do you mean *now*?' I say, joking. 'I was always too cool to hang out with you idiots.'

They roll their eyes, scoff, laugh, do the guy thing. It's good to see them.

'You guys know Faisal, and this is Nida.'

'We just met Nida,' Mania says, looking quite pleased. Faisal they all know and there's an exchange of handshakes.

Faisal lights two expensive imported Bensons, gold-rimmed and flashy, handing me one. He lights one for Nida, chivalrous and all, holding the lighter steady, making sure it's fully lit before moving away. Then he passes around the pack, knowing that most of the RJs are struggling middle-class undergrads studying finance or marketing or computer engineering—boring-ass shit they're forced to do to please their fathers.

Faisal makes himself comfy on the cracked pleather, resting a brand-new Nike'd foot on the table, dangling the cigarette between his lips, doing his best Brad Pitt. Always a hero in his own mind, even while sitting beneath a poster of a shirtless and oiled Right Said Fred. Nida stands next to me, watching, observing the culture. The station lounge is grimy as hell, one tube-light flickering in and out of consciousness above my head, a ripped two-seater sofa and littered coffee-table, behind it two open cubicles with restricted Internet and viruses up the wazoo.

I take a long drag on the dry bitter cigarette. Faisal's imported cigs are always brittle and tasteless, like smoking a dead man's finger. He thinks the gold pack impresses the chicks, and it does until they take a puff.

'So what the hell have all you losers been up to?' I ask jubilantly.

'You didn't hear? Well our good buddy Razzle-D here is getting married,' Mania says. 'He's biting the bullet and resigning to a life of shaadi torture.'

'What?! Are you fucking serious?' I say.

He nods resignedly. 'Parents found me a girl, yaar. And there's nothing bloody wrong with her. She's not pretty, but not ugly; not smart, but not retarded. I'm fucked,' he says morosely. He looks down at his cigarette, studying it as if it contains a clue to his freedom.

'But you're, like, eighteen,' I say. 'You're way too young to be married.'

'I turned twenty-one last month. My mother thinks if I don't get married now, then I never will. I've reached my singles expiry-date, yaar. My sperm is apparently losing its potency.'

Flash elbows him to remind him of Nida's presence.

'Well, at least you'll get laid,' Faisal says, always looking at the bright side.

A hint of a smile plays on Razzle's lips. That's probably what he's thinking, the one bright star in a lifetime of conjugal darkness.

'I'm sorry to hear about you leaving the pack,' I say to Razzle. 'She's not your first cousin, is she?'

'No, thank God. But she's Ahmedi too, and you know how rare these chicks are.'

'It must be like hunting a unicorn huffing up K2,' Nida says. We all laugh.

'So have you heard the latest news?' Faisal asks, the question open for anyone to answer.

'Of course,' Flash answers. 'We don't live in a bubble. Can you believe it? It's crazy shit, yaar.'

'What?' I ask. 'What news?'

'It's a proper political scandal, yaar, with proof and papers. We never get that shit. We're never that lucky. It's bloody beautiful,' Flash says, getting up and grabbing another cigarette from Faisal's golden pack.

'Beautiful? I think it's fucked-up as hell,' Faisal says.

'What do you mean "papers"?' I ask, my heart starting to beat a little faster.

'This could cost him the election,' Mania says. 'Even before he really gets started, it could be over.'

'What the hell are you guys yapping on about?' I ask. 'Is anyone going to fucking tell me?'

'Don't you ever read the news?' Faisal says. 'Salim Chaudhry announced today that he has some bank documents that prove Mian Tariq has been stowing away money in Panama.'

My stomach takes a thirty-thousand-foot drop.

'Yeah, illegal funds and dodgy properties. That's what Chaudhry is saying,' Flash adds.

'That fucking figures, yaar,' Razzle-Dazzle says angrily. 'Just when someone honest comes along, you find out he's the biggest crook of all.'

'I don't know, I'm not buying it,' Faisal says. 'I'm still holding out for my main man MT. This sounds like total bullshit.'

'Totally, I agree. Salim Chaudhry is just up to his usual dodgery,' Mania says. 'These are the final acts of a desperate man.'

'I'm not so sure,' Flash says. 'He said he had proof. He was practically vibrating during the press conference.'

My eyes meet Nida's. She licks her lips quickly, holding her cigarette out in front of her. I feel nauseated.

'Hey, Bugs, don't you have a final link to do?' Razzle-D asks.

Fuck, I forgot all about the damn show. I stagger, like I've been back-stabbed, towards the on-air booth. I do a quick parting link, my voice sounding distant and disembodied. Fuck the Top 5. I lower the Arctic Monkey's 'Knee Socks' so it's barely audible and queue up Audioslave to end the show.

I call Moby. I don't think, I don't ponder what the fuck is going on, I just call him and pray he picks up.

Moby answers before the third ring. Before he can get past his usual 'Bugsy, yaar, what's up?' I interrupt him.

'What the fuck is going on, Moby?' I ask him nervously, my voice loud and shrill. I'm grateful for the on-air soundproofing.

'So you've heard the news. I should have called you before you heard—my bad, yaar,' he says.

'The bank documents . . . They're the same documents I delivered, aren't they? The ones you gave me?'

He says yes and tries to explain but I cut him off.

'What the fuck, Moby? What the hell is going on?'

'Listen to me, Bugsy,' he says slowly. 'We need to meet. Immediately.'

My heart begins to hammer as he says this. This is not good.

'But first, breathe. Okay?' he says. 'Just relax. It will all be sorted. Where are you?'

'Station.'

'Meet me at Monsoon's.'

'I'll be there in twenty.'

Outside, the boys are gone. Faisal and Nida remain, waiting for me.

'Everything okay?' Nida asks. 'You look pale.'

'I'm fine. Just a little tired. My sister called and she needs the car now,' I say, lying. 'Faisal, can you give Nida a ride?'

'Totally. I'd love to,' he says, giving me a cheeky grin.

'I'm sorry you have to go, Bugsy,' Nida says, 'but I had a great time. Maybe we can see that movie you talked about sometime.'

'Sure, I would really like that,' I say, giving her a kiss on the cheek goodbye.

'What movie?' Faisal asks.

But I'm already out the door, thinking about 'Shadows on the Sun', strangling Moby with my bare hands and Nida's smell of sweet jasmine.

When I arrive Moby is already in the basement cafe, sitting in a corner booth. The place is empty—as is usual on such a sweltering summer afternoon—the air conditioner whirrs in pain, the lone refrigerator vibrates wildly in a desperate attempt to cool the cheesecakes splitting like volcanoes.

I motion to the dull-looking boy behind the counter for a bottle of water and pull up a chair.

Moby wipes his cake mouth with a tissue. The idiot is wearing his black trench coat despite the heat. He's sweating buckets as he sips his coffee, trying to look cool.

'I'm glad you came, Bugsy,' he says.

'You didn't leave me any fucking choice.'

He nods but doesn't speak. The boy brings me a sweating Pak Crystal that has an odd colour and an even stranger taste. In the background, miraculously, John Coltrane and his tenor are tunnelling from the cafe sound-system. Moby keeps looking past me, at the door, adds more sugar to his coffee. I feel like punching him in the face.

'Do you want some cheesecake?' he asks, his voice fluttering.

'No, I don't want any damn cheesecake. What's going on, Moby?'

'I've got a good one for you, Bugs. A paan-wallah's wife is in a coma . . .'

'Are you fucking shitting me?'

'Chill, yaar. Listen. There's a paan-wallah sitting by his wife's bedside in hospital.'

He keeps telling the joke obliviously like he's on crack.

'She's in a coma. He's rubbing her arm, and by mistake he rubs her tit and she moans. He rubs her other tit and she sighs. He runs to the doctor and tells him what happened. The doctor says: "Quick, man, go back inside and try some oral sex." After five minutes the man comes out and tells the doctor, "Doctor, she's dead." The doctor says, "Dead? How could she be dead?" "I don't know," the husband says, "I think she must have choked."'

He pauses, waiting for my reaction. I don't laugh.

'Are you done?' I ask him. 'How about singing a fucking song? Wanna recite a poem?' I say, pissed. 'Quit fucking around, Moby. This shit is real. You had me deliver Panama Papers, for fuck's sake! What the hell have you got me into? You said we were helping Mian Tariq. This is so messed up, yaar. This couldn't possibly get any worse.'

He sighs deeply. 'Mian Tariq knows you delivered the documents to Salim Chaudhry.'

'What?' I say. 'What the fuck are you talking about, Moby?'

'He just knows. But don't worry, this isn't as bad as you think.'

'Really? This isn't bad?'

'He just wants to meet you.'

I'm dumbfounded. I just stare at him. He tries to put his hand on my shoulder. I slap it off.

'Bugsy, it'll be okay, I swear, yaar.'

'This is bad. This is really fucking bad,' I say. 'Mian Tariq wants to meet me, the idiot who delivered his political death sentence. I'm totally fucked.'

'Will you shut up and stop being so damn filmi? This is okay. You'll just meet him, tell him what happened, that's all. You did nothing wrong.'

'Are you nuts? There's no way in hell I'm going.'

'Listen, yaar, Bugsy, listen. You'll go to him, okay. He's expecting you. And you'll take him these papers.' He brings out another envelope from a briefcase at his side, exactly like the one I delivered to Salim Chaudhry. I hadn't even noticed a briefcase. It has suddenly materialized like a bad prop. Moby has already thought this through. He's planned this.

'And then you'll clear your name,' he says. 'These are the same documents Salim Chaudhry has.' He holds up the envelope and gives it a shake. 'The ones you delivered. Mian Tariq wants a copy so he knows what he's up against. And when you give them to him, like he's requested, you'll tell him you have no idea where they came from. Do you understand?'

'So let me get this straight. You want me to meet Mian Tariq? And give him his own dodgy Panama papers? And tell him I have no idea where they came from, like they just shot out of my asshole?'

'Yes, exactly, as long as you don't know anything, you're safe.' He lays the envelope on the table in front of me gingerly, patting it and moving it away from my perspiring water bottle.

'That's not going to work! He's going to think I'm an idiot. What, I just deliver random documents for people I don't know? I'm not fucking DHL.'

'I need to remain anonymous,' Moby says. 'That's the entire point. Make some shit up, who cares? Just don't tell him it was me.'

'And why the fuck would I do that? Why would I do any of this?'

He pauses and wipes his forehead with a napkin.

'For my family, Bugs. For Ayesha, for Nour, for my unborn son. Bugsy, I'm going to have a son.' He gets all emotional and chokes up. The cafe door opens and a young couple make their way in and take a table next to the door. I can't believe this ridiculous shit.

'I saved your ass once,' he says. 'That crash could have turned out differently if it wasn't for me. This is the last thing I'll ever ask of you. I swear. You have nothing to lose.'

'I have my life, I can lose that. Oh, and by the way, congratulations on the unborn son, asshole.'

'You won't, yaar. You're immune. You don't give a shit about politics. You're a famous star. And your father's a big shot in the army. You're protected. These guys aren't stupid. Nothing can happen to you.'

'Fuck you, Moby. Why is this so important to you? I don't get it.'

'My father's lands. They're in Salim Chaudhry's district and he's holding them hostage. My father had debts. This is the only way to get them back. You know how Salim Chaudhry is.'

'And why the hell should I trust you with this now? How do I know you're not going to fuck me up further? How do I know that MT is not going to fuck me up?'

'Trust me, it will be all right. Just tell him you have no idea who's behind all this, which you don't, and get the hell out of there.'

'Why didn't you do all this yourself?' I ask. 'Why did you involve me?'

'They all know me, Bugsy. A favour for one makes an enemy of the other. What do you think I've been doing these past ten years? How do you think I make a living? This is what I do, Bugsy. I dig the dirt. I do favours. I get shit done. They all know me.'

I stop and stare at him, try to making sense of this fucked-up revelation. I always knew Moby was a dodgy bastard but I never thought he could be the slime between the slippery handshake of Pakistani politics. He's going to get himself killed. He may get *me* killed as well.

Moby motions for the waiter to bring him the bill. I stare blankly at the couple, now whispering and holding hands secretly under the table.

NIDA

She looks like a boy with her boot-cut jeans and tight white T-shirts. Her chest as flat as the Punjab, short hair, make-up-free; she thinks she's the Paki Salman Khan with her menthol cigarettes, barbed-wire-tattooed bicep and a permanent sneer. She has everything minus the penis. She's no direct relation to Omer and yet she stays as a family friend, day after day, well into her second week.

I think maybe there's more than just innocent family friendship between them. She's too comfortable in his room, walking around braless in his silk pyjamas, her rude nipples piercing the flimsy silk, eating cereal as she strolls, spilling milk on the floor and crushing the wet flakes with her calloused feet. I'm observing her from Omer's sofa while smoking a joint, one I made and plan to burn through before anyone named Billi can come and steal it. I will covet it until the last black ash is done. Thankfully, she doesn't seem to notice.

Omer sits on the floor, cutting neat rows of cocaine on his glass Versace table. It's still breakfast time in Omer's wild kingdom, just after 3 p.m. The afternoon sunlight and heat press against the heavy drawn curtains. Omer is readying his after-breakfast lines as

Billi inhales her cereal. She's already consumed all the other food on the tray—eggs and toast, halwa-puri from Main Market—and claims through mouthfuls that she's just a growing girl. At 5'11" I don't know how much she plans to grow till—the moon? I want to tell her she should grow herself back to Karachi but instead quietly drink my tea and grab the television remote.

Billi stands over Omer. 'Make mine two,' she orders. 'I like a little glass through *each* nostril.' She smiles proudly at me, displaying a crushed mouthful of cornflakes. Occasionally, she acknowledges me, offers the briefest of eye contact. From that I'm supposed to gather that she's including me in the conversation. If I speak she waits until I'm finished and then resumes with what she was saying, often not bothering to answer or acknowledge that I've spoken. She could be ruder, downright vicious like most girls, but her passive way of ignoring me is a subtler death. Now Omer often mimics her disregard and I sit around wondering if I should just leave and let the two of them entertain each other. I don't know how much I'll be missed.

'Oye, Omer,' I say from my seated position on the sofa. 'What are you doing?' I know what he's doing, I can see him clearly.

He grunts. Billi answers. 'What do you think he's doing? He's lining up the coke, OCD-style, so we can post it on Instagram, #perfectlinesofcoke." You know we're going to snort it in like point three seconds, right?' she adds.

He ignores her. It's his ritual, 'perfect lines for the perfect high'. She would know that if she paid any attention, but instead she walks around bitching and talking about her life in Karachi, so obviously fabulous she refuses to return to it, waving her spoon in the air, hawk eyes ready to pounce right after Omer does the first line. She sits down on the sofa next to me and crosses her legs, balances the bowl precariously in the wide gap. She lights a cigarette. She smokes as she spoons the caramel-coloured milk from the bowl—gulp of milk, puff, gulp of milk, puff. It's disgusting.

'I can't believe you stay home all day. Isn't there anything else to do around here? Other than eat? This place is a total shithole. There's no beach, no nightlife, no Sindh Club. Two words: French Beach.' Billi talks non-stop, like the nondescript voices on an American sitcom, always with the same accent, the same jokes, the same fake laughter, played for comfort rather than content.

I realize it's useless getting Omer's attention with me sitting silently, with Billi huffing away like a cow next to me. So I get up, yawn loudly, lift my arms and stretch, and crumple the roach in an ashtray. I make a show of my actions, all the while fully aware of my pathetic attempt to grab his attention. 'Achcha, Omer,' I say. 'I think I'm going to go. I promised my sister I would take her shopping.'

Omer stops perfecting his lines and looks up. His eyes are small bloodshot planets orbiting loosely in their sockets. With Billi staying over he's been partying non-stop. My cousin Ali has been over almost daily, twice sometimes, delivering drugs, occasionally dragging me into a corner to distil desperate advice about me ditching Omer, begging me to return to my previous dull and depressing existence.

'Leave? What, now?' Omer says. That's gotten his attention. He stands up from his crouched coke-cutting position. 'What do you mean *go*?'

'I told you I had to take my sister shopping. We have that wedding in two weeks, remember?'

'Wedding? Who the hell gets married in August?' Billi asks loudly.

I shrug. 'It's not my wedding,' I say.

'Can't your sister go by herself?' Billi asks.

'No. I have the car.'

'Don't you have other cars?' she says. 'Doesn't your sister have a boyfriend or something who'll take her?'

This is no good. I'm now negotiating with Billi, who seems to have a confused agenda. She should want me to leave and be alone with Omer, and that I would understand, but apparently she wants what Omer wants, and knows it even before he does. She's now the voice of Omer, speaking before he can even think. It's the perfect takeover.

'Omer, can I talk to you please?' I say, attempting to be firm. 'Alone.'

Billi ignores me. 'It makes no sense why she should go,' she tells Omer. 'I mean, who will do her lines?'

She's doing what my mother used to do, talking about us in the third person.

'Let's do the lines first,' she says. 'Then Nida can leave.'

Omer leans down and snorts the line so fast I wonder why he even bothers to make a line, why not make a small mountain *Scarface*-style and thrust his stupid face into it. After seeing Omer do mountains of jaali drugs brought in from god-knows-where—I imagine a cave somewhere in Afghanistan where old men are filing their toenails into a fine white powder—I doubt the boy can overdose.

Billi gets down on to her knobbly knees and gets comfortable, taking the thousand-rupee note and re-rolling it into a tighter spiral. I start to walk towards Omer's bed, wanting to avoid the theatrical display of Billi snorting drugs into both her cavernous nostrils. Omer follows me.

'Listen, Omer, I really need to go,' I say firmly. I don't really want to go, even though spending time with Omer hasn't been the same. It's like dating Frankenstein, along with his dead-eyed bossy bride. I tell myself shopping with my sister might not be complete torture. But it's maddeningly hot outside. I don't want to drive in mid-day mid-week Lahori traffic. But I don't want to stay here either. I don't know what I want. I'm bored, I'm stoned, I'm annoyed, and I want Billi to piss off back to Karachi. I want to go swimming in Omer's pool, where it's always nice and cool, as if even the sun understands there are some places it should not shine too brightly.

'Don't be a silly meow. You're not going anywhere. Shopping in the middle of the day? You must be crazy. You'll die of heat exhaustion. Come, let's do a line and we'll watch something fun. What do you want to do, kitty cat? My little pixie-dust. Don't go.' He grabs my arm tightly and walks back towards Billi, towards the TV, which is playing some terrible action movie on mute.

'Move, Billi. Let Nida do her lines.'

Reluctantly Billi relinquishes control and stands, vigorously gumming the powder into her teeth. She may be the least attractive person with a nose ring I've ever seen.

'Let's order Chinese and have a party,' he says, hugging me. 'Would you like that, my little Tinkerbell?'

There's a loud splash and Omer pulls back the curtains. Billi has jumped into the pool in her underwear and tank top. She waves at us, splashing out pool water, and motions for us to join her. She just has to get all the attention. What's next, jumping off the roof into the bushes? Maybe I should suggest that to her.

'Come on, Nida,' Omer yells and dives into the pool in his pyjamas.

I contemplate leaving once more. Let Omer miss me while I trudge around Lahore with my sister. But I realize I have to bring out the big guns if I'm going to win this competition. I pull off my shirt and jeans and stand in my bra and underwear. Omer hoots loudly and splashes me with water.

'Get in, get in!' he yells. 'Don't tease me with that sexy body.'

I run back into the room and do a quick snort of the last line, thin and white, sparkling in the light.

I wake suddenly, anxiety-ridden. It's late-night and dark. My throat hurts from the raw air-conditioning. After two days of constant partying, Omer finally sleeps. They both sleep. Billi on a mattress on the floor, Omer and I on the bed. And now I'm awake with a headache, wishing I had not slept. The same dream keeps recurring, waking me up sweating under the thick hot duvet.

Next to me Omer is snoring obnoxiously, his arms splayed out wide. He is the king of his world, without a fear or thought in his head except his next indulgence. Billi breathes loudly, buried beneath her own floral duvet. I turn towards Omer and lean over his sleeping face, watching his heavy mouth breathing, his leg shuddering every few seconds as if he's trying to run away. His sleeping breath is a strong, sour exhale. I get out of bed. The floor is sticky and my chappals grip the floor as I walk. I hold my breath, afraid to wake them. Billi mumbles in her sleep as I gently pull away the curtains and look at the night-lit pool, cerulean blue beneath a clear moon.

I walk into Omer's bathroom, which is even colder than his bedroom. He likes to 'shower, shit, and shave' in the cold, he says, and leaves the AC on high permanently. In my house in Garden Town I awake miserable and crying in the heat of load-shedding, here it's a cool indifferent darkness. His bathroom is almost spotless, the maid coming in every hour to wipe the muddy footprints, the bleeding noses, the tracks of hash and coke smudged between the tiles.

Yesterday, after spending an hour in his bathroom, Billi came out and fell on to the sofa next to me, exhausted.

'I just got off in Omer's bathroom,' she whispered to me confidently, proud of her accomplishment, then closed her eyes, head thrown back on the sofa like an actress, and napped. There was a fine film of sweat around her crown, her short hair spiked with water.

I dreamt the same dream. It repeats, circling like a vulture waiting for death. I'm stuck in an elevator and it's crashing. Tonight a brown bear put a sliver of ice in my mouth and pushed me in. I'm inside, I'm alone, the elevator starts to swing. In my dream I understand that it's a dream, but I can't stop it. I close my eyes and then it starts to hit the walls and churn and teeter; it falls and halts until I'm on the elevator floor hysterical, grasping for an emergency button to press. I press every button for every floor and punch the board. I grab the emergency telephone, my mother answers and I scream for her to help me. I know she is weak and that she will fail, I know this even in my sleep.

In the bathroom I find a joint, ready to be smoked, sitting in the soap dish. I hold it in my hand and pull off my slippers, slide the door to the outside slowly and walk barefoot, the grass rough against my feet, towards the pool.

I stand in the silence and look down at my reflection, the water so still I can see the dust settled on the bottom.

'Beautiful, isn't it,' a clean voice says behind me, causing me to turn quickly and almost slip into the pool. I look around and see Ifti sitting in the gazebo beneath dimmed lighting.

'You scared me half to death,' I say.

'My sincere apologies, it wasn't my intention to startle you,' Ifti says with soft authority. 'I didn't expect anyone to be awake. Would you care to join me?'

I step away from the pool and head up the two gazebo steps to where he is sitting. He motions to a small cushioned wicker chair and I sit awkwardly, my heart still beating from the surprise. He's wearing a blue silk robe, similar to Omer's red silk pyjamas, his hair is wet.

'What are you holding on to so tightly?' he asks, smiling, pointing to my balled-up fist. In my shock I've squeezed the joint and it looks a little mangled when I uncurl my clenched hand to show him. He takes it from me and gently rubs the thin paper, straightening it carefully back into a familiar shape.

'Trouble sleeping, too? Join me for a nightcap,' he says, sounding and looking almost like Cary Grant in an old Hitchcock black-and-white.

The gazebo is a small hexagon of cushioned sofas under a thatched roof, three wooden pillars laced with thick pink bougainvillea, bleeding flowers into the pool. Ifti sits like a king— quite like Omer would, but with legs crossed and robe modestly covering what's beneath. He's neatly shaved and combed and perfumed, even this late at night. I wonder if he's ever dirty or dishevelled, sweating on the Lahori roads or in a gym. I highly doubt it. A cigar is puffing smoke in a crystal ashtray and a book, *The Emperor's Handbook*, is downturned next to him.

'So Nida, what would you like?' he asks, as if we're dining in some fine restaurant. 'I have a wonderful cognac. I think you might enjoy that.'

'What's on the menu?' I say, joking. He smiles patiently. I decide to keep my mouth shut and let him talk.

'Try the cognac. I think you'll enjoy it.'

I have the sudden urge to bite my nails and consciously hold my fingers away from my teeth. I sit on my hands.

Ifti gently snuffs out the lit cigar and leaves it sitting at the edge of the ashtray. He pulls out his iPhone and sends a quick message. Somewhere in the house I imagine an army of servants scurrying. In a few minutes Zakir, the house manager, comes out, his uniform still pressed and pristine. He's wide awake—I'm guessing no one sleeps until Ifti lets out his first snore.

'Zakir, bring the Pearl, and two snifters . . .' He looks at me, 'Ice water?' he asks. Before I can answer Zakir pours me a glass full from a trolley in the corner—a golden trolley set with place mats and an ice bucket, glasses and a large jug of water.

'Bring some of those spring rolls and the prawn toast,' he adds, and looks at me: 'I have no time to eat during the day, and at night I eat junk, luckily the stress burns it all away.' He says this patting his stomach that appears tight and fit beneath his silk pyjamas.

'Junk is my entire diet,' I say. 'Is there any other kind of food?'

He laughs. His laugh is slow and deep and quite lovely. I'm pleased to have made him laugh.

'Yes, well, if I was your age still, I would think that too.' He picks up the joint and takes a box of long matches from Zakir's tray. 'Enjoy it while it lasts, Nida. It never does.'

He lights the joint, takes a long generous drag and passes it to me. 'Oh, don't look so shocked. You think I don't know what goes on with you kids? Who do you think funds his sordid lifestyle? It's not so different for me, but I also find time to work. Balance is everything. Work hard, play hard. But to play well one must work. For Omer this critical part remains unlearned. He's only interested in half the bargain.'

'Yes, the good half,' I say. 'He's gifted that way.'

He passes me the joint and gives me a quick wink that makes me smile. I take a long smooth drag, beginning to finally relax. It feels good to be outside smoking, even though it's a stifling humid night and I'm sitting with my boyfriend's father. In the distance I hear thunder.

'The monsoons are finally here,' he says. 'It's about time. They're late.'

'Don't you feel uncomfortable sitting outside?' I ask.

'Not particularly. I acclimatize well. I grew up in a Lahore without air-conditioning, just high ceilings, fans and sleeping outdoors on the roof. Artificial air gives you artificial security. Really, man can live anywhere. Being too comfortable isn't always a good thing.'

'I'm glad I'm born in a time of air-conditioning,' I say. 'And flushing toilets.' A giggle escapes me. The hash is good, strong and fun.

'I suppose you would be. It's too late to go back now.'

I'm high and spinning, and it seems so is Ifti because he takes another quick drag, holds it in his lungs and then places the rest of the joint—almost half left—next to the cigar. Then he gives me this sly grin. Great, I'm smoking with my boyfriend's father. That's something to write about in one's diary.

The gazebo is lit in a tawny glow. A digital clock hanging on a pillar reads 3.25, a lizard stands guard next to it, its legs motionless, tongue darting out to catch mosquitoes and floating insects.

'My parents have an account in your bank, you know,' I say, quite randomly.

'Which branch?'

'My mother has a locker too, at the branch in Cavalry. It's where she keeps her wedding jewellery.'

'I'm glad to hear of it. That is one of our first and most prestigious locations. A lot of history there. That's the branch that I use personally.'

'When you own a bank, can you take the money out whenever you want?'

'It doesn't quite work like that.'

'Why not? You own the biggest bank in Pakistan, aren't you able to do whatever you want? I mean, isn't that the whole point of having your own bank?'

He laughs. 'I think you're thinking of Scrooge McDuck. And I can't say I've never daydreamed of diving into a pile of gold coins, but we do the next best thing, we grow, make more branches, expand. We're going to be in Singapore, Dubai and Panama City by next year.'

'Wow, Panama City? What's that like?'

'Interesting. A bit like Miami, surprisingly modern, and they have some of the freshest oysters you've ever tasted.'

'That sounds fun,' I say, unsure what fresh oysters might taste like.

'But enough about banking. That's all I do during the day. At night I have to force myself not think about it. Let's talk about you instead. What have you been up to this summer, Nida?'

'Not much, really,' I say, trying to remember what we've been doing, the joint not helping my memory. It's a vast unanswerable question, considering that yesterday is a blur.

'Is Billi still here?' he asks. 'She's like a stray dog, isn't she.'

I laugh, enjoying the image. 'She refuses to leave,' I say.

'She's always been like that. Her parents are exactly the same, leeches, always wearing out their welcome, sucking everything dry before they finally push off. A lot of people here are like that. In Pakistan boring lives always lead to bad manners.'

'I wonder if she'll ever leave,' I say, more to myself than Ifti.

'Omer will get bored and kick her out. It's an old story, really.'

I wonder if that will happen to me. Will Omer eventually get bored of me as well?

'You think too much, you know that?' Ifti says, studying me.

'What do you mean?' I ask, startled. I didn't realize I was being watched.

'I'll tell you something that I learned quite late, Nida, something I wish someone had told me in my twenties: don't think too much. Thinking gets in the way of doing, and doing is what life is about. There's simply no point in it. Whatever is supposed to happen will, and it'll never be what you expected. You can analyse and think until your teeth hurt, but you're wasting your time. Here we are, on this wonderfully muggy night, in good company, a good smoke, and soon we'll have some fried food . . . You must learn to enjoy the randomness of life. Did you ever think your summer would go like this?'

'No. Never.'

'Exactly. And if you had spent all last winter thinking, you still wouldn't have guessed anything as random as this. All that good time wasted, and for what?'

'It's not bad logic,' I say. 'Especially living in Pakistan, where there isn't much you can control, particularly as a woman.'

'Exactly. It's great logic.'

'But if we don't think of anything, how do we know if we're living right or making the right choices?'

'You don't have as many choices as you think, Nida. It's usually binary, a yes or a no, a left or a right. And they never turn out the way you expect. A good decision can turn out bad, and vice versa. You just make the choice at that moment and hope it works out.'

'Isn't that just luck?'

'Sure. Luck, God, kismet, whatever you want to call it. It's all the same. You're just not controlling as much as you think.'

'So basically you're saying I shouldn't think about consequences and instead should do whatever I want, whenever I want?'

'Something like that. Not exactly, but close. Of course, there are always stupid things one shouldn't do.'

'Yes, and there's always guilt.'

'Ah, yes, guilt. Lovely beautiful societal guilt, as significant as a puff of fog on a desolate midnight road.'

'But shouldn't one at least self-analyse?'

'Why? What for?' He leans forward, his hair gleaming jet black under the light, not the slightest strand of silver to be seen. The shadows of the gazebo cut through his face, slicing the jaw and nose into thin contours. 'Self-analysis breeds insecurity. A very nasty trait, especially in this part of the world. It's considered weakness, not intellect. You fix yourself, be the best that you can be and all that nonsense, and to what end? You're still dealing with common stupidity, weakness, laziness, the list goes on. Pointless.' He leans back and I notice he's not wearing a wedding ring. There's not even an indentation to where it should be nor a tan line where it was. His hands are perfectly smooth, the nails manicured and glossy.

'You sound like a disillusioned religious figure,' I say.

'I should have my own cult. *Dianetics* for the dissatisfied desi.'

'Dia-what?' I ask.

Ifti shakes his head in amusement, as if he doesn't know what to do with me. I hear glasses clinking and Zakir appears holding a tray. Ifti points to where he wants him to put everything: glasses in front of us and an ornate bottle. I watch Ifti arrange everything in an almost compulsive fashion—napkins, silverware placed precisely, a perfect pour from the bottle.

'Too much?' he asks me, catching me observing him. 'Don't bother hiding your expressions from me,' he teases. 'I'm a master facial interpreter.'

'Really? A master facial interpreter,' I repeat, slightly slurring the words.

'God, you girls and your low tolerance. Here, drink this.' He hands me a massive glass, almost as large as my face, filled with the smallest amount of amber liquid. I swirl it and stare at the shifting colours in the light. A light goes on inside a bedroom upstairs and someone, it looks like a woman, pulls the curtains shut.

'Where is Auntie?' I ask.

'On her usual summer escape to London. Haemorrhaging my money on worthless bags and shoes.'

'I would like to escape to London,' I say. 'I don't care about bags and shoes. I just want to escape.'

'You and everyone else, my dear.' He holds up a stunning glass bottle, heart-shaped, with small shards of glass like a fish spine protruding from the curve. There's an indentation in the middle and a beautiful fleur-de-lis stopper, also in glass.

'Do you know what this is?' he asks me. I shake my head no.

'This is a LOUIS XIII Black Pearl, a rare and magical luxury in Pakistan. Well, anywhere really.'

I try to copy him and hold the wide-bottomed glass in the palm of my hand, the stem inserted between my middle fingers. It's bigger than my hand.

'Take it very slowly,' he says. 'You don't need to gulp it, just the smallest little sip at a time. Breathe it.' He inhales his as he swirls it, like Omer swirling his whisky. 'Let's celebrate. To those of us left to rot in Lahore.'

'To rotting in Lahore,' I say, lifting my glass. It smells strong, pungent. I tip the glass to my lips, the rim touching my nose, and take the smallest lick of a sip. The liquid is sweet and intense and it warms my throat as I swallow, heating my entire body. It feels good, like solid footing on a rope bridge.

'Amazing stuff this is, a little bit of heaven. It was a gift from a very wealthy businessman from Guangzhou. I helped him finance some factories and he sent me this, by private jet, no less. There's nothing like a magnificent cognac to seal a perfect night.' He leans back in his chair, closes his eyes and takes another taste. He hums to himself as I sit sniffing and drinking. I feel a little guilty he's wasting it on me, someone who would be more than satisfied with a cold nimbu-pani with sugar. I'm not that difficult to impress.

Ifti's leaning back in his chair, eyes shut, the glass globe resting on his hand. He doesn't look like your average *daddu* desi politician. No strange hairpieces, bloated jowls, puffed chests and pot bellies; eyes that rove from one lie to another, incessantly arguing over nonsense as if it's the gospel truth. He's the polar opposite of Salim Chaudhry, and it's a little difficult to believe that they are friends; Salim Chaudhry, the man who complained on national television that a foreign president didn't serve him biscuits with his tea.

'Uncle Iftikhar, may I ask you a question?'

'Please, my dear—Ifti. We are not related.' He makes a sour face.

'It's strange calling you Ifti.'

'It's infinitely better than being called uncle, so please, Ifti.'

'Okay, Ifti,' I say, still feeling strange.

'How did you end up working with Salim Chaudhry?'

'Oh no. Politics on such a wonderful peaceful night as this? What a shame.'

'Sorry,' I say, feeling like I've overstepped some boundary.

'Just this one. So you want to know about my long forged relationship with the distinguished prime minister? Such heavy material. You can light it again if you want,' he says, pointing to the joint.

I lean forward, past him, and grab the joint, starting it with his heavy silver lighter, the flame hissing a solid blue. Bits of tobacco cling to my tongue, the flimsy roach curled yesterday by less-than-sober Omer.

'You know, I don't think politics,' he says, once he's taken a few short puffs. 'I just do politics.'

'What does that even mean?' I can't wrap my head around the sentence. It's like unformed jelly falling from the sky.

'Ours is quite a long story, and honestly, quiet dull. Let's just say politicians require influence and I am always in a position to help them acquire popularity.'

'Do politicians have to buy votes to win?'

'Don't be ridiculous, of course not. I'm a big proponent of clean campaigns and clean elections. I just helped him realize his full potential. Helped him run a better, more organized campaign. But I find that, sadly, Pakistani politics has degraded over the past twenty years, the campaigns are plunging downhill in a direction that I do not approve of.'

'But hasn't there always been rigging? My father complains every election. He says he can't remember a time when the elections weren't rigged.'

'Well, yes, of course. Rigging is in the national blood. But personally I feel that it makes no difference in the larger scheme of things. Usually, rigging happens in small-time provincial, district-based elections, with low-income voters. More on the nazim scale than the prime minister. Pakistan is a big country, it's impossible to do nation-wide rigging. I've found that the candidate the country most wants is usually the one who wins. The margins are never determined by a few hundred thousand, especially when you have millions.'

'So you think Salim Chaudhry wins every election because the people love him?'

'Of course. Why else would he win?'

'And all his campaigns are honest, corruption-free?'

'Absolutely,' he says. 'It's always about the issues—our economy, international trade, industry, terrorism. All this talk about bank accounts, it's rubbish. It's the issues that elect leaders.'

'Do you actually believe all this? Or are you just telling me what you tell people on TV?'

He gives me a quick wolfish grin. 'You are quite the *laal mirch*, aren't you, Nida?'

'I'm just asking. I'm curious as to what you really think, not what I can hear you say on TV.'

He exhales and stares at the smouldering end of the joint, as if the answers lie in its orange glow. I've seen Omer do the same countless times before—contemplate the universe (or at least appear to) from the tip of man's greatest discovery. An ancient wisdom unlocked by staring into the fire.

'We live in an age of sophistry, Nida,' he says. 'Perhaps it's just who plays the better, smarter, game.' He picks up his glass and takes a sip, leaning back more comfortably in the chair, crossing his legs so his ankle rests on his knee. He's wearing shoes a bit like my grandfather's, brown house slippers that cover the toes but are open in the back. I can see a few dark hairs curling from beneath his silky pyjama hem.

'We're not monsters, Nida, trust me. I'm simply an investment banker. I merely finance and advise campaigns. Make no mistake, in the end all politicians are quite identical, despite the gloss and glitter of campaign slogans. Does it matter which one is in power?'

'One has to be better than the other, surely?'

'You might think.'

'It feels like two bitchy girls competing in a popularity contest,' I say.

'And the more popular bitch wins.'

'But Salim Chaudhry is not the popular princess in this election.'

'He may have finally worn out his welcome.'

'So what are you going to do? My father used to say those who enter politics half-way dig their own graves.'

'He's seems a smart man. In such a case, then, it's always important to be ready with a clean shovel.'

As he says this I hear footsteps and then see the fat cook plodding towards us carrying a TV tray. Behind him are Zakir and two running dogs. They're Ifti's racing greyhounds, usually kept as far away from Omer as possible. They bound towards Ifti, jumping up to greet him, the charcoal-grey one nuzzling his chest with her muzzle, the biscuit-coloured one pawing at him and whining gently.

'Zeus, Ares, sit!' he commands, and instantly they cower and sit, their eyes obediently fixed on his face. This is the first time I've seen them up close; they're beautiful, with tall, graceful necks and delicate muzzles, powerful shoulder muscles like steel waves. They ignore me, aware only of Ifti and this unexpected late-night opportunity to worship him further.

'Why the hell did it take you so long to fry two damn things?' Ifti says angrily to the cook.

'Sir, there was nothing left. Omer Saab and his friends ate it all. I had to make everything from scratch.'

I'm glad Ifti doesn't look over at me, because I was definitely one of the friends eating those spring rolls earlier. Instead, he just huffs.

'Well, you should prepare beforehand. What else are you doing in there except cooking? Do you have any other job? You don't even wash the dishes or serve. When something finishes, your job is to replenish it. If you can't even do that, then . . .'

'Sorry, sir. It won't happen again.' The cook stands there with an ashamed look on his puffy sleepy face.

'And what have you been doing all day?' Ifti asks Zakir. 'Because you're definitely not supervising them. If you let them get lazy again, Zakir, I'm going to send you to the farm. I brought you back because you promised, and now this.'

It's now Zakir's turn to look ashamed. I turn my face away and stare out at the pool water, radiating soothing turquoise from beneath, the pink bougainvillea floating towards the edges. I never like to watch servants get scolded, but apparently it's the only way to get work done. Fear is the desi way to get results. This is the lesson we all learn from our fathers.

Ifti angrily waves them both away, as if too disgusted to see their faces. As they leave, Omer's French bulldog, Bruno, waddles out from behind some bush and climbs into my lap. He's smelt the food and knows I'm a sucker for an adorable smooshed face. Bruno is completely unlike Ifti's greyhounds and, as I attempt to eat, he steals a shrimp toast off my plate without remorse and licks the ketchup off my fingers, while Zeus and Ares remain in their poised sitting positions, erect and upright, not the slightest hint of a beg or whine escaping their throats. Like master, like dog. I pet Bruno, the little fatty, and he rubs his cold wet nose into my palm. He's been hanging with us, stoned, most of the day, sleeping and eating, then sleeping again.

Ifti puts down his plate once he's done and the dogs lay their long faces on to his lap. He absent-mindedly pets them. I decide to stay away from any more serious political discussions, even though I'm dying to ask if he thinks MT is corrupt. I guess it doesn't matter even if he is—who isn't? At this point it seems it only matters who is the least destructive. Pathetic.

'So Nida, apart from talking about me all night, why don't you tell me about yourself?' He's swirling the glass again, the liquid, as if to keep it alive.

'What is there to tell?'

'I'm sure there's plenty, you seem like a fascinating young lady. What do you want from your life?'

'From my life?' I laugh and then shrug. 'I have absolutely no idea.'

'Oh, come on, you must have some idea. I'm sure you have dreams, just like every young woman. That's when you should have dreams, big ones, insane ones. Not at my age, where dreams enter a state of permanent fade.'

'Well, I have a dream I get into an elevator with a bear.'

'I'm talking about life goals, Nida.'

I shrug and take a small sip of the strong drink. Bruno, annoyed by my movement, jumps off my lap and wanders off somewhere.

'Honestly, I don't know. I don't have too many, I guess. I don't know what I want. I've been so busing trying to survive each day, I don't have time to really think about the future. I don't think I have much control over it anyway. It'll just rush up towards me and I'll brace myself like I've always done before.'

Ifti doesn't say anything, just nods slowly, looking serious. I take a few more warm swallows from the giant glass. It gets better with every sip.

'It's important to have real dreams,' he says thoughtfully. 'To have goals to work towards. Without that we're just living like the poor, hand to mouth, day after day. It's almost a waste to exist.'

'I had dreams when I was younger. I thought maybe I would like to make movies or write books. Something arty like that. My brother used to tease me about always talking to myself, making up stories in my head, walking around the house having conversations with imaginary people. But after he died . . . I don't know. It seemed stupid.'

'Your brother died?'

'In an army helicopter crash.'

'I'm sorry to hear that, Nida. That's never easy. As if life isn't hard enough without death thrown in.' He pauses and pours more alcohol into his glass. 'You owe him a better life for yourself.'

'I guess so.'

'In this digital age, nothing is beyond reach,' Ifti says. 'That was the excuse of our fathers, of my generation. Now you can find all you want online and figure out a way to get there.'

'I don't know. You make it sound easy. My parents can barely pay for my education at Lahore College.'

'There's always funding, loans, scholarships, grants.'

The greyhounds, lying sleeping on the floor, stir at this speech and readjust themselves. Bruno is back from his wanderings and has fallen asleep on one of my feet.

'You really think so?' I say.

'I know so. All you have to do is look and ask. I can even call some of my contacts, if you want, and see what's possible.'

'That would be nice,' I say, unsure of what I would even ask for.

'Of course. No problem. Just tell me when you're ready and I'll see what I can do.'

He reaches out and touches my arm. I didn't realize how close we were sitting until he leans forward, his face inches from mine.

He softly runs his fingers over my skin, giving me goosebumps. I turn my body away from him slightly and look out towards the pool. He's leaning forward, close enough for me to hear his breathing. The dogs stir, but otherwise it's silent. The last of the night insects chirp and till greedily, mating and eating and surviving for one more night. His hand now squeezes my shoulder, gentle, no pressure.

'I'm glad we had this conversation, Nida,' he whispers.

I turn my face slightly towards him and nod. I can feel his breath against my neck. I can feel him watching me, his eyes studying the side of my face. Out of the corner of my eye I see him lean back in his chair and relight his cigar, relaxed and at ease with himself and the night. I exhale slowly.

He leans forward again, removing the cigar from his lips and holding it away, scrutinizing my face and body in such a way that it's embarrassing. I feel a frightening pulse of electricity rush through my body.

'What?' I ask, the word coming out in a half whisper.

'The pool looks inviting, doesn't it?' he says. 'It's my favourite feature in the house, the one thing I personally designed. Do you want to go for a dip?'

He gets up without waiting for my response and grabs my arm, pulling me up. We walk down the gazebo steps to the edge of the pool. His robe falls to the grass and he undoes two of his top buttons and pulls the silk shirt over his head. His chest hair is sparse but it gets darker and more purposeful as it connects down into his pyjamas in a perfect silken black line. He grins and pulls down his pants in one swift motion, stands there looking at me, and then dives smoothly, almost perfectly, into the pool.

I watch, flabbergasted, the pool lights wavering over him as he swims underwater. He appears at the other end and breaststrokes casually back towards me. He stands in the shallow, motioning for me to join him, the water barely reaching his flat stomach.

'Take your clothes off, otherwise you'll be uncomfortable,' he says, then turns around and smoothly swims towards the deep end of the pool. I watch his body and the undulating bougainvillea flowers that crowd the corners as the waves push them away.

I feel the ground sway violently beneath me.

BUGSY

Past the normal check-post of sandbags and barbed wire, Mian Tariq's crib is a proper desi gothic horror, complete with peeling paint and creeper vines, it's one of those houses that screams old mental institution. I almost expect crazy old farts to lurch out screaming with their robes flung open. Even though MT has made a small fortune in real estate, I can't help but wonder if he's taken the No Corruption joint a bit too far.

The privately hired security guard checks my name at the gate and gives my crotch a once-over. Apparently a healthy crotch says a lot about your terrorist proclivities. Mine says: *stoned privileged motherfucker in old-ass jeans with loose sweaty balls.* I see the sour expression on the guard's face that says: *let him pass before his big-shot father fucks my shit up.*

I'm in, rounding the semicircular driveway towards the pillared entrance. A handful of drivers lounge on the burnt summer grass, sitting in small cliques like girls on the Kinnaird College campus, smoking and sharing gossip about their big kahunas, who, at this moment, are probably inside kissing MT's ass. They clock me as I make my way up the steps to the front door.

The doorbell echoes through the house with a loud clang. It's like bad Poe short story—'The Haveli of MT Usher'. A greasy-looking cook waddles past with a tray of nimbu-pani, heading for the thirsty sun-baked drivers. Beyond him, a tall Kabir Bedi–looking motherfucker on security stops my entry. Crotch-checkpoint two: the extra feel-up. I expect to be jerked off if there's a third.

'I'm here to deliver an envelope,' I tell him, waving the envelope so it looks legit. I've decided to play it cool, despite the internal sweating at meeting MT. Moby's face flashes in my mind, which makes me want to punch something.

He gives the envelope a rough and tumble and then eyes me some more. I'm not wearing a burka, I want to tell him, where the fuck would I hide my bomb? My asshole isn't big enough for dynamite.

'You will have to wait for someone to come get you. No one goes inside unescorted,' he says in a deep booming voice. I give his impressive handlebar moustache a once-over, checking out the flawless blend of shine and wax, the exquisitely curved tips.

'Why can't you take me inside?' I ask, to which he gives me a stern look and walks away.

Standing in the hallway, I look at my watch and realize I'll be leaving in darkness if this takes any longer. I'm giving myself another five minutes—and if no one comes to escort me, to hell with Moby and MT, I'm bailing.

A short bald man in cheap creased black rayon pants and a yellow tucked-in button-down finally comes to get me. I'm surprised by his appearance. He doesn't look dirty, just low-class, awkward in shirt and pants. He might be MT's peon. He seems to have all the requisite qualities: paan-stained teeth, jaundiced eyes, prominent cheekbones, rubber chappals instead of real shoes.

The house is cold and feels bare, despite the dense splash of crooked black-and-whites—MT's pre-Partition relatives, some newer colour glossies of a young MT posing with presidents and prime ministers way past dead. There's even one with him hugging a wrinkled Mother Teresa, and one with the Bhutto family, all members still intact, smiling. You can see the progression of MT's ageing and his political career through the cheap frames and fading pictures—his hair growing whiter, his face slowly wrinkling, but his eyes sharpening, his smile growing wide and ever more confident. Somewhere between the pictures of him posing with Benazir and a goofy George Bush Jr, his hair gets darker again, his skin tightens. I look again and recognize the cheap technology, definitely some Just for Men hair dye, probably a little waistline liposuction, a little Botox to round it all up into the twenty-first century.

As we progress deeper into the house, the air grows musty, like in a broom closet. This used to be MT's father's home, but now it seems fully stripped and operational, a headquarters fit to conquer Pakistan and the whole Western media circus.

'If he's busy I can give you the papers,' I tell the man as I follow him reluctantly. 'I have to be somewhere, so I don't have too much time.'

'Don't tell this to me, tell him,' he says and opens a door. Inside there's an office and another dude standing, this time dressed proper, with a tie and all. Unattractive, but proper. Fat and sweaty, but a definite upgrade. He takes the envelope from me and opens it, ignoring my protest that maybe MT should do it himself. I sit across the desk, as per his instructions, and watch him carefully as he lays out the papers magazine fan-style on the desk and places a yellow pad and pen next to them. He pours a glass of water and places that too on the desk. From a drawer emerges a gold cigarette-holder and a matching lighter. All quite posh. Those too are staged near the papers. Then he makes a call.

'Mian Saab. Come,' he says, and goes to stand behind the desk, hands folded in front.

Mian's office is a vomitus homage to full British-windbag style—ass ugly, dark-wood panelling, Afghan carpeting, large chairs in red–green tartan upholstery and a massive wooden desk. The cushions, all two of them, are more tartan, in green and blue. And the colonial cherry on top? The room smells like old wet dog. This could be where Mountbatten, Mountblanc, Mount-whoever busted his last Indian nut. But somehow, despite the dedicated sentimental effort, it doesn't quite stand up. Take, for instance, the massive gilt-framed tapestry of a camel caravan hanging adjacent to a painting of rolling British countryside, with sheep and Tudor farmhouse and all. It's like something out of *Yes Minister*, Saudi edition.

Now there's nothing to do but sit and sweat, observe the fat man, who stands so still it's eerie, like the Queen's beefeaters. He doesn't even look my way. I analyse his saggy bulldog face, his large hairy knuckles, the folds of fat and grease layering his neck, his bursting buttons, the Kashmiri chai-coloured shirt, the yellow tie, the brown pants, looking quite a bit like a Neapolitan ice-cream bar. The fan above us is whirring, there's a weak air-conditioner, but it's still warm enough for him to sport soggy armpits. I squirm and shift in my seat, my ass and legs falling asleep at annoying intervals.

Finally, when I'm at the point of giving up, Mian Tariq enters. He walks in as if he's onstage, door swung open, full rock-star mode—host and politician, man in charge, man about town, man in tight white Pak pyjamas. I get up to shake his hand and he waves me away. Not a great sign. He looks exactly like his posters, like he did fifteen years ago, a lowly minister sitting near me on a PIA flight to Karachi. He's clean-shaven, wearing salwar-kameez. Even from five feet away he smells like a California redwood.

He points for me to sit and goes around his desk. Bulldog pulls his chair out for him, then goes back to his regular butt-plug stance. MT adjusts the already-perfectly arranged papers on his desk, shuffling them around a bit, pushing them further away from him. From his waistcoat pocket he pulls out a small case, in which a delicate pair of silver glasses are folded. He unfolds them, like a hand puzzle, and they balance on the edge of his sharp nose. He glances at the documents, as if he already knows the secrets they hold, then removes his glasses and sets them on the table carefully, moves the water a few inches to the right. It's all very elaborate, like I'm watching a silent black-and-white Borzage. He's big-timing it, even for me. I wonder if he can turn it off any more, if he's become another showbiz whore. He lights a cigarette from the golden monogrammed case and holds it delicately between his fingers, the case clicking shut, and I imagine someone yelling out: *Action!*

'So . . . You've come,' he says.

'Yes, sir. And those are the papers you requested.'

He looks down at the documents and touches them lightly with his fingertips. Then he pushes one away from him slowly, as if it's infectious. He inhales and exhales quickly, and then abandons the cigarette half done, mutilating it in a small crystal ashtray.

'Do you know why I asked to see you?' he says, looking me up and down in quick assessment.

'No, sir.'

'I don't know you, Bugsy, although I am told I have heard you on the radio. I do not know your father, either, but I have heard of him and of his valiant service to our country. I feel it is my duty to meet the son of such a man and set him on the correct path, because—and I don't know if you know this—this is a very dirty and dangerous direction you are taking.'

I don't know what to say. I'm frozen, my brain unable to process anything intelligent. All I can think of is how I never noticed his strange British BBC accent before. He hides his Oxford education on television, hoping to appeal to the uneducated everyman, similar to Benazir Bhutto covering her head at public appearances. My school art-class project of her in shorts flashes in my mind. I suppress a mad urge to laugh.

'I'm starting to realize that, sir,' I say. 'It isn't what I wanted. It wasn't what I expected. I was just helping a friend. I didn't think it would turn out like this.'

'Hmm.' He looks down at the documents, frowns. 'You know, a man is defined by the friends he keeps. I'm sure you know this and think it's common sense, until you realize how it isn't. We as a species tolerate a shocking amount just to be accepted, to be part of a community, an organization. But if you are willing to tolerate moral flaws in others, even the small seemingly insignificant ones, then you too are of low moral fibre. I firmly believe this. Loyalty is one thing, but it is often confused. Some people are not worth your loyalty. People think friendship is looking the other way, not judging, allowing people to be unscrupulous. But that is not friendship. That is the fear of losing friends. True friendship is bold. It has boundaries. It has high expectations. It has been my attempt in life to have such friends—bold, trustworthy, honest, respectable people, whom I am honoured to associate my name with. These people are the ones who have supported me through this campaign. I have worked exceedingly hard to keep out the riff-raff.' He pauses, whether for effect or because he's emotional, I can't tell.

'But now, with these documents . . .' He looks down at them and sighs. 'With these I can deny their entry no longer. Only garbage can clean garbage.'

'I don't understand,' I say.

'These documents are from my personal foreign account. I'm not a poor man. I never claimed to be. It's money I've made over the past thirty years through my businesses, careful investing, saving. A poor man does not run for prime minister.'

'Why don't you just tell the masses that?' I say. 'I mean, if it's just your business money, they'll understand.'

'It's too late now. The word is out. I have untaxed foreign accounts. It's a significant amount of money, my supporters will not understand.' His lip curls in disgust.

'To succeed in this election I have to let in the devil now,' he says.

'I didn't know this would happen,' I say again.

'It's how it works. The naive are always taken advantage of.'

Uptight Bulldog standing in the back moves, readjusts himself. He's been there the entire time, standing firmly behind MT. I don't know if he's listening or singing some Nusrat Fateh Ali qawwali in his head.

'I wanted to meet you, Bugsy. I wanted to judge you for myself. Our politics has been built on lies. On broken promises of bread, cloth and shelter. This government was created by crooks for the sole purpose of corruption. I have to beat a man with so much corrupt money he's going to rig half the Punjab. That's what we're up against—cheating and lying.'

'I'm sorry,' I say, not knowing what else to say. Every crooked politician thinks he's honest. At least MT isn't as big a douche as SC.

He sighs. 'Well, what's done is done. It's a lifetime of promoting illiteracy to get cheap votes. Of taking what isn't ours.

Of thinking there are no consequences. Of setting the bar so low it's hit rock-bottom. At some point we have to stop following the stream of our history and create something new. Someone needs to make a change.'

'You're right, sir. Absolutely. And if you win, I know you'll succeed.' I couldn't blow more smoke up his ass if he bent over and I puffed. But I do feel for him, he's at least attempting to make a difference, which is more than I can say about every other asshole who has come before him. It's unfortunate we can't know the impact of a leader until after he's done, when it's too late.

He nods slowly, as if exhausted. The man standing behind him steps forward.

'Aamir will show you out,' MT says, looking down at the documents.

Aamir is Bulldog? A surprisingly tame name for such a jowly pissed-off-looking *pehlwan*. MT remains sitting.

'I'm sorry again for the trouble,' I say. 'It was not my intention to make things difficult for you. I was at your rally. I support you. I want you to win.'

MT nods and gives me a weak smile.

I follow Bulldog down the hallway. It's all over and done with. I don't have to deal with him or Moby or any other damn politician any more. No more fucking favours, no matter who asks.

Bulldog stops. Right in the middle of the hallway, with the front door in sight. His fat body is blocking my way.

'Before you leave,' he says. He opens a random door and steps through, motioning for me to follow. I walk into an empty room, dirty white walls and an open glass sliding door at the end. He steps through and waits for me outside. The back lawn—a large expanse of thick manicured grass and golden amaltas trees in full bloom. There's a large haphazard circle of wrought-iron chairs with cushions. This is probably where many meetings take place, under the shade of those trees. Although right now it's ass-raping hot. The grass is wet and clings to my shoes. I follow Bulldog. I'm not sure where we're going, but until this point I presumed it was a faster exit towards my parked car. Now I'm not so sure. There's never a reason to be back in the servants quarters—unless you're playing with their kids, or wondering why the hell they haven't got you your afternoon mango milkshake and plate of chips.

I remain outside, observing the lawn and waiting. Sparrows hop around the wet grass searching for worms. I check my phone and message Moby that I'm done. No reply. I wait for Bulldog to return, giving him a few more minutes before I bail and find my own way to my car. Moby's phone rings until it doesn't.

One went in, but three come out. Bulldog is joined by the massive Kabir Bedi fucker from before and a greasy skinny dude with large ears and olive-oil-slicked hair. He's sporting a Chaplin moustache, jangling a large set of keys.

'Chalo, let's go,' Bulldog says to me, and gives me a slight shove.

'Where are we going?' I ask, starting to get worried. I put my hand in my pocket and finger my car keys, thinking I can either make a run for it or jam them in someone's eye.

We walk around the back to a private garage where four cars are parked. Bulldog walks to a white Toyota Camry and holds open the back door for me.

'This isn't my car,' I say.

'It isn't? Well, that's too bad, because you're getting in it anyway.'

'Have you lost your mind? I'm going to my car.' I back away from them and start to fast-walk towards the house.

Kabir grabs my collar and pulls me back, choking me. He then shoves me in, head first, with one move. He kicks my legs in enough to sardine himself next to me and slam the door shut. Bulldog comes in from the other side. I'm sandwiched. The skinny Chaplin dude slides into the driver's seat and starts the car, easing it out of the driveway and through another gate at the back.

'What the fuck is going on?' I shout.

'Chill karo. We're not doing anything,' Bulldog says. 'We're just driving you to your car. And while we drive you we thought we'd explain a few things. Just simple things. Like, for example, how much we support Mian Tariq Saab. And how we're here to make sure nothing—do you understand, nothing—harms him or his campaign.'

'Does Mian Tariq Saab know you're doing this?' I ask, making sure to emphasize their idiotic use of 'saab'. Their loyal display of MT love is a little freaky. I resort to the usual desi threats: 'Do you know who my father is? When he finds out . . .'

'Haan, haan, we know who your father is. Why do you think we didn't bring guns? We don't want to bloody his name. We just want to bloody you, a little. Enough to find out who is behind you and those documents.'

'I told Mian Tariq everything. I don't know anything more.'

Kabir grunts and rests his heavy hairy arm on my shoulder, pushing me down. I can smell onions on his breath, or maybe it's his armpit. We're out of the GOR neighbourhood now, driving towards the Old City. Greasy driver is attempting to hit all the narrow residential roads. That's never a good sign.

'You told Mian Tariq Saab that someone gave you the documents,' Bulldog says. 'So all you have to do is tell us who that someone is and we'll drop you off right here. Close enough for you to walk home.'

'What are you talking about?'

'It's not over until it's over,' Bulldog says, pointing a fat finger in my chest. 'Someone who wants to harm Mian Tariq Saab is out there. We wouldn't be doing our jobs protecting him if we let this person remain free.'

'I don't know who it is. Really. I was just given the papers to deliver. If I knew who it was I'd kick his ass myself.'

Kabir elbows me hard in the kidneys from the right side. I lean forward in pain.

'Don't lie, asshole.'

'I'm not lying, you idiots.'

This time they both punch me and I feel an elbow crack into my ribs, my face explode, blood gushes into my mouth. I lean over in pain.

'Look, yaar, I'd love to tell you who the asshole is who gave me the papers,' I say. 'Don't you think I'd tell you? But I have no bhenchod idea. So you can punch me again, go ahead, but it's not going to suddenly produce a name.'

'Do you think he's lying?' Kabir asks Bulldog.

'Who cares? Look, son,' he says, softening his voice, his breath closing in on my ear. 'Right now, we've just slapped you around a bit. That's nothing, we usually do much worse. But you know that already.' He puts his fat arm around my shoulder, like we're buddies. 'You also know that we can't do much to you. However, there are many ways to hurt someone. Do you understand?'

I nod.

'Good. We'll be in touch.'

Greasy stops in the middle of the road. There's not a single car in sight.

'If you hear something that's worth our while, give us a call. If not, at least remember us.'

Bulldog steps out and gestures for me to exit, like a fine limo driver at the Oscars. He pats my back like we're old friends and hands me a crumpled tissue from his pocket. He sits up in the front seat this time, the rightful location for his ego, and they're off. I'm left a bruised and battered dumbass, pissed off and standing mid-street somewhere behind the rickshaws and disintegration of the Old City. I can't walk home. My car's at MT's. And fuck, I check my pockets. I think I dropped my phone in the car.

NIDA

It's another long and lonely Lahori evening. I sit outside on my brother's dusty balcony, drawing out a feeble high from my last remaining smoke. I should have called Ali and asked him to top off my charas supply, he's been wanting to come over, but I don't want to see him, or anyone, right now. I haven't called Omer and he hasn't called me. It's as if he knows what happened. Maybe this is how things end, with everyone speechless.

The neighbourhood lights turn on in lethargic sequence— the streetlights, ageing and orange, then the gate lights with their swirling insects and, finally, the glow of bedrooms and living rooms, people moving about their lives in Islamic silhouette. In one hour the electricity will be out and life will move on in dark hours of candlelight and diesel generation. I think of Kasim, what life would be like if he were still alive. I always miss him in this shifting hour and the growing blacktop incandescence. It would all be so different if he were still here.

Sometimes hash is strong enough to connect me to my brother, connect me to all his things still neatly placed in his room, as if someday he might return. As if someday we might laugh and cheat at Ludo, fight over the last mutton *haddi*, or pack his army flight-bags again. Sometimes I can hear his voice and almost feel him.

I think of Kasim at thirteen, skinny with long arms, a fuzzy upper-lip, desperate to learn to drive. All his friends were doing it, the boys starting to drive the minute they reached the pedals, impressing each other by manically racing down Main Boulevard, hurtling towards death in rickety Santros and beat-up Suzukis. But Kasim was too scared to drive alone, and every Saturday he woke me up at four in the morning and made me sit with him while he laboured up and down our street, roughly switching gears and stalling the car. We rehearsed our alibi in case a policeman stopped us—I should pretend to be sick, maybe try to throw up, and he would say he was driving me to the hospital. I happily agreed. I would have given all the sleep in the world to be with my brother, and especially to share such a secret.

And then there was the dog we found, a mongrel puppy, lying in the middle of the road. It makes me want to cry when I think of that dumb dog, Kasim's love for the pathetic little creature, lethargically lapping at a puddle while he got out of the car and wrapped it in his jacket. Buffy, the cat slayer, who slept in Kasim's bed and followed him around the house, avoiding my mother's angry broom and incessant complaining. She made my father give it away eventually, when Kasim joined the army and left home. It broke his heart. I think it was one of the reasons he didn't visit much those first few years. I know my father feels horribly guilty about it now. His only son and he couldn't even take his side, help keep the little happiness he had in his short life.

Uff Allah, I'm becoming like those pathetic Lollywood drama aunties, who wear black shawls over their heads and weep hysterically over their misfortunes, over their wasted youth, their cheating husbands.

I peer down the balcony and watch the neighbourhood tomcat pass before the kitchen lights beneath me, his lamplit shadow long and elegant against the burnt grass. I can hear my mother's monotone ordering the cook to not be lazy, to *bhuno* the salan properly. I know she's cutting disaster articles out of newspapers at the kitchen table. It's the only activity that comforts her, slicing around the misery that befalls others. She stores them in an old Quality Street tin, never looking at them again or rereading them, just making every heart-wrenching headline a part of her sorrow-filled bond with the universe. My father is watching the *Khabarnama* news hour. I can hear the newscasters with their high Urdu, their clipped businesslike voices talking of bomb blasts, a woman stoned to death in front of the Lahore High Court, the upcoming election.

The sky has now become a deep charcoal bruise, the last rays of light melting away behind the trees of our small yard. Fruit bats dizzily whiz back and forth searching for water while the sparrows sit patiently in military rows on telephone wires. Soon, in a last gush of air and energy, the birds will start to fill the trees and by the time it's completely dark they will be perfectly balanced, fast asleep. I can hear a bicycle ringing outside, the repetitive high whine of a peddler trying to sell mangoes off a cart, the sound of dogs barking. It's never silent here, all perpetual motion, no direction. Across the tight gulley, not too far from where I sit, is another small balcony, lined with hanging laundry—large white sheets, a pair of starched pyjamas, salwar-kameez dejected and wrinkled, not the slightest breeze.

My phone glows, vibrating against the dusty plastic table, but I ignore it. It's probably Saadia letting me know about her next dance practice. It might be Omer, but I doubt it. He hasn't called or messaged, and I don't know if he's moved on or if he's waiting for me to make a move. If I never do, I'm sure drink and drugs will wipe me clean from his memory. A few days of no contact and it's over. Apparently I'm easy to forget. Years from now I'll see him in some local shop and he won't even know who I am. I'm the one stuck with the burden of memory. So much, for so little.

I smoke and sweat profusely. I haven't stepped out of my morning pyjamas and they stick to my skin in the unbearable humidity.

Suddenly a light comes on from the balcony across. I can hear the creaking of the metal door as it opens and I see my childhood friend Mara step out into the light with a laundry basket. I haven't seen her in ages. For some stupid reason I freeze with uncertainty. She looks different, mature and older after marriage and the birth of her daughter. Her hair is longer, hanging down past her shoulders. Her body is rounder, bigger after the baby, same blank face. She looks worn out. She pulls the laundry carelessly off the wire, dropping the shirts on to the floor, then lethargically bends to pick them up, loosely folding the sheets and kameezes before setting them in the plastic basket. I can see her perfectly under the soft orange light, her moon-shaped face, the cheap rubber chappals on her feet, her cream kameez and hooped gold earrings. She hasn't noticed me sitting in the dark.

She looks around the balcony absent-mindedly, touching her earrings and then gently touching her belly. She's daydreaming and humming softly to herself as she pulls out her phone, which she has tucked into the elastic waistband of her salwar. We're so close, if she threw her phone at me I'd be able to catch it.

She stays for a few seconds checking messages, then tosses the rest of the laundry in the basket and is gone. The birds have now seated themselves in the trees and are silent.

I'm surprised at seeing her. It's like suddenly glimpsing a scene of the past—us running in the garden with a hose, chasing each other, laughing—like a blurry home-video; friends falling, playing, crying; videos we never made. Another reminder of my brother, the games we played as kids and how Mara always insisted on being on his team. Maybe she would be my sister-in-law if he were still alive. Maybe he would have changed her life as well.

I faintly hear Kasim's bedroom door open and shut, the sliding window behind me—for a moment I expect his voice. But I know it's Fatima, the only one other than myself who comes into my brother's room. The days of my mother weeping on his bed are over; she can't take it any more and stays downstairs, occupying a dismal triangle of bedroom, kitchen and bath.

'Ugh, it stinks in here. Are you smoking?' Fatima drags an empty chair next to me, the sharp noise hurting my ears, and dusts it off as best she can. She makes a face as she sits. 'You know everyone can smell you, right? Just because you smoke back here doesn't make you invisible.'

I shrug, who cares, whatever. I'm too tired to care if the entire neighbourhood has me on tape.

'Guess what? Mara's home,' I tell her.

'Really?' she says, suddenly interested, shifting in her seat to look at the balcony across. 'What did she say?'

'Nothing. I don't think she saw me. She was taking down the laundry.'

'Well, I'm sure she smelled you. What did she look like?'

'The same, I guess. Chubbier. Pregnant again, I think. Longer hair.'

'Did she look good?'

'I don't know. She looked . . . like nothing. Older. Not happy. Not sad. Normal. Now that she's married, I'm guessing all those crazy dreams of becoming a doctor are gone. Nothing too exciting.'

'It depends on who you marry and what you want in life,' Fatima says.

'Oh, please, as if you know anything about marriage. The first time you see a *lun* you'll pass out and wake up with a house and six children.'

She laughs, thinking I'm being funny. Fatima's a traditional homebody, happy to spend the evening at home cooking or praying or watching bad TV serials. She'll make some boring uncle a great wife. She'll have a million children and never look back.

My phone vibrates again. Fatima looks at it, then at me. She looks surprised.

'You're not answering your phone? What, has the world come to an end? Are you ill? Are you dying, Nida?'

'Ha ha, you're so funny. Shut up.'

'Should I get it?' she says, reaching for the phone.

I snatch it off the table. 'Mind your own business.'

'Trouble in boyfriend paradise? That's okay, I'm sure you have tons more as backup.'

'Don't you have anything better to do?' I ask her.

'My friend Nermeen told me she saw you in a sports car with some boy. You were kissing.'

'You shouldn't believe everything your dumbo friends tell you,' I say, annoyed. She's ruining my mood. I try to think of when her friend could have seen me kissing Omer. I can't recall ever doing that in public.

'You're not the same any more, you know,' she says. 'You've gone to college and changed. You're never here. You come home late, sometimes you don't come home at all. And I know you've been lying about being at Saadia's. You've become a total slut. I can't believe you're my sister.' She chants a string of religious phrases, cleansing her soul and, apparently, mine as well.

'Don't worry, Fatima, I won't ruin it for you. I'm sure you'll find some boring loser to marry you regardless,' I say meanly.

I close my eyes and take a deep breath, my lungs expanding as I lean against the warm plastic chair. My butt and thighs are asleep, I can feel the numbness creeping towards my knees, making its way past my ankles to my toes. I like this anaesthetized feeling of life held at a length, reality through a layer of smoke and sleep. I talk with my eyes closed, letting the feeling paralyse my body.

'You know, Fati, you don't have to take responsibility for *all* of our souls.' I open my eyes and look at her. She's pouting self-righteously, lips pursed tight. I hate it when she looks like that. It makes me want to slap her.

'This whole pious routine is getting on my nerves,' I tell her. 'It's just an excuse to be judgemental, to think yourself superior. But it's bakwas.'

'I don't know what you mean,' she says, turning her face away towards Mara's balcony and crossing her arms. 'It wouldn't hurt for you to pray once in a while.'

'It won't make the slightest difference. And you know that. You pray constantly, is your life better? Has something changed for you?'

'It doesn't work like that. It takes time, you know.'

'It still doesn't guarantee anything, stupid,' I say loudly. 'Look at us. What did we do so wrong that this happened? We were good kids. Did it make a difference? You can pray every single minute of your life, it still won't guarantee happiness or health or money. You still die alone.'

She looks at me, horrified, like she's either going to wail or punch me. I prefer a punch. I breathe slowly, calming myself down, and touch her arm softly.

'I'm sorry, Fati. I don't know what I'm saying,' I say, retreating. 'I guess I just want you to learn to take care of yourself, because we're on our own. Our behaviour doesn't guarantee anything. Religious people have difficult lives too.'

She gets teary-eyed and I pat her back. 'Relax, I'm not trying to be so serious. I'm just telling you what I think. You never know, things might turn out amazing. There's always hope.'

She sits on the edge of her chair and stares out at Mara's empty balcony. I can't help but imagine our alternative futures. If Kasim were still alive maybe we would have had different lives. But now, with comatose parents, we have to settle for whatever we can get. And no more Omer to stoke the embers.

We sit silently for a while, the darkness starting to wrap itself around us. Bugs flitter and the lizards come grabbing out. The neighbouring lights allow me to see her well enough, sitting slumped next to me. Her long skinny feet rest on the balcony grill. I pull a cigarette out of the pack lying on the table and she reaches for one as well. She lights it awkwardly, puffing slowly, the cigarette precariously balanced between her fingers. She doesn't cough when she inhales, and I realize she's smoked before. I have no idea when she tried her first cigarette; there are so many things I don't know about her. At some point she might have been smoking in her bathroom while I was sitting alone in mine doing the same. I've been so desperate to live a life, some life, that I've forgotten her. So strange to think how disconnected we are, living in the same house, performing the same actions, not sharing any of it, even if it's just a single bloody smoke.

'I'm sorry, Fati. Just be yourself, okay,' I tell her. 'Do whatever you think is right. And if you need anything, I'm here. I know that isn't much, and that you want Ami, but I just want you to know . . . you know, that you can come to me and I'll try my best to help you.'

She's silent, but I see her nod. I watch her smoke, her face crumpling in disgust with every bitter inhale.

'And stop fucking smoking.' I yank the cigarette from between her fingers and toss it over the balcony. 'It'll just blacken your gums and give you cancer. And you look ridiculous.'

'You smoke,' she says accusingly.

'And that's why I'm telling you to stop.'

She gives me a look, like I'm full of shit, but I can see she's already feeling better. She adjusts herself in the chair so she faces me and tells me some silly school gossip.

BUGSY

I'm lost in my own city, disoriented, bruise-soaked. Heckle and Jeckle could have at least dropped me off near a main road—somewhere familiar, respectable—like a post office or girl's college campus. Instead, I'm lost in a tangle of old Lahori gullies, my cell phone lost in the ass of some *gunda*'s car. The street is dense and stacked with the cracked and peeling backs of cheap concrete havelis looming over me on either side. I hear a servant shouting out, a familiar and welcome sound; in a high-pitched whine he curses and calls for someone named Nasreen. Apparently she has washed all his dish towels, and he is not pleased. At least normal life continues. Lahore will survive long past me, past Mian Tariq, past all these political assholes. It's getting dark, lights flicking on, mostly kitchens and stairways. I walk up the street hoping to find a random puttering rickshaw or friendly motorbike driver willing to give me a lift.

At least there aren't any seriously dangerous neighbourhoods in Lahore—that I know of. You can walk almost anywhere, at any time, and minus the occasional dickhead, it's pretty chill. The neighbourhoods distinguish themselves according to the various levels of human curiosity—rich neighbourhoods not giving you a second glance, the poor ones clocking you like you're a walking talking Japanime character. In this neighbourhood buffaloes bathe in puddles and the servants gives you a quick once-over from the balcony. One in particular lays into the woman named Nasreen, who screams back. A seasoned veteran, she tells him to shove his dish towel into his black hole. I chuckle and pain shoots down my side.

After a few turns and a few goggle-eyed stares from donkey-cart drivers, I make it out to a main road. The traffic is shit, pushing me to one side, where I step over some garbage and try to find a street sign.

'Salaam, grandpa,' I say to an old man squatting on the roadside smoking a cigarette. 'Where am I?'

'Jilani Road,' he says. 'Behind Data Darbar.'

Okay, good, I'm in the Old City. That's not so bad. From here it's a not-too-terrible rickshaw ride to the Walled City and Moby's haveli. I need to find him, tell him what happened.

'What happened to your face?' the old man asks.

'Gundas,' I say. He nods understandingly, as if we've both been wronged by the thugs of the world.

'Do you have money?' he asks.

'Does it look like I have money?' I say. 'Do I look like I would be walking around this dump if I had money?'

He shrugs and goes back to his cigarette.

I search my pockets for my cigarette pack, something the goons decided to let me keep. I hand him a cig and he gives me a massive toothless grin, his face wrinkling even further, looking like an old-ass rotten apple.

'Fancy,' he says, and places it in his kameez pocket.

I lurch towards Data Darbar, where it'll be easier to find cheap transportation. I'll figure out how to pay for it later. Maybe Moby can foot the bill, the bastard. He owes me big. I touch my face gingerly. It's pretty swollen. The pain isn't too bad though. It feels like a tomato, but the nose has stopped bleeding and the bottom lip has crusted. The ribs and kidneys are another story. It'll hurt more tomorrow, but nothing seems to be broken. I wonder if this was a warning, if they'll torment me until they get a name, or if it was just a one-time ass beating. I wonder if MT knows about this or if this is standard backdoor shit. Either way, I'm starting to understand the full extent of political thuggery. I am sure that stashing millions is just a fraction of dodgy desi politics. Beneath all the high-line Pakistani finance and elegant speeches there's always a dirty goon-load of ignorant chuts swinging meat clubs. Even if MT takes a personal interest or not.

Some small kids run past me, touching my jeans with their grubby little fingers, laughing at my miserable state. A giant of a man walks out of a small restaurant holding a massive metal daig filled with biryani. My mouth waters. People who come to the Data Darbar to pray, with its emerald-lit minarets and bleached marble, give money to the small restaurants to cook food for the poor. I remember coming here with my mother, giving the men money and watching as they distributed handfuls of rice and meat to the sick, the orphaned kids, the heroin addicts. It almost seems like another lifetime ago. I weave through heavy evening traffic, eyes peeled for an empty rickshaw. While I stand on the side of the road staring out stupidly, watching the pehlwan ladle out steaming rice, a lazy blue-and-green rickshaw teeters over to me.

'Oye, *mundé*, what the hell happened to you? Are you standing there drooling for fun or do you want a ride?' a wrinkled grizzled rickshaw-wallah, probably in his forties looking like his sixties, leans out and calls me over.

I tell him Moby's address and he shrugs, he doesn't care where we go as long as I pay him. He's going to be pissed when he finds out I don't have jack shit. I step up and through the back flap on to the hard wooden seat. The rickshaw still has its back flaps, a rarity in desi travel. I'm alone in the back, the space tight and constricted, dark and smelling of the driver's greasy skin, his pungent foot odour, cheap plastic China-made seat covers. Barely two adults can fit but I've seen about four fat aunties and a gang of kids huddled into the back, three wheels drifting on two. The space between me and the driver is open and I can see that there are no side-view mirrors, that's he's driving barefoot, his slippers discarded and flopped near the motor that sits next to him like a vibrating passenger, humming loudly like a coked-up mosquito. And next to the motor: his gas tank. Safety first, of course. And as if God-sent, I hear the brief chime of a text message coming from his body. A cell phone.

'Uncle,' I say, using my most charming tone, 'can I borrow your phone for a minute?'

'What for?' he asks.

'I need to make a quick call. Fast, I promise.'

'Where's your own phone,' he asks suspiciously.

'I was attacked, they took my phone. I just need to make one quick call. That's it. Super fast.'

'Do you have money?' he asks, turning his head around to look at me. 'Because this is not a charity, telephone, lunchtime rickshaw.'

'My friend will pay you when we arrive, I swear.'

'Fine, if you swear. You look bad enough for me to believe you.'

He hands me his phone, an old beat-up Nokia with a urine-yellow cover. I call Moby's cell phone, then his house phone, which doesn't even have the courtesy to give me a proper ring tone, just a strange TB cough and then it disconnects. What the fuck is going on? Have they found Moby already? I start to imagine worst-case scenarios—of arriving at Moby's to find the door blasted open, bullet holes, dark blood pooled at the front door, his wife and daughter missing, a discarded doll near the staircase. I shake my head, I've watched way too many Hollywood movies. Most likely he's just left his phone somewhere, or they've gone out. But the image of the pool of blood doesn't fully leave me.

'You have blood on your face,' the driver says when I hand him back his phone. I wipe my nose with the bottom of my shirt.

'How were you attacked?' he asks me. He's your typical charsi rickshaw driver—stoned bloodhound eyes rimmed in black *surma*, drooping with sleep and hashish-filled lethargy, a rancid-looking set of teeth, a few missing. His face is shining with sweat under the streetlights.

'It's a long story,' I say.

'What did you do?' He lifts his eyebrows quickly in a gesture of curiosity and gives me a mischievous grin.

'I didn't do anything, okay? Stop asking.'

'Did you have a car? Was it stolen? Because I have a nephew who finds stolen cars.'

Translation: my nephew steals cars and will return yours for you for a nice sum of cash.

'No, it's not stolen. I just left it at a friend's house. Okay? Happy now? Can't a guy take a rickshaw without a full interrogation?'

'Because you have nice fancy shoes, still white on the bottom,' he says, turning his head and looking down at my blue Converses, 'but your face looks like cow shit.'

'*Shukriya*,' I say, sarcastically thanking him.

He shrugs and goes back to driving like a maniac. I open the flap and stare out at the Lahore traffic, the Old City looks totally different from a rickshaw. I've never seen it like this before, with all the smells—frying samosas, grilling chicken tikka, diesel fumes, fresh garbage, donkey shit—and the sounds of honking, people yelling, clopping horses. Everything is so close I can touch the bus's dust next to me, feel the cycle-wallah's heat as he waits at a traffic light. Lahore has never been this loud. I stick my head out and let it rush in, a city of no hope. The record needle stuck on tunes of 1601 AD. We live in the past on these streets, with farting, shitting donkeys, wild teetering rickshaws and drugged pedestrians. We run on our own time, flowing backwards. I watch a heroin addict crawl out from under an ancient Mughal archway to throw up.

The rickshaw honks sharply and the driver curses. I can smell his stale breath from back here. I sweat balls and wipe my dripping nose on my sleeve. I feel like a menopausal auntie —one minute I'm amazed at how awesome Lahore is, beautiful in its Third World rot, and I want to stick my head out and wave to the crammed world of my fellow countrymen; the next I'm irritated, wanting the fucker to driver faster, sick of being stuck in this old-ass line of transportation history, the cars and wagons becoming the distorted shapes of elephants and horse-drawn carriages, the blur and vibration of honking, braying Old Lahore, every form of man-made transportation choking these roads to death through the ages.

I curse Moby in my head. He better be fucking bleeding, because if he's not I'm gonna kick his ass.

By the time I reach Moby's haveli it's proper dark. His house is black and lifeless behind the tree branches and veiling leaves. The rickshaw driver says he'll wait, looking at me suspiciously, unsure whether I'm going to bolt, sceptical about if there really is a friend with cash behind the dark closed gate. I tell him to relax, there will be money.

Moby's street is empty. There isn't a sound to be heard except for the summer insects. The Walled City is never quiet and I wonder if I'm going deaf. I start to feel a building panic, my head throbs. I push open Moby's gate and stop, wait a few seconds, wait to hear something, an indication of life inside, someone moving or talking. Nothing. Maybe they're not home. Moby wouldn't have known I was going to come over. I stand outside his front door and yell his name, hoping that from somewhere in the belly of the house I'll hear his comforting call. Nothing. Not a sound. Not even the shouts of his servants and their children. I hold my breath. The faint sound of music far away on some rooftop wafts past me.

I ring the doorbell, it vibrates through what sounds like an empty house.

Moby has an old-fashioned wooden door, the kind that has lasted through generations of use, thick and ornate with rusted metal bands and detailed arabesque. I've admired the painted patterns of faded turquoise and amber a thousand times, but right now I kick the shit out of it trying to force it open. It doesn't budge. I walk around the outside trying to see through the dusty grilled windows.

Either I'm blind or the house is empty. There's not even furniture covered in vacation bed-sheets, no sofas or beds or pictures on the walls, only glaring white cut-outs where once hung family portraits. And then I realize: Moby and his family have blazed—bailed, left, absconded. For a minute I stand there in a stupor, confused, my eyes adjusting to the darkness. He's ditched me. I look around the garden for signs of struggle, sign of a massive last-minute pack-up, but there's just the same old tree-swing and rusted slide and nothing else.

I don't understand. It would take days for them to organize a move, to disconnect the phone, the electricity. To get the family ready. The servants and their children.

It hits me, harder than anything else: Moby isn't coming back. And what's more, the fucker planned it ahead of time. When we met earlier, at the cafe, he knew he was leaving. He knew this was going to happen. That I'd look like a fool. The fucking piece of shit. Like a fucking idiot I believed him. I came all the way to warn him and all along he was planning his escape.

I slowly wind my way up the outdoor metal staircase, exhausted beyond comprehension, and sit on his roof. It's not as dark there, the city lights brighter above the rooftops and trees. It forms a bitter halo of washed-out orange beneath which the streets are visible in their crooked pattern, a steady flow of headlights endlessly leaving and entering the Walled City like haemorrhaging blood. There's nothing left on the roof. Even his *manji* is gone. All the cushions, the tattered lawn chairs, the water cooler with bottles of Murree beer, all gone.

I light a cigarette. I reprimand myself for being so blind, so stupid. I think of Moby, his wife, Ayesha, all the years I've known them, and I feel crazy anger. The tobacco gives me a buzz, making me feel a little dizzy, which is perfect because it eases the pain and the nausea rising in my throat.

After a while the neighbours come out on to their rooftops and I realize I've been sitting on the edge of his roof for quite a while. I must have smoked half a pack of cigarettes at least. I didn't even realize I was staring into the neighbour's living room until they turned on the television. There's nothing left here for me. My short horrible stint into Pak politics is fuckin' over.

On the street I tell the rickshaw driver, who is still waiting with an amazing unexpected patience, my house address, which is miles away, and tell him I'll pay him double if he doesn't speak. He bobs his head and smiles as we putter off towards home.

NIDA

Saadia's wedding blazes closer, like some billowing fire that can't be put out. And with no more boyfriends and the summer break from college, I have placed myself in the centre of the flames, gathering every night at her house with all her friends and relatives to dance and smoulder. I just wish I could be enthusiastic for her, excited about her upcoming wedding and month-long honeymoon, but really I mope, joke and smoke to survive the commanding nasal voice of her peppy dance-practice coordinator; hours of nonsense to immune myself from Saadia's domineering watch over my pathetic uninspired dance moves. I want to burn in the fire of her happiness and re-emerge a phoenix; a believer in love, in fairy tales, in Cinderella stories and happy endings.

I just need to remember who I was before Omer. But I can't seem to find that girl.

Standing on the edge of Saadia's landscaped garden, shaded from the day's heat-crush beneath a thick twisted chinar, three of us quickly puff out a joint. Even this far outside the thumping Bollywood of Saadia's disco-dance line-up penetrates.

With Saadia's two male cousins from Dubai, I manage to get enough distance not to care that she's bossing us around like a

Bombay street pimp. We make fun of the hired choreographer, a tedious Christian half-pint named David who claps his hands spastically commanding us to, 'Put more razzmatazz into it, *naaa*!'

This is the fourth dance practice this week and it's only Wednesday. The soles of my feet are bruised, it's agony to lift my arms in the air, but we press on—the mehndi is this Saturday. Saadia has demanded we master our routines or be publicly humiliated by the groom's side. Apparently they too have hired a choreographer and are the more musically gifted family. Sacred millennium-old rituals have been reduced to a cheap *antakshari*-style dance-off. We dance and provide the entertainment while Saadia sits high on a stage clapping and laughing, pretending she hasn't just spent the last few weeks grinding us for two minutes of a semi-coordinated 'Choli Kay Peechay'.

I'm flying high as a kite under this chinar tree. We've managed to smoke an entire joint between the three of us. The two cousins look totally bombed, their bloodshot eyes so puffy they look Chinese. One of the cousins sits limply down on the grass and looks as if he's about to pass out. The other is too blasted to care. Amateurs. My phone vibrates. My cousin Ali has answered my message, finally, with a smiley face and a promise that he'll try to make it tonight. I hope he does, I haven't seen him since that last night at Omer's house.

'Oh my God, Nida, what have you done to them?' Saadia screams, peering down at us from the balcony. 'Are they sick? I knew I shouldn't have trusted them to you.' She throws her dupatta at me in protest, it flutters down harmlessly. 'Pick them up and get up here. The mixed dances are starting. We need the boys.'

'I don't know how effective they'll be now,' I say, looking up at her. I push the boy laying on the grass with my foot. 'I think

he's sleeping, Saadia. Don't you have any real men in your family?'
At this manhood insult they both rouse, groaning in protest.

'Come on, let's go, otherwise Saadia will kill us,' I say to them,
helping the sitting one up. He's limp like a rubber band and I tug
at his arm trying to get him on his feet. 'Let's get you guys some
Pepsi, that should wake you up.'

Inside Saadia grabs my sweaty wrist and pulls me towards the
middle of her living room, where a huge white kapra spread out
on the carpet acts as a dance floor. 'You start and everyone will
follow,' she says.

'If you say so, but I don't know if you want everyone to follow
my rubbish dance moves.' I toss my own dupatta on to a chair,
adjust my kameez—I've gone full summer with turquoise flowers
on eggshell. I throw my shoes in a corner.

Across the room, sitting on a large sofa holding court, is Aliya.
She gives me a dorky thumbs-up. She's the last person I want to
see. She's come to the last two dance practices, and unlike the
entire time I was with Omer, she's actually being nice to me.
Apparently she's some distant relative of Saadia's. I give her a half
smile and look away, not wanting to encourage more contact.

I stand behind the choreographer, along with Saadia's school
friends, two sisters, cousins, and mimic his overeager dance
moves. There's a token white couple visiting from somewhere
in America, the boy smiling, open-faced and eager to ask stupid
questions, discuss the most mundane of Lahori facts like a child
at the zoo pointing out the tiger's stripes. The white girl, tall
with short blonde hair, stands in the front row and painfully tries
to match the dance steps, her large white feet moving gingerly,
uncoordinated. She's wearing a lilac salwar-kameez with gold
trim—nicely playing the tourist part. Her dupatta drags on the
floor with every buttock-swing *thumka* of her hips, every twist

of her arms above her head throws the fabric over her face like a bandage. But she just grunts, adjusts and catches up again, earnest about her international duties. She's the choreographer's wet dream—determined white girl, natural blue eyes, First World passport.

Aliya comes and joins us, inserting herself between me and Saadia's sister. She makes no effort, but stands, swaying a little, mocking the white girl's gangly giraffe-like movements. Despite my best efforts, I giggle. I'm too high to be a bitch, or follow the choreographer's steps, and now Aliya and I can't stop laughing, tripping over the white kapra which is starting to bunch as we drag our feet.

'Fuck this,' Aliya tells me mid-step. 'My feet are killing me. Let's go sit.' Relieved and wanting a break I follow her to the end of the room where the sofas are stacked against the wall to make space. I'm shaking a little and need water, some time to allow my body to adjust to the high. I drink directly from the bottle, enjoying the feeling of its icy coldness against my teeth and throat. Aliya comes and sits next to me.

'God, when will these people stop fucking getting married?' she says. 'I don't think I can attend another wedding. Who gets married in summer? So paindu. I should just start recycling all my old outfits.'

I highly doubt Aliya would recycle her kitchen trash, let alone her warehouse of pricey outfits. 'It's because Hassan's brother works in America,' I say, feeling the need to explain. 'He could only get time off in August. He is the groom's brother.' She shrugs as if she doesn't really care.

I sit next to her on the long sofa and take her in. She's dressed simply, in a white cotton salwar-kameez with pink and red flowers, no dupatta. It's the first time I've seen her dressed normal, without serious contouring and shimmering highlighter. For the first time Aliya doesn't look sharp-featured and Western, but rounder and full-faced, very Punjabi.

'I don't have it in me to do this dance practice bullshit any more,' she complains, rubbing her feet. Her red toe polish is chipped at the edges, making a jagged line against her nails.

'Well, I can't get out of it,' I say. 'Plus it helps when you have nothing else to do.'

Aliya rubs and squeezes her toes and watches me from the corner of her eye. She looks like she's unsure of what to say. The music stops and the dance kapra is rearranged. Saadia kneels down and yanks it taut from under everyone's feet, bossing a maid to do the same from the other side. Beneath it is a large red carpet, meant to serve as padding. The bottom of Aliya's feet are black from walking around barefoot. Then the music starts again, the song plays from the beginning. I sip more cold water.

'I'm sorry about you and Omer,' she says finally, attempting sincerity. She fails.

'Thanks,' I reply, equally insincere.

'He's an ass. It would have happened sooner or later. Omer's just like that,' she adds, saying it as casually as if she's sharing her favourite ice-cream flavour.

Sip more water, remain silent, I tell myself.

'He's not bad,' she says, pointing to the tall American boy who's bhangra-shrugging his shoulders to the music in a way that looks almost legit. 'There's probably a huge white hot-dog inside that wholewheat bun.'

I look over at her, surprised, and she laughs me off. 'What? A girl can dream, can't she?'

Aliya's trying to be friendly, for what reason I can't imagine. Maybe she doesn't like being alone in public. At least she's funny.

But despite her friendly attachment to me at these dance practices, I know I'm only a brief second-class passenger in her life. She adjusts herself, tucking a bare foot underneath her butt and shifting her large pile of coloured hair to flow over one shoulder. The other side, the uncovered side, is angled towards the room, so anyone looking can see her clearly, posing.

'The pest from Karachi has left,' she tells me. It takes me a few seconds to realize she's talking about Billi. I've forgotten all about her.

'Achcha?' I say. 'I guess she had to leave eventually.'

'Yeah. It took forever. Finally her brother came and got her. They had a huge fight and she pushed him into Omer's pool. It was hilarious. Pity you missed it.'

'Pity.'

There's an awkward silence. Then she turns towards me and tosses her hair back with purpose.

'Okay, enough of this chit-chat crap. I'm dying to ask. Did Ifti hit on you?'

'What? What makes you think that?' I ask her. My pulse increases. I try to control my expressions, masking the surprise I feel with an attempted nonchalance.

'He did, didn't he?' Her eyes are filled with enthralled interest. 'Oh, relax, he hits on everybody. Every desi model has been through him, and he through them,' she says, laughing at her own joke.

'No,' I finally say, finding my voice behind my parched tongue. 'He never hit on me.' That night by the pool, I've told no one about it, and there's no way I'm going to tell Aliya, of all people.

'So then why did you and Omer break up? I thought it was because Ifti hit on you. I mean, that's usually how it ends.

Personally, I think Omer and him have a deal, like when Omer's sick of a girl, Ifti swoops in and breaks them up. They both get what they want and it gives Omer a great excuse.'

I'm horrified. 'Are you serious? That's so . . .' I'm barely able to formulate a sentence.

'Oh, I know. It's really disgusting. Men are such dogs, I swear. But I'm glad Ifti didn't hit on you. I actually liked you.'

I feel a sudden wave of nausea.

'There was this one girl Omer dated a few years ago,' Aliya says. 'Some journalist who . . . well, let's just say someone who didn't particularly take to Ifti's seduction method. Poor girl, she's still reporting from the Gaza Strip. But I'm glad you broke up for your own reasons, Nida. It's probably for the best. Omer's gone crazy. It's all that bloody coke. He's not capable of handling complex relationships any more, which is such a shame. He used to be kind of sweet. Now he lets his father shag his girls and doesn't have the balls to break up with them himself. But I'm really glad Ifti didn't hit on you. Although you'd be the first.' She stares at me like a hawk at a shivering mouse. 'I guess you got lucky.'

I just nod miserably, waiting for her to finish. I feel like she's clutching my throat with her skinny fingers, choking me to admit Ifti hit on me. I'm shaking and I don't want Aliya to see. I get up abruptly, dropping the bottle and spilling water.

'Oh my goodness, ladies.' The choreographer comes up to us, fluttering in his overdramatic English. 'This is no time to sit around and gossip. The mehndi is almost upon us. Join the dancing and practise your moves.'

'Your dance moves are shit,' Aliya says sharply. 'Any fool can watch Hindi movies and piece together some pathetic moves. Even my dog can do that. You're not doing anything special.'

He gapes like a fish.

'What's going on?' Saadia asks, coming over.

'These two fussy-pots don't want to dance,' he bleats to her.

Instantly I'm overwhelmed by a feeling of loathing. I feel like grabbing Aliya and the choreographer by the hair and knocking their heads together until they bleed.

Saadia sees my face and suddenly takes action. 'Aliya, why don't you join the others on the dance floor? Nida, come and help me with dinner.'

I squeeze her arm gratefully as we enter the steaming clamorous kitchen.

'What did that crazy *haramzadi* say?' Saadia asks, weaving between the cooks and bearers engrossed in preparing an elaborate desi dinner. She pulls up a high chair and motions for me to join her on the marble island.

'Nothing.' I take a deep breath. 'You know her. It was nothing.'

'Was she talking about you and Omer? You know you can't take her seriously. She's just a bitch. And he's a huge asshole. You need to forget these people.'

I pick a sliced cucumber off a serving plate and dip it into a little ceramic pot of red chilli powder. The heat hits my tongue first but lasts until the end, circling its way around my mouth, igniting my taste buds, sharply pricking the sore spots where my teeth have rubbed against my cheek. Saadia only knows what I've told her, which isn't much. I told her that I stopped calling Omer and that he didn't bother to call back. I think of Islamabad, of Ifti, and feel my face burn. All for nothing. Even the laughs are now charred black memories, like the burnt skin of chicken you throw away.

'Nida, are you okay? You're biting that cucumber like it's one of Aliya's fingers.'

I feel Saadia's hand on my shoulder. She's shaking me gently.
I abandon the rest of the cucumber, now just a spicy red-fringed
tip. 'What?' I say, forcing myself to speak. I want to lose my voice,
stay silent until there's something worthy to say, go for days with
my tongue expanding in my mouth with the starchiness of silence.
But Saadia's looking at me all concerned, her eyes bugging out a
little, looking scared. 'What?' I say again.

'You're freaking me out,' she says. 'Where are you? Please stop
thinking about him. He doesn't deserve your lift.'

'I wasn't thinking of him,' I lie. 'I was just . . . I don't know.
I feel kind of ill. I think the stuff we smoked is making me sick.'

I sip the bland lemonade she hands me. It's awful, without
enough sugar or salt. A seed floats to the surface. The kitchen is
unusually busy. Massive metal pots bubble on the stove, the cook
removes a lid and sprinkles in a large pinch of garam masala. I see
the fluff of rice from the chicken biryani. I watch him as if I've
never seen anyone cook before, pretending to be so absorbed in
his chopping coriander that I can't hear Saadia. He wipes his wet
hands on his apron, the green coriander smearing along with all
the other herbs and spices he's handled today. He grins at me,
enjoying the attention, and rewards me with a plate of mooli,
perfectly white, cut long and sweet, arranged like the spokes of
a wheel, a floral tomato the hub. I dip the ivory radish in the
chilli powder, in the salt, in the black pepper, and let it burn my
tongue. I unravel the tomato rose and let it lie open and disfigured
in the middle. A waiter in uniform drops a fork. I look up and see
Ali walk through the kitchen door.

'Here you are. Goddamn it's hot. Why are you two hiding in
here?' he says.

'We're not hiding idiot,' Saadia says. 'We're talking.'

'Well, your tortured dance troop is looking for you.'

He picks a mooli and jabs it into the chilli powder, munching it loudly with his mouth open. Saadia rolls her eyes at me. Then she lowers her voice, as if telling him a secret I shouldn't hear. 'She's not feeling well. That *kutti* Aliya said something to upset her. I think she's really high.'

'I'm fine.' I look up at him with the most sober look I can muster. 'I'm totally fine. I was just zoning out.'

'Are you sure?' he asks.

'Yes, I'm bloody sure. I think I would know. All these cooking smells are making me sick though.'

'Ali, take her to the balcony. Get some fresh air. I'll go deal with the dancers.' Saadia stalks out of the kitchen, reminding me of our bossy school headmistress.

Ali gently links his arm with mine and lifts me out of the chair. My legs feel like jelly. My head spins. I feel the cool gush of air conditioning as we walk through the living room, the smell of possible rain as we step through the open window, the dust as he sets me down on a chair and pulls one for himself. The entire time his eyes are on my face, watching me with worry. He goes back and slides the window closed. The music is now faint.

'Here, drink this.' A bottle of water. I shake my head.

'Everything is spinning,' I say.

'Are you going to throw up?'

'I don't know.' I breathe in and out, calming myself. It's not working. I can feel the waves of anxiety building, crawling up into my chest. It's growing.

'It's good if you throw up. You'll feel better. There's an empty planter over there.'

I vaguely see what he's pointing to, hidden behind some large green leaves. Then I'm leaning over it, throwing up into some old weedy dirt. I can feel his hand rubbing my back. I can taste the mooli. My body shakes as he helps me sit back down. I sip the water.

'Feeling better?'

'A bit. I'm sorry, I don't know what's wrong.' Tears run down my face.

'It's okay, yaar.'

'But I don't know why I'd throw up. I was feeling fine before.'

'Maybe you ate something. Who knows? Or it was shit hash. Was it mine?'

'I don't know. I don't think so. I think Omer's.'

He's silent. He's always silent now when I mention Omer. I lean back in the chair and stare up, the sky a wash of city lights, faint grey clouds. I see one star, probably the North Star—the only one visible on most Lahori nights. I can feel the heaviness of monsoon rain in the air.

'I'm sorry about, you know . . .' Ali says. 'I'm glad it's over, it's for the best, but I'm sorry.'

'Don't be,' I say without moving, still staring up as the North Star disappears in grey. The moon appears briefly, a neon vanilla beacon. Then it's gone too.

'It's my fault,' he says. 'I shouldn't have taken you to his house. I should have known better. I'm an idiot. I wasn't thinking.'

I look at him. He's sitting hunched with his elbows on his knees. An unlit cigarette dangles between his fingers. He's staring down at his shoes. There's something different about him, but it takes me a few seconds before I realize.

'Your hair, Ali. What happened to your hair?' He's gotten a major haircut, short. No more crazy wild curls. I didn't even notice. He's still wearing the same old stained T-shirts and jeans though, the same torn joggers.

He grins sheepishly. 'Too hot to have long hair.' He lights his cigarette and smokes in silence.

'It's not your fault, Ali,' I finally say. 'You didn't know. I didn't know. I wanted something crazy to happen and it did. Be careful what you wish for, right?'

'But I should have known, yaar. I hang out with these people. I saw that he was interested in you and I wanted you to be happy. But I should have protected you. Instead I let things happen. Your brother would have murdered Omer.'

'That's probably true,' I say with a smile.

'He would have killed me too. No matter how much I try, I just can't be like him . . .'

'Stop, Ali, please. Stop torturing yourself. You couldn't possibly have known. And now it's over. Maybe it was meant to be this way. Maybe this is part of my life plan. Who knows? Everything is okay now, and except for Saadia's planter, we've survived.'

He nods miserably. I kick him gently on his shin. He looks up surprised and I give him a smile. 'Don't be so filmi, Ali,' I say lightly. 'Omer, who the hell is Omer? Let's forget him, achcha?' I say. Just like he's forgotten me.

'Do you feel better?' he asks.

'Yes, I do.'

'Maybe you just had to throw up.'

'Or destroy a planter.'

He grins lightly.

'Come, let's go inside and make fun of the dancers. It's hot as hell out here,' I say.

'You go. I'll finish the cig and come.'

It feels good to be inside. The cold air-conditioning feels great against my face and skin. I can feel my scalp tighten as the sweat dries. I sit on the sofa and give Saadia a thumbs up. The girls are attempting to learn some slutty boob-shaking moves from the video 'Desi Look'; on the mounted TV an actress with an incredibly padded bra and feathered angel wings is shaking her hips and biting on a massive pink lollipop. I picture Saadia in the same goofy outfit, tonguing a swirling lolly at Hassan, his bafflement at how to remove her bra and the sticky lolly from his pubes.

The girls are attempting to mimic the actress's exact moves. I laugh at their lack of coordination, their hurling limbs, their pathetic hip and boob thrusts.

Aliya snorts as the white girl trips over her trailing dupatta and falls to the floor. The music stops. The girl's face is a bright red. Time out, servants to the floor: white woman down.

Saadia declares it dinner time. The steaming food comes out and an instant crowd forms in front of the table. Ali is back, sitting next to me, reeking of tobacco.

'We'll wait until the rhinos have had their fill,' he says.

'Good idea.' It's never smart to infiltrate a desi food line, especially during wedding season. A limb could be lost. Or worse, bitten off.

The first person to grab a nimbu-pani is the gori, gulping the drink, beads of sweat dripping from her hairline. She's wearing a full-sleeved kameez in this heat, the material beneath her armpits dark and staining. She's also wearing ridiculous multicoloured socks.

We wait until we see Aliya get up and grab a plate. Then Ali elbows me. 'If the princess is in line, then let's go, before she takes all the juicy chicken legs.'

I follow him and stand behind Aliya, holding a large warmed dinner plate in my hand.

'Where are you from?' Aliya asks the white girl, standing behind her in line yet speaking loud enough for all to hear.

The girl gulps some more lemonade, and some air. 'California.'

'I have an aunt in Santa Monica,' Aliya says. Trust her to bring the conversation back to herself. 'Where about?'

'Orange County.'

'That's too bad,' Aliya replies. 'If I had to live in LA, I'd live in Brentwood.'

The girl plays at ignoring her, ties and reties her short hair into a tiny ponytail. She's not very pretty, just very pale and angular, foxlike. Even her eyelashes are blonde. Her coolest feature, dark thunderous blue eyes, are raw and squinty.

'Did you go to school there?' Aliya continues with her third-degree. 'I had friends who went to UCLA.'

'I went to college in the Bay Area, Berkeley.'

'Do you live there now?'

'No. Tom and I live in DC.' She stands uncomfortably, holding her empty glass. She doesn't offer any more information and she doesn't ask any questions.

'Do you want another lemonade?' Aliya asks.

'I think I'll have some food first.'

Saadia does her best hostess duties and attempts to explain the food, searching madly for accurate English descriptions to describe the haleem and the box of Nirala mithai. I laugh at her attempts to break down the desi ingredients, something we all think we understand until we have to explain it to clueless foreigners.

'I don't know what this is made of,' she says. 'Or this. Maybe some sort of wheat and sugar. Lots of sugar, that I know. I think that's food colouring. I don't know how else it would get so yellow.'

Ali and I fill our plates, now that the buzzards have left, and sit near the dining table, where the chairs are placed haphazardly against the wall. Aliya doesn't eat, she hovers, picking at random bits of salad, nibbling a little roghni naan she's snipped off at the edges.

Saadia makes the white girl sit next to me, making sure her plate is overloaded and a second helping is close at hand. On Ali's side sits the boy, who introduces himself as Tom. I feel like we're at some bad school function. UN day or something similar: Adopt a Dopey White Tourist Day. I watch the girl battle with her food, balancing the naan on her knee, the plate held above it, fork wrestling with the large bits of boned meat, salan spraying on her kameez.

'It's okay if you use your hands,' I say to her. 'We won't judge you. Use your naan like it's a utensil. Save the fork for the biryani.'

She mumbles a thank you but I get the feeling I've offended her international sensibility of white-girl-knows-all. She still battles with her fork, balancing a piece of mutton and some salan on its tongs. She's going to starve that way. I let her be. Maybe she saw a Nat Geo programme on India and now knows everything.

'So what do you do?' Aliya asks, loudly munching a carrot. 'I'm Aliya by the way, and this is Nida. I don't know who he is,' she says, pointing to Ali.

'Thanks, Aliya,' Ali mumbles. 'We've only met a hundred times.'

'I work for a non-profit education organization,' the white girl says. 'For refugee children.'

I can see the distaste streak across Aliya's face like she's watching some ugly fat man shaving his legs. She's already bored. She goes back to her plate, nibbling like some anorexic mouse.

'How do you like Lahore?' I ask the girl.

'It's . . . different. Interesting.'

'Is that good?' I ask. 'How is it interesting?'

'It would take all day to explain,' she says, as if we've asked her a horribly inconvenient question.

'Yes, I'm sure,' I say. She's probably had to answer the same dull question since she arrived, desi people lining up to ask her if she likes the city, the food, the people. We're relentlessly inquisitive and we don't believe in personal space or personal questions.

'I've had food poisoning since we arrived,' she says. 'We've been staying in a place called Johar Town. I've spent more time in bathrooms than anywhere else. So I can't really comment.'

'It's the spicy food,' Ali interjects. 'Not everyone can handle it. Either it agrees with you or it just explodes out of you like a fire hydrant.'

'Hmm,' the girl mumbles. Both Ali and I nudge each other, imagining the hilarity of her sweaty and exhausted face fixed to a pot in some dinghy bathroom in Johar Town.

'I've been okay,' Tom says, finally speaking. His plate is almost empty. 'I love spicy food. I mean, give it to me, no problem, Thai, Indian—it can't be spicy enough.'

'That's good to know,' Aliya says dryly. 'Congratulations.'

'I didn't realize how much people party in Pakistan, though,' he says. 'I mean, there hasn't been a moment where I haven't been drinking or hanging out with people . . . Brunch, tea, dinner, pre-parties, after-parties . . . For a country where booze is illegal, you all sure as hell drink a lot.'

Ali and him talk about something. I've stopped listening. It's impossible to eat comfortably with so many people hovering over you, talking, watching you shovel food into your mouth. I put my plate down, grab a nimbu-pani and reclaim my comfortable spot on the sofa. I'm starting to feel a little better, but my stomach is still queasy. Saadia's father refused to pay for alcohol at these dance practices so usually after dinner most people leave, unless Saadia bullies them into more dancing.

'How are you doing?' Saadia comes over and asks me.

'Better. But I threw up in your planter. Sorry.' I give her my best apologetic mouth-stretch eye-squint.

'Eww, Nida. Gross.'

'It was empty, if that helps. But better remove it before it fills up with rain.'

'Yuck.'

'I'm going to wait to dance though.'

'Good idea. Let's keep that mystery of half-digested biryani alive.'

She pats my knee and gets up, claps her hands loudly. 'Oye, listen,' she announces, 'no one is leaving until we master these dance moves, okay? So don't eat too much, and get ready.'

The music starts again and the few people who are done with dinner line up on the kapra for round two. I close my eyes. A different song comes on, we're doing the Old is Gold collection now—the exquisite nostalgia of Lata Mangeshkar fills the room, melancholic and numinous, her alto-soprano singing tragic tales of lust in high Urdu. I inhale and miss being young, listening to songs such as these for the first time on grainy Technicolor videos, Amitabh Bachchan in sky-blue bell-bottoms running through a field of Amsterdam tulips. Only the drama in films was important, real life was simple.

Ali comes and sits next to me. 'Dancing after dinner? I bet there's a lot of sneaky gas happening around that square of cloth right now. Maybe we should crack a window open.'

'Ali, you're disgusting,' I say. But I laugh.

Poor Lata is cut off, the choreographer's voice cutting sharply over her melodious harmony to order and reprimand.

'No, no, the same song!' He stamps his foot. 'Practise until perfect.' And we're back to our original version of Bollywood hell—'Desi Look' and lollipop biting.

Aliya comes back and sits next me.

'You know, you look very familiar,' she says to Ali. 'Where have I seen you before?'

Ali rolls his eyes at me. 'You saw me near the dinner table ten minutes ago,' he says. 'Smoke up less, your short-term memory is worse than mine.' He grins at me and winks. Aliya gives him a blank look, then shrugs it off. Ali doesn't look important enough to expend too many brain cells on.

'You know, the gora is kind of hot,' she says to me. 'I love tall guys.' She gives him a not-so-subtle wave when he turns our way. He smiles and waves back. Suddenly his dancing improves, a big toothy California smile plastered on his face. When the dance ends she waves him over to us and he does a slight *Baywatch* jog, grabbing a bottle of Coca-Cola on the way over. He's tall, reddish hair and brown eyes, pale freckled skin.

'Hello, ladies, what's up?' he says.

'We thought you could use a break,' Aliya says, immediately flirting. 'I hope your girlfriend doesn't mind.'

'Who, Cynthia?' he says, sitting down next to Aliya. He crosses his long skinny legs and gets comfortable. He's not handsome, but maybe cute. He looks a bit like a tall Spiderman, without the skintight suit. A waiter comes by and clicks open the Coke.

'Shukriya,' Tom says, his desi not too bad. 'You know, this is the first event I've been to where there's no booze.'

'That's nice. The blonde girl, she's not your girlfriend?' Aliya cuts right to the chase.

'No, we're officially broken up. We both went to Berkeley with Haroon,' he explains, referring to Saadia's older brother. 'It made sense to travel here together.'

'Oh, well, then that's perfect,' Aliya says, moving a little closer to him, flirting shamelessly. He grins at her, open and naive, without the slightest apprehension. I think of warning him, saying something witty about a black widow spider, a cobra, a scorpion sting perhaps, but then what's the point? Who cares?

'So are you having fun, Tom?' she asks.

He grins and runs his fingers through his thick red hair. 'Fuck yeah! Amazing food, awesome people. I can't get enough. And the mangoes, oh my God.' His rolls his eyes back dramatically, then lists every item of food he's eaten for the last four days. Aliya listens and takes every opportunity to correct his pronunciation, teasing him gently, touching his arm as she laughs. Ali and I watch them, fascinated, acting like a live audience at a carnival show.

'I think all I've done here is eat and party,' he says. 'I haven't been this drunk since college. I don't know how you get any work done.'

'We don't,' I say. He looks at me, as if he's suddenly noticed my presence, and laughs.

'That makes sense. I'm really glad we came though. My parents weren't too excited about us visiting, what with the election and everything. I don't know what they thought, that everyone would run around strapped with bombs and AK-47s. Stupid.'

'How long are you here for?' Aliya asks, assessing the amount of time she has to pounce—should she bring out the big guns or her little TT pistols.

'Just until the wedding is over. We fly out the next morning.'

'That's so soon,' she says, pouting. 'Have you seen the sites? Lahore Fort, Badshahi Mosque, Shalimar Gardens?'

'Not all. A few. We saw the fort and the mosque.'

'Then we must meet and figure it out. Take my number. Maybe tomorrow we can go to Shalimar Gardens. And Cuckoo's Restaurant, of course. I happen to be quite free this week.'

He pulls out his iPhone and feeds in Aliya's number. Ali and I exchange a look—poor gora, he has no idea what's in store for him.

Saadia comes over, holding a camera. 'A quick picture everyone, get close. Say: Butterflies! Great. I cut you off, Ali, your teeth were scaring me.'

Ali gives her the finger and she gives him a scrunched-face look. 'Nids, are you feeling better?' she asks. 'Because you're in the next song.'

'Yes, much better.' I get up and walk towards the makeshift dance floor. 'Good timing,' I say to Saadia. 'Otherwise we would have had to witness Aliya's praying-mantis sex dance. She's going to bite the poor gora's head off.'

Saadia giggles. The choreographer stands in front of us, the red bandana that was tied around his neck now around his head, Rambo style, and starts to mime some dance moves. 'Come on, girls,' he whines. 'Think Kareena Kapoor, not Shammi Kapoor, naaa.'

I laugh and try to move my hips to the bouncy bhangra beat. Aliya continues to hit on the unfortunate gora, who is loving the Asian attention, while the white girl trips over her dupatta and gives Aliya the evil eye. It's a right proper drama ready to detonate. Maybe the wedding won't be so bad after all.

BUGSY

And so the desi shuffle begins, the wedding season starting off six months in advance, in the middle of a sweltering August. From now until March we'll all be stumbling around town in our best starched salwars and socks, getting drunk and celebrating the oh-so-cheaply-bought milestone of desi marriage.

For me, the season officially begins with Aliya's high-pitched nag, enough to pierce the machine-gun rattle of *Call of Duty* and the Black Keys' 'Next Girl'. Her finely tuned alto whine ruining the thumping bass of my well-timed headshots in an effort to guilt me into a shower and a mehndi.

Upon arrival it's no surprise that it's the same as all the others—last season's Bollywood hits spilling out on to the road, the melody lost among the crush of random punters and the irritated honking of blocked traffic. Inside it's as hot and steaming as a monkey's ass. They've gone the usual route—high budget, low quality. I follow Aliya through the quivering multicoloured tent and watch her kiss people hello, greet aunties in her fake good-girl voice, show off her emerald sari and gaudy jewels. It's unnerving how she inhales compliments like bong hits, instantly high off the envy and lechery of old-ass uncles who want to bone her, or marry her to their sons. I let her do her thing, distancing myself from her, scanning the room for any of the jokers I know.

No matter whose wedding, or where it's located in the city, you will always bump into at least a hundred people you know. Lahore: a twelve-million strong Punjabi village masquerading as a metropolis. I shake hands with some random dudes and immediately go on the hunt for a bar or a wedding *sharabi* with a bottle of whisky and some ice hidden in his chuddies.

'Faisal's here,' Aliya nudges me. 'I told Saba to bring him along for you.'

Apparently the girls feel they are now in charge of setting us up for playdates. Faisal comes over and rolls his eyes, but I know the fool, he's tickled bubblegum pink at being officially presented as Saba's boyfriend. It was just a matter of time for him to be sucked into the marriage trap.

'Where the fuck have you been, man?' Faisal asks me. The girls swish off to say hello to the bride on stage. The dancing hasn't started yet, but now that the bride is here, it's only a matter of minutes.

'Home. Where else would I be?' I reply.

'I don't know, you could be on freakin' Mars for all I know. I called a shitload of times, why didn't you pick up? What's been going on, yaar? Why are you such a fucking hermit, bhenchod?'

'Nothing's been going on. I was home playing Xbox. What can I say, I'm bored with going out.' I do the nonchalant shrug and control the high pitch of tension in my voice.

'Bullshit. You've never been bored of going out before. Have you been hanging out with Moby again? Because that man is super dodgy.'

'Thanks for the advice, dad. Maybe I was just sick of your ugly mug. Especially now that it's stuck up Saba's ass.'

He gives me a goofy grin. He's a goner. Happy to be bloody whipped.

'Is there a bar in this damn place?' I ask.

'Dry mehndi,' he says, 'but I hear Tabor has something in his car.'

Tabor, some snaggle-toothed dude we know through Omer, is holding a little private party in his parked Pajero. We knock on his window and he opens the door, letting us into the back seat, already quite crowded with boys. Tabor sits in the driver's seat, one guy in the front, two next to us, all drinking out of plastic cups. Once we're in the car we notice three more boys in the back, crouching on fold-out seats, grinning sheepishly. Tabor's driver stands guard outside. The windows tinted, AC and music on full blast, a trance something-or-the-other remixed. He pours us both a cup of warm piss. It's a cheap knock-off, something local in a foreign Black Label bottle that will probably make us puke our livers later tonight, but it's fucking loads better than wedding sobriety. Such a condition can quickly lead to some awful hallucinations, grave images of ball busting and a house with twelve screaming kids. All very dangerous foul shit. I take my chances and sip boldly.

The dude in the front seat calls himself Robbie, lights a fatty and is willing to share. By the time we exit the car we've added three random numbers to our cell phones, know by heart a list of possible 'hotties' at the mehndi, have been invited to a sausage after-party, and know one more banker, one more real estate dude, and another drug dealer. Overall it's been successful—connections have been made, we're drunk and shit-faced high. This is how to wedding in Lahore, with copious alcohol and drugs gushing through the veins.

'So you're not going to tell me what you've been up to?' Faisal asks as we drag ass back into the sweltering tent. Faisal, despite all the distractions, still manages to retain his annoying persistence. I contemplate my options: tell him, don't tell him. He's my best friend, he'll be pissed if he finds out, if one day in some drunken haze I blab—which is very likely to happen.

'Moby's gone,' I say, settling on an abridged version of the story. One that doesn't include me looking like a total douche.

'What do you mean gone?' Faisal gives me a dumb look, the exact same look he got in computer class—a dumb brainless look, with his jaw hanging in full retard mode. C++ was not a good period in Faisal's life.

'I don't know,' I say. 'I don't think he's dead. I went by his haveli and all his shit was gone.'

'What do you mean *gone?*'

I sigh. This will take longer than I thought. 'I went to his house and there was nothing there. No car, no furniture, no kids, nothing. I looked through his windows and it was all gone.'

'So where did he go?'

'How the fuck would I know, Faisal?' I say, exasperated. 'Otherwise I would tell you where he's gone, nahin?'

'So he's in shit?' Faisal says with a gleam in his eye. He's never liked Moby. Moby always thought Faisal was weak and pampered, Faisal thought Moby was a dick. They were both right, and every attempt to get them to become friends had failed. After the car accident Faisal was always adamant that Moby was no good for me. I'm sure he feels pretty good about himself now.

'Probably,' I say.

'And he didn't tell you about it?'

'Nope. Not a fucking word.'

'So he bolted. But why? And why would he take all his shit if he's running away?' he says, making a very good point, one that I've been furiously pondering ever since. 'I mean, it's not easy to escape with kids and shit, beds and sofas. Most just dump their family at their parents' or some shit and fly off to Dubai.'

'I have no fucking idea. All I know is that he's gone.' I grab the cigarette Faisal's smoking and take a drag.

'So it was planned? I mean, he had to have organized it. So he knew he was ditching way beforehand. He just didn't tell you. Did you know he was in trouble?'

'Sort of. He mentioned it. His father died, he got involved in some heavy shit, he wanted my help, he came to my birthday. But he was gone before I could properly talk to him.' Here I lie, brazenly and without guilt. This is as far down the road as I'm willing to go.

'Well, he probably fucked with the wrong man and had to bail, yaar. Dodgy bastard. Good riddance. He was trouble, you're better off with him gone.'

I guess I am. I don't bother telling Faisal about the little after-party with MT's goons. That's just for me to know, and hopefully forget.

Some hot girls pass, close and perfumed like toxic flowers. We stop talking, stand up straight, offer smiles as they pass.

'Oh, and did you hear? My MT sexy news of the day?' he says.

'No, what?'

'Shit, you really have been in hiding. Ifti has thrown his lot in with Mian Tariq. There's no way Salim Chaudhry is going to win this thing now. Ifti has the mega bucks, yaar. Isn't that fucking sexy? See, I told you my man MT was on the up and up.

And this makes his position even better. He's gonna win, yaar. Now it'll be smooth sailing for MT until election day. See, the good do win.'

'I thought the good die young.'

He rolls his eyes at me. I wonder what transpired to bring Ifti into the fold. Is Ifti the devil MT was referring to? I'm exhausted by politics, who can keep up with the bullshit?

'So are you coming back to the real world now? Or are you still going to be a moody bastard?' Faisal asks.

'If this is your idea of the real world, then I'm going to remain a moody bastard.'

'Why do you have to be such a pain in the ass?'

'Why do you have to be such a lun?'

'A lun? Seriously? We're digging out school cusses now?'

'Yeah, I'm bringing lun back.'

'You're bringing dick back?'

'Yup.'

He laughs loudly. 'Asshole. Don't disappear on me like that.'

'As if you noticed, floating in your Saba bubble.'

Some fatty aunties smile at Faisal, one asks him how his parents are doing. 'Fine, auntie, they're doing well,' he says politely. They walk away, find a comfortable place to plant their jiggly asses to watch the dancing.

There's a commotion around the dance floor, some clapping, people crowding around. Everyone gathers around us and the loud speakers squeal their authority. Faisal has picked a choice position, near a tent pole, where the view is pretty decent. Far away enough to talk, close enough to see the tits and asses bounce.

'Are you going to do something about Moby? Find him or something?' he asks.

'Nope. Not a thing.'

'Good idea. He was trouble anyway. Better to stay clear.' I can hear the triumph in Faisal's voice. And now Moby's permanently gone. Our friendship severed. And he doesn't even know the half of it.

'Hey, isn't that Nida dancing next to Aliya?' Faisal says, pointing. The girls are lining up for their first dance. I haven't seen Nida in ages but I heard Omer and her broke up. She looks pretty fucking fantastic without Omer. Good riddance.

'Yeah, that's her.' I stand a little taller to see her over the tops of everyone's heads. She's looking fit in a tight yellow-orange salwar-kameez (standard mehndi colours), hair up in a ponytail. I wave to her and she waves back, rolling her eyes and pretending to slit her throat with her finger. The music comes on loud and the girls start their choreographed dance, enjoying the attention rained upon them. There's a mad rush of people, the music a signal to abandon all food and drink, and they push and shove to find a good spot to sit or stand. Seated aunties and girls ring the dance floor, which is a slightly raised wooden stage covered in white sheets. The uncles and boys stand around the back, near the exits, within alcohol range. People synchronize, clap to the song, cheer and hoot; kids run around like mad, weaving through the stage in excitement.

Aliya dances well enough, her golden-shimmering belly exposed beneath the emerald green of her sari. Her eyes are everywhere, less on her moves and more on the crowd watching her adoringly with their mouths agape. I can't tell if she's attempting Shakira or Kathak queen Sitara Devi. Saba stands next to us, close to Faisal, whispering to him. Every few seconds they giggle and point to someone. It's nauseating.

And then from the back Nida steps forward, close enough for me to see her clearly. She glows orange beneath the lights, her face beaming in some sort of excited glittery illumination.

She's really quite good, delicate with her tiny feet circling the carpet, her ponytail bouncing as she turns. Her dupatta is tied around the small curve of her waist and it highlights her cleavage and low neckline. Her eyes meet mine and she sticks out her tongue. I smile at her and, as a bonus, she leans down, part of the dance apparently, and allows me a brief glimpse down her kameez. Her bra flashes, ever so brief, in my direction, and then it's gone in a twirl, a twist of the waist, a flick of the wrist, back to the second row, corner of the carpeted stage, out of my sight.

'Yaar, I think she likes you,' Faisal says.

'What?' I say, trying to hear over the loud music.

'I think she likes you,' he yells into my ear.

'Who? Nida?' I yell back. 'Yeah, that's all I need, Omer's ex. As if I don't have enough issues already.'

'Well, I don't know about that,' he shouts back. Saba tiptoes on her heels to hear us better, sniffing out the gossip from our breath. 'But she's single. So why not?'

'The last thing I want is Omer on my case.'

'Come on, like Omer gives a fuck about girls, or anyone. He won't even remember her name in a few weeks.'

That's true. Omer's not really into counting his exes. He doesn't even break up with them, preferring the ignore until she gets the hint method—a sort of female self-combustion, where, without looking at the object he hopes it will evaporate, slowly melt into nothing, ice to water to vapour, and it usually does. He has it down to an art, reducing the number of hangouts and phone calls until it reaches zero, like a slow bleed-out. I doubt it's as painless as he thinks.

'Well, what I heard was that she just left one night and didn't come back,' Saba says.

'What do you mean? Like, just walked out?' I ask.

'Yes, just walked out. Omer has no idea why.'

'That's a first,' I say, slightly impressed.

'What's with all these people just leaving?' Faisal asks. 'I mean, what the hell? So she just disappeared?'

'Clearly not, Faisal,' Saba says, pointing to Nida. 'Something must have happened.'

'Maybe she came to her senses.' I watch her dancing, beaming under the lights like a rock star.

'Well, Omer would have ditched her eventually,' Saba says. 'He was probably already losing interest. It's been an entire summer almost. That's long for Omer.'

'Well, whatever. Fuck Omer, he's an idiot,' I say.

'So . . . What you gonna do about it?' Faisal asks, grinning like a bloody goon.

I look over at her, catching glimpses of her from the second row. She looks pretty damn good to me. She's shaking her hips in this sexy way and grinning sweetly, every few seconds looking over in our direction, meeting my eye and giving me a wink or a glimpse of the tip of her tongue as she licks her lips.

Game on.

'Omer's a fucking moron,' I yell over the next song, a dance replica of a British pop song in Urdu. 'I can't believe he would let her get away.'

'He's an ass,' Saba says, grabbing my shoulder, 'but you're not.'

Nida dances in three songs before she gets a break. Some kid walks up to her and hands her a rose. She smiles at him and holds it up to her face, inhaling, and then she comes over to where we're standing.

'Hi everyone,' she says shyly, giving Faisal and Saba a quick hug. 'What are you all doing?' She looks soft and pretty, the dancing making her cheeks glow a rosy pink.

I shrug and attempt coolness, 'Nothing much, just standing around, watching your moves.' I can feel my heart starting to beat just the slightest bit faster. 'You're quite the dancer.'

'Why do you sound so surprised, Bugsy?' she says, teasing. She pokes me in the chest with a thin sharp fingernail.

'I'm not surprised, not at all. I expected it.'

'Really, did you expect it?' She laughs and hugs me tightly, her sweat and perfume smelling sugary and light like cinnamon.

'Here,' she says, and pushes the rose into my hand. 'For you.'

The golden glitter on her eyelids sparkles as she blinks, the strong tent lights illuminating the particles that have fallen over her cheeks. She's not wearing any lipstick and keeps moistening her pink lips with her tongue. She seems nervous, excited by the dancing, breathing heavily, and her eyes are wide, pupils black. She keeps biting her lips, smiling and licking. I'm mesmerized by the movement of her mouth.

'How many more dances are left?' Saba asks her.

I hear Aliya's high laugh coming somewhere from the right, where she's standing between three boys fawning over her.

'Umm, I'm not sure. I think there are two more with the boys, then one more with just the girls, and then I'm done and I never ever have to think about dancing at a mehndi again,' Nida says breathlessly.

'Cool, so I get to see you a few more times before you write off dancing forever,' I say, attempting to flirt. 'It seems like a sad end to a very promising career.' I ignore Faisal and Saba's smirks and google-eyed looks.

'Oh my god, Nida, you were fabulous, just fabulous,' a familiar male voice says, and Alfie pops up behind me, putting his arms around my shoulders and leaning down to kiss Nida at the same time. Nida tiptoes up and her ponytail brushes past my face. She places a hand on my chest to steady herself, her cheek grazes against mine softly as she lowers herself back on to her feet. It's the briefest of contact, but enough to feel the sparks. She looks away quickly, busying herself in talk with Alfie, but I can see the excited smile lingering on her lips, the fire in her eyes. I see her glance at me from the corner of her eye.

'I'm so excited about the photo shoot,' Alfie says to her. 'Do you want to see what it'll look like?' He removes his arms from around me and shows her some pictures on his phone.

I do the casual, pretending to be immersed in Faisal and Saba's *gup-shup*, but unable to comprehend a single word they utter. I glance blankly at the dancers, the groom's family trying their best to show off. All I can think of is Nida next to me, so close I can feel her heat. And as she talks to Alfie she makes sure some part of her body touches mine—an accidental swipe of the hand, a quick lean into my chest, a soft touch on the arm to look at something. Every few seconds our eyes meet and everything lights up. It's a high-school-style affair, everything relayed through a series of microscopic sexual signals. I breathe out and think of my rotten-tooth chowkidar from Peshawar. He should do the trick.

'So what are you guys doing after?' Nida asks.

'Post-mehndi party!' Alfie yells loudly, making sure all hear.

'I have to get dropped home soon after,' Saba says, which means Faisal will be out of commission, taking the long way home, driving slow and hoping to get a little hand-holding action, possibly a kiss, at a deserted red light.

'I don't know if I'm up for a drunk fest,' I say, hoping to sound cool. 'I've done the obligatory hour. Aliya seems able to handle it from here.'

'You're going? So soon?' Nida says, suddenly looking miserable. It's the perfect reaction. Exactly what I wanted. Now I just need to figure out a way for us to be alone.

'Well, after your dances, of course,' I say.

'Do you have a ride home?' Saba asks sneakily, nudging Faisal, who obediently nudges me. I elbow him back. *Yes, I get it, you fool.*

'Well . . .' she hesitates, 'my parents were supposed to come, but I guess they changed their minds.'

'Don't worry, I'll take you,' I say on cue, trying not to sound too eager.

'Really? Are you sure, Bugsy?' she asks.

'Yeah, of course. It's no big deal. I have nothing else to do. And it would be irresponsible of me to leave you here without a ride.'

Thanks, Bugs,' she says and kisses my cheek, a little more slowly than needed, and then runs off towards the dance floor to resume her dance position.

'You guys are real luns, you know that?' I say to a very grinning, scheming Faisal and Saba.

'But smart luns,' Faisal says. 'You're welcome.'

I can't help smiling. 'Yeah, whatever.'

NIDA

After the mehndi, when the dances are over and spittle flies slovenly from drunk men's lips, after Saadia's exuberance has led to bridal exhaustion and the adults have reluctantly filtered out of the multicoloured tent, once Bugsy and I find his car among the dark shadows in elephantine shapes, escape the clamorous panhandling of the wedding *bhaand* and see jittery aunties wrenching off heavy gold from sore earlobes, I reconsider Bugsy's late-night invitation to his house. I accept.

It's almost midnight and my feet are sore, my body is exhausted. But I don't want to go home. That voice inside me says *No*, it practically shouts it.

'Relax, Nids,' Bugsy says when he sees me hesitate at the front door. 'My sisters are home, probably awake and up to no good. We're just gonna hang out, okay? Watch a movie, maybe listen to some music. Or we can each go our separate ways and I'll drop you home. It's up to you.'

Downstairs his sisters smile sweetly when they see me in my shiny shaadi attire and cheap wobbling silver sandals and offer me popcorn and a seat next to them on the large family sofa where they ogle the latest teenage horror film. I want to say yes, join them in familiar female comfort, knowing what will follow—chatting through the boring bits, screaming at the gore. I recognize them from Bugsy's birthday, which seems like ages ago. I feel embarrassed that they saw me with Omer, probably drinking and dishevelled. I search their faces for judgement but find none. There's no recognition, just three normal pretty desi girls asking if I want to see what happens to the cheerleader kissing the boy in the back seat of an American car. But before I can open my mouth Bugsy grabs their bowl of popcorn, teasingly throws a few puffs in their direction and leads me upstairs to his room. I wave to them but their eyes are back on the screen.

Bugsy's room is cold, the air conditioner running, the TV broadcasting a local music channel. Above his bed a jumbo glass-encased Freddie Mercury poster hangs on his wall, glowing golden-yellow beneath the light like a holy deity, a Vishnu or Shiva or some other multicoloured, multi-armed, terrifying godhead. In feng shui, mirrors opposite beds are bad luck. I wonder what kind of luck a giant framed dead rock star brings.

'I don't remember that from your birthday,' I say.

'Yeah, it's new. A birthday gift from my sisters. They like to indulge me.' He says this looking a bit embarrassed.

'I've been listening to the CD you burnt me,' I say, digging my hand into the bowl of warm popcorn and filling my mouth with its crisp blandness.

'Yeah, that's right. I forgot about that, everything's been such a blur. What did you think?'

I think back to the music, the punch of sound in my bedroom, the thick delicious voice of this man, this Queen, vibrating against my old cracked walls and rupturing life.

'I listen to it before I sleep,' I say. 'I think I love it.'

'That's awesome,' he says, tossing some of his rumpled clothes into the bathroom.

'I'm sorry it's so messy, I wasn't expecting anyone,' he says, throwing in a wet towel and slamming the door shut. 'The maid is useless.'

He brushes crumbs off the blue sofa and reorganizes his pile of remotes and game controllers. His television is massive, mounted flat on the wall, almost the size of his Freddie Mercury poster.

'Your sisters couldn't get you a bigger poster?' I tease. I shovel more popcorn into my mouth and sink deeper into the soft velvety fabric of his sofa. 'What kind of a fan are you if he only takes up one wall? Your TV is bigger. That, I'm sorry to say, is pathetic.'

'Ha ha, very funny. I don't think he comes any bigger. Unless you stuff and mount the man himself.'

I take my shoes off and feel instant sweet relief. I rub the red lines the straps have dug into my skin and inhale the cold Axe-deodorant smell of his air-conditioned room. 'Your AC's been running all night?' I ask.

'It's on a timer. It turns on a little before midnight.'

'Brilliant,' I say. 'The AC in my room barely runs at all, let alone manage an internal clock and timer. *Bechara*, its electrical buttocks are hanging halfway out the wall and dripping on to the driveway.'

'That sucks. Pablo here is a pretty amazing creature,' he says, and points to the sleek Korean-made air conditioner with a digital display in electric blue.

'You've named your AC Pablo?' I can't help but laugh. 'You're a very strange lad, Bugsy.'

'Yeah, well, I tried Waheed, but he just wouldn't accept it. Pablo was what he wanted, and I obliged.'

'So,' I say to him as he continues to run around the room cleaning and sorting, 'I've heard the music and I understand the appeal of Queen. But what is it about Freddie Mercury specifically that you love so much? I mean, yes the man can sing, fine, but I'm sure there are others who are equally talented. So what is it about him that turns you on so much?'

'Jeez, Nida, you make it sound like I lay on my bed every night and wank to his picture.'

'Well, I wouldn't be surprised if you did.'

'Thanks for the confidence. Now you've hurt my feelings. What type of guy do you take me for, yaar? It's not like that.'

'Then tell me what it's like?'

He's standing near his bed, rummaging through the drawer, taking out a fresh pack of cigarettes and a lighter. He stops and sits down on the bed, looking up at the poster.

'I don't know. I've thought about this a lot. On my show I always say it's because he's kind of everything. He's ugly and he's handsome. His skin is fair but he's pure chocolate-hero inside. In blood he's one of us. Well, *was* one of us. He walked like us and looked like us. He belongs to us, no matter what anyone says, like Sting belongs to the Brits, David Lee Roth to the Americans. He transcended in a way that's impossible for desis. We always seem to carry the white man's stereotype with us, like a hunchback. But he transcended, yaar. He managed to break the racial boundaries, and he did it in such a way that people still worship him. It was almost like a magic trick, a miracle.'

He pauses and slowly unwraps the plastic from the cigarette box. He throws it towards the dustbin and misses.

'Most of these gora fuckers have no idea he was from India, a fucking Gujarati, for shit's sake. It's kind of awesome. You gotta love watching the Brits bow down and pretend he's one of theirs.

A proper English gentleman—with fucked-up teeth, Aids, and all.' He laughs and gets up off the bed. He comes and sits next to me on the sofa.

'For me, living in Lahore, a lowly-rat RJ playing rock music to a few desperate lonely teenage boys, Freddie really lives, yaar. He was one of us and he wasn't broken. He did what he wanted, he told everyone—his family, the system, the class—to fuck off. He was better, the best, and he succeeded. He was gay and weird-looking and desi, and yet he was a righteous magnificent angel.'

'I like that,' I say. 'A righteous angel. Although I'm not so sure he wasn't broken.'

'We're all fucking broken, yaar. Maybe that's the way it's supposed to be. Bored and broken, ascending a ladder of global misery just like our parents.'

'So you're just as disappointed as I am?' I say, surprised. He looks at me funny, his face all serious, his eyes locked on mine. He frowns.

'Do you want something to drink?' he asks. He's changing the subject. 'Beer? I have Heineken, I think.' He kneels down on the carpet and opens a small white fridge next to his TV, filled with Coke cans, Nestlé Pure Life bottles and beer, nestled among a dozen varieties of chocolate. He pulls out a long large golden slab of wrapped chocolate and two frosted green cans of beer. The cans sigh as they pop open, fizzing over the side. It's ice-cold, making my hands ache. He breaks the chocolate—a fruit-and-nut bar—in large uneven squares and passes it to me.

'By the way, I've been dying to know, what happened with the whole Salim Chaudhry thing?' I ask. I catch him off guard and he chokes up beer. 'I was at the radio station with you and Faisal when you heard the Mian Tariq news, remember? Then you rushed off. I figured you had something to do with it. So? What happened?'

'What happened?' I consider not telling her and keeping my mouth shut, like I did with Faisal, but Nida's the only one who has been present the entire time—from Salim Chaudhry's mujra to the radio station and, now here, in my bedroom. 'Nothing happened,' I say. 'That's what. I ended up at MT's, where he quasi-lectured me about loyalty, friendship and morals. I think he just wanted to assess the threat level. And after it all, when I thought, okay, this dude isn't so bad, and I felt like shit for delivering dodgy docs, his fucking goons slapped me around and threatened me.'

'Seriously? Are you all right?'

'Yeah, yeah, I'll live. It wasn't major, they just wanted to scare me and show me who's boss. They even returned my car. I found it in the driveway when I got home.'

'So, wait, I'm confused. How did you end up getting involved in all this?'

'A friend of mine, Moby. I've known him since we were kids. He needed a favour, someone who could get to Salim Chaudhry and deliver the documents, and he knew I was friends with Omer. Later I found out that he was just using me.'

'That's horrible. Did you know what you were delivering?'

'No, of course not. Otherwise I never would have gotten involved.'

'So this friend of yours, Moby, he basically set you up?'

'Yeah, and you wanna know the best part? He has now disappeared.'

'What do you mean disappeared?'

'I mean *gone*. Like gone gone. With family and furniture, blank white squares where pictures once hung, telephone wires dead on the floor.'

'Where did he go?'

He shrugs and lights a cigarette. Smoke filters out from his mouth as he speaks like his tongue is on fire.

'Who knows? Family lands? Maybe up north to the mountains like the von Taliban family. A giant fuck-you, Bugsy, you trusting fuck, see ya later, you stupid gaandu. The fucking bastard. I swear, if I ever see him I'll fucking kill him.'

'Well, if you feel like murder and you can't find your friend, you can always take Omer out for me,' I say jokingly.

'Omer? Hah. That asshole doesn't deserve the effort. Omer doesn't care about anybody other than Omer. Trust me, I've known him since we were five. He's a selfish bastard.'

'I know this now,' I say.

'Well, you live and learn, I guess. I'd like to think we're both a little less stupid than we were a few months ago.'

He laughs dryly and rests his bare feet on the table, long fair feet that are strangely effeminate. He leans back, taking a gulp from the can of beer. His mehndi kameez is thin cotton and I can see the outline of his chest and his arm muscles through the off-white fabric, the soft tan skin of his neck dipping into the wide ivory kameez that covers him, the alcohol bobbing its way past his Adam's apple.

'I don't know,' he says absently, tapping the side of his beer can with his fingers. 'Things are not as they seem. Not as I thought they would be, that's for sure. I'm a shitty judge of character, that's what I've discovered.' He wipes his mouth with the back of his hand.

'You're not the only one,' I say, thinking again of Omer. He doesn't answer, but looks at the television. It's local cable, the picture fuzzy, showing Fashion TV girls in distorted colour.

'Are you comfortable in that?' he asks me. 'From what I've been told, sequins are mad itchy.'

'Haan, it's like sandpaper slowly trying to slit my throat,' I say, pulling the kameez's low neckline away from my body.

'Well . . . do you want, you know, to wear something of mine? I have clean pyjamas that are comfortable, a T-shirt, maybe some trackpants?'

'Really? You don't mind? Because that would be great.'

'Obviously not. Why would I mind?' He gets up and opens his closet door, the hinge squeaking loudly enough to make me turn my head. The inside of the wooden door is decorated with a faded poster of Carmen Electra, a sexual homage to breasts barely covered, forward leaning and overflowing, hair a wild mess of extensions and style perfection as the mouth opens, the eyes narrowing in pleasure, in pain, for the camera. She's magnificent in a red full-piece *Baywatch* bathing suit, holding the signature-red lifesaver. I can't help but laugh, surprised at the unexpected burst of male adolescence.

'Now I know why desi men are so unhappy,' I say. 'They want Carmen in their bed, not some fussy, conservative, goody-two-shoes wife smelling of doodh and tarka.'

Bugsy blushes, as much as a brown boy can blush, and sheepishly offers an explanation on how it's been there forever, how he can't seem to remove it, it'll take the veneer off the door if he tries.

'Yes, Bugsy, I'm sure it's the closet wood you're worried about,' I tease. He grins like a kid caught red-handed. 'Relax. My brother use to have a few naughty magazines hidden under his mattress,' I tell him. 'I used to sneak a look while he was out. Then my mother burnt them when he died. I think she was attempting to cleanse his soul, or her own.'

'Faisal and I have a blood pact: if either of us dies, we have to go to the other's house immediately and destroy all the porn.'

'Where does one even get that stuff here?'

To this question he grins wickedly. 'It's a secret, yaar,' he says and hands me the pyjamas. They look like standard boys' pyjamas, blue cotton bottoms, the T-shirt a soft grey Smiths print.

'That's not fair, why is it a secret?' I ask. 'There's so much that Pakistani men do that's a bloody secret. It's unfair. And honestly disgusting.'

'That's why it's a secret, because we're bloody disgusting. If you knew all we did, you'd want to burn your eyes out. Anyway, I'm sure there's tons of shit women do that's just as nasty,' he says.

'Like what? Recipe exchanges? Children's diaper routines? Complaints about the maid? As if you guys don't control everything we do anyway. As if you'd be okay with us having secrets from you. It's a one-way road buddy, don't have any doubt about it. You want to know everything and say nothing.'

He just smiles and shrugs, like that's not his problem. And there's the whole male–female desi relationship—a shrug-off.

'How about a funny story instead?' he says, coming back to the sofa. He has already started grinning at his story.

'When we were in school Faisal once went porn shopping, somewhere down the Mall. That was the horny desi male hotspot then, some cheap video store that also sold porn. Anyway, he'd been out all day in the sun and hadn't had time to eat. So he collects the videos from the shop, like this tall pile of twenty or thirty movies, because he's fucking lazy and wanted enough to last him the rest of the year. As he steps out the door with this massive pile, his blood pressure drops and he passes out. Just like that, thump, out cold, in the middle of the road like some drunk fuck. When he comes to he finds himself being helped by some auntie and her teenage daughter. Here he is, all passed out, surrounded by a pile of hard-core Asian shit and German threesomes, and some sweet auntie is gathering his movies for him and giving him a banana. She even helped him to his car, her daughter holding the movies. He said the auntie wouldn't make eye contact with him when he tried to thank her. He felt so guilty, we made fun of him for years. Every auntie we'd see we would ask, "Is that her? How about that one?" Needless to say, he's very happy he can now just download that shit.'

I laugh at the thought of poor Faisal and some shocked but sweet auntie. 'I can imagine Faisal doing that. He seems the type.'

'He is the type. Don't tell him I told you though. He'll kill me.'

I change my clothes in Bugsy's bathroom, cringing as I remember the last time I was here. I was inhaling lines off his sink counter like some cheap addict. It seems like that was years ago, when I was a different kind of Nida. Was I that naive? That desperate to have a good time? Maybe I'm still that girl.

I remove an eyelash from my cheek. Wipe the sides of my lips. Wash my hands.

'How do I look?' I ask Bugsy as I step out of his bathroom.

'Great. From now on you should wear all my clothes.'

'Maybe. I could use a new wardrobe.'

He's changed the channel to some eighties movie, the volume on low. Arnold Schwarzenegger's biceps fill the screen.

'Is this okay in the background?' he asks. 'I don't like to be in a room without TV. It's a social disease.'

'Sure, of course. I like it.'

I sit back on the sofa and notice that he's on his second beer. I quickly sip mine, not wanting to fall behind. He leans back and slumps down. I gently extract the cigarette from between his fingers, take a puff and carefully plant it back. He gives me a lazy smile, eyes on Schwarzenegger beating someone into a bloody pulp.

'How's your show?' I ask.

'It's okay, I guess. I haven't been going all that regularly. They've been playing old shows, the best of *The Rocket Launch*.'

'How come?'

'I don't know. I feel . . . weird.' He turns his head slightly towards me, resting it on the sofa cushion, his body still facing the TV. 'For the past few weeks, with Moby and MT, I don't know. I've been thinking stuff. Things feel different. It's not normal, the way we live our lives, you know? All the drugs and booze, the endless parties. We don't do anything worthwhile. We just throw our lives away. I feel as if I'm throwing my life away. I don't know if it's just Pakistan or if every place is like this. I can't seem to grasp it.'

'What do you mean?' I say.

'I feel that things are broken,' he says. 'Or not worth my time. And usually I don't give a shit, I've lived in Lahore my entire life, I know how to block out the broken and the bullshit. But for some reason I'm finding it impossible to do it now. Maybe we're getting older, or we've just had enough and reached our limit, but . . . I mean . . . Well, to tell you the truth, Nida, things are badly broken. And I don't think there's a possibility of repair.'

'Broken? What do you mean *broken*? With the station?'

'Not just the station. Everything. The entire fucking system. The government, our friends, our parents, our families, our roads, our economy. All of it. Fucking busted. And everyone we know is broken.'

'Tell me something I don't know,' I say, half laughing, referring again to Omer. He doesn't laugh.

'Don't you see it? Look at this place, this city. I mean, if there's an example why we're broken, it's Lahore. Poor beautiful fucked-up Lahore. Load-shedding for twelve hours a day, sometimes fourteen, and no one to pay the city's electricity bill. Politicians would rather pocket the money and buy apartments in London. The richest man in the city, our resident Donald Trump, lives on a broken potholed road. Inside he stores his Porsches and BMWs, but outside everything looks like shit. This place will never get fixed, and you know why?'

'Why?'

'Because no one wants to fix it. It's broken and people like it like that. They like it because it makes them feel good. Seeing others walk in shit makes their pathetic lives a little less dim.'

I nod to let him know I understand. He's all worked up, forgetting he's holding a cigarette. The ash is threatening to collapse on to his carpet. I point to it and he crushes it out in a plastic skull ashtray.

'We feed ourselves bullshit lies daily: it'll get better, it'll improve, no worries, yaar, someone will help us. The Americans will help us. The Chinese will help us. God will help us. The economy will grow. Everyone thinks it's just a matter of time and then boom!—like a fucking lightning strike, one loud blurted inshallah—we'll proudly enter the twenty-first century.'

I burst out laughing. 'And with my luck, I'll get electrocuted, just like every other desi girl.'

'Oh, please, don't give me that,' he says. 'You girls have it easy. No job pressure, no money tension. All you have to worry about is what colour contact lenses you'll wear at your wedding.'

'That's not true! We're not animals, you know? We have feelings. We have ambitions. You all just don't want to hear them or give a shit. But I have real worries. And marriage isn't a solution. It's just a cryogenic state,' I say, punching him in the chest.

'Jeez,' he says, breaking into a smile. 'Okay, sorry. Don't get so worked up, yaar.'

'Don't be stupid and I won't. Everyone deserves the freedom to destroy their own lives.'

'Well, we're doing a bang-up job then.'

'If things are so broken, why don't you fix them?' I say.

'How do you fix something that everyone wants broken? I've come to realize that the real power, the real money, is not in fixing things, but in keeping them broken. On the *promise* of repair, not on the actual process itself.'

'Because if things worked, then what would people lie about fixing?'

'Exactly.'

'Poor Bugsy, it looks like we're both sinking in the same existential ship. Welcome to the upper deck.' I gently mess up his hair and he gives me a cute smile. He has the slightest dimple on his right cheek and I touch it gently. He doesn't move away but sits still, letting my finger caress him. He has smooth skin, completely blemish-free, soft like a baby.

'Do you want some charas?' he asks.

'Charas? Weren't you just talking about wanting more from life than drugs?'

'Yeah, well, I think that's why we need to memorialize this moment, our sad reality, by getting good and blasted.'

He gets up and walks towards his bedside table. 'I don't know what I have, but I'm sure I can dig up some random shit. Whatever people give me I throw in here.'

I see him rummaging in the drawer, pulling out rolling papers, lighters, a Chupa Chups lollypop, other random bakwas. I get up and walk over to him, sit on his bed and peer into the drawer. It's a proper mess, with old hash stuck to the sides like gum and bits of dried tobacco and torn Rizlas. He pulls out a small baggie with two tiny white pills and a foil strip of medicine.

'Okay, so after inventory, we have some E, old-ass E from a few years ago. I don't know if it's still any good. And one, two, three, four Xanaxes. Some not-so-shitty hash. Mashed Dunhill Lights. No coke, crack or heroin, though, sorry.'

'Ha ha, very funny,' I say, pulling the bag of E out of his hands. The pills have little umbrellas on them. 'As if you'd know what to do with heroin if you had any.'

'And you would?' he asks, concerned.

'Of course not. What kind of girl do you take me for?'

'The kind of girl that rolls a mean joint,' he says, laughing.

'Thanks, but I don't do anything that will kill me. Just a few brain cells. Make you a little less whiney.'

'Oh, is that how it is?' he says, pushing me back on the bed. I lay back and look up at him, standing now. I put my bare foot on his stomach. I can feel his abs against the pads of my feet. He wraps his hand around my ankle. I feel the heat of his hands.

'So, what's your poison?' he asks, waving the baggie above me.

I gently grind the ball of my foot against his abdomen. The foot slips and lays against the edge of his salwar. I can feel where the elastic scrunches around his waist. A little lower and I'll be able to feel all of him, the flimsy fabric holding nothing back. I pause my foot's downward slide and lazily grin at him. Why am I flirting with him? I can't help myself. He's cute. Even cuter now, looking a little dazed, unsure of where to go from here.

'So? Are we gonna do this or not?' I say, taking charge.

He takes a light step back. 'Sure,' he says as nonchalantly as he can. 'Why the fuck not. Tomorrow you're homeless, tonight is a blast.'

'What?' I ask. I've taken back possession of my foot. I don't want to come off as too forward. 'What are you talking about?'

'Tomorrow you're homeless, tonight is a blast,' he says louder, almost in wild singing. 'It's a lyric, by the Dead Kennedys. Tomorrow you're homeless, tonight is a blast. Come on, baby,' he extends his arm to me. 'Let's fuck each other up.'

'If your parents are asleep, why are we still smoking in your bathroom?' I ask him this while sitting on a small plastic stool next to his high-tech glass-encased rain shower, which, while giving me a demonstration, he ended up accidentally soaking his hair and shirt with. He's now in pyjamas too and looks adorable in red-and-blue-chequered cotton bottoms. We look like a couple of silly American kids on a sleepover, like in the movies.

'I like it here,' he says. 'Bathrooms are peaceful. With the blue tiles and this wonderful fuzzy floor mat.' He rubs it lovingly, like he's rubbing a dog's belly. 'What's more private than your own bathroom? Plus after all the years throwing up and passing out, I have a special relationship with this one.'

'You're such a strange one,' I say. He's making the joint on the floor, sitting cross-legged on his thick bath mat, a magazine in his lap filled with cigarette innards and a smoking red ball of hashish dangling off a hairpin. He's at the mixing stage. He's not bad, a little too cautious with the flaming ball of hashish. If he doesn't rub it in well the mixture will separate into lumps. He tells me to turn on his small CD player mounted on the wall and to my surprise it's jazz that comes through.

'What?!' I say, feigning shock. 'Famous rock RJ Bugsy, caught with *jazz* in his WC. Shocking.'

'Yeah, yeah. Sometimes you need to cut the rock with something beautiful, like Chet Baker. He's my bebop rock 'n' rolla, don't tell anyone. Play song number three, "Time after Time". After a tinkling of piano the warm voice that arrives gives me goosebumps and I immediately wonder if Bugsy does this with all the girls. Has he shared a similar moment with Aliya? I shake it off. Who cares? Just enjoy the moment, Nida.

'You have such an odd assortment of things in your bathroom,' I say, getting up and examining all the colourful bottles and tubes on his counter. 'Seriously, Bugsy, you have more useless products than I do, and I thought *I* was obsessed. I mean, what's this?' I hold the pump bottle sideways to read the label. 'Organic Herbal White-Tea Soap? Tea soap? Why would you want to rub your hands with chai? What, drinking Lipton not good enough for you?'

'I have sisters, okay. They just give me their old stuff. Usually it's shit they bought and didn't like.'

'Do you use it all?' I twist open the top and smell it. I make a face of exaggerated disgust. 'This is awful, like essence of goat.'

'Yes, Nida, that's what it is, pure essence of goat. Essence of goat for my face,' he says. 'Obviously I don't use all this shit. But you never know when some girl or the other might need it,' he says, winking.

'You mean when she'd like some goat essence?'

'Exactly. You never know when some good *bakra* behind the ears might be sexy.'

I laugh and twist open more bottles, rub a little sugar scrub on the back of my hand, dab some perfumed lotion on my neck.

'Do you have a lot of girls wearing out your cosmetics supply?' I ask casually, hoping I don't sound too nosy.

'Hardly. This is Lahore, after all. Faisal's used more of these products than all the girls I know combined, including my sisters.'

'So basically Faisal's the main female presence in your life.'

'Unfortunately.'

He rolls a decent-looking joint and lights it up, still sitting on the floor. His bathroom is nice and airy, with a lot of light. It's almost as big as my bedroom. Everything is blue, from the towel hanging off the back of the door to his blue Lux soap sitting in a blue glass dish. I get the feeling his mother or sisters buy everything for him, making sure everything matches for their darling son or brother. He smokes slowly, enjoying it, holding the smoke in his lungs and letting it out slowly, like I do when I need a smoke badly. He leans back against the cabinets beneath the sink and rests his head. There's peace as I watch him smoke, his profile striking. The shadow from his nose frames his lips, enhancing their sharp shape. He runs his fingers through his soft brown hair, daydreaming

'What are you thinking?' I ask.

'What?' he says, looking a little confused. 'Oh, nothing. Usual bullshit.' He picks a bit of tobacco off his tongue and flicks it carelessly.

I sit on the floor next to him, my shoulder touching his, my back against the hard wooden cabinet. I put my head on his shoulder and he adjusts himself to make me more comfortable. His body feels warm. He intertwines his fingers with mine and it feels incredible, as if we have always been holding hands. I feel myself sink into his body, my head becoming one with his shoulder, our arms merging, our fingers moulding.

'The charas is kicking in?' I whisper.

I pass him back the joint, feeling my limbs relax, my heart speed up. Everything feels clear and new. I am new again. A new person, in a new world. Spaces shift and a simple bathroom suddenly becomes an expanse of possibilities, makes the worn fresh again. I inhale and move my face back into Bugsy's neck. I smell his skin. He smells so safe. He skin feels so soft. His cologne lingers, of lemon and earth and air. I can feel his breathing. I press my cold nose against his skin.

'I think I'm high,' I whisper into him. I nudge his ear gently with my nose. I feel like his ear is the only thing in the world. Me and his ear. Everything else is gone. I close my eyes. The lobe looms large in my head.

'Yeah, me too.' I hear his voice break the slightest bit. It quivers. I lick his earlobe slightly. I think I've lost control of my brain, because it's not following anything I'm saying. It's gone rogue, chasing after an ear. My tongue has lost its self-control and darts out without permission.

He inhales sharply and turns his face towards me, his nose almost touching mine, his lips so close I can see the soft pink ridges in the fullness of his lower lip. A trumpet plays on softly.

'You're tickling my ear,' he whispers hoarsely.

'Mmm, am I?' My heart is expanding through my chest, his face so close his breath is against my cheek. I'm afraid he'll hear my heart thumping, feel its shiver of nervousness. He moistens his lips with his tongue and leans towards me, his eyes searching my face. He's going to kiss me and I stop breathing. He moves in so slowly it feels like forever. Suddenly the electricity goes and we're bathed in darkness. I'm afraid it'll throw him off. I whisper his name and he whispers mine back, so close I can feel the words against my lips. I'm grateful for the dark.

We kiss, slow and languid at first, lost in the blackness of the room, floating through its stretched jungle space like we're in warm water, gasping for air as the energy builds. He moans as we kiss—or is that me?—and at some point we roll on the floor and press our bodies desperately against each other.

Wrapped into each other we make out shamelessly, sweating in the bathroom, our tongues sliding against each other, our bodies pressed tightly. His hands move deftly over me, feeling every part of me as if committing it to memory; my body burns with each caress his fingers make against my skin. He doesn't bother kissing my neck or any other part of my body; it's all about our lips. He pulls my hips against him and gently tugs my hair, moaning. I can feel him through the thin cotton, fabric so fine it's as if we're already naked. I reach down and insert my fingers through the waistband, feeling his stomach, when as sudden as it went, the electricity hums back to life and the lights in the bathroom reveal our sweating lascivious faces. We look at each other, shocked, a little embarrassed, and pull apart, but it's too late for modesty.

'You are so beautiful,' he says, breathlessly and strokes my face slowly with his fingers. He runs his fingers down my nose, around my lips. I kiss them nervously and peer into him. I try to read his eyes, I see the lust and sexual desire, but also a sweetness, some apprehension maybe, tenderness.

'You know, I don't think you have a clue how beautiful you are,' he says, looking seriously at me. 'I've been dreaming about you, about this, for a long time.' He kisses me softly and takes my hand, opens the bathroom door and leads us out.

In the bedroom the cold air is heaven against my flushed skin. The oscillating breeze blows back my sweat-damp hair and dries my lips. Bugsy stands behind me and kisses my neck, his hands moving up the shirt until it's crumpled against my bra. We spill on to the bed, pulling each other's clothes off, touching our own bodies to see if this is real, then touching each other in validation. The blankets are cool and I push them away from me, toss the pillows on to the floor. He tugs the blue shirt over his head and stands over me, his body beautiful. He has no fat, just muscle. I can't help but compare him to Omer, who was sloppy and half drunk, his body soft and fleshy like a child's. This is different, this is a new awareness I've never felt before. I'm present everywhere, in every pore and every sigh, every finger touch and tongue lick. He touches my thighs and I am two thighs, then two breasts, a hungry tongue, lips that multiply with every kiss. I've broken into pieces scattered on the bed, each piece building, radiating passion. Everything feels magnified—the chilled air against my back, now the hot body above me, our rubbing and heated sweat against the cold sheets, his burning mouth. I hope no one can hear us outside, but I don't care. Right now I don't care about anything.

BUGSY

'I want you to stay,' I tell her. 'I don't want to come home and lay in bed alone, smell you on my sheets.' But she just smiles and kisses me. She strokes my face softly with her sharp fingernails and tells me she will see me tomorrow, but for tonight it is best to sleep in our own beds and miss each other.

'It's good to miss,' she says.

'I already miss you,' I tell her, and she kisses my eyelids.

In the car I let the radio play for a change. It's *Jazz After Midnight*, and Miles Davis exhales his wistful trumpet into my soul. I let it slow-dance through me as déjà vu consumes me. I feel as if I've lived this moment before, in another life maybe, another time. The quiet inside me. Nida sitting next to me holding my hand. This mellow feeling.

'I like this music,' Nida says sleepily. 'Now it will always remind me of you.'

'Yeah?'

The song changes to something faster, with more energy, the saxophones blare, the snare drum in the back almost pulling itself forward.

'Hey, are you hungry?' I ask, suddenly feeling famished.

'I always am,' she says, laughing. 'Especially when I'm with you.'

The drive-through is full, the line of cars extending out and around the road, past the *challi* cart that's still serving roasted ears of corn. It's the weekend bustle, despite it being almost one in the morning, and families are willing to wait in their chilled cars for fish fillets and McFlurries. People don't sleep in Lahore, and definitely not on the weekends.

I pull up behind another Honda, a long distance from the fast-food window. Four skinny goofy kids in cheap China Chowk print T-shirts climb up their back seat and point at us from their rear window. They giggle when Nida shows them her tongue. They then show us theirs.

'I love that people are up at night,' Nida says. 'I love that Lahoris don't like to sleep and that people go out together as a family, even if it's for junk food. I would hate to live in a city that's quiet at night.'

'Yeah, me too. My sisters and I still go out at night. Sometimes just for the drive, listen to music, buy a pack of smokes or some paan.'

'We don't any more. My house is like a bloody cemetery. We used to go out all the time. My father was addicted to chicken Zingers.' She laughs wistfully. 'Did you ever do that with your parents?'

'My parents? Ha! No way. My father is so not the driving-for-food-at-night type. He's not even the driving-for-food-during-the-day type. He's so army it's ridiculous. He eats his dinner without us if we're late.'

'And your mother? What is she like?' Nida is curled up on the seat, legs beneath her, leaning against the door to face me. I love how comfortable she looks in my car, as if she's back in my room sitting on my sofa. She's also back in her shimmering mehndi kameez, looking a little tired but happy.

'Honestly?' I say. 'I don't know. She used to be more fun and chill when we were kids. She'd play board games with us all night, let us bunk school to go shopping with her. Once she jumped into a tube well at a farm with all her clothes on, shoes and everything, and pulled us into the water with her. But now, she's become kind of rigid. I think my father's military uptightness has finally consumed her. I mean, she was always a bit aloof. My grandfather was in the air force, and he's one strict bastard, and my grandmother died a long time ago. I think she's just been squashed flat by the Pakistani military complex.'

'I guess everyone has something that crushes them. With us it's my brother.'

I nod and she grabs my hand and holds it tight, rubbing my thumb with hers. I inch the car forward through the main drive-through gate. We're moving, one small hungry car at a time.

'You know, despite Lahore being such a pain in the ass sometimes, I really love being here,' I say to her. 'Like, right now. This is awesome. I mean, yes, I fucking love to bitch about the place, we all do. It's in our Lahori nature, to trash what we love.'

'We complain because we care.'

'Exactly. But I would miss this place if I didn't live here. No matter what, in Lahore you're never alone. People are always up in your business. In a way we take care of each other.'

'That's why people stick around,' she says, 'or come back to retire.'

I pull her hand that's still intertwined with mine and kiss it slowly. She sighs ever so slightly and leans forward, putting her head on my shoulder. I kiss her hair and forehead and at the same time inch the car forward a little bit more. There's a tapping at the window, a young kid in Mickey D's finest with a smirk.

'Your order, please,' he says, as I lower the window.

'Um, what do you want, Nida?' I ask her, and lean back in my seat for her to yell over.

'Chicken nuggets, Happy Meal,' she says loudly. 'Six nuggets, not four, achcha? Coke. And a girl toy. The boy toys are useless.'

'And I'll have a royale with cheese, Coke *ke saath*,' I say, and the waiter grins, nodding, writing it down quickly on a piece of scrap paper.

Nida looks at me with a raised eyebrow.

'*Pulp Fiction*, baby,' I tell her. 'He understands. Oh yeah, and one . . . You want Oreo or Butterfinger?'

'Butterfinger,' Nida says in excitement.

'And one Butterfinger McFlurry.'

'Please pay at the window, sir,' the waiter says, pointing about ten cars down to the yellow-lit window, and hands me the receipt written on a piece of paper.

'How the hell does he know what a royale is?' Nida asks.

'Come on, everyone has seen *Pulp Fiction*, yaar. Especially the guys working at McDonald's.'

'Really?' she asks.

I laugh. 'I don't know, maybe. Probably. I come here lots, this dude knows me. He knows what I order, that's all.'

'Ahh, sneaky,' she says, settling back into her seat. 'God, I'm really starving. I didn't realize how much until now. I can already taste the French fries.'

Down the line we roll until I pay at one window and retrieve our food at another. Instantly Nida's organizing the bags—pushing the drinks into the cupholders between us, unwrapping my burger halfway and handing it to me, squeezing ketchup on her fries, balancing the box of nuggets on her knee, the square tub of hot mustard open and balanced precariously on the lid. She shoves fries into her mouth and feeds me three at a time.

'Are you sure you don't want to go back to my place?' I ask her. 'It's close. We could eat in peace. I can always drop you later. Maybe early in the morning?'

She shakes her head, signals a 'no' with a mouthful of food.

I drive even slower, reluctantly, the taste of burger, pickle, ketchup occupying my attention for a while. Greasy crap never tasted so good. Every few seconds, delicately like a nurse, Nida gently places fries into my mouth. I watch her dunk her nuggets and she shares a few bites with me.

I take a left, a shortcut through Cavalry, the smaller quieter roads maze-like and concealed, the perfect place to drive slowly and talk. Maybe even steal a kiss or two in the dark tree-lined streets. We've devoured all the food, only the melting ice-cream left to share. She feeds me spoonfuls as I brake over the million speed bumps, and on a silent dark road I lean over to her and we kiss with cold milky tongues.

'This is fun,' she says, holding the McFlurry between her thighs. Searching through one of the bags, she pulls out a silver packet. 'My toy,' she says, sounding like a pleased six-year-old. She rips the wrapper with her long fingernails and wrestles out a Hello Kitty doll.

'Yuck,' she says, looking at the toy oddly. 'I already have one of these.'

'Not a fan of Hello Kitty?' I ask. She just shrugs and drops the doll in the paper bag of trash.

At the end of the street, near the major exit out of Cantonment, I see the regular army checkpoint and slow down. I hope they don't give us trouble this late at night.

I slow the car to a crawl and lower the window. Nida sits up straight in her seat, tossing the ice-cream container and crumpling the paper bag closed. She runs her fingers through her hair and wipes her make-up clean in the sun-visor mirror.

The checkpoint has been reinforced, soldiers walking about in camouflage, waving down traffic and signalling at cars to move on or come to a complete stop. Even this late at night there are plenty of cars. They're peering into every passing window, and every second or third one is being searched. There's a bit of a jam, we're four cars down from what seems to be a new barrier. To my left on the side road a white Suzuki van is pulled over, a driver being questioned. He looks nervous as he hands his licence and registration over to the soldier. The soldiers are all wearing military web gear, the stand-issue G3 rifles and MP5s. Some even have hand grenades hanging off their belts.

They remind me of my father, his younger days when he wore his uniform to work. I would go into his room and all his small tightly packed possessions would be spread out on his bed. As he went over a long serious list I would help him check off the items and offer as many unhelpful suggestions as I could think of to make sure he came back limb-heavy and sane-plenty.

I hear shouting. The soldiers are yelling at a bus to stop. Behind the barrier there's a truck with a massive machine-gun facing us.

'What's going on here?' I ask a solider as we move closer. He gives me a salute after noticing my dad's military decals.

'Sorry, sir, but there have been bomb threats to the city,' the soldier says, bending to peer into the car. 'You should be careful. There is news of trucks loaded with explosives coming in from the motorway. We are attempting to locate them.'

'Trucks with explosives?' Nida asks with fear in her voice.

'Good luck,' I say to him and raise my window.

'Thank you, sir,' he says, quickly waving us through. The soldiers salute as we pass.

'That's crazy,' Nida says. 'What's this place coming to?'

'Well, hopefully, it won't be a truck filled with explosives blowing up.'

'Omer and I saw a bomb blast last month, did I tell you? From the Palace Hotel.'

'Yeah, I remember.'

'One minute we're eating sushi and then boom!—there's a hole in Mall Road. I've never seen anything like it before. I mean, there have been bombings, but always in the Old City, or in other cities. Never right in the middle, where we live. They're getting closer.'

'And they're getting desperate.'

The traffic slows at a red light, hunched and wheeling in slow motion—a cyclist on his way home, a Daewoo bus, a red-eyed driver gaping at the traffic lights. I imagine the trucks with explosives loose in the city. I wonder where they are right now, which neighbourhood they're roaming. A lone rickshaw putters past, sleepily weaving between the lines, breaking the red light and magically avoiding collisions. I sigh and slouch a little in my seat. Nida places her warm hand on the back of my neck and gently runs her fingers up my hair. It feels amazing. I swivel my head so she can touch every part of my neck, her nails scratching away the stress.

Despite the news, the bombings, the fundos with their fucked-up ideals, I feel safe. Lahore always feels safe, familiar. A right turn and I'm at my uncle's house, a little further and it's where we played soccer as kids. This is my city, and even when it drives me crazy and I need to run away to some Western place to recover, I know that Lahore is always there, always the same city where I know every shortcut, every friend's house, every midnight turn I've taken at high speed.

I look over at Nida. She's sitting pretty, cross-legged on the seat, her bony knees pressing against her thin salwar. Her eyes are glued on the road as if she's scouring the dark alleyways and side streets for terrorists.

'Are you nervous about the trucks?' I ask her.

'Not really. I just like the city at night. It's so quiet. And clean. Seems almost like another world.'

'Yeah, I know what you mean. Driving at night is my favourite. We're almost at your house,' I say. 'I forget, do I take a left or a right?' She motions left with her hand.

As we near her lane there's another checkpoint—three officers wave a hand motioning us to stop. One of them has a Kalashnikov. Just seeing him with a machine gun makes me nervous; our local police force is not exactly comprised of the most trained or educated of personnel. The missing trucks must be pretty serious. It's a new checkpoint, and there are no cinder blocks or barriers. A car is parked behind them, blocking the road.

'Shit,' Nida says, sounding worried. 'I understand checkpoint-ing all the main entries into Lahore, but why the hell here? This isn't even near a main road.'

'God, I hate these bastards. Army I can handle, but police-wallahs are real dumb shits.'

There isn't any traffic at this stop, we're the only ones. It's a small quiet road, set away from the big houses that crowd the main road. A large policeman comes up to us and walks around the car, slowly checking the vehicle. With the new crackdown laws on terrorism the police have become unpredictable, ready and eager for an occasional roadside battering.

The policeman taps the window with his knuckles. The sound of his metal ring against the glass is loud and harsh. Something about it makes my skin crawl. I make sure the car doors are locked.

I lower the window slightly, just enough for me to hear what he has to say. 'Yes?' I ask in my best polite but impatient voice. It's almost 2 a.m. and I want him to know I'm not up for a conversation or interrogation.

The policeman peers into the car. 'Is that an alcoholic drink you have?' he says in some serious village Punjabi.

I follow his eyes to the large McDonald's Coke wedged into the cupholder. 'No, it's a Coca-Cola.'

The policeman frowns as if he doesn't want to believe me. I'm guessing he was wishing I had said it was a Scotch and soda. His eyebrows are thick and meet in the middle beneath his frazzled blue wool beret. He eyes Nida the best he can in the dark. 'What business do you have in this neighbourhood?' he asks.

'I'm dropping my cousin home after a mehndi,' I say, not straying too far from the truth. It's better to keep it simple, and in the family, than bothering with some snarky comments about my freedom to drive wherever the fuck I please. Altercations with the police are best held when there are no females present.

'Is she your wife?' the policeman asks. 'Do you have your marriage licence? It is illegal to have a girl in the car without papers. Please get out and show me your papers.'

I sigh. These buffoons are bored, looking for a bribe. This isn't uncommon, police hassling couples—even brothers and sisters, mothers and sons—for some quick cash. And most kids, young and on secret dates, deathly afraid of their parents, pay up. Occasionally the police plant some hash in a car full of boys and haul them to the station for a finder's fee. But this is the first time

I've ever been stopped with The Brig's army decals. Nida looks over at me, worried. I pat her knee reassuringly. At least we know their intention.

'First of all,' I say to him calmly, in the cleanest Urdu I can manage, 'I just told you she's my cousin. So that would make her *not* my wife. I have no papers to prove she's my cousin because there is no such thing. Also, if there's a law saying it's illegal to drive with a girl in the car, I would like to know more about that law. Would you kindly show me where it is stated?'

I can hear the irritation in my voice and I take a deep breath. There's no use arguing with this ignorant village prick. God, they really know how to push my buttons. He's making shit up so either I pay him or he gets his late-night police-brutality fix. But I know he's seen the military decals and it's money he wants. The problem is that I don't really have much, not enough to appease a few policemen. Not after the McDonald's splurge. I'm more likely to piss them off by offering a miserly bribe than get them off my back. If I stand my ground maybe they'll get fed up and let us go.

'Get out of the car,' he commands and attempts to open the locked door. I roll up my window and tell him firmly, 'No.'

He stands there, stuck now. He's not sure what to do. The policeman stares at Nida, his eyes open ridiculously wide, bulging out from his darkening face. He stares at me, at Nida, at me again. I'm afraid his eyes are going to pop right out of his haggard face. He's searching for an answer where there is no answer, his anger bursting at the seams.

I look past him, to where the police car is blocking the road. The driver's door is open and one of them is standing close, as if ready to go. The one with the gun starts to walk towards us, looking fucking dodgy with his hand on the trigger. The two police-wallahs meet in front of the car and talk, pointing to us and then conferring. What the fuck are they talking about?

'Bugsy, what's going on?' Nida asks. I can hear the worry in her voice. 'Why aren't they letting us go?'

'I'm guessing that they heard about the trucks and thought it would be a good idea to create their own roadblock. Maybe threaten some scared civilians and make some money.'

'Are they even policemen? Did you hear his Punjabi?'

'I don't know. Probably. But who knows.'

'So give them some money.'

'I don't have any money, unless they're willing to accept some ketchup packets and a tossed Hello Kitty doll.'

'Seriously? I don't have any either.'

'Well, then we go to Plan B.'

'Plan B?'

'Argue until we exhaust them, or until another car comes along.'

They walk back to us, the moustached man walking to my door, while the other with the gun, a grizzled-looking dude who looks like no policeman I've ever seen, with bloodshot eyes and a serious hair-lip, walks and stands in front of Nida's door. This does not look good.

'Get out of the car,' he says to me.

'Are you crazy? There's no way we're getting out of the car.'

The dude yanks at Nida's door handle, trying to open it. Then he raps loudly on the window with the barrel of the gun.

'Open your door,' he yells. 'Get out or we'll shoot.'

'Bugsy!' Nida yelps, squeezing my hand painfully.

'Fuck off,' I yell, letting go of her hand, putting my car in gear, revving the engine loudly. I see the man near the police car jump into the driver's seat and shut his door. We might just scare them off.

But I hear the barrel of the gun rapping loudly against the glass, and then I hear the window explode and Nida scream. The door is open. He's dragging her out. I try to reach her, hold her, pull at her kameez, but he's already got her halfway out, pulling her by the hair. I swing my door open, hitting the policeman with all my might.

'Nida!' I shout. I run outside and try to reach her. She's jerking and twisting, trying to escape the man's bear grasp. The policeman behind me tackles me with a force and speed that I didn't expect.

I yell loudly.

The gunman continues to drag Nida to the car, while the driver gets out and runs towards me, swinging a foot to my head.

The light comes back slowly, the haloed blur of a streetlight, the intense headache, the humming of my car, door open, seats empty, air conditioner blasting. I lift my head and my eyes explode into darkness. Nida screams my name and I hear a loud slap, a door shut, a car screech away, smell the rubber. I force myself to sit, my face throbbing madly, and call out weakly to Nida. Nothing. I get up kneeling against the car. She's gone.

Inside his office Ifti's wide awake, as if he's been up the entire night. He looks fresh and lucid, ready for anything. Omer, however, I can't say the same about. He came to the gate dead drunk, and even though I'm sure he's tried to sober himself up for a meeting with his father, he still looks like shit. His eyes are watering, hair a long tangled mess of uncut curls, skin a pasty grey, sickly translucent with dark circles under his eyes. He looks like he hasn't seen sober since high school. His white shirt is buttoned crooked, spotted with stains, and he's in pyjama bottoms and torn plastic house slippers. Omer has a tendency to start the summer fresh but by the end the partying takes its toll and he looks like something that should be stored in a cage in the basement. He looks confused to see me, despite my desperate explanation on the phone, and a little uneasy.

After a pathetic sobbing bleeding drive around to find the car, and some severe panic, I called Omer. Ifti's in with all the police chiefs in the city, and if anyone will know about a dodgy police checkpoint, it's him.

He sits behind his desk, very old-school Hollywood in a silk robe, staring out the window overlooking the lit swimming pool, talking on the phone. Zakir hands me a wet towel for my crusty face, a bag of ice for my cut forehead. From what I've been able to assess the asshole's foot split my forehead. It's all utterly humiliating.

Omer and I sit on the small sofa arrangement Ifti has in one corner of the office. Ifti is quiet and not all that affected after I relayed the events of the night.

'The chief of police doesn't know of any checkpoints in that area,' he says, putting down the phone. 'Some trucks were found outside the city earlier. They were empty. Apparently it was false intel.'

'So then who were these police-wallahs? Where did they take Nida?' I ask frantically.

'How would I know?' he says. 'I only know the legit officers, not all the gundas posing as policemen. They could be anybody. Police uniforms are not hard to acquire. They were probably after some money and when you gave them a hard time they took the girl.'

'Won't they be disappointed,' Omer says crudely.

'Fuck you,' I say.

'Why the fuck were you with her anyway,' he asks. 'Were you trying to get some ass too? Thought you'd hit that as well?'

I shove him hard and he falls to the floor, smirking.

'What do you think is going to happen to her?' I ask Ifti. I'm almost too scared to ask.

'I don't know,' Ifti replies. 'Nothing good. They'll ask for a ransom probably. Someone in her family will pay it, or not. That's usually the way it works.'

'What's the worst that can happen?' Omer asks, with a strange mix of fear and fascination on his face.

'Be quiet, Omer,' Ifti says.

'Isn't there anything you can do?' I ask. I feel nauseous.

'What am I supposed to do? Do you know how busy I am? I'm in the middle of a new election. I'm not here to clean up your messes, to find some random girl you two have been playing with. It's nobody's fault but your own. I've told you time and time again, you need to wake up. Stop with this incessant wasteful partying, the drinking, the endless drugs. Where do you two think you are? This country is a serious place. And this is the kind of shit you get into when you don't grow up.'

'The Mongol horde is coming,' Omer says. 'From China. They'll fuck us all.'

'Shut up, you fool,' I say. 'You're fucking nuts.' He gives me a wide toothy drunken grin.

I think of all the horrible scenarios Nida could be going through. She isn't somebody's daughter or wife or mother—she's nobody. Who'll help a nobody?

I lean back against the sofa, the pain in my forehead radiating through my face, and sip some cold water. I did this. It's my fault. She was at my house. I was dropping her home.

I want to cry and throw up at the same time. I think of her family, who to contact to let them know about her. I know nothing about her, but I remember her drug-dealer cousin, Ali, and look over at Omer. He's hunched down, staring intensely at his phone. For a minute I think he's maybe finding Ali's number, thinking of who to call, formulating a plan, and then I hear a melodic beeping and hear him curse.

'What are you doing?' I ask him. I grab his phone out of his hands. 'You're fucking playing candy crush,' I say, shocked. 'You're fucking playing candy crush?'

'So? I just got all my lives back.'

I stand up and throw the phone at him. 'You fucking asshole. A girl you dated all summer is missing and you're playing bhenchod games on your fucking phone. Have you lost all your humanity?'

'What? She's missing, not dead. I'm sure they won't kill her. They'll ask for some money and that's it.'

'Really? Are you a fucking kidnapping expert now?'

'Why would they kill her? They're just scaring you, yaar, that's all. And it's working. She was in your car, you told them she was your cousin. Relax. They think you'll pay up. Don't be such a little bitch. They'll return her.'

I punch him in the mouth with a quick sharp jab and his head bends back like a whip. He gives me a stupid surprised look.

'You fucking asshole,' I say. 'How will they find me? Who will pay? She's not my fucking cousin.'

'How the fuck would I know?' he says, injured, pressing his lip. 'Maybe they have your licence-plate number.'

'You're a real fucking idiot, you know that?'

'Stop it, you two!' Ifti yells. 'If you want to kill each other go do it in your own room. I don't have time for this bullshit.

You got her into trouble, you fix it. I don't have the time or the energy to worry about some stupid girl who wanted to play Cinderella.'

'I don't know why they chose to take the girl,' Ifti says to himself as we get up and walk out of his office, 'when they could have had you two idiots instead.'

We step out into the corridor and close Ifti's door. I lean against the wall, breathing and sinking, feeling another wave of nausea coming over me. She's gone. And no one gives a shit. My father is going to kill me, but maybe he'll be more of a help. I call and send a message.

'Faisal just messaged me,' Omer says. 'He's on his way.'

'You dickhead. This isn't a fucking movie.'

He shrugs nonchalantly.

And so it begins, the city flocking towards the smell of blood.

'Want a drink?' Omer asks me as we walk towards his room.

I could use about a million.

NIDA

The car has stopped, I hear voices, and then the boot pops open. Two men stare down at me. It's dark, it's difficult to see them, my eyes adjust from the almost complete black, their bodies form more concrete shapes, but their faces, I can't see their faces. I lay my head back down on the gasolined carpet. My scalp hurts. A tear runs down the side of my nose and wets my lips with its wretched saltiness.

'Get up, this is no time to sleep.'

I feel his fingers dig into my arm, pull me up. It hurts but I don't resist. I can't. I fall limply, exhausted. I can't even lift myself up. All I want to do is sleep. Another hand is on me, pulling at me, and they both heave me out of the boot and let me lie on the damp earth. The earth pulls me in closer. It's consoling, warm, immaculate like a womb.

'So this is what they caught,' the bigger of the two says, leaning over me. He's dark-skinned and difficult to see; he has a lot of hair, as black as the night. His voice is thick and heavy. He leans down and slaps me across the head, not hard enough to see stars, but enough to feel slapped.

The other laughs, high and feminine. He squats down next to me, moves his face in for a closer look.

'You're not bad,' he says, tightly grabbing on to my jaw and moving my face to get a better look. His fingers dig painfully into my cheeks. He reminds me of a teenage kid some mother has spoilt. He still has acne around his chin. 'Not bad at all,' he says.

'So, what do we do?' he asks the other, standing up and moving away from me. I twist in the mud and look up at them, tall figures that loom like beasts. What do they want from me?

'What we were ordered to do,' the man says. He's big and square, the type of man you see on bad Lollywood posters, where the man stands looking wild and angry, red paint staining his face, hairy chest out, some kind of ridiculous gun clenched in his fist. I'm shivering uncontrollably. He leans down and grabs my kameez, lifts me up with one hand as if I were air and pushes me against the back of the car. The metal digs into my spine and pain shoots up my body. My legs wobble. My shoes slip in the mud. My teeth chatter.

'Relax. We're only going to hurt you a little bit,' he says with a lecherous look on his face. He blows me an air kiss that squeaks.

Thunder rumbles above, a jagged bolt of lightning illuminating an empty field somewhere far and forlorn. There are no houses, no mud-walled villages, no cows or buffaloes or birds. In the distance is a thin line of trees framing empty fields, ploughed, worm-infested, wet. The dim halo of city lights, Lahore seen from miles away, is invisible. The monsoons are here in their exquisite timing. It starts to rain. I sink back into the earth, knees into dirt. They pull me back up and shake me.

'Let's see her better,' the skinny boy says. 'It would be a pity to waste such a pretty face on the darkness.'

The man grabs me and drags me before the headlights. My sandals plough through the mud, it oozes between my toes, and when they pull me up the Punjabi soil steals them. I don't know why, but being barefoot, feeling the ground beneath me, thick and familiar, gives me strength. I stand up. I stare at them, two idiots gaping in the rain.

'This is a mistake,' I say. 'You've got the wrong person. I don't know anybody. I have no money. I'm nobody.'

'Wrong girl or not, you're here now,' the man says, and then he smiles a dark smile. He moves in close, so close I can smell the food on his breath, the tobacco on his skin. He grabs the V-neck of my kameez and rips it down with one pull, the zipper at the back roughly giving way. The rain beats cold at my back while I cross my arms across my chest. He just laughs and pokes me, tries to touch me, motions for me to pull down my salwar.

'No,' I say, turning my body away from him. 'Stop it. Don't do this. This is a mistake.' The sound of my voice, its desperate tone, makes me cringe.

They laugh and the skinny one grabs at me, touching me with his long bony fingers, jabbing them between my legs.

'Get away from me,' I scream. 'I know Iftikhar Ali, he's a close friend. He will murder you both when he finds out. Stay away from me.'

They both laugh loudly and shake their heads in amusement, as if they're watching some television comedy.

'Okay, enough gup-shup,' the man says. 'We're not at some tea party. Keep your mouth shut, girl, otherwise I'll break it shut.' He punches me hard in the stomach. I collapse. It feels as if I've been hit by a truck. I regurgitate. It comes out burning, like acid. I can't feel my body. I'm crying, every sob hurting.

He nudges me with his foot, as if to see if I'm still alive, and then lunges like some starving wolf, grabbing at my breasts, trying to pull off my salwar and his at the same time. I try to press him away, turn my face away from his, the rain so heavy it fills my eyes. And then I dig my fingernails into his neck and bite him. I feel the iron warmth of his blood in my mouth. He jumps back, eyes wide open, mouth hanging, my teeth marks bleeding on his face.

'You fucking gashti!' The man rubs his face, looking incredulously at the blood on his hands. He's yelling curses, yelling at the boy. The boy steps forward and kicks me. Something cracks inside me, something breaks. I feel my body loosen, searing pain. I dry-heave into the dirt. The skinny boy lifts me up by my neck. I see stars, hear myself gasping for air as he presses harder.

And then sweet oxygen gushes through me. I can feel him pressing himself against my leg, trying to rip off my clothes, his hand digging into my underwear and scratching me with his fingernails. I can smell his smelly breath. He pulls my hair, jerking my head back.

I'm soaked through, the rain thick in my hair, seeping into my eyes, my underwear. I breathe and inhale water. It floods my eyes and blinds me. I gather all my strength and push him away from me. He stumbles back and looks at me stupidly. He grins. I see all his stupid crooked teeth.

'You're fun,' he says. 'You're liking this, aren't you?'

He comes towards me again, and with everything I have, I kick him between the legs. He howls in pain and bends over, falls backwards. Fumes of the wet soil submerge me and I sink into the sludge, my fingernails caked with the same earth that runs through my blood. I make a fist in the dirt and try to sit up. I have grown up breathing this earth, swallowing it. I will die in it.

The boy whines and cries, curses me. The man starts to laugh, his laugh fragmented, distorted by the million raindrops that engulf us. Still holding his testicles, the boy staggers up, tries to punch the other but misses. Then the man hits him hard and he falls to the ground, crying, clutching himself.

'You bhenchod *cussie*,' the man says to the boy. 'Get your ass up and go get the rope.'

'You fucking go,' the boy says indignantly. 'I'm in pain.'

The man kicks him in the behind and knocks him forward. The boy reluctantly stands up, staggers towards the car, moaning the entire time. Then he yells back towards us, 'Where are the keys?'

'What do you mean where are the keys? *You* have them.'

'I don't have them.'

The man curses loudly and walks towards the car. I hear him hit the boy and he cries out again.

I lie in the rain, overwhelmed with pain and nausea, my body heavy and burning. I can still feel his tentacles against my throat. They argue like fools, searching the wet ground for the keys. Lightning breaks overhead—the barren field, the car, its headlights, the men searching in the muck, the trees in the distance, a safe haven. I try to crawl away, my knees sucking deep into the mud. If I can get far enough, they may not be able to see me. If I can just make it to the trees.

I crawl as fast as I can. I try to stand up through the pain and run, but I slip and fall, the rain and mud impossible to wade through. I try to get up again. And then I stop, a cry escapes my throat, a wail that breaks through the heavy deluge. The man is standing over me. He squats down and looks at me. I try to hit him. He moves slightly back, still crouching. I spit at him and curse his mother, his sister, his entire family. I wish upon him every horror that man can imagine. I can see the emptiness in his eyes. He looks like every man I've ever seen—driving a rickshaw, cycling down the street, begging for money, delivering milk or newspapers, working in an office, discussing politics on TV, running for prime minister. He looks like an entire country, and no one, at the same time. He's the invisible man I will never forget.

'You stupid girl,' he says. 'Where did you think you were going?'

'Go to hell,' I say.

The rain hardens, pouring down its misery upon me, its cosmic understanding—I'm just a girl drowning in a wet field. I close my eyes.

BUGSY

Inside the walls of Crescent-Kasoor First Asia Bank there are no special economic zone shark-suit power pit chowmein-flooded Jiǎng Jīn PSX collapsing balconies, upticking bull, bear, water buffalo, FOMO, no go, why go, windows into the optic asshole of the financial world. Here we will gladly take all your money, guaranteed 6.5 per cent return and a ready lukewarm cup of chai for as long as we stay solvent—God bless Pak–China friendship.

'Hello. Yes, this is Bugsy. *Former* RJ,' I say into the phone, correcting her. She apologizes, as if she's called my mother a whore.

A woman's voice, attempting a Brit accent, slightly hesitant, out of breath. She's from some dorky new magazine called *Play*.

'Happy New Year to you too,' I say.

It's February, yet the New Year mubaraks are still going strong. I transfer the telephone receiver from the left ear to the right. She's already irritating, but any distraction is better than work.

Apparently she wants to do a human-interest piece on me for their new entertainment and lifestyle magazine: rock RJ to irreverent asshole banker. She must really be on the bottom of the rung, or they've run out of every possible mediocre desi celeb from here to Gwadar.

'Sure, why not? Talk is all I've ever done anyway,' I say, unable to fully hide the irritation in my voice. I lean back into the ripped leather swivel chair and put my feet on the table, cradle the phone between ear and shoulder.

Inhale. 'Well, I'm hardly a banker. Don't really feel like one. All I do is account chase . . . mostly stealing clients from other banks, offering them something rotten buffed to fresh. Occasionally I battle on the phone if someone steals them back . . . Wait, don't write that.' I pause until she agrees she won't. I don't particularly believe her, but what does it matter anyway. I can hear her typing in the background. She asks about RJ voice-recognition.

'Yes, I suppose it helps sometimes. Very few clients recognize my voice though, most aren't even aware we have an English radio station. And the few that do recognize me are not all that willing to trust some ex-rock RJ with their money.'

She laughs and types furiously. I can hear her nails clicking against the keys. I try to imagine what she looks like. Sanya? I think that's the name she gave. I imagine her with long hair and deep cleavage, looking full-sexy librarian. I'm probably wrong; she's likely some mousey girl who looks like one of my sisters' friends, but somehow I'm hopelessly indoctrinated. Hollywood. Bollywood.

'Why did I shift jobs?' I repeat, trying to listen instead of imagining her naked. I've been in this damn office too long, staring at blank white walls and censored computer screens flashing with paltry monetary investments. I look out, at the space beyond my office door, the bank lobby, filled with anxiety-ridden loafers in cheap suits and uptight women in baggy cardigans. I pull at my starched shirt collar, loosening the red-navy-striped tie my father gave me on my first day. And for my first day at the radio station? He called me a DJ and told his friends it stood for Dumb Job.

'Well . . . it's a long story,' I say. 'I guess I didn't want to hear the music any more. What? Yeah, it's been a while.'

I courtesy-laugh at what she says next. It's like an idiot wrote these questions, but it makes sense, idiots will read them. 'No, I don't position my career choices towards a political career. I'm not really into politics. I would like to keep my political affiliations to myself, but yes, that's correct, Mian Tariq's win came about a month after I left the station.' I fiddle with a ballpoint pen, doodling mountains and W-shaped birds, the only things I can doodle, on to my business cards.

'Sure, I guess everyone was excited, it was a big election. Exactly, no one was sure until the very end. Let's see what it means for business, you know, in the long run.' She agrees with me so vehemently it's funny. I can imagine her violently shaking her massive tits in agreement. 'Yes, that sure was a surprise. No, of course I didn't see it coming.' I stab through the business card, right through the name, the corporate logo, my email address. I thread one card through, than another, another, until the cards are holding the pen up, vertically suspended in the air.

'I mean, how could anyone have known? No one expected Iftikhar Ali to jump ship to Mian Tariq's camp,' I say.

'Sure, Omer and I went to school together, but his father's business is his own. Omer running for office? Really? No, I had no idea. You seem to know more about this than me. No, I haven't noticed the posters. Work is busy, what can I say? What I think? I think it's good for him, of course. It makes sense for Omer to go into politics, especially after his father was made chief minister. It makes sense that a chip off the old block would be next in line.

No, I rarely see Omer nowadays, we're both very busy.' I twirl the bizarre pen contraption and watch my business cards spin.

Adil, a fellow degenerate banker and computer geek, peers into the office. 'Hey, Bugs, done with those files, yaar?' he asks. I point to the files on the desk. He gives me a quick salute and leaves to transfer my newly mined contacts to the main computer, to follow up with investment packages and credit-card deals. A free trip to Dubai if you spend six lakh in six months. No one ever goes to Dubai.

I swivel away from the door and face the window, which overlooks the backside of another cubicle office where some poor schmuck like me talks on the phone all day, drinks mad chai and watches the slowest-loading porn late-night.

'Sorry, some work stuff,' I tell Sanya, who holds patiently. 'Where were we? Hercules told you about that? Yes, he did offer me a publicity manager position. You've really done your homework. Thanks, that's sweet, always nice to talk to a fan. Well, to be frank with you, Sanya, once I decided not to be an RJ any more there was no reason to stay on at the station. It was always about the music.'

And then, as expected, Sanya the reporter for a silly fluffy magazine, asks me a slew of obnoxious questions I can't and don't want to answer—*Do you miss the radio? The music? The fans? Do you like your new job? Do you miss being a celeb?* Blah blah blah.

'Honestly, I haven't really processed all the changes yet,' I answer as truthfully—and elusively—as I can. 'I'm just living in the moment, going day to day. I try not to reflect on what's happened too much, you can't change the past. Just concentrate on tomorrow.

'Thank *you*, Sanya. I enjoyed talking to you too. Yes, that sounds great, you can send a copy to the bank, if you like. I look forward to seeing it.'

I sigh deeply. The pen arts-and-crafts monstrosity I toss into the trash. I'm sure there are plenty of Bugsy business cards lying in countless trash cans throughout the city. Adil returns. 'Oye, Bugsy, where is the Abdul-Hamish Carpets account?'

'I need to call him again,' I say. 'He's a difficult one. He's too happy with his current bank.'

'Did you tell him about the Dubai package?'

'He doesn't use credit cards.'

'Our special offer of a three-lakh loan? No interest for three months.'

'He laughed and said he makes more than that in a month, why would he want a loan? He has a point. It's a wack loan. I mean, anyone who can add and subtract understands they're paying triple for three bloody lakh. It's a shit offer.'

'Well, keep on him. Maybe he'll be interested in our international investment packages. You can have Bilal talk to him.'

'I thought we weren't internationally linked to the other branches?'

'Yeah, technically, we're not.' He grins. 'But once he's in, there are tons of ways to keep his money busy. Great customer service.' He points a finger at me and clicks his tongue like some idiot, like he's memorized some shitty movie on how to be an investment banker. A chutiya in a shit brown ill-fitting business suit.

'Well, you get two days, and then he's mine.' Again the clicking finger.

I rummage through the desk drawer, find the carpet dude's phone number, which I scribbled on a napkin while having lunch, and unwillingly punch in his number. I have no interest in making him switch his bank, and I know he's going to repeat yesterday's argument: Why switch when satisfied? Soon he will get fed up and become rude. Yet here I am, listening to the empty ring of his cell phone. Don't answer, I pray. Don't answer. Be taking a giant shit. Eating with your fingers. Fucking your wife. Just don't answer.

Around me phones jingle incessantly, constantly demanding attention. Printers cough malfunction, the noise of construction rumbles next door, clanging and thumping and whirring and vibrating through the walls. The chai-wallah comes around again, round four, for Kashmiri tea, swapping the used cups for new. The sharp screech of cheap leather shoes against the cheap marble floor is constant, like an animal caged. It smells like school.

I sit at my empty desk until dark. Until the din of office wears itself out and the men who dominate the desktops are at home pillowing their cheeks with chicken pulao. The lamps are dimmed, soft lobby light sliding through the cracks through the door to illuminate a dingy and wrecked commercial world. Paperwork sprawled on my desk purposely abandoned. I light a cigarette.

Maybe there is still some hope, I think. She may still be okay. No one has heard from her since that night. Nida and Moby, both gone without a trace. I lean back and try to remember the details in her face, her laugh. The way she smelt. Her kiss. But it was so brief, just one night.

I scroll down her Facebook page, at all the questions people are posting—'Where are you, Nids?', 'You got all As, yaar, you lucky girl!', 'We miss you.' The last picture of her is at some dance practice, where she's sitting on the floor with Aliya and some gora, smiling with her head tilted. Her hair is up in a ponytail, looking pure and spectacular, so much better than the others, and I wonder what she's thinking in the picture. The beginnings and endings. There are no new pictures, it's always this same one I see over and over.

In my car I adjust the heater and accidentally bump the stereo. Freddie's 'Sheer Heart Attack' comes on, thunderous and flashy. I yank out the CD and toss it out the window, hear the crack as it hits the street. I put the car in gear and swing out around into thick Mall Road traffic. It's choked, alive, primordial at seven o'clock in the evening. A rickshaw-wallah cuts me off, throwing fast-food trash into the lane. I yell at the driver uselessly, honking my horn like the steering wheel is going to come off. He just shrugs and keeps on keepin' on.

Goodbye Freddie Mercury.